The KING
of CORSICA

The KING of CORSICA

A Novel

MICHAEL KLEEBERG

Translated by
David Dollenmayer

Other Press • New York

First published in 2001 as *Der König von Korsika* by Deutsche-Verlags-Anstalt, Verlagsgruppe Random House.

Translation copyright © 2007 David Dollenmayer

The publication of this work was supported by a grant from the Goethe-Institut.

Production Editor: Robert D. Hack

Text design: Natalya Balnova
This book was set in Janson Text by Alpha Graphics of Pittsfield, NH.

10 9 8 7 6 5 4 3 2 1

Library of Congress Cataloging-in-Publication Data

Kleeberg, Michael, 1959-
[König von Korsika. English]
The king of Corsica / Michael Kleeberg ; translated from the German by David Dollenmayer.
p. cm.
ISBN 978-1-59051-256-2 (hardcover : alk. paper)
I. Dollenmayer, David B. II. Title.
PT2671.L38K6513 2007
833'.92—dc22

2007013931

For Petra

Flüchte du, im reinen Osten
Patriarchenluft zu kosten.

Flee to the pure Orient, there
To breathe the patriarchal air.

Johann Wolfgang von Goethe, *Westöstlicher Diwan*

Prelude

THE STAGE IS DARK and empty.

If I close my eyes, it expands into a universe. Beneath my hand, the moist surface shaggy with tiny mosses becomes the relief map of my freedom as—a blind Odysseus—I feel my way with fingertips along the continents, the isthmuses and deltas, the islands and plains and plateaus, wherever my innocent dreams lead me.

My memory glides through the ether, an eagle circling so high up it discerns only the faults of the era but not the victims of my own life. Or is it more like a fluttering bat, careening through the vaults of my past and snapping eagerly and in vain at my few unregretful recollections?

Light!

His Majesty wants light!

Light is coming!

A bright gleam coaxes stalagmites and stalactites from the endless blackness. Steps scrape across the stone. Where the candle flame flickers, walls loom out of the void. As the passage closes in, undulating shadows announce approaching candelabra.

I've always been too interested in myself, but by God, I'm a subject deserving of more interest than others.

Now they're set up. The light gives birth to stone that spreads a narrow vault all the way down to my hand. The mossy, imaginary map beneath my fingers is extinguished.

I've lost everything except hope. It's as stubborn as the lice and I'll need to have my skull shaved of illusions to finally get rid of it.

Music!

His Majesty wants music!

A heavy wooden door slams shut. The hundred tiny flames tremble and smoke. Iron fittings or a ring of keys clatter.

The musicians are ready!

A humming tone, firmly bowed, emerges from the wall, flows through my cranium, breaks against its rear wall and ebbs back. A siren voice flits along beneath the vaulted roof, floats down and nestles around the bass hum, then both are swallowed up in a shrill noise. As if on secret command, it narrows down to a single tone, only to burst open anew into purring cellos, hysterically trilling violins, trumpet fanfares, breathy flutes, and the call of a bassoon in rut. A whirlwind trapped in the vaults erupts and settles back down again.

A chair for my guest!

His Majesty wants an armchair for his guest!

I was always afraid. Afraid of the world. Afraid of death. Afraid of stasis and afraid of change. Afraid of people and, above all, of the absence of people.

An armchair is coming!

The chair is dragged in and brushed off, making the dust

dance in the candlelight and setting its tassels aquiver. In the backlighting the thing throws a shadow like a scaffold.

My throne!

His Majesty wants his throne!

The throne is coming!

Again, doors slam and footsteps scrape across the flagstones. A bearded fellow in a stained doublet and with stringy hair carries the tall, scratched chair above his head, so that its lathe-turned feet with their peeling gold leaf stick up like antlers.

Set it up here, my dear William.

The horned man is the same one who fetches my food from the kitchen, so a little investment of friendliness pays off. The velvet brocade cushions are threadbare, their colors faded, between the bronze rivets it looks suspiciously like excelsior leaking out. But as soon as I sit down, even this wreck becomes a throne.

Play!

Four staccato chords, then the *Tafelmusik* sets off, striding and trotting. I peer into the arched vestibule where my desk stands at the barred window, a narrow funnel of sunlight. The musicians crowd so close together that with the sun behind them, they form a dark billow on which dusty powdered wigs nod like a crown of foam. Now a bow, flourished high, catches the candlelight, shimmering like a fishing rod in the earliest morning light.

It's seldom this bright in here. Unfortunately, I can see myself more clearly than I like. My thick, gristly joints, the crooked ends of my fingers. Almost like a claw. And my joints are as painful as if pliers were pulling them from their sockets.

And yet I used to be a handsome man.

A psyche!

A what?

Good God in heaven, you idiot, the cheval glass!

The mirror for His Majesty!

The full-length psyche is carried in. It has a double cherry-wood frame, the inner one pivoting around the transverse axis of the outer one. The candles are doubled; they waver, glide past, disappear, reappear, and take a bow without dripping.

Put it so that we can see each other from both chairs, then leave us.

The fellow in the mirror looks at me like the deformed, retarded uncle one pretends not to know when there are guests in the house, but who is permitted to stay because one shares with him the secrets of crimes committed together. His hair is gray and no longer very thick, cut short to deprive the lice of a winter home. A hard face, I've got to admit, without a trace of the wisdom of age (to be sure, the mirror's not the best quality). But I still love this face with tender sympathy, like an old lapdog who just lies on his sheepskin rug all day and can't hold his water anymore. It's a face that allows of no more hope for any kind of future.

And yet I've always hoped for something, believed in something, something above us, guiding our fates. But if we humans must bring everything to pass by ourselves in this life, without the Almighty, then no one can absolve us but ourselves.

My responsibility to think things through to the end begins to glow in this emptiness, and even though I would now have time for the task, I have less taste for it than ever, and not enough powers of reasoning in any event. There's this blind spot that flickers and blurs as soon as I approach the skin of a thought—or of a woman, by the way.

I admit it: I've never thought about anything except myself. I'm garrulous, but brilliant.

And besides, money is more important than any kind of cogitation. I know what I'm talking about. A letter of credit backed up by sufficient funds is like having your own box in the theater: the catharsis has already been paid for, so you can leave during the intermission and not be late for supper.

I look at the psyche again, but now I see the painting there, and I can close my eyes. It will be that last thing that I see, and in the end I shall finally understand it.

There is the sunny landscape, overhung with thunderclouds, that I first saw in Venice. The walls of the houses on the right bank of the river are still reflecting the light. Above them the sky, green with electricity and massing clouds, gives a first flicker of lightning. In the foreground the young beauty wearing only a cloth over her shoulders nurses her child. Her left knee is bent, the leg turned slightly outward, and in its attempt to support her body, the left foot strokes through the grass like a mother-of-pearl comb. In serene equanimity she gazes back at—or rather, through—the viewer.

She's definitely not looking at the wayfarer who is departing the city and escaping the storm. He has paused and, leaning on a staff taller than himself, looks across at her, smiling. He wears a white shirt and over it a red, open jacket with wide sleeves. His short breeches have an elaborate pattern. His right hand caresses the hiking staff in contemplation. The tension, the space between the two of them, into which the lightning bolt is striking, cries out for resolution, like a dissonant chord.

PART ONE

Tout notre raisonnement
se réduit à céder au sentiment.

All our reasoning
comes down to yielding to feeling.

Blaise Pascal, *Pensées*, I/274

Chapter I

*C*ONVIVIALITY REIGNED IN THE house of Pujol. The oak door on the ground floor, where the office was located, stood open. Hired torchbearers lighted the guests in, as if that were necessary what with all the noise and the aromas exuded by the steeply gabled house. The doorbell jangled without pause and the maid on the upstairs landing held out her arms and took charge of the coats, capes, and hats.

Between the kitchen—where pigs and pheasants were roasting and pies baking—and the ballroom there was a constant to-and-fro of attendants whose swaying silver trays laden with roast chickens and cakes, quiches, wine carafes, glasses, and tankards of beer were like Spanish galleons being plundered and emptied at the hands of Corsairs before ever reaching their destinations.

The wide, lofty room was dappled with yellowish-green light from the bull's-eye windowpanes. Furbelows swept over the polished parquet, pantaloons rustled whenever someone furtively scratched himself between the legs. Fan-waving ladies clucked in groups. Men puffing on pipes stationed themselves by the fireplace. "How were the prices for Verviers wool today? Did they finally lift the siege of Brussels? Have you seen the Italians yet? Priceless!"

A brooding Spanish official, dignified and black, sat on a chair whose tall, elaborately carved back and arms kept his flanks and neck protected. Two French colonels and a handful of prosperous farmers from the Hainault region and Limbourg represented commerce, while several prelates and professors of theology from town represented intellect.

Pujol, who dealt in cloth and textiles but also provisioned the French army, furnishing it with boots, greatcoats, muskets, and powder, sat enthroned at the head of the largest table, applying himself with gusto to the dishes spread out before him, and expounded to his neighbor—with a gesture that encompassed the hall, paintings, draperies, furniture, mugs, and carvings before coming to rest above the quail on his plate—his love of things, of what was around him, what one could see, touch, grasp, smell, and taste, and what belonged to him.

He was a florid-cheeked, gray-haired man in his fifties with waxed mustaches whose twirled-up ends tickled the heavy bags under his eyes and were counterbalanced by a fuzzy little Vandyke beneath his fleshy lower lip. He was dressed in a fancy black jacket decorated with colorful embroidery representing flower baskets, entwining vines, and overflowing cornucopias. Like two peaceful white doves sleeping on his shoulders, the points of the collar encircling his neck just under the chin spread over his lapel. And since the host was eating and talking at the same time, the collar exhibited several gravy stains.

In the middle of the hall, two large macaws, one red and one bluish-yellow, were installed on the crossbar of a meter-high pole. Their tail feathers reached to the ground and golden chains on their right feet prevented them from flying away. They cocked their heads and turned them in little jerks from left to right and back again, observing the strange goings-on with steadily blinking eyes.

Pujol had received the two birds as a gift from abroad. Whenever he gave a reception, he had them brought out of the cage where they vegetated away during the week, and the guests gaped at them as if they were black African chieftains. The merchant regarded them with something of the same gormandizing pleasure he took in the other furnishings of his home, and with a peculiar mixture of awe and contempt.

Even after hours spent in the hall, the birds refused to blend into the ponderous décor, remaining a glaring splash of color from another world. Monitoring the look in their button-like eyes, vacant from the melancholy of imprisonment, the master of the house felt a slight revulsion, as he did toward every thing and every person who was dependent on him and disproportionately weaker than he, yet belonged to a higher sphere. The parrots' colorful plumage was like a helpless protest, less tolerable the more brazenly the birds provoked the master with their prisoners' autonomy.

Just now there was a young man kneeling by the parrots and when Pujol caught sight of him, the host's eyes and the corners of his mouth remained motionless. The youth raised his index finger and the red macaw opened his beak and said, "Al-fons is be-eautiful!" And the bluish-yellow one added, "Al-fons is vee-ery be-eautiful!"

Pujol silently nodded. One could hardly argue with the beasts. The brown-haired young man dressed in shimmering black moiré seemed among the other guests like a drop of quicksilver among balls of lead. He was younger than most of them, his comely face an oasis among all the warty, smallpox-scarred deserts, the bulbous noses and goiters, the ham necks and jaundiced eyeballs. His laughter as well as his grace of movement set him apart from the men whose fingers were made for counting money or putting dirt into their mouths to test its fertility. Alfons von Neuhoff hailed from the Westphalian Mark, a protectorate of the prince elector and margrave of Brandenburg. There on Pungelscheid Hill was to be found the castle of Donnersfurth-Bruchmühle—it was called a castle, but was more like a house with windows and doors—where the barons of Neuhoff had resided for generations. For the past six months, Alfons had been living as a lodger in the house of Pujol while studying theology at the University of Liège. He was twenty-six years old, a lieutenant in the French army, and an apple of discord between his parents, who were both inordinately proud of him.

Life in the castle of Donnersfurth-Bruchmühle was to life in the house of the merchant Pujol as Lent is to carnival. In the end, what were the Neuhoffs except farmers with large holdings of field and forest? The war had killed their farmhands, devastated the village, and scattered their rent-paying tenants in all directions. It had slaughtered their cattle and requisitioned their horses, cut down their forests and transformed their granary into a cesspool. It had pilfered window frames, carts, tables, and cabinets. Thistles grew in the kitchen garden. Gallows outnumbered the trees, and flapping crows congregated on the faces of the hanged. Army units and freebooters marauded through the country, bayoneting the men, slitting the bellies of unbaptized infants to facilitate their souls' flight to purgatory, and impaling the women. It was a savage, desolate wilderness through which echoed as if across an empty stage the fanatical singsong of wandering monks and the tinkling bells of those sick with the plague.

Alfons's grandfather before him had served in the French army and still held an officer's commission from that time. Although Alfons's father, whose nose jutted out over his ruff like a musket over a breastwork, had only experienced the war as a child, he was more martial in temperament than an active soldier, as is often the case. He wore a uniform that had been in fashion fifty years ago, but who cared about fashion in Donnersfurth-Bruchmühle? Who gave a fig for etiquette, table manners, or any other refined product of peacetime, the cities, and human interchange?

All the more astonishing, then, that in that soot-black, moldering house Alfons matured into bright resplendence and seemed an inexplicable reminder or anticipation of better times that had skipped several generations. His father was not at all pleased that his son liked to sit with the women, held his cup of chocolate with his little finger extended, and—dividing his attentions and charm between young and old with the wisdom of Solomon—wove a web, delicate as a sigh, out of little favors and *histoires*, in which women got so tangled they couldn't tear themselves away from him.

He learned French and Latin faster than horsemanship. He never learned to chop wood or guzzle beer, and his father bought him a lieutenant's commission in King Louis's army to make a man of him. His mother, on the other hand, held up her son like a monstrance of light in a tabernacle and dreamed of making a churchman of him, a churchman of a different order, to be sure, than the crow-like Capuchins, wandering the countryside with their fanatical faces like Grim Reapers, or the pastors who were filling the parish parsonages with their consumptive wives and twelve children ever since the change of confession decreed by the authorities.

With the *patres* of the Jesuit College in Liège, Alfons discoursed in Latin on the relative merits of the marquises de Montespan and Maintenon and the Duchess de Lavallière. Evenings of wine, cards, and dice in a back room of the guildhall went on until dawn, and in Pujol's house he freely came and went, part son and part older brother for young Amalia. He was the guest of honor, a credit to the bourgeois establishment, and a hardship to be suffered with a jovial smile.

Above all, Alfons was relieved to have escaped the constraints of life at Donnersfurth-Bruchmühle. The prosperous, hectic town on the Meuse with its tradesmen shouting their wares, ladies of easy virtue, witty Jesuits, and solidly appointed burghers' houses was Alfons's bohemia. Aside from occasionally requiring his presence in the Metz garrison, his lieutenant's commission was no burden at all, and after the rigidity of a childhood filled with tales of murder, war, privation, and misery he reveled in the anticipatory state he considered his present life to be, here in this comfortably furnished in-between world. He felt he had a right to be carefree and, like many charming young men who see only the smiles they conjure up on the faces that surround them, had the impression that the world conceded him that right good-naturedly, without sensing that he was perhaps benefiting from someone's longanimity, but rather that anything done in the service of the blithe life he led must necessarily make the doer more blithe and happy as well.

Alfons's main creditor was old Pujol, with whom the young man, tongue-in-cheek, both cultivated and played the part of a son. He was full of admiration for the financial freedom in which the merchant moved as if in a comfortable waistcoat. Alfons himself was a gentleman, so it didn't bother him that his host wasn't. But Pujol's worldly causerie, his ability to have something to say about any subject—nothing earthshaking, but just getting his mouth open to say something—made life so much more pleasant. Pujol impressed Alfons as the sort of man who had enthusiastically sown his wild oats and given others some slack in his day, and who would regard the same impulses in a young man with a benevolence steeped in contented memories.

If Alfons approached him concerning the deferral of his rent payment or told him about his gambling debts over a glass of wine, Pujol reacted with the dismissiveness of an implicit accomplice—"Please, Baron, let's not talk of such things. I'm very well acquainted with that sort of temporary difficulty. One more word about it and you'll be insulting me, my young friend!"—so that the Westphalian princeling was at times convinced he was doing the master of the house a favor by letting him pay his debts or loan him money.

And in a more complicated way than Alfons imagined, he was not incorrect in thinking so. Pujol felt an honest affection for the young gallant. At a gathering such as this evening's his pretty countenance and carefree good humor were worth their weight in gold. Moreover, in the evenings after supper, it was pleasant for the widowed merchant to be able to chat with him man-to-man. The pretense of father–son intimacy in which Alfons indulged—while taking care to maintain a distance of formality and avoid misunderstandings—amused Pujol for the same reason it amused the younger man: it lacked the element of accountability.

The young Neuhoff overstepped his bounds only—but more and more frequently since he detected no stirring of resistance in his interlocutor—when he found himself in pecuniary difficulties. The first time and perhaps the second time too, Pujol had advanced him money out of politeness. The third and fourth time he did so because the earlier loans had eventually been paid back. The fifth time, because—not although—Alfons had fallen behind in his payments and the merchant discovered that in this case, the unpaid balance didn't annoy him but rather filled him with a previously unknown sense of satisfaction.

Not that he would have wanted to compare himself to the Fuggers or the Medicis, but not everyone was able to continue to afford something that brought him no profit, and without being capable of analyzing his own thoughts very deeply, it nevertheless seemed to him that this situation was somehow connected to the new era and its shift in values. Sometimes he even got fancies into his head, such as the possibility that through his tactless handling of Pujol's money, Alfons was voluntarily creating moral compensation for the fact that he was unable to respect Pujol as much as he perhaps would have wished to because the merchant was a venal man of commerce.

Pujol's eyes still rested on Neuhoff, kneeling next to the parrots and teasing them.

"Bar-rone," inquired the red macaw with a croak, "is it true that all phenomena may be explained in terms of motion and extension?"

"As a pupil of Gassendi, I maintain that matter is inert," cried the bluish-yellow one.

"What are those beasts talking about?" someone asked Alfons.

"About Leibniz's theory of monads," replied the baron, "but they lack a proper understanding of it."

"Monads are souls!" squawked the Gassendian.

Meanwhile, the guests had turned their attention to a young girl just entering the room, cradling a viola da gamba in her arm. She blushed as she crossed the floor and entered the music room. All the guests followed her including Alfons, who was to be her accompanist, while Pujol remained seated at the table. He was expecting someone.

This black-haired girl was Amalia, the daughter of the house. She was wearing a floor-length, high-necked dress and before the jostling, staring friends of the establishment she lowered her long-lashed eyes in the most delightfully chaste manner. She was tall and slender, and the dress that billowed out more widely toward the bottom enclosed her body like a metaphor, expressing everything and revealing nothing. Her somewhat straddle-legged walk, almost the rolling gait of a sailor, contradicted the image of a lady without affecting the charming impression she made. The same was true of Amalia's unplucked, naturally prominent eyebrows which dominated her entire face so that the observer at first concentrated on them, only then noticing the eyes themselves and her rosy lips. On account of these thick and mobile eyebrows one couldn't really call her a beauty *à la mode* but, said Alfons to himself, what's more boring than perfection?

The contradictory impressions continued as soon as Amalia sat down on her stool and began to play.

She perched there with legs spread wide, the warm wooden body of the instrument nestling between them, and drew the bow with a powerful movement of her arm. The sight reminded Alfons of a peasant woman holding a lamb in a headlock and shearing it, except that the sound produced was no panicked bleating, but a throaty melody which, together with eyes that were closed and seemed to be listening inwardly, a furrowed brow, and gaping mouth, produced an appearance of knowledge —of experience and pleasure—to which Alfons's sweat glands reacted with alarming activity.

After all, it's not the person as such who awakens our appetite (Alfons had spent months at Amalia's side without ever having other than fraternal feelings for her) but a sudden eruption in our perception, a slight shift of perspective. Suddenly the shell that until then was the only thing we had seen seems to open, and the hidden kernel, the fruit, reveals itself.

He wished to see again and again that expression of keen rapture on Amalia's face, and above all, *he* wanted to be the one to evoke it and himself to occupy the gamba's place between her legs. With stiff fingers Alfons struck his cords until Amalia tapped him on the shoulder and called, "Stop, Alfons, the piece is over."

Alfons had already been in love with Amalia in a brotherly, innocent way. This inclination was so carefree that it contained within itself its significance and limitations just as did his entire life at present, and until this evening it had not occurred to Alfons to make any plans based on it. It consisted of glances, jests, brief moments when their hands touched, shared effusions of sentiment, and anecdotes from their childhoods. It was like a summer day in the dunes, when wind and sea are soughing and it's utterly unnecessary to discover what lies beyond the two or three sand hills where one is playing.

But this evening, Alfons's psychic satisfaction was troubled by his suddenly awakened erotic impulse, which squeezed a few drops of unattainability and hopelessness into the limpid water of his harmless sibling love, in a flash transforming the beverage into an incomparably more attractive bitters.

At the same time that the house music was playing in the side room, the accompanist Alfons was discovering his desire for Amalia, and the instrumentalizing young lady was completely absorbed in the melodies of Sainte-Colombe with their clean, Jansenistic division into black and white, without the remotest idea of the fantasies of her friend nor feeling anything similar herself, the evening's guest of honor so urgently awaited by Pujol had finally arrived: the well-to-do farmer Xavier Hainaut.

Without hesitation he made for Pujol and motioned him into the study. The doors were closed, and after some time, Hainaut emerged and trundled back down the stairs with the same hurried steps that had brought him here. He had not deigned to cast even one glance toward the festivities, nor had he greeted the daughter of the house. But the host remained out of sight. Alfons learned of all this after the musical performance, and since he was by nature no Parsifal, once the guests were gone he knocked on the door of the study and asked if Pujol were all right.

Pujol was not, and he was much too agitated not to reveal his misery, or at least a part of it, on the spot to his youthful friend, for by giving voice to his worries, he also was putting them in order in his merchant's head, which was then able to decide what to make known to an outsider and what not to.

"My dear Master Pujol, if the meeting with your guest has plunged you into some sadness or embarrassment in which I can be of some assistance by putting myself at your disposal or simply by lending you my ear . . ." began Alfons in his flamboyant way, which, out of a sense of politeness and genuine generosity, always promised a little more than it could or would deliver.

"You're a good boy, Baron," said Pujol and told him that for ages now he and his old acquaintance and supplier Hainaut had been agreed that their children would marry each other and that the contract was supposed to have been notarized today.

He was on the point of allowing himself to get carried away by Alfons's expression of concentrated attention and mentioning as well the financial necessity of the union, admitting that he needed evenings like the present one to maintain the appearance of prosperity in order to protect his reputation, when a servant appeared with the parrots and asked where he should take them, and Pujol decided to say nothing about these things.

To be sure, what he said instead shocked his listener much more than the admission of poor financial health would have, which the young man could all too well have understood and accepted. Pujol revealed that Georg, Hainaut's son, had not put in an appearance because he had gotten pregnant a young girl from the hills of Herve. Her family was now out to get him, and as a consequence his father had dispatched him to France and into the army as quickly as possible and as far away as possible, you understand, until the situation could be brought to an amicable conciliation. So the marriage to Amalia would have to wait at least a year. Pujol looked so upset and unhappy because while speaking he was calculating in his head whether he'd be able to survive that year or not.

For the first time in his life and not without some pride, Alfons felt himself touched by the fatefulness of life. He saw the coach of his existence rolling away before his very eyes, driven by an unknown coachman. He was now compelled to dash after the receding vehicle without delay in order to salvage what could be salvaged.

More in confusion than friendliness and politeness, he succeeded in maintaining good form and withdrawing, but there was no hope of going to sleep. In this alarming condition, all his sense organs turned inward to come to grips with the revolution seething within him, he left the house and hurried to an inn down by the river where he collapsed onto a bench in a corner without casting a glance at the other late-night patrons, and ordered beer.

Only then did he ask himself why the news that Amalia had been promised to another should plunge him into such panic. That it was able to, he reasoned, must mean that I love her, and reaching this conclusion, he noticed that now he did in fact love her. But even love didn't warrant his horror that Pujol wanted to wed her to a farmer's son. Did he then intend to marry her himself? Not up to this moment, but now that question stood before him, large and awkward.

Vaguely he understood, or more accurately sensed, that he was being called upon to react and act in some way or other, since the world was simply ignoring his in-between existence, his blithe anticipatory state, and continuing on its way. Obviously the condition he was in only became virulent at the moment he gave it a name. The fumbling thought "I love her," once said aloud, created an irrefutable fact.

I'm afraid of being cheated of my happiness, that's what it is. It's only odd that the fear itself first created my awareness of the condition of happiness that's now suddenly missing. He was a young nobleman who had fallen into the well of bourgeois morality. And then he understood what was in fact new and unsettling about his situation: he had become aware of himself. Who am I, actually, he wondered, as if Pujol's story had torn the keystone from the arch of his life. What am I actually looking for in this world? And he answered his own question: to be happy! At the moment, what stood in his way was the realization that things happened that he couldn't control or even necessarily know of.

To be happy meant to possess Amalia, and to possess Amalia meant marrying her, and that was in every respect such an unheard-of thought that the pure madness of thinking it, to say nothing of the mountain of impossibility of ever realizing it, made it seem the only adequate reaction to the shame that Alfons felt.

What will become of me if I lose this happiness, if I fail to win Amalia, he asked himself and he thought about the girl wielding her bow with eyes closed, the shiny brown animal between her thighs, and then about his dreary homeland where all his education was good for nothing, and about this mercantile world in which one had to work hard and dirty one's fingers for a bit of the good life.

To carry out a marriage to Amalia against all resistance was possibly the only great thing someone like him could perform and accomplish: a decision the likes of Columbus's embarking on his voyage of discovery. But the happiness he sought to find was a continent of heresy, expunged from all the charts. No feeling or personal appetite, however powerful, could justify a *mésalliance*. The enormity of his revolution of love took his breath away but nonetheless didn't frighten him. Until he had acted, nothing could happen and thus one couldn't know what might happen, either. That is, theoretically one could know very well: it risked scandal and social ostracism, but it was like playing chess, when an unprotected bishop challenges the queen. She could capture it, and there was really no reason why she shouldn't, except that she still had many other possible moves. And if he didn't move himself, he would never find out how the world would react.

Pujol's reaction was anything but joyful. It was a struggle to remember to declare himself honored before beginning to persuade Alfons of the absurdity of his request. And he couldn't even mention the real reasons for his negative response. But the higher the barriers that rose up before the resolution Alfons had now expressed, for better or for worse, the more stubbornly and eloquently he insisted upon it. He even went so far as to break into well-tempered tears and accuse the merchant that even he for whom Alfons had the greatest possible respect, even Pujol, was the enemy of his happiness, while that very respect and the knowledge that Amalia was her father's rod and staff, the apple of his eye, would of course prevent him from ever marrying her against his will.

Amalia herself was impressed by Alfons's determination and interest in her. Without knowing whether she loved him as well or attributing any special importance to that question, she found it quite proper to follow the man who, after her father, was the most attentive to her. She too knew nothing about the state of Pujol's finances, and even less, by the way, about those of her suitor.

When Alfons's hysterical courting began to make living together unbearable and in the end he fell into a sort of psychosomatic fever which even several blood-lettings could not alleviate, and when through what one might call a contagion of spiritual solidarity Amalia also took seriously ill, Pujol had no other choice—all the more so as Hainaut sent discouraging news with regard to his son—but to grant the hand of his daughter to the delirious Alfons, *in articulo mortis*, so to speak, whereupon in less than a week the young man had risen from the dead and the wedding could take place.

The rest of Alfons's story and life is quickly told. For unfortunately, the heroic decision to make personal happiness the center and goal of his life against all the conventions of his class would remain his greatest moment and sole triumph. The wedding took place in October 1693; the groom was twenty-seven years old.

First of all he set about informing his parents of the marriage. It took him several days to compose the long letter, for once he had actually gotten his way, he was seized by a kind of mental laxity and having accomplished so much already, he unconsciously expected that others would of necessity follow him with goodwill and also contribute to the success of the undertaking.

His sentences grew longer and longer, apologetic parentheses surrounded his straightforward statements like giant octopi, and imperceptibly his missive acquired the form of a cry for help, understanding, and (financial) support.

The answer, in his mother's hand, took a long time to arrive and when it finally did, was as brief as it was devastating. The baroness forbade any further importunities addressed to her deeply disappointed husband, prohibited Alfons from ever again visiting his parental home, and informed him succinctly that he was disinherited and neither parent had the slightest interest in hearing how a son was faring who had so miserably compromised himself in his very first entry into the world.

From a clear-eyed point of view, something of this sort could have been predicted, and yet it shocked Alfons deeply, and he was crushed to discover that his sunny disposition and ingenuous trust that life would favor him thanks to his charm had abruptly reached their limit and from now on counted for nothing. In the short interval remaining to him, it became clear that he had exhausted his resources with his decision to live for happiness, and that he had no reserves left to cope with the rest of his life.

Less than a year after the wedding, old Pujol died and, once his business had been liquidated, left his daughter a modest eleven thousand gulden. Tellingly, he had never suggested to his son-in-law that he take over the business himself, for if the attainment of happiness justified the baron's compromising marriage, it would never justify a compromising activity. So the only option was a military career. Alfons used the dowry to raise a company of soldiers and as their captain assumed the command of a fort near Metz in one of the newly conquered pockets or *réunions* that had been formed near the embattled front line during King Louis's war in the Palatinate.

The fort was one of the brilliant constructions of Vauban, that is, it was brilliant as a defensive post. As a place to live, especially for a pregnant woman, it was a nightmare. Drafty corridors whose moisture encouraged the proliferation of poisonously yellow mold on their ceilings; the icy wind of Lorraine that roared across the plateau, got ensnarled in the inner courtyard, and blew through their lodgings; the noise of the soldiers' drills that echoed through the private rooms of the captain; the eternally overcast sky; the garden of pale vegetables that Amalia nursed along by the courtyard wall of the commandant's apartment. The yowling songs of the soldiers, sung in various broad dialects, and their drunken bellowing; their furtive, animalistic glances at the young woman—the granite fort on the plateau was a cold purgatory, and the more time went by, the more likely it seemed that they had been sentenced there for life.

Every one of Alfons's requests for transfer, every application for promotion, remained unanswered, was denied, or got postponed. Except for a few skirmishes, life in the fort was peaceful, too peaceful. The men were bored, had to be disciplined, kept busy, and paid, since none of them was getting killed. Alfons, more weakened than hardened by military life and the granite gloom of the walls (he'd begun to cough), had to admit sadly that his heroic deed against all the odds had turned out only for the worst, and he wondered how long fate would continue to cheat him. Basically, he still expected some kind of reward for his act of courage, and ultimately, for his person as such, quite apart from his deeds.

When Amalia began to throw up on a daily basis, he rented the Flea Tower in Thionville, where on the twenty-fourth of August, 1694, his son was born and christened with the names Theodorus Antonius Alfons. Amalia's confinement was extended, for she continued to bleed after the delivery of the large, sturdy boy, and when she finally returned to the fort with the child and a wet-nurse-cum-charwoman named Minne, who hailed from

Westphalia like the Neuhoffs, the skin at Amalia's temples had a translucent shimmer and a tracery of blue veins like bone china.

The following spring she was again expecting and nothing had changed. The latent state of war, the rain, wind, and cold, the dank, dark rooms of their apartment that caused the clothes to rot in their wardrobes, Alfons coughing and spitting more and more often, the graying temples and emaciated face which made him seem even more handsome; no transfer, no promotion, no money, and thus not a trace of social life.

The couple still treated each other with the same exquisite courtesy and amiability as during their engagement. Whenever he led his wife into the drafty dining room for a frugal supper, Alfons looked at Amalia with such smoldering, hypnotic eyes, it was as if he were trying to convince her that the only reality was the airy bridge that connected them, that all their adverse circumstances were only an illusion, and Amalia must also do her part to maintain this fiction, must in no case, by word of complaint or reference to their hopelessly miserable life, break the magic spell through which he kept at bay a confrontation with the realities. She learned to maintain this silent denial of the world; the power with which his eyes transported her into a kind of levitation in which her feet no longer touched the grubby ground of the facts was a last echo of the power he had displayed in order to win her hand.

Amalia did him the favor of never touching upon this fiction. Which didn't keep her from perceiving their dead-end situation with complete clarity. She had followed Alfons because she neither wanted nor was able to resist the ardor so intensely directed toward her. To be sure, she had expected that something or other would follow on the heels of this initial drive. She saw her husband's weakness without illusions, his—let's not mince words—inability to master the quotidian. She had been used to a different, more comfortable life, but while her situation became more and more miserable, Amalia assumed her husband's stoic pride, and a consciousness of her own power took root and grew within her. At first, it was more of a slumbering treasure, a subterranean fire, but it warmed her from within in the dank cold of their exile. She knew she was superior to her husband. With each passing day, as she watched Alfons's decline, her will for self-preservation grew. And she continued in her stalwart denial of reality when, shortly after the birth of her second child, a daughter christened with the names Amélie Viktoria Elisabeth Charlotte, she could no longer keep secret even from herself that Alfons was suffering from consumption and the horizon of his future was closing in. They didn't waste a word on it. "Actually," said the baron, wearing a woolen scarf around his neck and shivering at the breakfast table while the north wind whistled through the cracks in the walls, "actually it's about time I was promoted to colonel and transferred to Paris. Don't you agree? I expect to hear any day now. What do you think about Paris? I can hardly stand to wait. But it's been very nice here too, hasn't it?"

"Certainly," said Amalia. "It wasn't so bad here." She looked lovingly at her husband. Yes, she loved him. She despised his weakness and was disappointed at his lack of good fortune; she loathed him on account of her dashed hopes. She became aware that these were the first deep feelings she had ever had for him. And one needs concrete feelings for the other which one can then call love, for "love" is a collective term for a combination of precise perceptions which may be quite contradictory and generally are simply silenced by the big word that gets tossed over them like a hat.

In the late fall of 1697—the Peace of Ryswick had just been signed and the fort had lost its strategic importance in the contested theater—Alfons von Neuhoff died and his widow moved away with her children and the wet nurse Minne, and with what money remained bought a house in the country on the edge of the Argonne Forest.

Chapter II

THE COUNTESS DE MORTAGNE, a confirmed country woman who missed nothing of what happened in the surrounding countryside, wrote to her spouse (the chamberlain of *Monsieur*, the king's younger brother), with whom she conducted a primarily epistolary and therefore frank and harmonious marriage, ". . . and by the way, everyone here is talking about a lady, apparently of German nobility, who reportedly lives in utter poverty in a hut of straw and, despite not possessing a second dress to change into, devotes all her time and energy—apart from the education of her two children—to the poor and sick of the canton, and never misses a Mass. The peasants call her the 'Black Madonna' since she cannot be persuaded to stop wearing mourning although her husband, an officer in the Royal Army, passed away years ago, if I am not mistaken. Were this not a challenge to your well-known *générosité*? Especially since the lady is said to be a beauty beneath her rags, so your idealistic aspirations would not have to be in conflict with your aesthetic sensibilities . . ."

Not all the information in this letter accorded with the facts. Thus, Amalia was by no means living in a straw hut, but rather in a three-story house with windows, a pair of fireplaces, and a well-tended garden. Nor did she lack for anything in her toilette. But presumably she would not have been upset to be seen in this way, for being in such a condition would have contributed to the world's bad conscience toward her, something she incessantly demanded.

Ten years after Alfons's death, Amalia von Neuhoff was a thirty-year-old matron, dressed in black, whose stern pride forbade her to lower her eyes and thus spared her the sight of her wooden shoes among the droppings on the muddy cartways. Her lips were as tightly closed as the gates of a city under siege that has vowed to perish rather than surrender. Life was Amalia's foe—or rather the circumstances of her life. She contemptuously ignored them, and to what she couldn't ignore she refused to concede any deeper reality.

Her denial went hand in hand with defiance and a superior sense of insult, which expressed themselves in her regal walk and struck her with a subtle form of blindness, for even after ten years in the wretched village on whose edge she lived with her half-orphaned children, she barely acknowledged any of her neighbors as she strode past them, head held high.

This proud denigration of the world was paired with a determination to subjugate it to her children, and it was not always completely clear which world she was raising the two of them for, especially her son: was it the world that must have existed behind her defiant look and stitched-tight mouth, or the actual world her mud-spattered shoes were splashing through?

The years since her sad farewell from Liège were a black, swampy nightmare through which she had waded, her heart full of fear and holding her children by the hand, constantly turning to look back when a noise struck her ears, unceasingly on the alert to forestall in time all the dangers lying in wait, filling her eyes with misery until they were black and swollen like the bloated corpses in the roadside ditches, so as to prevent the children from seeing what could poison their gaze.

The roads were not safe. Robbers could club her son to death, rip the clothes from her daughter and herself and take advantage of them. Marauding soldiers took women wherever they found them: in occupied towns, in requisitioned houses, for fun, out of boredom. She knew them from experience. A Capuchin preacher might incite the peasants and before you knew it they were running amok in their sullen, drunken, self-righteous fury, incinerating Jews and Saracens in their houses and wagons.

How many cries one heard in a lifetime! Cries of the dying by day, cries of poor souls at night, in their sleep. Neither confession nor absolution could prevent them. The screams of people being burned to death, the piteous squeals of people being stabbed, the ghastly rattle of the plague victims, the lepers, the consumptives, the animalistic bellow when a crushed arm or leg got amputated. The festering wounds, the ubiquitous fat green flies laying their eggs in suppurating flesh, the hanged swinging at the crossroads, their bloated blackish-red bodies whose stink you could smell a mile away, so sweetish. The squat peasant cottages illuminated by tallow candles and the bleating of sheep on the other side of the wooden partition against which lay the straw mattresses, so that the humans could benefit from the warmth of the animals, and the billy-goat stink of the greasy woolen jerkins of dirt-encrusted peasants and their brood with their scurfy eyes, the gelatinous white of their eyeballs and their moronically wagging heads. And she was never certain she was doing the right thing. The priest accused her of pride and he was right. To atone she applied salve to the mange of stinking peasant children and said prayers with them. She had planted the sin of pride in the heart of her son as well, but how would he ever survive without it? Mosquitos and horseflies and stench everywhere, and the morass whenever it rained as if it would never cease, and in the bare chamber of the priest the handwriting on the wall: a green, cabbage-sized fungus on the whitewashed ceiling, the hollows in the wood of the prayer stool, and on the rough-hewn shelf, glass jars with rats and toads in alcohol. And again and again fear of pillage, of the blade slicing into her flesh, the bestial, gnawing fear that something could happen to the children, an illness could carry them off: they're being bled, their bright-red blood bubbles out, suddenly they're white as a sheet and perish without a last word, without the sacrament, or a tumor grows within them and they rot from the inside out while still alive and their eyes call to her, their mother, for help, and she can do nothing.

Sometimes, as if suffocating, she would lean her face into a tangle of honeysuckle or in June into the calyx of a peonie, just to rediscover a fragrance as exquisite and clean as the freshly bleached sheets of her childhood or the speculatius biscuits in the ashwood breadbox or the little sack of lavender in her linen closet back home in Liège.

She never spent one restful night confident that she could look forward to the following day. No comfort except in the biblical Beatitudes, which she read again and again, and no refuge except her barricaded heart. No one relieved her of the burden of responsibility. Her father had left her in the lurch, then her husband. Only God had not, but God helps those who help themselves.

She went to confession with her mouth grimly set. "If the world refuses me the means to do what I nevertheless do, so much the worse for the world." The world looked on guiltily as she performed miracles of cool love for her fellow man and impersonal ministration to the poorest in the parish while neglecting her own impoverishment, but since there are no miracles in financial matters, Amalia Neuhoff was over her head in debt to the baker as well as to the bank where she had mortgaged her house, and if she was still running around a free woman, then only because her personality made her creditors feel ashamed that this woman owed them money.

His whole childhood, Theodor loved his mother like a fruit loves the tree from which it hangs. Amalia was convinced that fate was exclusively a consequence of one's character, and since her son was the image of her deceased spouse—the same gentle eyes, the same soft, dark, furry hair, the same full lips— she was at pains to purge Theodor's character of the dross of paternal defects. For this was Amalia's credo: the elect are no martyrs. Whoever intends to earn laurels must first of all endure and survive and not let himself be simply carried off, like Alfons, as if there had been no one else whose turn it was to die.

When Theodor was still small, his mother's upbringing consisted entirely of stories. There were only two heroes in them: Alfons and Theodor himself (for Amalia's pride was perhaps surpassed only by the narrowness of her education; she had no more heard of Odysseus than of Lancelot, Parsifal and his striped half-brother Feirefitz, Iwein the Knight of the Lion, or even Don Quixote). Amélie, on the other hand, learned by lending a hand to her mother and the servant woman.

It was a sort of fifth gospel preached to the six-year-old Theodor in which he himself played the role of the divine child, and he became firmly convinced that he must bring this book to a good conclusion by succeeding his father in the responsibility for his mother's happiness.

But sometimes, in the intimacy of their reciprocal contemplation, which in time intensified to the point that they saw right through each other, Amalia complained bitterly to her son about the man who had left her alone in this vale of tears.

At other times, she seemed suddenly to start awake in the midst of the intimate reveries with her little son and would peer at Theodor, dumbfounded and with an expression close to disgust, as if she noticed how absurd and chimerical was the idea that a child could replace a husband. When Theodor took these sudden shifts in her attentions as an expression of a widow's mourning and dared to lard his consolation with two or three phrases that called his father's halo into question—phrases repeated word-for-word from Amalia's complaints—she cut him short or even slapped his face and began to cry from despair that her son would sully the memory of her sanctified spouse.

Nevertheless, Theodor never grew tired of his mother's company. It wasn't that she represented the world for him, she *was* his world, and its poles were his own greatness and his own nullity. He saw no need to look around for another world and lived constantly in her memories and visions, exclusively in "once upon a time" or "some fine day," no matter which. The present was nothing but a raised shooting blind from which one could comfortably survey past and future.

Theodor liked to watch his sister working in the garden; it gave him an agreeable feeling at the back of his neck, as if he were a dog being scratched. She kneeled on the ground and pulled weeds and didn't see or hear him. He observed her quiet concentration with a pleasure free of all envy, like a master craftsman appreciating the skill of a colleague from a different trade. Her trade was life. And his?

Amélie was his only confidante, his only friend. He loved and admired each of her infrequent words, every one of her harmonious movements. How much more beautiful than all striving and activity was this body kneeling there by the flowerbed in its gray cotton skirt, the heart-shaped face that lay invisible in the shadow of a wide-brimmed straw hat, protected from the afternoon sun! These sinewy, sun-browned forearms and the strong hands that glided over the dry earth, began to dig at the base of a thistle plant, and then with a jerk pulled it out by the root, which looked like a naked white worm and measured almost a cubit. Beside her stood the large willow basket into which she threw the weeds, taking it under her arm when it was full and carrying it to the compost pile while Theodor observed the tensed muscles and sinews on the arm encircling the wide-bellied basket.

In dreamy hours like this he lost all sense of being bound to the earth and was only a pair of eyes resting on his sister with complete sympathy and inner approbation, as if it were utterly sufficient that she live and act for both of them. What use would it be for him to learn to pull weeds and start doing it today, if by tomorrow something great and unknown awaited him and already required a certain preparatory meditativeness?

The half of life located in the here and now and never varying from the snail's pace of everyday tasks belonged to Amélie. The other half—the one that lacked the tranquillity to begin some interim activity or other, given the evanescence of memories and the longing for what was to come—that was his. He knew very well that some small-minded person blind to his sensitive constitution and his destiny might think him a dreamy layabout, and even though he would have found such an appellation inappropriate and ignorant, he would nevertheless have been the first to agree that of the two of them, Amélie possessed the more trustworthy compass in her head, the more reliable judgment, the greater heart—in short, that she was the better person. And there was no one besides his sister whom he would more happily concede to be a better person than he. The gifts had indeed been fairly distributed between them: she was their mother's support and he her pride.

He rose, took Amélie by the hand, and said, "Come, let's play prince and princess."

His sister sighed at the whims of her sometimes excessively childish brother, but his firm hands grasping her shoulders and his sensuous faun's gaze—it reminded her of the mythological prints in which long-lashed youths offer grapes to the drunken god—bewitched her. Like their mother, Theodor had the ability to wrap you in velvet and silk with his hypnotic eyes, so that you forgot your gardening and everything else and changed into a princess beneath his gentle, respectfully affectionate fingers.

There were several variations of prince and princess: verbose and imaginative ones in which the two of them took sedate and dignified strolls through their parks and estates, graciously greeting trees, sheep, and unsuspecting peasants to their right and left, exchanging civilities and imaginary court gossip, and paying each other compliments in all the languages they had mastered, whether fluently or only in fragments, including an atrocious parody of the local dialect larded with gurgling gutturals and nasals; then historical, action-packed ones in which they played English aristocrats driven out by the brutish Roundheads and then restored to their rights after years of exile spent wandering in privation and humiliation; and finally intimate versions with a physical emphasis, ladies' chamber versions of the game, so to speak. Here they performed all kinds of affectionate services for one another, knelt to help each other put on their shoes, file their nails, and comb their hair, freely exchanging and taking turns at slipping into the roles of master or servant. What Theodor most enjoyed about this game was the proximity of breath and hands all around his body, this gentle cocoon of fragrances and fleeting contacts with his skin, when all the little hairs on it would become voluptuously erect.

They took each other by the hand and strode from the apple trees to the linden, bowed to the nodding sunflower heads that constituted their guard of honor, while the rustle and rattle of the foliage in the breeze that heralded the evening sounded like the admiring whispers and murmurs of their royal household as they led each other to the dance floor. Now their fingertips touched at the ends of arms outstretched as if in a fencer's prima invitation and gracefully, their insteps flexed, they placed their feet onto the earth toes first and strode back and forth to the inaudible tones of a minuet. Now they took hold of each other, held each other by the hips and whirled faster and faster around their common axis like peasants at a village dance. Amélie laughed aloud at the pirouettes of this royally plebeian dance and exuded the fragrance of hay and fresh sweat; the centrifugal force of the rotation tore them apart and they fell into the grass, holding their heads.

By their twelfth winter in Lorraine, Amalia was finally and irrevocably insolvent. All the obscure springs from which the bare necessities had continued to flow had iced over. After several days, the children noticed that the house was getting cold and they were being served only cold food, then only bread crusts, then nothing at all. Their mother's lips were pulled ever tighter, her clenched jaw trembled, and her tall, slim figure braced itself like the flying buttress of a Gothic cathedral to divert the pressure of calamity from the heads of her children.

Now she nourished them only with the angry pride of her glances. Better to die, better to sacrifice son and daughter than to eat humble pie, go begging, duck your head to enter the stinking peasant cottages and plead for milk and flour.

For Theodor and Amélie, it was at first a little ascetic game, then it turned into privation and finally, torture: vomiting, diarrhea, and a listless state in which they heard as if in a trance Amalia's attempts to distract them through adjurations and Bible readings, until they had reached a condition of such drowsy vacuity that they were ready to receive the last rites of their exceptionality.

At that point, the Count de Mortagne showed up, taking advantage of one of his inspection tours through his lands to look in at the house of the woman his wife had written him about. He wrote back to her immediately, "I am now able to confirm your information in two points, *ma chère*: she is a Catholic of flaming piety, and she is a beauty."

Whereupon his wife replied, "*Mon pauvre ami, je vous souhaite bonne chance.*"

But Mortagne was not content simply to admire her in silence during Mass. He introduced himself to Amalia, exchanged a few words with her, and entered the village where she lived the next day, causing a crowd to gather.

His coach-and-four with a coat of arms emblazoned with a lion, his tricorn hat with a red rooster feather that bobbed out of the coach before his shiny top boots were lowered onto the footboard and with the next step into the mire, his medal ribbon, wig of black curls, twirled mustachios, pointed and thin as protruding, horizontal pipe cleaners, the cloud of rose water rising from his frock coat and the lace handkerchief he held before his nose while descending to then heedlessly let it drop into the filth, whereupon a scuffling tangle of village children was instantaneously rolling in the mud until a victorious, dirty little hand held the object aloft like a recovered regimental flag and was tossed a copper coin by Mortagne's coachman—his arrival at the house of the "Black Madonna" was an event. The peasants gaped, manure forks over their shoulders, until he had disappeared into the house. The priest stood at the garden gate, bowing to the nobleman like a majordomo.

That a gentleman like Mortagne, a man whose influence at court was not to be underestimated, took the impoverished little family under his wing was a cause of neither surprise nor amazement for Theodor. For this much was certain from the beginning, it was Amalia who was honoring the count by allowing him to help her. The count was a consummate player of this game. He brought bread, meat, dried fruit, perfume, clothes, candied fruits, nougat, and sugared almonds, and Theodor began to eat as he had never eaten before. His palate and taste buds staggered from one ecstasy to the next, with the result that six months after being edematous from malnutrition, he had swollen into a plump lad who for the rest of his life could never again bear having to wait for anything, having to suffer for anything.

Naturally, he noticed that he had become fat and immobile and it didn't fit his image of himself. If he looked at the skinny village boys with ribs you could count and shoulder blades pushing up under their red skin like the stumps of wings, and then compared his own round white belly and his padded, womanly hips, it was impossible to dispute that something had gone wrong. He complained to his mother of his shame and displeasure, but Amalia utterly denied that he was overweight. He was slim, he was perfect, and she fixed her magnetic eyes upon him as she always did when she intended to draw him into her world.

But this time Theodor noticed that her gaze was more bottomless than usual, and by fathoming it he felt himself becoming more mature: in the midst of the opaque darkness of her eyes was a hole into which he could plunge as if into a cistern at whose bottom there gaped yet another cavern. And there, in the deepest depths, she no longer required blind belief, but solicited his complicity. Let us not give things the names they are called by a world that is not ours.

Perhaps it was no accident that Amalia granted Theodor this insight into the wells of her eyes precisely at the moment when once again, a grown-up man was beginning to take an interest in the life of their family.

With Mortagne's entrance into their life, Theodor began to receive regular lessons. To give Theodor private instruction, the count engaged Monsieur de Broglie, a former member of the Academy who, because of a scandal the nature of which was left indefinite, had to avoid the capital and had lost his position there.

Theodor learned to read, write, and do sums as a fish learns to swim: he was in his natural element and automatically made the proper movements. It soon transpired that he also had an ear for foreign languages. He absorbed the grammars of Latin, French, and Italian as a plant absorbs dew.

All the greater was the shock when his conviction that it was only a matter of time before he had learned *everything* in his customary, vegetative way collapsed at the point where de Broglie began to introduce the fundamentals of higher mathematics: algebra, calculus, and analytic geometry, which had progressed by leaps and bounds in the last half-century thanks to the researches of Pascal and Fermat.

What Theodor didn't understand was that here, for the first time in his life, he would have to think, that an obstacle—deaf, dumb, and incorporeal—had been placed in his path, an obstacle that one could neither circumvent nor impress and mollify with a quick word or a gorgeous image. Simply the existence of such resistance made his heart sink into his boots.

In the first lesson, at the first "Can you follow me, Baron?" he was as shaken as the time when he had wanted to follow some village boys who were chinning themselves on a branch and realized that he obviously had no muscles in the required place. Now he had to fight down a feeling of panic as he sensed that he lacked some muscles in his brain as well.

How was it that his mother had never mentioned to him the eventuality of obstacles? That such hindrances were normal, indeed, that life possibly only began when one struggled with and overcame a few of them—of that he had not the slightest notion. He felt himself deceived and personally insulted. It was his conviction that each person is born complete and can learn nothing that is not already within him, by nature. Any kind of study was therefore more an awakening of knowledge slumbering inside, and the only difficult task for the future was not to struggle with something foreign to one's nature but to learn to ignore it.

No, young Theodor was no fighter! Lorenzini, for example, the *Maître d'Armes* hired by Mortagne, had even greater difficulty than de Broglie in teaching the adolescent baron to appreciate his art. It was evidently enough for Theodor to imitate the handling of the épée in an aesthetically impressive way: the en garde, falling into the invitations of sixte, quarte, octave, and prime (the latter his favorite because of the immensely snooty, patronizing position of the arm), a gentleman and fencing master from head to toe, but his not exactly muscular arm held the weapon so limply that any beat, indeed almost any bind, was enough to strike it from his hand.

"*Mà* . . . !" cried Lorenzini with mouth agape and shook his free hand, the fingers waving like a flower bud in the wind, "You're only play acting, Baron! You're not supposed to play the movement, you're supposed to carry it out!" In saying these words, the Italian looked so much like a mime from the commedia dell'arte that Theodor inwardly laughed aloud. But then he squealed like a piglet as a thrust from the weapon of his opponent, brushing aside his own sword, struck his soft belly with its cork-tipped point.

"*Mà què, Baron! Appliquez-vous!*"

But that was precisely Theodor's problem: applying himself, concentrating, and staying with a thing. He was in fact playing the invitations, indeed the whole business of fencing, but not, as Maître Lorenzini thought, because he didn't like it or didn't take it seriously. On the contrary: precisely in the things that mattered to him, the lightness of a beautiful gesture, visible to everyone, was of supreme importance to him.

For the most part, his thoughts dashed ahead or dawdled behind, his concentration began to flicker and blur, he moved through a bank of fog, freed himself from the Ariadne fetters of logic and replaced them with the gilded ribbons of his imagination.

If de Broglie were introducing the study of philosophy, Theodor, who listened with much less concentration than his sister, immediately preferred to hear something about the men who had uttered such great thoughts and to know how the thoughts had served them in their daily lives. After three or four sentences he was already inhabiting the skin of a Socrates and disputing in the Academy (while the further elaborations of his teacher rustled past Theodor unheard), eloquently defending himself, scoffing at the poison, suffering under the regime of his wife, sunning himself in the admiration of his pupils, and uttering the wisdom whispered to him by the almost incorporeal prompter de Broglie, while in the thundering interior of his head, precision and context were swept aside by the bow wave of his fame.

Abstract as it was, mathematics offered no such escapes. Theodor had to admit to himself that the *ars analytica*, operating with unknowns, marked the limit of his comprehension.

"Can you follow me, Baron?"

He shook his head. He hated equations; you couldn't talk to them and in their dark masks they evaded his eyes. You couldn't argue with Pascal's theorem about the projected sides of a hexagon—and why must it be a hexagon?—inscribed in a conic section, whose respective points of intersection lay along a straight line. *So what!* (English came to him more easily.) It was inhuman in the truest sense of the word. And de Broglie's ability to find that sort of thing beautiful lent him an air of inhumanity as well.

"And what do *you* find beautiful, Herr Baron?" asked his teacher.

"The sunrise, for example!" cried Theodor and made a despairing gesture with his hand.

Exultantly, de Broglie set out to explain the mathematical laws governing the movement of heavenly bodies, but Theodor closed his ears to them as if they were blasphemy. What made the sunrise something special and wonderful each morning was its fortuitousness. A sunrise wasn't the solution to an equation but a favor granted, and each individual one made his heart quake with gratitude because he was convinced that the sun could just as easily *not* rise. He needed the hope, the anxiety, in order to then experience the joy. *Not* to rely on the sunrise, because it could just as well *fail* to occur, *that* was the logic Theodor understood.

He was incapable of concentrating long enough to follow even a single one of his preceptor's proofs to the end. A premature intellectual exhale regularly put an end to his effort, as if he were trying to run once around the house while holding his breath and gave up, gasping, after three sides. "I don't want to die!" he would then protest, as though thinking were some subtle form of suicide to which they were trying to drive him.

No sooner had his concentration begun to fray at the edges than he would flee into conversations with himself in which he was a great mathematician, and in so doing would lose the thread of de Broglie's patient explanations. How could he continue to exist if he were not in every regard the person his mother had described him as being? This question transformed itself into, How could he hide from this realization? The only available refuge were his daydreams.

"Can you follow me up to this point, Theodor?" He shuddered with wounded dignity. It seemed he was already so stupid that he was no longer Herr Baron but only Theodor. He shook his head and gritted his teeth. Once again he hadn't been listening. This time, he pulled himself together and hearkened word for word as the wobbly tower of logic rose before him. At the sixth story, it disappeared into the clouds, and when Theodor paused so as to at least assure himself of the foundation, the whole thing collapsed and he burst into tears.

His one faint hope was that some day he would be caught up in such terrible storms of fate that in his existential distress, he would completely and forever forget about all these things, then once the danger had passed, would begin again and live as carefree as he had before they had begun to embitter his existence.

Why was his mind capable of the craziest nonsense, knowing intuitively, for example, how an Italian word he had never heard before must be pronounced? *Reviviscenza*, for example, or *spidocchiare* or *dapocaggine*—he didn't even need to have any idea what it meant, and would even accompany it with expressive gestures which, although de Broglie disapproved of them as *singeries*, delighted Lorenzini so much that he kissed his fingertips with emotion and homesickness.

But as soon as it was a question of abstract, analytical thought, when improvisation and flirting with happenstance and the imponderables of human nature were at an end, when there were no more sounds and pictures, Theodor's intellect went blind.

"All right then, enough for today, Baron." And how resigned the word "Baron" now sounded. It was even more humiliating than the earlier "Theodor." "We'll try again tomorrow."

Theodor nodded and swore to himself to go through the material that evening, and that night, and the following morning—as long as it took until he had understood it. And indeed, after dinner he sat over the lifeless pattern of letters that formed no speakable language, of lines that yielded no beautiful drawing, but immediately everything dissolved before his eyes, he heard himself arguing with Fermat about the theorem he himself had proposed—it had been hard work, he explained to the mathematician, let's talk about more cheerful things now—and his eyelids grew heavy. He swore to himself again: tomorrow, tomorrow for sure, but next morning the sun was shining and he fled into the garden, where his bad conscience made him perceive its beauties even more clearly than usual. Yes, he would have needed willpower and discipline, but who knows, he thought, those are things of which one only has a certain quantity in oneself, and one ought to save it for something more important than mathematics.

His mother overlooked the catastrophe of his ignorance in her time-tested manner. At first, Theodor was disappointed that she was so tolerant of the baser tendencies within him. He had hoped she would scold him and force him to learn, if necessary with the whip—that is, actually he hoped she would enable him to understand. But instead, she treated mathematics like a guest who had misbehaved: she banished it from the house.

Nevertheless, it was difficult for Theodor to suffer this intellectual humiliation. He escaped into sleep and fever. During this illness or convalescence, he became better acquainted with Count Mortagne, who visited him at his bedside every day, and whom he had previously seen only once or twice.

In his half-hour conversations with the patron sitting by his bed, Theodor understood for the first time what nobility actually meant. Amalia's words of instruction became flesh in the person of the count. Fascinated and as it were enlightened, the boy observed every gesture, every remark of this man in whom, in a wondrous way, the secondary was distinguished from the essential, the acting from the being, and this being unfolded into full blossom as soon as the count opened his mouth.

All the activity that constituted Mortagne seemed to be detached from him and to run entirely on its own, without him having the slightest thing to do with it himself. His coach traveled, his servants read his wishes from his glance, somewhere in the capital secretaries worked for him, his official duties were carried out, his influence was propagated. Somewhere in the country helping hands kept his chateau in working order, woodcutters cleared his forests, his peasants sowed and harvested without him even for a moment giving the impression that he must go to any trouble or exert himself, intervene in this clockwork, work or think. No, his entire material existence led a life of its own and the count was free to devote himself to his nobility.

And his words constituted this nobility. They were wrested from a weariness that had nothing personal about it, for Mortagne was a lively, urbane man who had just turned forty.

It was the weariness of the centuries, the burden of secular, worldly knowledge that preferred to clothe itself in aphorisms collected over generations and thus forestall the ennui that personal opinions—by nature impolite, presumptuous, challenging one to take a position—always elicit in conversation.

For Theodor quickly grasped this much: that language, when it was wielded by a person of nobility, served neither to set in motion some action or other, nor even less to assert one's personal opinions. Language was the most highly developed form of interior design: it made empty rooms habitable.

The first time that Mortagne sat by the bed of the ill or malingering Theodor, he said, "Baron, it's unworthy of great souls to make a public show of their perplexities." And, "One must approach serious problems lightly and insubstantial problems with earnestness."

Such sentences were kept impersonal enough that Theodor did not mistake them for instructions for behavior, but rather understood them as an invitation to continue the conversation. Mortagne was not interested in ruminating upon problems— like equations!—and possibly solving them. His language was in the service of speaking itself. However, one must on no account make the mistake of thinking that his conversation was just cheap talk. The materialistic opinion that words only have value when they lead to opinions, insights, and deeds was foreign to Mortagne's rhetoric, which possessed its own rules and laws and was more like music.

"For someone lacking in taste," said the count, "honesty is an unfortunate characteristic." And in view of Theodor's present despair, "Lamentation is women's work, Baron. Men must remember."

Thus, if the art of talking and conversation, as demonstrated to Theodor by Mortagne, was no one's handmaiden, and especially not the handmaiden of the deed, nevertheless it soon became apparent that it possessed a triple power: it transfixed men's consciousness like the red cape the attention of the bull. It distracted them from what was, which now, thanks to its force, was no longer. And it was a pilot able to steer the vessel of perception in the desired direction.

Once Theodor understood that, he was one step further than his mother. The counterworld she had created by denying the realities could, with the help of language, be beautified and turned into a pleasant and comfortable place where others would also gladly tarry.

"Success is ugly. Success nauseates me," resounded the parlando of the count's seminar, and Theodor understood from this sentence that it was ignoble to measure a person—and especially oneself—by results. That was what merchants did. The value of a nobleman was bound up with his existence, which, embodied in his language, could then be seen in the proper light.

Chapter III

*T*HEODOR'S FIRST OPPORTUNITY TO apply the knowledge acquired in his conversations with the Count de Mortagne was in Master de Broglie's lessons in natural science. When the latter, in defiance of the maternal proscription, once again threw his grappling hooks over the porous walls of Theodor's analytical intellect and started in about the projected sides of a hexagon inscribed in an ellipse and how they intersected at points A, B, and C along a straight line, Theodor looked at him with ardent interest and said, "When Pascal developed this theorem, wasn't he a member of the Académie Mersenne, the predecessor to the Académie des Sciences to which you belong as well, Maître?"

"Indeed," answered de Broglie in surprise and with a joyful, still tentative smile.

"Then I wonder," continued Theodor, "what it was that drove him to Port-Royal and flung him from mathematics into theology. Because from what little I can judge, there's a considerable difference between the logic of these conic sections here and the *logique du cœur*. Isn't this evidence of Pascal's starting to . . . well . . . slacken off?"

"Extremely interesting question, dear Baron, but I would most emphatically beg to differ with you. First of all, you must think yourself back into the intellectual—and spiritual—climate prevailing in the Academy at that time . . ."

Theodor noticed that this was a different tone than previously and the hour passed in pleasurable and informative conversation, interlarded with anecdotes from de Broglie's academic career, sallies against the casuistry of Escobar de Mendoza, speculation on St. Augustine's concept of the heart, and samples of existential optimism. Theodor enjoyed himself and was able to contribute interested and seemingly interesting questions and interjections that continually gave de Broglie the impression that they were having a dialogue.

At the end of the lesson, he was more satisfied with Theodor than ever before. That makes two of us, thought the latter with furrowed brow, and he asked himself in astonishment and some incredulity to what extent his interlocutor had only been playing along with him to be obliging while not for a second losing sight of Theodor's limitations, or whether it was in fact so easy to divert others' attention from anything one found disagreeable.

In the depths of their souls, did even die-hard logicians like his teacher crave nothing more than to have their existence and identity validated, a validation more indispensable than all their theory and practice, all thought and action?

But if Theodor thought that, thanks to these initial rhetorical ruses, he had solved all the problems de Broglie posed, he was quickly disabused. One day his teacher sent Amélie, whose presence during school hours was usually tolerated, out of the room. For on this day he intended to inform Theodor, whose education was meant to be a pyramid rising level upon level from the Bible and the pre-Socratics right up to the latest scientific discoveries, of the recent discovery by Leeuwenhoek, with the aid of his two-hundred-seventy power microscope, of spermatozoa.

"*Comment*, Baron?" The preceptor's eyes widened in astonishment. "You've never . . . never? Not even about the meaning of the secretion in the palm of your hand?"

The utterly sheepish expression on Theodor's face made him pause.

"*M'enfin* . . . But you do know . . ." He pointed below Theodor's belt at his wide breeches. "You must know what that thing's for?!"

The young man, or at this moment, the blushing lad, knew only one thing: lying in bed by himself and dreaming of the past or future, recalling the images of that afternoon's games with Amélie in the garden, their innumerable, intertwining encounters with mythical and historical figures—traveling, fighting, crowned with laurels—when he lolled on his belly and tossed and turned, stretched and rolled himself into a ball, his member (which seemed to be what de Broglie was talking about) would enlarge and stiffen, while languorous shivers ran through his entire body; it was like being tired out from riding or walking or swimming and finally being able to stretch out your legs in bed.

He got the same feeling when Minne gave his shoulder-length hair a thorough combing; in that case it began on his scalp and from there ran down over his temples and clavicles in tickling rivulets like a warm rain—or when Amélie stroked his arm so that the little hairs on the nape of his neck and his arms stood up, or when his mother's cool hand lay upon his forehead, twisting his locks between her fingers.

It was a feeling that flourished only when he was completely still, when he surrendered himself to whatever was happening to him; it was like doing the dead-man's float on the glittering, sun-struck surface of the lake, with the sweet, dizzying sense of never ending. It began as quietly as an afternoon breeze, gained speed and force, and then slowly subsided again. The fact that something seemed to be missing lent a tension to this blissful feeling like a dissonant chord left unresolved, coupled it to a certain nervous expectation in his skin and limbs of something more, made it tingle in the tips of his fingers and opened up prospects of broad valleys of the imagination across which, as the feeling subsided, somewhat melancholy shadows quietly fell.

In short, it was agreeable, extremely agreeable, a lethargic pleasure, the most pleasurable physical state he knew. But so what? What was the old Frenchman getting at with his talk of Leeuwenhoek's whatchamacallums?

The old Frenchman asked no more questions and, curiously enough, requested an interview with Theodor's mother. With cool gray eyes she listened impassively to the schoolmaster's remarks.

"*Non, Monsieur, je n'ai pas l'habitude de surveiller la quequette de mon fils,*" was all that Theodor, listening at the keyhole, could understand, and he concluded from all this that he was suffering from a fatal disease that de Broglie had discovered through some weakness or other that Theodore had betrayed. And so his life was already over, and all his dreams had been hobgoblins, illusory chimera. He collapsed on the flagstones. Wiping the cold sweat from his brow, he began to pray: Lord, if thou . . . The door opened. Theodor had just enough time to disguise his posture as polishing his shoe buckle, and Amalia and de Broglie emerged. The moribund boy glanced from mother to teacher and back again, and even more unbearable than the certainty of death was the indiscretion of this man who had known the most intimate of all secrets, namely his imminent death, before he did himself. Moreover, the most monstrous thing was that the Frenchman was smiling, for even if he meant it to be comforting, it was a dreadfully inappropriate expression for the present tragedy.

In the wagon that brought mother and son into the market town, Theodor learned that he wasn't going to die, only to be operated upon. From hints she dropped he started to put two and two together, most especially (and this was worse than death, because more embarrassing) that without knowing it, he had apparently been living in an inhibited, unnatural, infantile state and was thus some kind of retarded freak. Suddenly the dozens of innuendos and boasts of the village boys that he had overheard without being able to make sense of them acquired contour. During the ride, his suffocating fear of getting the short end of life's stick without, for the present, being able to explain exactly how and by what means, expanded to a feeling of nightmarish displacement from reality when his mother said, more to herself than to him, "We can't leave such an important thing up to a barber or a quacksalver. It's got to be done by a *mohel*." Theodor couldn't understand what she was mumbling. Suddenly he had the impression that a stranger was sitting with him in the wagon.

The bearded man with ringlets wagged his head circumspectly at the sight and gave a servile bow. "Your Highness, is more complicated with big *yingl* like young Highness than with little infant . . ."

Amalia jingled a little sack and the bearded man gave another bow. Theodor was determined to take whatever awaited him like a man. But when he saw the fellow honing the double-edged blade with the rounded tip and attaching it to a flat, protective handgrip, he lost consciousness in the silvery shimmer and the ominous scraping noise of the whetstone.

"Young Highness has sensitive constitution," commented the *mohel* sympathetically.

Amalia gave a tense nod. "To be sure. Now discharge your duty."

"Wouldn't your Highness perhaps prefer . . . Is possible not good for delicate nerves."

"Never," cried the Baroness, "would I leave my son alone at a moment like this!"

"*Barukh haba*," replied the *mohel*, and it sounded like, I wash my hands in innocence. The incision followed, blood spurted, Amalia cried out, "He's bleeding to death! He's bleeding to death!"

Theodor regained consciousness, saw the blood, and knew he'd been mutilated.

The man in black curls reassured his mother. He said the loss of blood, which he sopped up with several rapidly saturated bandages, was normal for a fourteen-year-old whose circulation was, after all, already completely developed at the location in question.

Every time the encrusted bandages were changed, the wound opened up and bled anew; it took days for it to begin to heal.

When everything had healed over, Theodor took a close look at the ugly, burned-looking red knots of skin surrounding the pale pink glans which he discovered with a certain sentimental commiseration, reminding him of a dead chick fallen from the nest, and he made a decision to ignore and forget this zone of his body just as he had always done. The thing was unnecessary except for making water. And as an aging commander, after repeated defeats, might resign himself to writing off forever a piece of territory he had conquered and occupied, so Theodor forsook any conscious notice or use of this appendage, this vessel of such painful memories.

It was months until, one sleepless night, listening to the sound of his sister's measured breathing drifting in through the open window from the next room, he was perishing from loneliness and needed something—anything—to hold onto so as not to be swept away by the current of his yearnings. The only solid thing his hands could find was his member.

It was not exactly unpleasant to knead that misshapen red bulge of skin he refused to look at, but the tender sensations that had earlier suffused his entire body now flowed together at this tip; it was both an increase in intensity and an impoverishment. Since it was becoming apparent that his bodily fluids were striving toward this one location like a river toward a waterfall, its bed growing ever narrower and steeper, he fell into a milking motion that half relieved, half exacerbated the peculiar itch. This much was certain: something or other was about to happen. This crescendo must culminate in some kind of final chord and crash of drums. While he was still ruminating about what it would be and how it would manifest itself in surprise and terror, while his brain in quick succession was proposing and rejecting images that could serve to illustrate and translate this revolt of his senses until it finally settled on details of Amélie's body—her strong, work-roughened hands, the veins and tendons in her forearms—a movement suddenly began halfway up his spinal chord that every other part of his body hearkened to intently, a sort of column of quicksilver inside a narrow canal ran with single-minded determination down his back, then rose up diagonally from his buttocks through his abdomen, past his testicles, and out into the light.

A brief paroxysm, a fleeting cloud sweeping over his consciousness, then comfy flaccidity once the tension had burst, and immediately thereafter the insipid, sordid anticlimax, waking from the trance with moist, sticky fingers. Theodor shook himself back into his right mind and two thoughts took shape in his consciousness: Leeuwenhoek and Original Sin.

So this was what his mutilation had been for, to uncork the sacred vessel so that he might become like everyone else in this effusion that made relieving oneself a little too easy. Sin has a *horror vacui*; it can't stand to have anyone deny himself to it and remain in a state of innocence. In exchange, it rewards us with physical pleasure to make us forget the shame that follows. Hadn't the Dutch scientist described his spermatozoon, the agent of this sinfulness, as a sort of flagellate? God had made them into flagellants, given them the form of penitents, atoning for man's urge to drag everything into the light, his desire to see everything and his need to show everything.

To rub his skin raw and cause this effusion at a single point signified not only a loss of purity, but above all, the disclosure of a secret. The denouement was banal like all denouements, and half to punish himself for his unfortunate curiosity, half in the hope of perhaps being able to discover something more about the matter after all, he soon began the exercise again. But there was nothing more to be learned except that, disappointingly enough, one's body prefers banal pleasures to sublime frustrations.

De Broglie returned to the subject of spermatozoa and their role in copulation.

"Well, Baron, this little eruption of lust, which you have probably experienced by now, is strictly speaking not actually necessary for reproduction. Animals apparently do not experience anything of the kind. Perhaps it is the human soul that makes us susceptible to it. So we are confronted with a remarkable phenomenon. It looks very much as though the bliss we experience is nature's way of thanking us humans—and us alone—for perpetuating the race.

"Nature," Theodor replied coolly, "pays in small change."

He hated his teacher since this affair. The other knew too much about him, had dragged his life down into sinful banality, the sight of him became unbearable. And since Theodor settled all his inner conflicts, worked through his hopes and fears in hundreds of constantly varied and newly initiated inner monologues and dialogues, there suddenly occurred to him in one of these imaginary conversations an evil sentence which got lodged in his everyday consciousness and started growing there like an abscess, until one day Theodor couldn't help saying it aloud, whether to get rid of it or to see how what had already happened a dozen times in his daydreams would function in reality.

And precisely because he had already silently said the sentence so many times and in so many different intonations, it crossed his lips in a very credible and convincing way when the Count de Mortagne inquired about his progress in school and Theodor whispered it into his ear in a well-rehearsed tone of shock. Nevertheless, he was glad that his patron only nodded and didn't mention it again.

So now he had become wicked as well, but since it was de Broglie's indiscretion that had burst the hermetic bubble of innocence in which Theodor had existed (as he interpreted the affair) and he found himself in a state of original sin, at this point it didn't matter anymore.

The next morning, de Broglie bid farewell to Amalia. Pressing notarial affairs required his presence in Dijon. His successor would be dispatched by the count in the next few days.

He cast a melancholy smile on Theodor, who was white as chalk and at pains not to let the ice in his eyes melt.

"*Au revoir, Baron. Je n'ai plus rien à vous apprendre.*"

Theodor discovered that he was incapable of keeping a secret in manly silence, in dark acquiescence to his own wickedness. It was as if he were trying to keep the lid pressed down on a pot of boiling water. Not twenty-four hours after de Broglie's departure he confided in his sister with the intention of submitting himself to a judgment that was morally irreproachable but also shaped by love and understanding.

"You said *what* to Mortagne?" she asked, appalled.

"You heard me right," whispered Theodor contritely, not wanting to repeat the words.

Amélie regarded him sternly. "You disappoint me, Theodor. I wouldn't have expected that of you."

The sinner trembled as if at the evil augury of a fortune teller. At the same time, however, the reproach having been uttered, the worst was over and by bravely listening to the verdict, he had already gone a good way toward atoning for it and come a good deal closer to being forgiven.

"Amélie, please tell me that everything will be all right."

"Everything will be all right if you tell Mortagne the truth and ask for forgiveness."

"Yes, I will do it!" Theodor fervently replied. "But will you still love me?"

"Of course I'll still love you!"

And of course, Theodor said not a word to Mortagne; he resolved so long to do it, and he formulated the sentences so often in his mind, that at some point he almost felt as if he had spoken them aloud. This partial alleviation was enough for him and he left the rest to time, and Amélie was too high-minded ever to ask about it again.

But although de Broglie was gone, Theodor couldn't forget the humiliations he had suffered through him. He moved through the house, the garden, and the village as if he were stained scarlet and he regarded everyone with secret antipathy and vindictiveness. Most of all he wished he could dissolve into air, disappear and go somewhere where he was a blank slate, where the only thing that counted was what he was and not what he—inadequately—did.

But when the Count of Mortagne announced that in order to complete Theodor's education by transferring it to one of the first establishments in Europe, he intended to procure for him a position as a page at court to *Madame* (Princess Palatine, mother of the Duke of Orléans, and a compatriot of Theodor's, who liked to hear around her the sounds of her native idiom), Theodor had only one hope: that his mother would *not* let him go.

Amalia herself was not quite sure what to think about losing her son to Versailles, although she admitted to herself that this was the only way to bring to flower the seeds she hoped she had planted in him. It was only that she would have liked to see them blossom with her own eyes. Ever since her son's birth she had been his familiar shadow, the chronicler and guardian of his existence, and if he should now be torn from her, what would remain?

The Count de Mortagne had his own plans and suggestions in that regard as well, and conveyed them to Amalia one evening behind closed doors. The windows of the adjoining room, however, were not closed, and Theodor and his sister stood there listening with baited breath to hear what the judgment on their future would be.

They didn't understand the question Mortagne was asking. Theodor looked back at Amélie who shrugged her shoulders.

But then they heard their mother's quiet "No" and took each other by the hand.

Apparently Mortagne had stood up, knelt before the fire, picked up the bellows, and was pumping. The flames responded to the whoosh-whoosh of the stream of air like angrily hissing snakes.

The sound that followed didn't seem to make any sense.

Again, Amalia's voice could be heard, "No, Count." And again there followed noises about whose significance the siblings exchanged puzzled glances.

After a disconcerting pause in the conversation, they again heard their mother's voice. She said only one word—"Ah"—but in a tone they had never heard from her before.

They didn't see her again until the following morning, when she informed Theodor at breakfast that Mortagne, who had already left, would return on the following day to take him to Versailles. It was in his best interests and a matter of the greatest pride to her.

He tried to submerge himself in her eyes, but the wellheads were covered.

And so, without warning, the day of farewell had arrived. Now everything, his whole life, seemed to have gone too quickly. The house, the garden—everything became weightless under his relinquishing gaze. Everything turned to dust as under a scorching sun and Theodor wondered if what his eyes could no longer see continued to exist or whether the world collapsed into nothingness behind each of his steps.

Amélie, with whom he had not exchanged another word about the previous evening, was in the garden, and a feeling of transience drove him into her arms. He held her tight, as if she herself were fleeting time. She looked at him in surprise and amusement.

With a curious mixture of despair and badinage, Theodor said to her, "Let's play prince and princess once more."

To his astonishment, she agreed. Arm in arm they strolled through the garden. He asked for a dance and they started with graceful steps and turns, became more and more wild, at the end were twirling like dervishes, and at some point found themselves lying dizzy in the grass.

When Theodor wanted to keep going, Amélie raised her hand in protest. She'd had enough; she didn't feel well. He let go of her immediately. Unlike the rubes from the village, he was fascinated by the lunar secret of women. He felt a not very well thought-out but nevertheless genuine respect for Amélie during her period, a little as if she had stigmata. This invisible wound she bore with such dignity, this mysterious opening in her body from which she regularly spilled her blood without having to die, lent her in Theodor's eyes something martyr-like which he wasn't able to reconcile with the image of his utterly worldly and quietly cheerful sister. On days like this he secretly wished he could worship her like a saint or question her like a sibyl.

As he cooled down from the heat of the dance, the pain of parting suddenly set in. Like a magnifying glass for his senses, it made him experience everything as closer and sharper: the enormously alive and yet so plebeian odor of perspiration exuded by his sister's hot armpits, the masculine veins of her forearms and her dirty boy's fingers in his manicured hand whose palm itched painfully with the memory of the sticky moistness of the de Broglian and Leeuwenhoekian spermatozoa he had only just recently conjured up yet again. Amélie's lunar, fluid indisposition and the vague image of that opening, that source of blood in her body—there was a blind spot in the center of the pattern, something both alarming and enticing.

In the next breath, for the space of a heartbeat, he entered a trance in which he was blind and deaf to his own gestures and movements. Then he felt his sister's hand on his chest, opened his eyes, and found himself an inch from her face. With dry lips, she kissed him on the mouth and whispered, "We've been deposed, Your Highness. Now we shall die together." She lay down flat on her back; he followed obediently. They lay there like the *gisants* in Romanesque basilicas, two stone sculptures with their hands folded on their breasts, speechless, motionless. All that was missing was the faithful dog at their feet. Theodor opened his eyes and responded belatedly, "Yes, we shall."

He remained in this condition of weary, wounded sensibility the entire rest of the day. From the enervating tick-tock of the grandfather clock that seemed bent on bursting his head he fled to the attic and chewed persistently on a dry heel of bread until his mouth was so full of sweetish-sour, tangy-mushy tastes that he almost lost control and had to spit it out. And on top of all that there was his fearful anticipation of the imminent departure. In the evening, he lay wide awake in his bed. He felt the need to pray, or rather, to have a dialogue with God.

Believe me, my French is not half as good as you all seem to think, and I haven't the slightest notion about court etiquette. I'll make a fool of myself and you know how porous and threadbare my education is. It will be like walking on eggs. You've got to help me wangle my way through, make myself invisible or make the others blind to my weaknesses.

For Amélie, the life of a lady was being planned. Mortagne would marry her off sooner or later. With the fledging of her children, their mother's destiny had been fulfilled. Without wanting to admit it to himself, Theodor knew that it was impossible to stop the clock of his life at this point and let it fall into a Sleeping-Beauty slumber until he returned and awakened everything to renewed life, without having missed a single second.

The throb of his heartbeat lay cradled in the softer rhythm of his sleeping sister's inhale and exhale, which he thought he could discern through the open windows, and again, as had happened that afternoon, Theodor fell into a deaf, blind trance under whose spell he involuntarily arose, opened the door, tiptoed across the corridor, and glided noiselessly into Amélie's chamber.

The sphere of silence that was this room awakened Theodor from his stupefaction. He felt like a nocturnal animal, a cat with whiskers erect and moving silently, seeing and hearing everything, and as if electrified by the air surrounding its body.

It was a simple room containing only a bed, the washstand with its marble top on which stood a water jug and a bowl, a linen chest, the inlaid sewing chest on which lay the *métier*—the tambour frame stretched with a piece of as yet unembroidered linen—as well as the pattern and the cushion. Everything was bathed in a bluish-silver glaze of moonlight to which Theodor's eyes quickly adjusted.

Amélie's body was completely covered. Only a shock of brown hair was visible and her left arm, hanging down from the bed.

Cautiously, he took a few steps, took hold of the three-legged stool standing before the little chest with her needlework, placed it next to the bed, and lowered himself onto it without a sound. If he were to stretch out his hand now, he could touch Amélie. He hitched the stool a little to one side, fearing that his breath on his sister's skin could awaken her.

To make himself even more invisible, he adjusted his breathing to fit that of the sleeping girl and of nature itself, until he had become part of the décor, which expanded and contracted like the quietly creaking wood.

At regular intervals sounded the pure, whistled C of a toad. He listened to his sister's breathing and it became the distant murmur of a river, the rustle of the wind in the poplars. He smelled the potpourri with its predominant fragrance of lavender and the warmth of the sun trapped in the linens. Like a corona around the moon, a faint scent of rosewater surrounded the flacon on the night table.

The sounds and smells that flowed through him congealed into images, idylls of his life on whose horizon the future flickered like lightning and which seemed to be painted on a bright ground, and on closer inspection it turned out to be Amélie's arm his eyes had been staring at the whole time.

The softly modeled, longish biceps was crisscrossed by a fine network of veins. Two delicate transverse creases ran across the inside of the slightly bent elbow and there beneath the fair skin sat a vein like a dark blue scarab, which after disappearing beneath the snowfield of the forearm soon reappeared at the wrist like a subterranean river, subdivided, and emptied into the delta of the hand.

The change of color from the smooth pallor of the arm to the reddish, bulgy heel of her palm was shocking, like a hymn ending with a curse. This half-opened hand seemed obscene compared to the arm, so fleshy between the constricting folds of its palm, a tropical plant whose motionless petals, the fingers, seemed just waiting for the moment when a victim, lured by the shiny redness, the moist warmth of the calyx, disappeared into it, when it would close upon him.

Theodor instinctively leaned forward to bring his nose closer to this swamp flower and inhale the smells of earth, sweat, onions, and rosewater stored in its pores, but then he reined himself in. How unprotected this white arm lay, half hanging, as if it had already capitulated. How transitory it was. And what a feeling of urgency in the face of this life that was so vulnerable, so surrendered to death. Whose urgency? Theodor didn't know. It was a general, all-encompassing feeling of urgency. A night, a day, the blink of an eye, and already everything was falling into decay, would be only the memory of a life and evaporate like dew in the morning sun.

Theodor's pulse increased, his breathing grew shorter. The longer he sat beside his sister, the more overpowering his desire to stroke her arm, to squeeze her hand until the blood was forced out, leaving behind white pressure points which would slowly be resuffused from the edges toward the center. But then, the merest breath away from the object of his yearning, he realized how intensely he relished precisely the tension of not being able to bridge the last few centimeters if he didn't want this state of consummate happiness to end.

Shivers rippled down his shoulders and thighs, a weakness settled onto the back of his neck and knees, and his scalp prickled. His glance became sharper and he had the impression of more tautly filling out the skin now covering his nerve endings like a lizard-skin glove instead of flapping around them like a woolen mitten.

He saw his sister as one flawless, closed sphere and himself as another: closed, flawless, while between them flickered flames like St. Elmo's fire. How much sweeter was the secret, the ultimate lack of focus, than the banal, cold logic of resolutions. He had no desire to apply the probing, dissecting scalpel to these two spheres. What he wanted was the tension, the unresolved tension in which yearning slowly spiraled upward, as if an orchestra were playing the same theme again and again, each turn of the screw transposed a half tone higher, without ever coming to an end.

Toward morning he tiptoed from the room and out of the house.

With both hands he scooped water from the jug and splashed it onto his face and chest. The cold from the flagstones on which he stood barefoot crept up his legs and into his elbows and the roots of his teeth. Outside, the birds greeted the awakening day with deafening chirps and twitters. Swallows sliced through the hazy air. Shortly before the sun appeared, the slate-colored sky boiled up into white radiance, then the wind became warm and the larks rose—one could make them out as black, dancing specks against the light—and Theodor felt as if on this morning he could effortlessly follow this country lane around the whole world, his face continually turned back toward where the landscape of his past, receding deeper and deeper, confirmed the wealth of his existence.

And what had happened then? Already he was sitting upon the coach box of Mortagne's barouche, traversing the Argonne Forest whose beech trunks gleamed like oxidized copper, dropping down from the Lorraine plateau into the hot, sunny valley of the Marne. There in the distance, like columns of smoke, the steeples of Chalons were already emerging in the hazy sunlight. What had happened? He had secretly put on the tight corset that made him sweat, turning the journey into a torture, but made him look to the eyes of Mortagne and the rest of the world as slim and noble as he was expected to. He had lain in the arms of his mother, who had looked at him all through the afternoon as if she were reading a book she already knew by heart. What did she look like, actually? Could he possibly have neglected to internalize her image so that he would never forget her? What had they said to each other in farewell? And Amélie? She was gone, everything already gone as if it had never been, and he swore to himself to return as soon as possible and to continue living this life that had only been interrupted, alongside the new life toward which he was now being drawn.

In the inn where they stopped to change horses, a maid-servant gave him a frank stare, then sauntered straddle-legged into the barn, turning twice to look back at him over her shoulder.

Once they drove past a dandelion-yellow meadow where lethargic sheep were grazing and a shepherdess in a brown dress lay in the grass, chewing a stem. How strangely the sight of this girl touched him, a girl whose life he could just as well have led as his own. He had the feeling that his soul could migrate without effort from his body into that of one of these figures by the wayside: the fisherman or the bargeman on the towpath next to the river.

Mortagne's trundling coach swept him off through space and time. He no longer knew if he had said farewell to mother and sister at all. What would become of them when he was gone?

"Youth is past, Baron," called Mortagne as they retired to their rooms. "Tomorrow evening we shall be in Versailles."

Chapter IV

𝒪H DEVASTATING DÉJÀ VU! Theodor, believing that Mortagne's coach had spirited him away from all painful memories, found himself at the end of his journey confronted with the task of solving an equation that proved far more complicated than all the ones he had failed at in Master de Broglie's mathematics lessons.

In a visually impressive imitation of the cabbalistic world of geometric figures, Theodor was attempting to divide the palace of Versailles into horizontal planes of importance and vertical columns of spatial affinity, with the individual levels connected by diagonals and flights of stairs. But that was woefully inadequate. He had to complicate the already incomprehensible diagram even further with various circles at whose centers sat little fixed stars, surrounded by their satellites. The realms of functions and tasks spread a fine-mesh grid over his doodlings, a grid that failed because in the end it was impossible to represent a kind of ripple effect: entire wings of the building were full of actions, uniforms, gestures and wasted days, scurryings and voices, dancing bodies and reverberating laughter that couldn't be attributed to anything or anyone—all this distorted one's perceptions, as when the wind blows across a lake and dissolves all the reflections into lights and shadows. Besides, the insane diagram would have had to undulate with irregular parabolas representing the rise and fall of a general tension that originated in unknown events: visits, departures, performances, festivities that set all the levels and all their interconnections, the circles and the flickering rasters into additional, unpredictable motion and jumbled them up.

To all this, moreover, accrued a fourth dimension that rendered the solution of the equation Theodor had been assigned utterly impossible: time, duration, the knowledge of tradition and longevity that enabled one to discern an infinite prospect behind every movement, gesture, and act, and to see everything as the consequence of distant, long-term developments and processes.

And all of this, the whole pulsating tangle, didn't even touch the inner sanctum, the invisible numinousness, the beating heart at the center, the sun that kept this cosmos alive, the ultimate circle around the ancient, bigoted king who hardly participated anymore in all the revelries and follies of this world, his most Christian Majesty Louis the Fourteenth.

And yet the first sight of it had delighted Theodor: a central perspective with a white, shining palace at its vanishing point, which quickly drew closer as the horses' hooves threw up sand and gravel and raised Avalonic mists that obscured his view of the modern Camelot. He had no eyes for the surroundings, stared straight ahead, and there it lay beyond the majestic, black *grille d'honneur*: golden-ocher, immense, overwhelmingly beautiful.

But that only lasted a short time. Soon the palace was revealed to be a three-dimensional labyrinth with a maze of staircases which mocked any sense of space, a Molech of stone that gobbled up and digested whoever strayed into it. New faces appeared without ceasing. Bodies and faces came and went, threw open doors, hurried through suites of rooms, disappeared down halls, and whenever a privy door opened, the trapped stench of urine and feces was liberated and, together with the tallowy smell of old sweat from beneath powdered wigs, made one recoil.

It was impossible to read anyone's face, to understand even one word, if you hadn't mastered the codes, the sign language in which people communicated here.

His first impulse, to seek some catalyst with whose help to make sense of all this activity, soon proved illusory. There was no such thing. And yet the whole business did not break down, the edifice was still standing the following morning, the trains of delivery wagons rumbled in, and the ballet that had continued somewhat more slowly and with a smaller troupe during the night began to accelerate again.

Perhaps, thought Theodor during his first sorties as a messenger, the whole opaque mechanism of this ark was nothing but the sum of such errands as his, larded with chance encounters, driven off course by digressions, missed turnings, and delays, raised to the thousandth power, each one meaningful and purposeful in and of itself, but agglomerated in its entirety into one gigantic, insane swarm.

In his first days, when even his facial muscles seemed paralyzed by the sheer magnitude of the palace complex and its forest of faces—all similar, all melding into each other, there appeared no hope at all of ever achieving anything like orientation or overview, even within the narrow confines of his immediate circle. Yet Theodor sensed that this was necessary for survival, if he were not to be simply crushed.

He saw his mistress, Madame (everyone referred to her as *la Palatine*), for the first time the day after his arrival, a massive old lady in green brocade whose florid, wrinkled visage reminded him of a fruit tree. Her broad face rested upon a double chin, a bloated collar of fat which concealed her neck and did not always participate in the movements of her head; the head turned away, the bulge stayed still. Her chicken mouth was pursed below the empty expanse of her wide, elongated upper lip, as pale as if the duchess had just recently shaved off a bushy gray walrus mustache. Her lively, constantly rheumy little eyes surveyed everyone with a keen, mistrustful stare (but who here was not mistrustful?). Whereupon her minced-up impressions apparently got stuffed into the sausage-casings of her memory, behind the beautiful curve of her high, smooth forehead.

As Theodor, whom a footman in an antechamber had informed of the protocol, approached the large woman bowing and scraping, she clearly already knew who he was. As he noticed to his satisfaction in the attention being paid to him by those in attendance, this was not a matter of course. She immediately used the familiar *du* to address him in German.

"All right, Theodor," she said once she'd heard his story, directing and channeling its recitation into forms and proportions pleasing to her by raising her hands (shorter, faster!), opening her palms (tell me all about it!), or fluttering her fingers (I didn't ask for all these details!)—"All right, Theodor, so now go over there into that room and stand by that window and keep track of when these people come and go, right? I've put 'em all down on this here list. The others can help you."

"*Oui, Madame*," replied Theodor in dulcet tones, flushed with pride that he had interpreted her gestures so perfectly, as if they were a code he had mastered years ago. So right at the beginning, he got a look at what the fortunate who didn't have to live there called the "sewer of Versailles," the "slum" concealed from outside view in the great interior quadrangle of the palace.

There stood several rows of unattractively built tenement-like houses with pointed gables, stretching from one enclosing palace wall to the other, packed together with little areaways in between. External wooden stairs led to the four stories of each one, yet the buildings were still lower than the two-story palace itself. They were interconnected by arcades which lay in the shadow of the palace as did the small windows of the low-ceilinged dwellings.

In this dim light and in little rooms no bigger than prison cells dwelt, as Theodor was to learn, several thousand men and women, most of them members of the nobility. Back home in the country they had lived in rooms a hundred times more comfortable. From all parts of the land they had thronged to the court to partake of the monarch's sun and they lived in a promiscuity that was difficult to imagine. Which was also the reason why, from the second floor windows of the palace, one spied on their comings and goings from room to room, from block to block, as la Palatine now had requested Theodor to do.

He himself did not have to start out at such a low level, but instead continued to enjoy privileges that provided ample nourishment for his inner conviction that he was one of the elect, only temporarily forced to appear incognito. He did not have to do any work in the lowly sense of the word. Mortagne, whom he saw only twice in the first few months, continued to see to his academic and aristocratic education. His refuge, his fixed points in the incomprehensible chaos of Versailles, became the hours spent with books in Latin, English, and Italian; the rooms in which he studied; the pale face of his new teacher, the Abbé Ducreux (convulsed by a tic that jerked his left eye toward the left corner of his mouth); and Madame's dusky pink antechamber.

There was also politicking in la Palatine's reception rooms, but it seemed to Theodor that it was done the same way as in every second room in the palace: in a hypothetical way, like a children's game, as if one met for a game of chess and afterward swept the men off the board and back into their wooden box, peevish and disappointed at all the wasted mental effort. There were intrigues about he knew not what. Circles of women met behind closed doors. Strange, powdered gentlemen with unhealthy-looking dabs of rouge on their cheeks scuttled in and out. The footmen and chambermaids gossiped and outdid each other in dropping mile-long names, none of which meant anything to Theodor. Petitioners waited in line. They came from the provinces, from the devastated homeland of Madame. On the strength of its sound alone, you could recognize their accent immediately through closed doors, even without being able to make out individual words. A great number of younger ladies and gentlemen sat around, came and went, driven by a strange restlessness, and conversed for hours— obviously in possession of unlimited knowledge of the place— about what one could do that afternoon, that evening, that night, the next day, in order to keep boredom at bay.

An immense amount of time (to be sure, a commodity amply available to the more or less permanent residents of the palace) was spent on the transformation, beautification, and metamorphosis of their bodies. Theodor was regularly in attendance when Madame was being made up before receiving her son for a five-minute *entrevue*. What at first seemed laughable and absurd to Theodor's youthful impatience began after a while to impress him. What perseverance and effort, so many creams, essences, bottles of perfume, batiste handkerchiefs, so many hands—of the wig-maker, the coiffeur, the seamstress, the lady's maids—so much concealment! A white foundation was applied to her skin, the beauty-mark relocated several times, the swollen ankles bandaged so they would fit into her laced bootlets, the light-brown liver spots on her hands powdered over, her wardrobe chosen to match the season, the weekday, the hour, the sunlight, the wallpaper of the room selected for the conversation—so much attention to the transformation of an ugly old woman into . . . well, into what? A woman who was still old and ugly, but out of politesse or vanity was assailing the impertinence of nature with all the means at her command.

Sometimes when Theodor had watched and assisted for hours, it seemed to him that appearance, the appearance of ugliness, was Nature's work, and all human effort served to tear back the veil of appearance and draw out into the light the higher truth of what was wished for. For wasn't there a direct connection between the retouchings carried out on Madame and the way the palace park was an extract of proportion and beauty, distilled from the rank wilderness of nature, or the way the old human longing for a roof over one's head was realized in the architecture of the palace?

As for the others, it was by no means only the women who spent hours putting on makeup and trying on clothes. Large numbers of men did the same. Some of them were enormously effeminate without shocking anyone in the least. They were all united by the same affectionate attention to their own persons, a constant concern to look good, be in form, make a brilliant appearance, a centripetal self-absorption that made them seem almost interchangeable with the women and submersed the entire palace-city in an androgynous light which blinded Theodor.

Truth be told, as soon as he had gotten used to this light, he found nothing to object to in it. Certainly he was a man, if only because back in times gone by God had divided humanity into man and woman in order to create a little order, and chance, after all, had to place Theodor on one side or the other. But did a physical given necessarily imply an existential one? He allowed the conventions of masculine behavior to have their way as if they were whining children, and they constituted the everyday wardrobe of his life, so to speak. But what was more natural than that other garments were also at the disposal of his rich inner life? If it was feminine to feel voluptuous pleasure in having his hair combed, well, then he simply had feminine attributes at his command as well. And if it was considered manly to elbow other men in the ribs, clap them on the shoulder like a ruffian, hold onto each other's pump handles while pissing, or spend the night getting drunk with a friend and, your tongue grown heavier and heavier, tell him all about the world and your own misery—in short, if his gender was characterized by a lack of dignity, reserve, and distance, then here was the point where he refused to play along. He felt it was unreasonable and impossibly restrictive to be expected to define his inner world completely from the perspective of the sex he belonged to.

Such thoughts owed much to the fact that Theodor remained innocent during his first months at court, observing the sexual topsy-turvy with neutral eyes. More than the question of whether one should be more attracted to someone of the same or of the opposite sex, he was preoccupied with whether anyone at all except someone of his own blood (namely, his sister) was worthy of insight into the tabernacle of his inner self.

Shortly thereafter, he learned that despite the flickering ambiguity of his sexual identity, he was able to set limits when push came to shove. His studies had repeatedly led him to the royal librarian, Monsieur de Cheisseux, in his sun-drenched kingdom of books on the second floor.

In Versailles, Theodor had seen men who were really women imprisoned in hairy and muscular bodies, unhappy and grotesque hermaphrodites. And he had seen men so masculine that their only goal was the pursuit of women and their happiest moment when they stood gazing down at their fallen prey.

Monsieur de Cheisseux, on the other hand, was completely masculine in a different way. He was so much a man that he simply didn't have any use for women. Not that he despised them, but in his world of intellect and enthusiasm for youthful lives, women just didn't exist.

If Theodor was sitting at one of the great cherrywood tables that gleamed reddish-golden in the light of day, turning the pages of a book and making dust motes dance wildly in the shafts of sunlight, it could happen that the librarian bent over him from behind, supporting himself with a hand on either side of the book, and then raised a hand up to stroke Theodor's hair or massage his shoulder while lecturing in a way that was more like pleasant narration. And Theodor listened all the more attentively because he had the impression that the librarian was talking to himself, and would have done so even if he were alone in the room.

For the space of several afternoons, while listening to the pedagogical words of masculine intellectuality, the young page enjoyed the massaging of the powerful hands with the same princely favor as he once had the hands of his mother or Minne, and feeling as flattered as if de Cheisseux had introduced him into an exclusive club.

Things could have continued this way, but suddenly the librarian brought the familiar *tu* into play, and what had until then remained ambiguous became instantly concrete: it was about him, Theodor, and the forty-year-old, clean-shaven man was looking at him quite differently than before, indeed, was looking him in the eye for the first time ever.

"*Allez, mon petit baron*, I see that youth is ready to let maturity lead it by the hand."

But youth was ready to do no such thing. Theodor slipped away from de Cheisseux and put some distance between them. He didn't completely understand at which point or for what reason the tone and mood had changed, but he grasped that the librarian had crossed a boundary, so to speak, by no longer standing behind but in front of him, by showing himself and looking Theodor in the eye.

The pleasure Theodor took in the caressing hands and intelligent talk was one thing, quite another the panting man who was now cornering him and saying, "*Soyez pas coquin*, you've been getting me excited for weeks." Theodor felt nothing for him.

"*Ne sois pas si réfractaire*, you rascal! The man with the deepest thoughts also loves things that are most alive. Let me open your eyes for you. What are you afraid of? My caresses?"

"Shouldn't we save our caresses, the *tu*, and looking people in the eye for the ladies?" replied Theodor uncertainly and at pains not to insult de Cheisseux.

"*Mais que m'importent les bonnes femmes*. I want you! *Allez, pas de manières. Ce n'est pas parce que je t'enculerai une ou deux fois que tu deviendra pédéraste . . .*"

He was tugging at Theodor with growing impatience, and the latter was thinking feverishly of how to avoid a wrestling match with uncertain outcome. He'd have to improvise, put things into words in a credible way, things of which he had no clear concept but which, he was sure, could not fail to have the desired effect. He assumed what he hoped was a sly, debauched expression and whispered his little sentence into the excited fellow's ear. De Cheisseux recoiled.

"*Petite crapule!* Why didn't you say so right away? Out of my sight! Away with you! I have to give you credit for your honesty, you poor lost child!"

"Back so soon?" asked the Duchess. "Did de Cheisseux try to give you any trouble?"

"I backed out of his private tutorial by pretending to have an illness which, thank God, I don't suffer from yet, Madame . . ."

"*Bien fait, mon petit.* These French are all filthy buggers, sodomites, and swine."

Theodor thought his mistress exaggerated. He was unable even to be angry at the librarian, for the grotesqueness and embarrassment of the encounter was outweighed by a muted emotion at witnessing how someone opened up to him, thereby humiliating himself, but without losing his dignity. Now he almost regretted turning down the privilege of following Monsieur de Cheisseux into his pure world, a world overcast by a certain tragic sterility, in which mature men planted the seeds of intellect into their young disciples, a world from which, as in a monastery, the foreign, frightening, mysterious temptation of the feminine was excluded.

But shortly afterward, Theodor observed the Baroness Valentini for the first time, one of the duchess's maids of honor, and the storm of hot and cold feelings unleashed by the sight of her made him thank the fates that he hadn't missed out on such an experience by acting too early.

His first sight of the Italian woman was so bewitching that he forbade himself a second look. It seemed to him that one must not tempt an epiphany by ogling it from all sides like a livestock dealer looking at a beef, but it had absolutely nothing to do with the form of her face or her body.

The baroness was a woman certainly twice his age, or barely less than that. He was incapable of describing her any further. And yet it was she, absolutely unequivocally she who so unsettled him.

More precisely, it was the contrast between the whiteness of her skin and the bluish tint of her wig and her nail polish and eye shadow to match. It made such a strikingly artificial and mask-like impression that it excited Theodor's imagination immeasurably more than if she had shown him her naked body. He was reminded of the dancing doll in Madame's chambers which he could watch for hours, fascinated by the secret mechanism in its interior.

He had no idea whether the lady, sitting with other maids of honor in an open carriage, had even seen him and in truth, it didn't matter to him in the slightest. But this whitish-blue porcelain mask was decidedly more promising than all the manly intellect of Monsieur de Cheisseux.

Theodor's first steps toward understanding the Minoan palace and helping himself slowly to overcome his disheartening bewilderment were of a geographic nature. On his errands, the missions of espionage Madame dispatched him on, as well as excursions through the estate in her retinue, he felt like a traveler stranded in a far-off land who registers the wonders of the foreign continent with nothing more than a nod and, concentrating his energy on surviving and returning safely to his homeland, gives no thought to understanding, ordering, or classifying things. Nevertheless, the geography of the place became transparent to Theodor.

He discovered which entrance from the palace side and which from the garden side led most quickly to the wing where Madame lived. He memorized the order of the suites of rooms and chambers. He reconnoitered the realm of Monsieur, the king's brother, antechamber for antechamber. In his mind he drew the outline of the part of the palace reserved for the king. He investigated the "sewer," the cramped world of the courtiers with all its little stairways, passages, and arcades. He sorted out the order of the outbuildings, this noisy, teeming Hades reeking with a hundred smells, full of hard-working cabinet makers, carpenters, blacksmiths, plasterers, masons, cooks, bakers, gardeners, scribes, overseers, seamstresses, spinners, weavers—all the faceless and nameless who made the world of Versailles possible.

He studied Le Nôtre's plan for the park, ascertained the paths to the Trianon or the Potager du Roi, had no trouble learning which window belonged to which hall or chamber, and after a few months in Versailles he had a perfect grasp of its packaging, if still no grasp of its contents.

Its hierarchies and intrigues, its enormous crowds of important, seemingly important, and unimportant people—all that remained a book with seven seals.

All the same, it dawned on him what a market of information the palace represented. Rumors, conversations, conferences, and colloquies were listened to, overheard, passed on, divulged, embellished, or suppressed. This was one of the most avid pursuits on all levels and in all jurisdictions. But the topics of these conversations meant nothing to him, no more than did the allusions to political decisions, diplomatic initiatives, military campaigns, sieges, and negotiations, haggling over appointments and offices, trouble in Paris and in the provinces, no more than all the names that were spoken in whispers, with respect, in doubt, with contempt, or with pleasure. Well, he could still get by without knowing these things, but he was condemned to silence and wide-eyed astonishment, and ultimately that didn't suit him.

Every second conversation in Versailles was about money, and that was a second great mystery for Theodor. The world of the palace seemed to function under the same laws as the life of the Count de Mortagne: an obviously independent circulation of money and work on the one hand, and individuals acting in independence on the other. But although everything one could want was there—food, clothes, furniture—although journeys were undertaken and people wallowed in luxury, talk of money (or more precisely the lack thereof and where one could get some) was omnipresent.

Theodor had heard that the indebtedness of the country, that is, of the king, was immeasurable, and as far as he could understand, everyone took that as a warrant for themselves to become attached to this life on credit and to speak the more contemptuously—but more often—about money, the more precarious their own situations became.

The Abbé Ducreux explained it to him: "The tension between the palace and Paris increases from year to year. It's a mystery how long the money will continue to flow from the city to us. In the meantime, have you noticed how many bankers are running around here?"

The mystery for Theodor was the question of how money would some day flow to him, once he had left this nest. But that was something that lay in the distant, unforeseeable future.

Once again, he noticed that he preferred mysteries to straightforward, easily analyzed situations. He found it more congenial to walk into a dark cloud, entrusting himself to fate and chance, than to be confronted with a task he had to think his way through. The former required improvisation and luck, the latter an effort whose results could be measured, and he felt that such effort placed unreasonable demands on his sense of self-worth. No, he much preferred to let things and people take their course, to let them surprise him.

Money—where it came from and how it disappeared again, the fact that one needed it, and what one could do with it—was one such mystery, a treasure-trove of possible surprises, and the Baroness Valentini was another.

A third resulted from his meeting with the Marchese Vanzetti, Madame's astrologer, to whom Theodor was sent one day. Madame had hinted that the marchese was not a real marchese at all, but nevertheless, with a full head of black curls which would tolerate no wig, a Richelieu beard, and a slightly theatrical black *houppelande* lined with red velvet, he proved to be a highly impressive apparition and introduced Theodor for the first time to that special branch of science for which the young man had a natural affinity.

For both astrology and the alchemistic experiments also pursued by the Italian were based on the premises of natural science, made use of its rules and vocabulary as well, but also opened a wide breach in the arrogant, self-sufficient system of numbers, through which could stream things open to interpretation: the imponderable, the uncontrollable—in short, everything that was amenable and deferential to the word.

Theodor was so full of ardent questions that the marchese soon had introduced him to the fundamental rules of astrological interpretation. And he learned as much as he always did, that is, enough to make any outsider believe that he knew something about the matter. In other words, he learned how to apply these sciences symbolically, and where Theodor's knowledge was in danger of unraveling, they were humane enough to allow themselves to be expressed and manipulated in sentences that sounded as interesting as they were vague.

The page loved alchemy even more than the science of the constellations, for the former rewarded both eye and ear. The most precise thing about it seemed to be the half Rosicrucian, half Catholic ritual of conjuration and consecration: gestures, invocations, and verses, a painfully precise arrangement of various minerals, metals, and implements, moments of concentrated stillness and hummed, Gregorian-like antiphons with which the science surrounded itself in order to create an auspicious spiritual environment for the success of its endeavor long before it proceeded to concrete manipulations. Together with the bubbling decoction in the copper cauldron, the glass flasks and vials, test tubes and retorts, the multicolored liquids flowing and gurgling through tubes, this ritual functioned and smelled and sounded (thanks to splendid words such as *conjunctio, maza, nigredo,* and *citrinitas*) so exceedingly fascinating that it hardly seemed necessary to expect a concrete outcome from such beautiful exertions.

All the same, Theodor asked the marchese rudely, "And what kind of results do you get?" But he did it in the vague hope of not being disappointed by a precise answer.

"Nothing, my boy," replied the astrologist airily and perhaps a little indiscreetly. "The path is the goal." Whereupon Theodor looked at him with such delight that the marchese asked la Palatine to permit him to make the page his assistant.

And so Theodor proceeded in his conquest of this world, although with an occasional stumble. A faulty deduction led him to believe for weeks that one of the Marshals of the Realm, a man who often accompanied Duke Philippe on his visits to la Palatine, was some obstinate deadbeat from the provinces, one of those country noblemen looking for money to finance some utopian project or other—draining swamps or reclaiming land—and Theodor greeted him with a raised eyebrow and a disparaging twitch at the corner of his mouth.

But with time, he learned to distinguish faces and to categorize the inhabitants and visitors in the palace.

The category Theodor found most fascinating and least transparent were those he called "endangered satellites," women and men who neither performed any useful function one could put a numerical value on nor held an office they could call their own. They had built themselves an insubstantial nest purely on the strength of their words and the agreeableness of their persons, a nest which at any moment threatened to fall from the tree. Their pertinacity; their stubborn determination to gain for themselves a place in the sun; the discipline they evinced in staying *à la mode*, brilliant, creative, witty, sharp-tongued, entertaining; the prodigious fog machines they cranked with all their might to conceal their utter superfluity to the course of events, were both admirable and alarming. With a professional eye he was not yet conscious of, an eye that humans of the same vocation and similar disposition have for one another, Theodor made himself into a sympathetic, commiserating observer of their heroic exertions. Heroic, for given the risk of a complete fall from favor and hence instantaneous disappearance from the most important stage in the world, no hint of those exertions must be allowed to escape into public view.

They were companions to the nobility, carriers of *billets-doux*, plotters on retainer and unofficial heralds, they were artists, half- and quarter-artists, artists of the good life, court jesters. Theodor got to know one of them better when la Palatine asked him to keep Monsieur de Mortemart company and perform services for him.

The slim young man with brown locks and cheeks flushed with hectic excitement tore Theodor from sleep at 5:30 in the morning.

"What I want from you, what I'm asking you to do," he explained, "is what the English call coaching."

Theodor quickly discovered just what that meant. After a vigorous two-hour ride in the first light, his own muscles trembling from the exertion, he had to pour buckets of cold water onto his overheated companion. He wouldn't even have treated a horse this way.

"There, now I'm awake," was Mortemart's comment. "Off we go to the study!"

Theodor watched as the assiduous young man got out the books he had brought along, opened them to premarked pages, and began to recite. They were collections of poems, apothegms, aphorisms, and aperçus from the Greek classics to Persian and Indian literature to contemporary French or English works. In addition, Mortemart possessed a quarto notebook into which he had entered his own witty turns of phrase and Theodor was to quiz him on them. The pupil's temples were moist with perspiration, but he made not a single mistake.

"All right, and now . . ." and at these words, he pressed his fingertips against his temples in a kind of vice of concentration, ". . . now talk to me. Talk to me about whatever comes into your head and then ask me for my opinion or demand I take a stand. Ready, go!"

Theodor extemporized, and at regular intervals Mortemart ignited pyrotechnics that exploded in multicolored arabesques of bon mots, jests, and rejoinders as if shot from a pistol, so that the page gaped in astonishment. Here was a true virtuoso.

"What time is it? Noon? Very well, now I'll rest for an hour, then take some light refreshment, two glasses of *mousseux*, and then it will be time for Madame's *déjeuner*. But first, if you'll excuse me, I've got to do my breathing exercises . . ."

That afternoon, Theodor was present at the bright assemblage in the park, concentric circles of toadies swarming around la Palatine and her *cour* like wasps around their queen.

More than an hour went by before Mortemart got his opening. One of the great ladies said something and before the sound of her voice had faded, the aphorism of the young *précieux* from the second circle sliced through the stillness, sharp as a carving knife. A heartbeat's pause, then laughter, applause, a rustling of fans, blushes, and coquettishly wagging fingers. Mortemart had earned his keep for the day.

Toward the end of the festivities, a countess turned to him and invited him to come again. With a nod to Theodor, he disappeared with his bag of books, stooping slightly like a tradesman returning home after a day's work, back into the nothingness whence he had presumably come.

And there were hundreds like him.

By contrast, there was the most privileged group of Versailles' inhabitants: the court itself, the gaudy, gleaming, brilliant, hypersensitive, decadent, bored, perverse, highly educated, and constantly jabbering flock of peacocks, none of whom needed to justify their existence (for it was financially and hierarchically secure), none of whom needed to work (except for performing symbolic activities: a cabinet meeting here, a gay, flag-waving campaign there), and all of whom thirsted for ways to pass the time like sinful souls athirst for salvation.

The collision of these two groups, the hungry social climbers and those who had already made it—their dialogues, love affairs, intrigues, their games and performances—threw off sparks and lent the court a splendor that radiated into the farthest corners of Europe.

Le Nôtre's park was the greatest stage in the world even though, as usual, people said that in the old days, when the king was still young and fun-loving and had participated himself, everything had been bigger, more beautiful, wilder and crazier. His head spinning, Theodor told himself he was right in the middle of it, envied by millions.

To be sure, those millions had no idea what it was really like. For if the court and the park were a stage, they were also a place where life and time were passing, where clocks ticked if possible even more remorselessly than elsewhere, and whatever energies were squandered on games and self-promotion were no longer available for one's actual life.

But what is one's actual life, actually, Theodore asked himself in bewilderment, as if looking into an infinite regression of mirrors. Is there really any line between what one represents for others and what one is for oneself? Beneath the shimmering surface made up of a thousand silent endeavors, were there depths as well? Or could it be that the surface was all there was, and that it simply had a certain thickness that concealed the nothingness below?

The lightness he loved so much—was it the element he consisted of, or only the varnish, the final layer of polish on a heavy, solid, boring substructure of work, study, and education. Did this substructure mean that all the brilliant personages at court were simply more conspicuous, cultivated kinsmen of conventional human beings, the dim rural population, just as in the final analysis, the peacock is nothing but a somewhat grander chicken?

Instinctively, Theodor sought out the old Palatine to help him regain his bearings. In the forty years she had lived here, she had been pruned, trimmed, grafted, and decorticated and yet her core had not changed or warped. She put up with

Theodor's filial or rather grandson-like dependence and for hours at a time he listened to her mournful stories of times gone by, back home.

In her shadow and under her protection he learned the complicated grammar of communication at Versailles: the standard formulas and their significance, the codes dividing and connecting the hierarchies, causerie, chit-chat, how to define oneself in words or a tone of voice. He explored the frontiers of this language-regulated world which resembled the patchwork of holdings in the east of the country: the necessary word, the permissible word, the tolerated word, and the impossible word were peninsulas of territory whose ownership was constantly shifting.

His lack of certitudes and opinions made Theodor a good listener, a deep vessel without a cover into which everything possible could drop, but was he also possibly a bottomless pit, he wondered doubtfully?

For the more he learned of the conditions in the palace, the city, the country, the less certain he felt about them. Everything seemed equally justified to him, equally important and equally fascinating, and after a while equally arbitrary. That is, without realizing it, he was learning irony: a benevolent skepticism about the uniqueness of things, the result of the deepest skepticism about oneself.

He did not let the first opportunity to open his own mouth go to waste. The Duke of Orléans, Madame's son, was getting hot under the collar—almost boiling—about a snide article in a Paris journal against which he struck the back of his hand again and again once it had made the rounds.

"What do you say to this?" he cried to those present. "Who do these people think they are? Do they think they're more competent than the king?"

In a moment of silence Theodor said, "Ink stains on a rat skin don't make it the royal ermine."

"How's that?" asked Philippe in confusion. "Say that again!"

Theodor repeated his little improvisation.

"That's brilliant!" cried the duke. "Ink stains on a rat skin? Completely exquisite!" And he turned to his secretary. "Disseminate this sentence as my answer! You've got nothing against that, do you young man?"

Theodor bowed. "It *is* your answer. I only made so bold as to read it from your lips . . ."

He remarked what a deep, life-affirming pleasure he took in being applauded and nevertheless felt his lip curl in disgust that the applause rewarded a second-rate performance. Some of the young courtiers and *précieux* envied him his intimacy with the great ones and said he was a sycophant and a schemer. But they were mistaken. He just got on well with the duchess and was captivated by her maternal severity, but for the rest, she had no influence whatsoever on the course of events. He would have found it much too laborious to range through the entire palace in search of a patron cut to his measure. La Palatine had simply been where he happened to be as well, and he confirmed her in her opinions just as easily as he would have anyone else.

Once Theodor had become too old to be a page any longer, his mistress suggested he take an apartment in Paris and report to her from time to time on what was being said in the salons and cafés.

Theodor thought it over. The capital, the "city" (as it was referred to, without further ado, in contrast to the "palace"), a two-hour journey through sunny forests, spread out between the river and the surrounding hills, was an aspect of life here that he had criminally neglected up to now.

"Don't be so smug just because you're sitting in this bird cage, permitted to twitter along with everyone else," a colleague had once advised him. "The eagles and the falcons live in Paris. I went to school there. Try as he might, the king can't break the back of the city. That's where life really gets lived. In the faubourgs, the salons and cafés. All the important people, all the real people swear by Paris. That's where they're thinking and taking action, not here on this stage set."

"I don't know," he answered la Palatine. "I wouldn't like to leave Versailles."

"Growing up means learning to forgo things, Theodor," the Duchess replied.

"Well, time will tell," he said.

Chapter V

*T*HEY HAD ENTERED A small cabinet at the university to which, as Theodor noted in pique, he was allowed access only when accompanied by Jakob Sternhart. On the table before them was the ominous apparatus, standing between lighted candles, like a monstrance.

Theodor gazed in boredom at the box with wooden panels held together by screws, a sort of perforated dial, rotating cylinders, and an iron track mounted on four copper feet on which the body of the device, provided with numerous pull-rings, could be slid back and forth.

"This," said Jakob, his small lashless blue eyes protected by the bulge of his domed brow, gleaming with admiration, "this is it: Leibniz's stepped drum calculating machine! The only one of its kind in Paris. Wait, I'll show you how it works."

Who would have expected such delicacy and solicitude from those peasant hands? Tenderly he took hold of the machine, lifted it up, and let Theodor peer underneath. Then he began to explain how it worked, and while his excitement about the outstanding intellectual achievement that he was trying to make accessible to his friend caused a thin film of perspiration to form on his massive, red forehead beneath the downy blond hair which every stray breeze wafted up in the air, Theodor wondered without paying too close attention how one could get so worked up about an idea—in this case, an idea that had congealed in the form of a box.

"This is the future. Take a good look at it."

"Yes," said Theodor, "but you can't use something like this to prove Pascal's theorem concerning the sides of a hexagon inscribed in a conic, can you? You still need human intellect for that."

Sternhart regarded him with a disappointed expression Theodor chose to ascribe to the inadequacy of the machine. The other unconsciously jutted out his chin in challenge. His features took on a look that was both combative and contemptuous, as if, imbued with his mission, he were looking the armed opponent of all scientific riddles right in the eye, far and away superior to such triflers who didn't know him and couldn't imagine the glory of the intellectual battle to come.

Theodor knew that this impoverished student was in correspondence with an Italian, a marchese, with whom or against whom he intended to construct an improved version of this calculating machine. He recalled the ugly words "sprocket wheel," as incomprehensible and uninteresting to him as "stepped drum."

He felt a rising resentment that at the present moment, the friend whom he usually had good reason to look down on a little despite their friendship, didn't think him capable of understanding. But he told himself that Sternhart was giving him a gift by bringing him here and letting him see the object of his passion. It was a very great gift from someone who had no money and no taste or feel for other kinds of presents. Theodor was perforce a little enthusiastic as well, even if he would have preferred to be treated to a glass of wine instead of being taken to this dusty chamber.

For Jakob Sternhart was the only friend he had found since he had recently begun to live part of the time in Paris, in the Faubourg St. Antoine, the quarter of the cabinetmakers. And although he would have rather devoted himself to pleasurable diversions, Theodor had his doubts about the value of anything that came too easily to him and believed in the moral and intellectual improvement to be derived from occasional exposure to the self-discipline of things that were excruciatingly boring.

Since he still received his monthly bank draft from Mortagne and didn't have to think yet about his imminent future as a soldier, he had taken a furnished room in Paris and was auditing some lectures at the Sorbonne to complete his education.

Actually, he was less interested in completion than in soothing his guilty conscience about perhaps selling himself too cheaply as a second-class *précieux*.

As the son of a tradesman, Jakob was impressed by the Westphalian baron's elegant language and nonchalant manner, while the latter, with a mixture of horror and admiration, recognized in his friend a scholar who was no ossified old fossil but a young man like himself. So obviously, people devoted themselves to thought and the pursuit of knowledge not just as a sort of self-punishment, once life was past and the body impotent. No, it was possible to learn and experiment from boyhood on. Of course, it wasn't any fun, but Sternhart never pretended to be out for a good time.

Jakob, Theodor brooded, is better read than most learned men in the palace, and yet I would never think of him as having spirit. So does spirit presuppose effortlessness? And what should one think of knowledge acquired in the sweat of one's brow?

But sweat or no sweat, Sternhart's knowledge was vast, and Theodor, who had always thought of himself as well-read, discovered to his dismay the gaps in his education, or rather, the ocean of his ignorance in which atolls of knowledge were rarely sighted anymore. Whenever Sternhart summarized centuries of intellectual adventure or juggled with cross-references, Theodor could only maintain face with the help of his time-tested tactic. With brash cheekiness he would toss things fleetingly heard and remembered into the conversation as counter-examples, punctuating Sternhart's fluid lectures with a knowing smile and interjections such as, "By the way, didn't he also write that . . ." and "Could be, but I don't like his style, and style makes the man," confident that his interlocutor's courtesy and zeal would keep him from asking embarrassing follow-up questions.

For Theodor these were excursions into the realm of the intellect, but afterward he was happy to return home again. His friend with the ram-like skull had a concept of life—that reading was work and one fell to one's knees before factual knowledge as if it were an epiphany—which Theodor found just as much of an exaggeration as the hedonism in Le Nôtre's park. The sanctification of thought was no more his own path than the trivialization of sin.

He and Sternhart didn't see each other all too often in any event, for the latter was forced to eke out his existence as a tutor. And when they did, the things they talked about were only the surplus of the Prussian's capacity for knowledge. His actual area of study was mathematics, and he spent the better part of each day tinkering with his accursed machines (and at the moment, learning Italian—he had a miserable accent both in Italian and in French—so he could correspond with the marchese on the other side of the Alps).

Two things that occupied Theodor more than Sternhart and his intellectual arrogance had entered his life, namely love and money, and both were intimately interconnected.

First off, in the Garden of Diana at Fontainebleau Palace, Theodor lost his virginity to the knowledgeable Baroness Valentini according to all the rules of the art.

He probably had no idea how lucky he was to have his first experience—for which no preparation is possible exactly because it's the first—with a woman for whom love was not a metaphysical problem but a practical solution.

For quite some time, of course, Theodor had been hoping to be initiated into the mysteries of physical love, but it was even more important to him to give the impression that he was already familiar with them. Without the Italian woman, it's possible he could have remained a virgin all his life, for the absolutely insurmountable problem consisted in the fact that in order to find out, he would have to let at least one person in on his secret, yet it was precisely the person from whom he thought he must keep his ignorance the strictest secret.

Moreover, he was made uneasy by a vague notion that the mystery of the sexual act was also a celebration of exquisite, unblemished beauty, a work of art where one piece fitted seamlessly into the other and the perfection of the whole was the sum of the perfection of all the parts. And since he knew himself to be far from physical perfection, he wondered fearfully if he would simply provoke revulsion and derision.

In short, he was making things more difficult than they needed to be, which also meant that he had grand ideas about the matter. To that extent, it was lucky that he had found the Valentini woman—but also unlucky.

Because for her, love was the logical extension and augmentation of the other activities at court: conversation, diversion, the intrigues, power struggles, and the common pilgrimage toward more savory, more outlandish pleasures.

She was saved from becoming a cold seductress by a happy disposition that allowed her soul, after an almost imperceptible interval of hesitation, to follow the lead of her physical desire and her consciousness. Whomever she made love to she really loved, and just as her feelings followed a half-measure behind her appetite, once the latter had faded they also cooled down only after a little delay, and in this interval of time she had recourse to the whole emotional gamut of romantic nostalgia and dolor. Although wallowing in it did not prevent her from finding a new favorite, it did make her sensible to the tragic progress of time and lent her embraces a kind of desperate weight and intensity, of demanding and surrendering passion that made her different from other women whose experience was equally broad but who played their instruments completely in time with the moment.

Against this dark background of *tempus fugit*, however, the Valentini woman's love was bright as day and guided by practical considerations. She liked visibility, clarity, consciousness, wakeful exchange, and fulfillment. With obvious exceptions, her caresses did not preclude conversation. She knew about the erotic power of naming, for originally, to name things was to conjure them. The names she gave to objects and actions supported the language of her body. Whatever her word called into life, her body immediately examined its qualities and behold, it was good.

During a game of blind man's bluff, she led Theodor with unerring determination into the dead-end of a hornbeam labyrinth amidst the giggles of the other young ladies and gentlemen, and once there, removed the blindfold from his eyes.

Directly before him he beheld her blue wig and large, geometric nose, which seemed constructed of nothing but triangles. She was so close to him that there was no hope left of escape or prevarication.

At this moment, he felt utterly devoid of excitement. The whole thing was too public. He could hear the others; they knew where he was hiding and were possibly listening for what was to come. And yet love seemed to Theodor to require secrecy, stillness, and concealment. Besides, it was too bright, and la Valentini's blue eyes had no misty, dreamy look to them; on the contrary, they were awake, concentrated, and curious—appropriate, perhaps, to the study of a problem in logic but certainly not when one was about to descend into the fog-shrouded realm of the body, which, thought Theodor, one should approach only with eyes and ears closed, half asleep and dreaming.

The moment was also uncomfortably like an examination, something Theodor had never liked and always tried to avoid. He didn't want to have to prove anything or learn anything, just to possess everything all at once and get it over with. He felt squeamish in his skin and when la Valentini, who soon sensed what the problem was, took the reins of the conversation into her own hands, he stiffened, his legs gave way, and he sank to the ground, which is exactly where his lover wanted him.

Now she'd finally like to have a look at him, said the blue-haired woman, which Theodor didn't understand at first since she was, after all, just a hand's breadth away, kneeling beside him in the bright sunshine. But her fingers fumbling at his clothes, half resisted and half aided by his own hands, soon made him understand. He clung desperately to conversation, as if it were the primary and important thing, the justification for their being together, and he had to speak calmly to keep an overwrought or drunken person from causing a scandal.

Finally he gave in to the situation and, always a blink of
the eye behind what was actually happening, he tried to keep
in order what he was seeing, feeling, hearing, and thinking,
so that in his increasing confusion he would at least be able to
say "Now" and to know what feeling, if any, belonged to that
"now."

The white, softly yielding thighs of la Valentini were
encased in the fine gossamer of her stockings, which ended
abruptly somewhere beneath the rustling of her dress, where
they were suspended from filigreed cordage, miniature shrouds
on which the corsairs of his lust, knives clenched in their teeth,
were coming aboard, but then he sensed rather than felt some
source of warmth and it made him hesitate. He pulled back and
in a classic displacement made a grab for her large, long, equally
white and freckled nose. Brusquely she shook off his hand, took
imperious hold of it by the wrist, and resolutely guided it back
to where its work had been interrupted.

This commanding gesture reminded him of when he was
learning to write and his mother's hand would calmly and firmly
guide his own hand which held the quill pen, and how this con-
joint motion had conjured onto the paper calligraphies and arabesques that Theodor found intensely fascinating. At the same
time, the sight of the ocher-blonde hair of the baroness, who
had tossed her wig into the bushes, made him think involuntarily of the hue of the stray curs that sniffed through the gar-
bage of the Aligre Market, of their sad eyes and curled tails. And
so his mind reeled back and forth between these unhelpful images and the sight of la Valentini, who patiently continued to
keep him at his work. Now she was expressing her astonishment
and, if Theodor understood her melodious voice correctly, her
pleasure that he was constitutionally unlike other men, those
"hasty visitors who, hardly arrived, take their leave again," and

apparently due to his being a bit thick-skinned at his center, was more patient and therefore much more likely to arrive at just the right tempo for the natural rhythm of the woman. But he mustn't be too patient, too passive in his enjoyment. It was a matter of giving as well as receiving, for which reason the baroness now hitched up her dress, pulled it down off her shoulders, and mounted him so that her heavy breasts sailed into the harbor of his torso like Spanish galleons and docked at the quay of his chin, while at the very moment he was fearing that his defenselessly erect sex would get crushed beneath her white, Rubenesque body, it glided into her in such a perfect, precise, and effortless way that he felt a satisfaction similar to what Sternhart must feel when one of his equations came out even, in a whole number.

But that had to be an inappropriate simile, for what he was just now experiencing had a blurred, unfocused remainder, some ultimate uncertainty that resisted conscious observation, a revelation that could not be calculated, but only hoped for.

The Italian song of his Amazon tore him from this feckless inner dispute. She was just picking up the pace from a light trot to a gallop, snorting and whinnying but not surrendering the reins. She was horse and rider in one, a genuine centaur, it occurred to Theodor as wild mythological images whirled through his head.

He looked up into her flushed face beyond which the innocent violet of the sky seemed ironical. She looked at him and issued a jubilant command in her native language, only a single word that immediately awakened in Theodor images of the fountains of gods in the parks, the stone titans and tritons with enormous limbs, spewing marvelous arching streams of water into the sun-glittering pools, and the graphic nature of her imperative, as well as the sound of the doubled consonant and the dark vowel, was so powerful that he almost instantaneously and without any help from his conscious mind answered her summons with a loud cry of release, just at the moment when three tremendous contractions which Theodor clearly felt without being able to localize them caused la Valentini to collapse on top of him like a dragon he had just slain, with a rasping exhalation and an explosion of smells: streams of salty sweat and lily of the valley and garlic and other unidentifiable things.

So that was that. Theodor gave himself an inner shake to regain his senses and be able to say what was required:

"*Grazie*," he murmured hoarsely, "*grazie tante*."

But the baroness wanted no words of thanks; instead, she wanted words of love. He obediently repeated what she recited to him, but still asked himself where the wished-for feeling could be, the feeling which—in contrast to lust—he didn't get even when la Valentini conjured it up with words. Instead, he felt he had climbed a mountain and now actually knew more than he wanted to. Between himself and the large-nosed Italian woman, in a way that was difficult to explain, there had been revealed at one stroke too much and then again not enough, and Theodor felt a sort of remorse, as if he had revealed a secret to someone whose discretion he could not be certain of.

So that although the image of her ripe body and the sound of her voice called him to regularly varied repetitions of their mutual experience, at the same time, something new had been set free within him that la Valentini could not satisfy—or rather, that he didn't trust her or want to allow her to satisfy. Therefore, hardly a week after his deflowering, he quite consciously and intentionally fell in love with another party, in search of an icon for his unsatisfied need to have something to worship and in a sort of psychic division of labor in which he functioned like a politician who never tells all his colleagues about all his thoughts and plans, but feeds each one only the tidbits reserved specially for him.

The name of the object of his love was Gertrud Holzacher and she was the seventeen-year-old daughter of an immigrant cabinetmaker from Franconia who ran a flourishing workshop with ten journeymen and apprentices in the faubourg, not far from Theodor's room.

Gertrud, whom her lover always called Laura in his thoughts, was a freshly washed girl with brown curls, a some-what receding chin, and arched eyebrows that were constantly raised in proximity to her rather low hairline by her consider-able pride in her father's business. Self-confident, comfortable mediocrity must have some physical charm to it, for that's what Theodor fell in love with, it still being covered, in Gertrud's case, with the down of innocence.

Nevertheless, one may wonder how the young man, now awakened and in possession of the favors of the well-to-do and willing Baroness Valentini, who in the bright light of day and with equally bright consciousness wanted to give and receive all the pleasure she knew herself capable of—how the young man could neglect to spend even one minute with her in order to loiter around in front of the cabinetmaker's, sending his ser-vant Larbi in with flowers, candy, and poems for the daughter of the house, who managed her innocence with the same pains-taking attention her mother paid to the workshop's cash box.

Theodor was aware of his folly, knew also (in a compart-ment of his brain only temporarily sealed off) that not only was Gertrud-Laura absolutely no match for the centaurian Valen-tini, but also that she was as dumb as a post, would probably despise an impoverished nobleman with fancy manners and—every inch her father's daughter—prefer a sturdy master trades-man, and that his perfumed *billets-doux* with their appeals to the divinity in the girl's nature were falling on utterly sterile ground.

Theodor knew all this, but it didn't bother him, for why did he need Gertrud when he had Laura, and above all, when he had la Valentini? Without his regular visits to the baroness there would have been—and Theodor was aware of this as well—no love for the cabinetmaker's daughter. So it didn't matter at all to him that the object of his devotion was fairly certain not to answer his prayers. On the contrary! The more distant and out of focus she remained, the easier it was to transform her happy laughter and her air of innocence at Mass (from his place in the back he could see her swanlike neck below pinned-up brown curls) into longing and poetry.

In his *cour* of the burgher's daughter, Theodor created for himself the distance that la Valentini was always ready and willing to bridge over. And to Larbi, who could only shake his head at it, he averred that he was serious about this passion. After several weeks of sweet humiliations—for example, when the cabinetmaker, who was in the picture, asked him about his income and his intentions (in that order)—he even toyed with the idea of committing suicide.

Yes, he was serious, if perhaps not deeply serious. And besides, can't we ask, as Theodor constantly asked himself, how serious can you be about something if you're able to remind yourself to increase or decrease the intensity of your seriousness, as necessary? Perhaps different people are capable of different levels of seriousness. In which case, thought Theodor in distress, he obviously didn't belong among those who were ready to die for their convictions, even though he found such logical consistency charming.

However, his love for la Valentini and his love for Gertrud-Laura did have one thing in common: they both cost money.

Since Theodor lived in Paris, he was forced to admit to an urgent need for money in general. All his undertakings, everything he wanted to obtain and do, required means he didn't have at his disposal. When he compared himself once again to Sternhart, he was bewildered by how his friend seemed to take care of himself and his modest needs from some powerful inner source and was not dependent on a steady stream of money to finance his affairs. But after all, the Prussian spent nothing on food and drink, clothes and wine, or on anything else that gives pleasure. He never gave a thought to inviting anyone over or treating anyone to a drink. He went only to the cheapest bordellos, had a frugal fiancée easily satisfied with his letters, and to top it all off, he worked as well. Learning and thinking, his only passions, cost nothing.

By comparison, Theodor gave gifts to la Valentini, hired coaches and *separées*, and had to see to his wardrobe, support his servant Larbi, pay for a horse and stable, and show himself to be exceptionally generous when courting Gertrud. This could result in such whimsical expenses as a fee for a poem. Larbi, who looked after his master's cash, said reproachfully, "Monsieur, just listen to this drivel! And the man wants a *louis* for this stuff!

> O Laura, my marsh marigold,
> When your image I behold,
> The gods of Greece, however mighty
> Are envious of my Aphrodite.

Aphrodite! It's utter nonsense! With your permission, even your poems are better than this."

"Of course, but I don't always have the time and leisure to write poetry. And besides, she doesn't read them anyway, if she can read at all, which I doubt. The point is to give her something that nobody else gives her, something elevating."

"But this bullshit doesn't elevate anybody. Really, this 'poetry' is an insult to any intelligent person," said Larbi, who had received a certain amount of education back home.

"It's the poetry in and of itself," Theodor explained, "the fact that I'm giving her poems instead of bologna sausage."

"I'd prefer the sausage," complained the servant and added the *louis* to the ever growing list of his master's debts.

Theodor was spending twice and three times Mortagne's monthly allowance, borrowing additional money on the strength of that nobleman's name, running up tabs at the tailor's, the hatter's, and the confectioner's, and trying his luck in the gaming clubs and betting parlors. In this city, money was everything, as the language with its secret codes had dominated everything in Versailles. Money was perhaps the only serious thing there was, and Theodor's deep lack of seriousness in handling it led him to extended meditations on his relationship to life as a whole.

On balance, games of chance were an interesting source of income, but only because he wasn't afraid to bluff nor to place large bets, even though—or precisely because—he could hardly ever cover them. He even went so far as to put up Larbi as collateral, and was surprised to discover that this momentary necessity could coexist untroubled, side by side, with his genuine affection for his servant. He watched in astonishment as his sweating, red-faced opponents chewed their nails as if their life were in danger. This was precisely what Theodor didn't feel. For *he* was in fear for his *life*: the prospect of getting massacred in the near future as a soldier in the Régiment d'Alsace, or of some evening falling prey to the knife-wielding denizens of the Boulevard du Crime (unlike the men he gambled with, it meant nothing to them to slit open a nobleman's belly and then, while his last breath rattled in his throat, recognize him as one of their own: a mortal man)—that's what frightened him. But not the possibility of losing money.

Now, was that a sign of unshakable confidence, he wondered, or of stoic despair?

He often gambled in a circle of envoys and diplomats he knew from Versailles, and the only one of them Theodor regularly lost to and whom he therefore greatly admired, was the English ambassador Mr. Montague, a free thinker whom he often compared in his mind to Sternhart, for both were men of great learning and materialistic worldview, yet could not have been more different.

Whenever Montague, over a glass of port or sherry, recounted the Battle of the Boyne in which he had taken part as a young soldier, or talked about the Declaration of Rights or the conquest of Gibraltar, whenever he spoke of the Two Treatises of Government and compared the freedom of trade in his country with the suffocating control over all economic activity in France exercised by the *Surintendant des finances* and his army of tax collectors, Theodor could see the shuttle flitting back and forth between thought and deed.

Jakob, on the other hand, had a horror of politics. He thought it beneath his dignity to have anything to do with it. His Prussian king had been installed by God, just like the Most Christian Majesty here in his host country, and both of them should do what they thought best, as long as they let him construct his calculating machine. For the rest, he aspired to an official appointment. And if among friends he made no bones about his contempt for the ineptitude of all administrators, still he was enough of a dialectician to keep his mouth shut as soon as he was in the presence of someone who might eventually be of consequence for his future.

Privately, Theodor thought Sternhart was a latent fanatic. His categorical belief in theories and axioms, his impatience with the glacial pace at which humanity crept forward, inch by inch, toward higher evolution and intellectual advancement, his exclusive love for thought and contempt for people who did not live by it—all these could lead one to imagine a future in which such optimistic impatience would turn into impatient terror, initiating a new Inquisition dedicated to Athena, compared to which the Spanish Inquisition, which still left open the possibility of divine mercy, would seem a harmless joke.

Once, they went to see a cockfight in a rear courtyard off the Boulevard du Crime: around the roped-off arena a surging, jostling crowd of shouting, sour-smelling men; the syncopated, falsetto cries of the bookmaker; the whole fauna from the *Cour des miracles*: convicts freed from the galleys, one-eyed men, men with wooden legs, beggars, drunks, pickpockets, pimps; and then the noble cocks, jet black, cardinal red, golden yellow in their cages; friends and advisers clustered around the owners who were sizing each other up like prize fighters; the erratic, blackish-yellow button eyes of the fluffed-up birds; the greedy, blood-thirsty whites of the audience's eyes. Then the cages were opened and the two cocks—two roaring hurricanes, too fast to see any details—flew at each other, merged in a slashing tangle of flying feathers, shrill squawks, and squirting blood. The mob held its collective breath and gasped in unison. The talons of the darker cock, fitted with iron spurs, buried themselves in the breast of his opponent. Then a little black marble rolled onto the white and red sand: the loser's hacked-out eye. His agony followed. Now defenseless, bleeding from a dozen wounds, he hung his wings while his opponent, as if hypnotized, continued to slash at him in merciless frenzy.

Theodor turned away. He felt sick. He didn't want to watch this martyrdom of an innocent creature. Sternhart observed everything with a deadpan expression and mathematical coolness, or as he himself put it afterward, "with interest." "You're too superficial and sentimental," he told his friend. And you have no sense of dignity, Theodor thought.

Unknown to you, there is dignity in turning away, in not wanting to see and know everything. Turning away preserves your own dignity as well as the dignity of whatever you don't look at. For there are looks, and your look of ice-cold interest is one of them, that rob the observed of dignity.

It was the same in the bordello.

Theodor, who abhorred factory-produced sex and had ordered only a massage for himself, left the common room quickly so as not to be driven into nauseated abstention for the rest of his life by its sounds and images. His friend Sternhart reminded him of an idiot child who plays the same game of peek-a-boo for hours on end, incapable and unwilling to do anything else.

All that interested him were his own empowerment and release. Anything about the girls that didn't serve the cause of penetration interested him about as much as the beauties of nature interest the peasant who steps onto his field, gives it an appraising look, and declares, "The furrow is damp; let's start sowing."

It's the eroticism of a scientist, thought Theodor with distaste, a reduction to the meshing together of two organs, the eroticism of a burgher, and one of its results is bourgeois morality: if for my trouble I end up with a three-drop yield, then it was pleasing to the Lord.

Wasn't it Mortagne who had said, "Success nauseates me"? How well Theodor understood what he meant!

And yet he couldn't forget the virtues that constituted the obverse of Jakob's odiousness, virtues he hadn't met with in Versailles and knew to be so underdeveloped in himself: diligence, perseverance, concentration, thoroughness. Then what was missing in Sternhart?

Theodor pondered that question as he put his clothes back on, dismissed the masseuse with a generous tip, and waited for his friend. In the end it was respect for the mystery, the mystery of love, of woman, of nature. Sternhart lacked any religious feeling.

Something he himself had in abundance. Yes, he was old-fashioned. Compared with men like Montague or Jakob he was an intellectual anachronism. He felt himself to be centuries older than they; indeed, here in this bordello, thinking of courtly love and mysteries while all around him it was like rabbits in a bunny hutch, he felt himself to be deeply aristocratic.

Shortly thereafter the ship of Theodor's life, in which he had sat facing backward, watching the receding shore, and using the rudder only occasionally since the current was carrying the vessel into the unknown anyway, ran aground.

First his two loves came to an end almost as simultaneously as they had begun.

The Baroness Valentini canceled one of their gallant rendezvous with a perfumed note which bore somewhat too ostentatious tear stains and took his arm affectionately next time they saw each other at court.

"I can't expect you to forgive me, Theodor, but if our great love has meant anything at all to you, then don't challenge him to a duel. I wouldn't survive it and would have to end my days in a convent if something should happen to either of you. I've fallen for him."

And with this, she pointed to a plump dwarf with his wig on crooked who was just then hopping around on one leg because his left shoe had got stuck in the soft earth.

"What, that homunculus?!" cried the rejected lover and, insulted, fought down an urge to laugh. "Vanzetti can pull five of those a day for you out of his retort!"

"Don't talk so meanly about him, you wrathful man. I can laugh so marvelously with him," replied the baroness and clung to Theodor's arm as if she really had to restrain him from throwing himself at his rival.

"With him or at him?"

"Even when I'm laughing at him, he laughs along. And he's insatiable . . ."

"I'd prefer not to think about it," said Theodor.

"Will you always remember me, beloved?"

He looked at her and now, for the first time, he got a queasy feeling in the pit of his stomach. He suppressed his tears and recalled the moments when she had pleaded with him to tell her he loved her. And now, just as obediently, he answered yes.

The end of the Gertrud-Laura affair was more embarrassing—much more embarrassing. Love has its own dynamics, and after having played so long at fantasizing about the soul of his beloved, the urge to press this airy vision to himself in the flesh became so overwhelming that Theodor left his poems in the drawer to storm the fortress with more practical weapons: the pretense of wealth and serious intentions. And no sooner had he abandoned his subtle approach to wooing and set about achieving his object in a vulgar manner, than Gertrud's bastion, her widely advertised virtue, began to waver, and she agreed to a secret assignation.

If only he hadn't chanced it, especially not just a few days after *la Valentini* had dismissed him! But who knows, there might have been a subterranean connection which Theodor himself was not completely conscious of. And now that the first affair was over, perhaps he needed to take care of the other one connected to it—one way or the other.

It turned out to be a traumatic experience, for his exaggerated, tender regard for her, the proximity of her innocence, the longing that finally sees its beloved object within reach with its pink breast exposed, completely blocked Theodor's ability to act.

What would have been required at this juncture would have been a tangible, Valentinian initiative on the part of the object of his adoration. Then everything could have turned out all right, but unfortunately, the obverse of innocence is dull-wittedness.

Before him stood his temple, insisting on being ravished but not helping it come to pass, and Theodor burst into tears, for he couldn't achieve both love for this girl and its implementation, dissolution, and supersession in and through the deed. Once Gertrud, panting heavily, understood this (and of course didn't understand that here was a tender, deep, almost sacred emotion, faltering before the crassness of its incarnation—all Theodor's fevered mind could see was Sternhart's white body smacking against the whore's, reminding him of pig slaughtering in the village) there followed some strong language. She snarled like a butcher's dog, tore open the door of the coach and sprang out in a rage, her bodice still half open, turned back and then spat against the windowpane behind which Theodor's pale face appeared, but it was the spit of a street urchin. With an ugly noise, she gathered the contents of her throat and nose into her mouth and spewed out a compact, not quite colorless gob of phlegm, and while she turned and hurried away, it ran down the glass in streaks through which the baron watched her depart.

But all these terrible experiences paled like dreams in the daylight of a much deeper shock.

Theodor, on a visit to Fontainebleau with la Palatine, had left behind unopened a letter from Mortagne, guessing it must be about his imminent entrance into the Régiment d'Alsace. Upon his return from the outing whose merry-making had left him with indigestion, a headache, and a moral hangover, he opened the letter and read that his mother had died of cholera.

A second letter arrived that same day and reported that her burial had had to take place in a hurry on account of the temperature and the danger of infection, despite the absence of her son who was nowhere to be found.

Theodor fell into a fever with sweats and chills. He went to bed, bade Larbi close the shutters, and stared at the ceiling. He wanted to cry and couldn't. It was his fault she had died. He wanted to find out how it had happened. He wanted to talk to her, hear her voice, feel her hands upon his face. None of that was possible. The moments of her death sped past him at lightning speed, again and again, different every time. He was always with her, spoke to her, helped her, saved her. Then in the middle of his relief at a happy scene he remembered: she's dead.

He had hardly ever written. He'd never visited her. He had been in no hurry, for he thought he could return his whole life long, whenever he chose, and would find everything and everybody just as they were the day of his departure, as if only a minute had passed. And yet he had also postponed a visit for fear that absence and time could have effected a change, and he would perhaps recognize nothing.

It was his fault. His unthinking love had not sufficed to protect her from death. He wanted to know how it had happened. It couldn't be true. What guilt it is to go away, what guilt, not to stay with your loved ones and protect them your whole life long!

He stayed in bed three days. Larbi sat up with him and waited in worry until the crisis passed. Theodor saw the house, the fruit trees, saw Amalia sitting at the table, her back straight, dressed in black, praying, and saw her eyes that shooed away the ugly world and saw right through him. He saw the dog running after his coach; he saw Amélie standing and waving goodbye. He saw the wind in the green fields of wheat and the high plateau and the big-bellied clouds with tattered edges in the pale blue sky and their gigantic shadows gliding across the plain and up the hills.

In the same rain that was falling onto the gray lawn and the orangerie outside his windows—from the next room one could hear a tirade of homesickness from the incontinent Palatine amidst her overflowing Westerwald chamber pots—he can see his mother returning home to the village from a charitable visit to the hospital over spongy roads in which the wagon wheels cut deep tracks. His mother asks the coachman to stop. She doesn't feel well. She tries to climb out and falls face down in the muck. Her children are far away. The alarmed driver jumps down from the wagon box. Has the baroness fainted? What a shock to see her black mantilla, her black—gray?—hair spattered with mud. Gingerly, he turns her over. Her eyes are open and rolled up into her head, showing their whites. Nausea forces open her mouth. A milky, grainy, foul-smelling gruel gushes out. The shadows beneath her eyes, her cheekbones, her hands turn blue and cold. She trembles like a jointed doll shaken by a giant hand. The hand of the coachman grasping her arm is shaken along with her. He drops her arm and flees. She lies alone in the mud and dies. But now, at last, he's there. He's heard the news in time. He looks at her. She opens her eyes, sees him, he saves her . . .

Amélie's letter arrived several days later and closed with the announcement of her engagement to the Count of Trévoux, whom she had met at Mortagne's chateau. Their patron had kept his promise.

When Theodor returned to Paris a week later, he learned that Jakob Sternhart, the newly minted doctor, had been admitted to the Prince-Electoral Brandenburg Academy of Sciences and was returning to Greifswald.

How fine the flame of triumph in his eyes! His perseverance had paid off, his life's plan proven correct. Suddenly, for all that he was a man of the third estate and without wit or manners, he overshadowed his friend Theodor. A member of the Academy and a professor earned ten times what a lieutenant did, to say nothing of social recognition. The humiliation was complete, and Theodor had nothing with which to oppose it: no knowledge, no money, no luck, no home. A brief, joyless soldier's life, like his father had led, was what awaited him.

Chapter VI

THEODOR KNEW HE WAS no scholar or thinker and also knew he did not want to be a lieutenant in the French army. But what fate had in store for him, and whether he would have to peel layer after layer from the onion of his soul before he could find out—that was still veiled in mystery.

He couldn't stand the thought that the pattern of his life's tapestry was ready and waiting and all that was left to do was fill it in, pushing the shuttle back and forth for the rest of his days. Why had they brought him up as a young falcon, if he now must bob along through the dusty lowlands as an infantry partridge?

A lieutenant's salary was miserable, though quite adequate to feed a modest, frugal householder and his family. For the rest, the future of a lieutenant was relatively straightforward: in ten years you could become a first lieutenant, in twenty a captain. If there were a war and if you distinguished yourself—and didn't lose an arm or a leg, croak from gangrene, go blind from powder burns, perish from dysentery, or lose your mind—you might even make major or colonel before your retirement. Then you withdrew to your estate in the provinces and died.

The only problem was that Theodor had neither estate nor province to call home. He had the impression that the whole world was open to him, but being able to go anywhere you wish also means not belonging anywhere. And upon closer inspection, the world he was able to survey consisted of innumerable little kitchen gardens surrounded by picket fences.

The people he talked to in order to gain more clarity about himself and perhaps inspiration from one of them were barricaded within the citadels of their religious, intellectual, material, or sexual identities, where one could of course pay them a visit, but never lure them beyond their walls.

Like a supple glove, Theodor would slide his words and gestures, his demeanor and convictions over those of the person he was speaking to at the moment, and for as long as their conversation lasted, would adapt himself to his interlocutor. But never other than the way certain insects imitate vegetable forms and structures, so that the eye cannot distinguish them from their background. But these creatures have no intention of becoming leaves!

From the elderly Madame de Ferjol at court, Theodor gained more profound insight into Jansenist thought than from Pascal himself, but woe to him if he pointed to a group of dancers enjoying themselves; she would cross herself and all but spit on the ground. The Count of Sully taught him so much about horse breeding that he might have become an authority on it, but when Theodor needed to catch his breath and struck up a conversation about books, the nobleman turned up his nose and referred him to his wife. And a judge in Paris with an admirable library where Theodor could recover from all that horse manure, did not invite him a second time after Theodor mentioned his infatuation with a certain woman. The judge made a face as if he had bitten into a sour apple, leaned back in his chair, crossed his arms defensively, and declared that his guest would have to decide what was more important, the intellect or women-folk and making babies.

From time to time, Theodor still saw Mortemart at Versailles, and with him he was able to switch conversational horses in midstream, but whatever the *précieux* had to say about any topic sounded as though he had learned it by heart from one of his exercise books, which was exactly what he had done, and his *déformation professionelle* consisted in always being on the lookout for weaknesses in his fellow men that could be turned into bons mots. So he never had anything good to say about anyone in the world.

Theodor concluded that the only choice was between wells and tidal flats, the former deep but constricted and malodorous, the latter vast but shallow.

He had gotten this far in his deliberations when the king died. It was reported that the state indebtedness of France amounted to around two billion *livres* and its annual expenditures to 184 million. Theodor felt under no moral obligation to live more frugally than the polity. If his debts made him so socially impossible that he was forced to leave the country, then perhaps he would escape an officer's career.

With a certain composure and fatalistic resignation, he awaited a miracle. A miracle, however, is nothing but the happy concurrence of happenstance and internal preparedness, and this preparedness was the only activity he could take pleasure in anymore.

On the evening before he was to join the regiment, he lay on his bed. His servant Larbi squatted outside the door, chewing his nails at the thought of having to follow his master into the army. Theodor had no plans other than to sleep until either salvation arrived or the day of general oblivion dawned. He had already half nodded off when his orderly knocked and announced a visitor.

A tall man wafted into the salon in a black, floor-length cape and equally black cocked hat from which hung a veil, putting his face in shadow. The lieutenant-to-be had in the meantime moved into a larger apartment in the rue de Grenelle which was still sparsely furnished, since his gambling winnings were gobbled up by his rent payments. Theodor received this curious guest in his housecoat and sent Larbi for some sherry, but the stranger refused the offer of a chair. He was clearly playing a serious game whose credibility would have suffered had he allowed himself to surrender to any creature comforts whatsoever.

Theodor automatically adjusted his posture, expression, and gestures and honored the theatricality of his visitor with impressive alarm.

"Monsieur," the other began, carrying things perhaps a little too far by ostentatiously disguising his voice. By this time, Theodor had already realized that he was speaking to the Abbé Conconi, an adviser of the Regent himself and one of Guillaume Dubois's men.

"Monsieur, someone in high position who wishes to remain anonymous is tendering you an assignment."

Theodor nodded and gestured to one of the armchairs, which the abbé now accepted after all, weighted down as he was with the burden of his mission. He accepted a sherry as well. He took his time sloshing it around in his mouth, then explained that Theodor's assignment would be to carry a secret dispatch to the Hague without being identified, hand it over discreetly to a certain person whose name he would learn from a second sealed letter, and then to follow the instructions of that gentleman, for the good of the king—the abbé concluded his remarks —and the Fatherland.

Theodor was astonished to discover that he was not overly astonished. He didn't even have to listen very closely, even less to think it over. From the first moment it was clear that he would accept the assignment, although he later sometimes asked himself if there would have been any possibility whatsoever of turning it down.

His existential gratitude was much too great for that, gratitude to have been chosen obviously not on account of any superficial merits of his own, not because he had exerted himself and waited in line for it, but simply because he was who he was, because his person had been found worthy.

At the same time, his gratitude included an ingratitude that the assignment might have something routine or banal about it, something ordinary. If that was indeed the case, however, his self-conception and his imagination would see to it that, at least in his memory, the assignment would have an impressive format. A character destined for greatness proves itself not just in confrontations with great obstacles, but also, if not by making every gnat into an elephant, then by deeply experiencing it as such.

After these considerations, he once more paid attention to what the abbé was saying and learned that they had chosen him for two reasons: first, because he could speak German, and second, because he had a totally unknown face, was a blank slate.

"I will not conceal from you, Monsieur, that should your mission be discovered, you must not count on any support at all. You will be completely on your own. If you fail, you will doubtless have to pay with your life."

So Theodor started perspiring a little beneath his housecoat and asked him after all to repeat exactly what was expected of him. At last—and he reserved the best for last—the veiled man spoke of remuneration.

His recompense for the assignment would be a sum—half of it to be paid immediately, the other half upon completion of the task—that represented five times the annual salary of a lieutenant in the Régiment d'Alsace and, as Theodor quickly calculated, the equivalent of that of a professor in Greifswald.

It was explained to him where he should appear the next morning to take possession of the letter and the money. He bid the messenger farewell (painfully respectful of the abbé's incognito all the way to the door), then sank into a chair, filled to bursting with the desire to talk about this miracle, tell everyone about it, and show off his money and his glory in his most pleasing, offhand, and self-ironic manner. That, however—and this was the only drop of gall in his euphoria—was impossible.

Once he had somewhat regained his senses, doubts began to surface. In half an hour, without deliberation, without hesitation, he had upended a secure future and given his life an utterly different direction which yesterday would have seemed impossible.

Had he perhaps made the same mistake as his father, who had to pay for his moment of thoughtless temerity with humiliation and an early death? Was there not in the career of a soldier a comfortable, temperate happiness and the satisfaction of having obediently followed the plans of Count Mortagne to the letter and to the end?

With a shock, he realized he had reached the first real crossroads in his life and had chosen his path without forethought or preparation, he who had never wanted to be in the position of having to choose.

"Larbi, we're traveling to Holland tomorrow. See to procuring horses and take care of the packing."

"And what are we going to do in Holland?" asked the servant.

"Invest some money," replied Theodor. The answer came without hesitation.

Theodor's plan had been formed so quickly and naturally that actually, one could hardly call it a plan. He would pass off his agent's fee as a maternal inheritance which he, the young, enterprising baron on his way home to Westphalia, intended to invest in the Hague.

To calm his agitated mind, he attended vespers in the monastery church of St. Germain and prayed for the soul of his mother, for his sister, and for his patron the Count de Mortagne, whom Theodor would now deny the satisfaction and joy of seeing him don a lieutenant's uniform and thus offend him as one can only offend those to whom one owes something.

He prayed for the success of his mission and above all, for his own survival. As he did so, he observed himself, and his worshipful gravity and devout kneeling accorded marvelously with a future in the service of unknown but doubtlessly high ideals.

A certain generosity was also in order, he thought, and since thoughts of Mortagne led to thoughts of Monsieur de Broglie, whom he had wronged, he decided to expiate this sin so he could begin his new life with a pure heart. That very evening he wrote his old teacher a letter in which he spoke warmly of his school days, enclosing a generous bill of exchange for an amount he could easily do without in view of his remuneration.

Months later, by the way, Theodor received by a circuitous route a reply to this missive from de Broglie's widow, full of effusive thanks for the gift that had helped her and her half-orphaned children out of the greatest hardship. He had not had the slightest inkling that his teacher had a family, but the count must have known about them and thus seen Theodor's accusations for the bald-faced lies they were. Nevertheless, he had dismissed de Broglie and never said a word about it.

The house that Theodor had been directed to and entered the next morning was unremarkable, as was the room where he was received by four men. They behaved with great formality and looked him up and down as if taken aback by his youth. Their spokesman was addressed as "Duke" by the other three.

Upon a table stood a wooden box with shiny brass fittings to which the duke now pointed. "You probably don't know what this is?" he asked patronizingly while the others exchanged smirks.

"But of course," responded Theodor nonchalantly and without dignifying the table with a second glance. "That's Leibniz's stepped drum calculating machine. The only one of its kind in Paris."

"It's what?" cried the duke. "What on earth makes you think we have a calculating machine here, Baron?"

"Well," said Theodor, "this calculating machine is the future, and that's what we're talking about here, aren't we?"

The men looked at each other as if he'd spilled a state secret that had been withheld from them.

"Although the stepped drum will soon be replaced by the sprocket," Theodor continued, "a development to which, if I might be permitted to observe in all humility, I myself have contributed with word and deed. What can one say, gentlemen? The future is changing from one day to the next. For the rest, excess respect would be inappropriate. You'd have a hard time using it to prove Pascal's theorem about the projected sides of a hexagon inscribed in a conic section."

"Yes, the future, Pascal, respect," stuttered the duke. "I see you're a mathematician, Baron?"

"Oh, I only dabble in it. It's a hobby of mine, so to speak. I'm actually more for empirical studies than for theories, which is probably the reason why you've asked me here, gentlemen."

"Quite right, quite right. But as for this machine here, I must disappoint you."

The duke looked guiltily at Theodor, who noticed that his tone of voice had become much more respectful.

"What you see here, Baron, is merely an encoding device, but the best of its kind, I assure you. A cryptograph constructed for the enciphering system of Monsieur de Vigenère. After all, we must protect the letters you are to transport."

"Of course," Theodor was quick to reply. "What was I thinking? They must be protected. With a cryptograph. What else would one use?"

As a presumptive scientist, Theodor was given a crash course in the encryption system, which used a keyword connected to the twenty-six alphabets of the Vigenère table. Afterward, he thought numbly, this is useful mathematics for a change, if you can call it mathematics.

"Only you will know the keyword, Baron. It's not written down anywhere. You must keep it in your head and then disclose it to the addressee so that he can use it to decode the letter. Which word would you like to choose?"

"Amélie," said Theodor, and the gentlemen smiled knowingly to each other and dismissed him.

It was Theodor's first trip abroad, and his eager anticipation of the voyage from Boulogne to Holland, his keenness to see foreign lands and cities, was mixed with a certain apprehension and the wish to get everything over with so he could talk about it.

In the evening, at an inn in Amiens, he drafted a letter to his sister. Next to the sheet of white paper lay open the second letter from his employers, containing the name of the man he was supposed to visit in the Hague: the Holstein chamberlain, Georg Heinrich, Imperial Baron von Görtz, minister of His Majesty the King of Sweden, at present confined to a prison in the Hague and awaiting extradition to England. So it was against England.

As young and inexperienced and ultimately indifferent to politics as Theodor was, he had nevertheless been able to get an idea from conversations in Paris and at court of the profound differences in standards between French and English diplomacy, so that he had no very high opinion of the machinations in which he himself had suddenly become a tiny wheel. One should work for the English, he said to himself. They do everything in a much more rational and modern way.

They had installed an agent in Amiens and another in Boulogne. Theodor spotted him immediately upon his arrival in the latter city, and if he himself had had a well-known or suspicious-looking face, he would not have escaped his notice. But so whole-heartedly did he play the role of the young, garrulous heir looking to invest his money, that he even forgot the compromising letter in his pocket—probably the best possible camouflage.

As far as he knew, the English wanted Görtz extradited because Sweden had abetted and helped finance the Stuarts' recent abortive landing, with King Louis himself behind the plan. Although Theodor's curiosity led him to want to learn in which game he was one of the pawns, still it seemed to him for the time being both wiser and safer to earn his money by doing nothing but carrying out his assignment to be a discrete messenger.

In Boulogne, before his eyes the forest of masts and in his ear the creak of wood against wood, his nose filled with the penetrating odors of tar and seaweed, he interrupted a game of dominoes with Larbi to continue his letter to his sister: "All I wish for myself is to be forty and to have accumulated enough money so as to retire somewhere in the country. I have made a start, and if I continue to have such luck and nothing bad happens to me, I will soon be able to put the life of an adventurer behind me. I envy you such a well-ordered existence, and my most fervent hope is finally to be able to take my little nephew Friedrich into my arms . . ."

He crumpled up the sheet and threw it onto a pile, then began once again. "Beloved Amélie! I have taken the first step toward fame! Only so much: I am about to enter man-to-man negotiations with the most important politicians in Europe concerning the future of the country. The brilliance of the international stage is terribly blinding, but as you know, I remain clear-sighted while others fumble in the dark. The only thing I still need to accomplish is to make myself heard. As soon as one achieves some understanding of the machinery of diplomacy, one realizes how much we are ruled by chance and vanity. Wouldn't it be enough to follow clear and unerring insights with equally clear and unerring deeds? . . . In Amsterdam, where my arrival is expected, I plan to purchase a big rocking-horse for little Friedrich, a white one with a real mane and red leather bridle . . .

. . . My only sister! How foreign to me are the flat greenness of this rainy landscape, the cow pastures and marshes and the salty tang in the air, the gray, endless ocean, churning within itself, and with wistful melancholy I think back on our childhood home, the enclosed garden, the smells, the trees in bloom, the cloud shadows on the hills, the safe, dark refuge of the house, the plainsong in church, our games. I just can't believe that all that is over and done with and our lives only move forward, away from all that we loved, away from all security. Don't you feel the same way, that things must first have happened before one can see them, smell them, and possess them? Don't you also sense that the real life we're able to survey and experience and savor to the fullest is precisely, tragically, what lies irretrievably behind us, and that the attempt to prepare for an uncertain future—like having to parry the attack of an invisible opponent—robs us of all leisure to see and experience what is happening today? The only moments of happiness I know are in remembrance of things past or the hope of what is to come. Have you learned how to combine the moment and its pleasure, your pleasure and your consciousness of it? But why am I asking you? You're a mother . . ."

Theodor succeeded at everything so effortlessly that it seemed suspicious even to him. Although he was never one to gauge the worth of an action from its difficulty nor regard the agony of carrying it out as itself a positive quality, nevertheless the large reward he had received begged to be justified by some difficulties, to avoid creating the impression that he had performed an activity that was beneath his dignity, which a lowlier person could have seen to just as well.

But each day and each step of the way proceeded undisturbed and unencumbered. He hired a ship and during this first brief sea voyage, stood at the bow above the choppy gray waters of the Channel, always in sight of the coast, letting the spray lash his leather garments and his face like an encouraging slap and felt he was being rejuvenated, purified. Contact with the elements, provided it's not titanic and dangerous, almost always has just such an effect on someone who lives mainly indoors. He arrived in the modest harbor, boarded the coach to the Hague, found lodging in a tidy inn. Each step and each day succeeded as if by magic. No obstacle, no danger was in sight, and into his euphoria there crept an ever-increasing anxiety.

He had enough familiarity with the old myths to know that the favorites of the Fates, the darlings of fortune, the immortal heroes, paid for their wings with a short life and a bloody death, and that the gods granted long life only to the boring.

Perhaps he would fall victim to some illness made more likely by the unhealthy climate and all the brackish water. For that very reason, before they had even left the harbor, Theodor ordered Larbi to purchase from an itinerant apothecary a sort of clyster syringe of interminable length with which a room, once its windows were tightly closed, was to be sprayed with a remedy for illnesses of every description.

After the first treatment, Theodor's chamber stank so badly that their eyes were running and Larbi had to tear open the windows and at the same time stir up the fire against the invading cold.

"Sir, do you really believe in this flim-flam you paid a gulden for?"

"By no means, my dear Larbi, no more than you do. But I find it reassuring to spray this odious stuff; it calms my nerves. It's an activity, and I've got to do something so that I'm not doing nothing."

"But it's possible that this very stuff will make us sick!"

"There's no denying it! But then at least we'll know what we're suffering from, and an illness you know the cause of is more reassuring than health that at any moment, when you least expect it, can turn into sickness."

"Sometimes, *Maître*, your logic astounds me."

"My dear Larbi, I wouldn't give a farthing for it myself, but at the moment we're having such a streak of luck that I'm certain I could scratch the gods under their chins and they would turn a blind eye just because it was me."

As soon as he learned that Görtz was under quite comfortable house arrest in one of the buildings in an inner court, he had himself announced as a distant relation and chatted with a captain of the guard in such a carefree and naive manner about the life of a soldier (substituting a regiment of Prussian dragoons for the Régiment d'Alsace) that he received immediate permission to visit his "cousin."

Görtz was a massive man in his late thirties. He was sitting at a desk in a room that was higher than it was wide, and glanced up briefly as Theodor was escorted in. His red, large-pored neck rose from a collar of white lace over a black vest with a dull sheen. His hair and beard were reddish blond and his glance instantly comprehended the scenery, yet seemed to concentrate on the essential elements, in this case the unknown visitor who had been announced as his cousin from Westphalia. Below his nostrils lay the dark shadows of snuff stains.

"Aha, here's my cousin . . . (a glance at the guard) . . . We must not have seen each other since you were a lad! Come, let me embrace you . . ."

Theodor was impressed. He had entered the man's ambiance and inhaled the scent of will and power. It smelled of snuff, sweat, and last night's cabbage. As if in confirmation, the minister broke wind explosively and Theodor, accustomed to the manners of Versailles, almost fainted from embarrassment. Instead, he drew his lips into a thin smile.

As soon as the guard had disappeared, he explained who he was in well-chosen words, withdrew the letter from his inner pocket, handed his interlocutor the Vigenère table, and uttered his keyword. Thereupon he remained standing and watched as Görtz tore the envelope open—or rather, into pieces—with his thick fingers.

Actually, Theodor had expected to be informed as to its contents, but nothing of the kind occurred. A smile, a nod, a pinch of snuff, the letter put away, a sigh, a sneeze, then renewed concentration. Theodor could tell from watching the man that he had just closed one chapter of his life and was about to begin a new one without lingering over second thoughts.

The young man immediately envied the older one his sifting, ordering, and evaluating mind, and on the spot took note of the gestures illustrative of his thought process, but it was with a certain reserve that he sensed he had come up against someone whose power pulled others to him like a magnet and then exploited them. Theodor had to hold himself in check so as not to blurt out an embellished version of his life's story in order to induce respect for his personality in this superior, before the latter even had a chance to make use of his services.

"Are you actually aware that the British crown has a hundred agents out to seize you?" Görtz now asked. "Do you even realize that they foresaw assistance like this coming from Orléans and were planning to prevent it from reaching me? I have friends here, but the agent they were expecting was not supposed to even make it into this land. My compliments, young man. How did you do it?"

Theodor clenched his jaws to prevent them from gaping apart in an astonished "Oh!," immediately regained control of himself, and answered with a smile, "Ah well, with time one learns to smell danger and evade it. I had quite an entertaining and pleasant journey." (For some incomprehensible reason, the image of the gigantic clyster syringe occurred to him at this point.)

"You seem very young, Monsieur. How old are you?"

"Twenty-two."

Again he nodded, looked Theodor over, took some snuff. Then he gestured: "Please sit down. I have a job for you."

Later Theodor would think back on this occasion with a smile. As far as he could see, it had been the only time he could have asked about remuneration for the mission which, measured by its importance, would have had to pay ten times as much as his first one. In this solemn moment, however, he considered it inelegant to put a brake on the momentum of events with anything as tasteless as haggling about money. For the rest, he had listened closely to Görtz's explanation so that at the next available opportunity he could sketch the most fascinating, demonic-comical portrait of his character and reap for himself laughs and admiration. But while Theodor allowed the sly fox to bewitch him with compliments, Görtz was playing on his vanity in order to get him to work for his enterprise for free.

Later however, in retrospect, Theodor would say to himself that had he been given the choice between compliments and money, he would have chosen the compliments in any case.

On the next day, still in his role as an heir, he and Larbi continued their journey to Amsterdam where, thanks to Görtz's letter of recommendation, they found lodging in the stately red-gabled house of State Councilor van Boon in the Herengracht.

He noticed that there were no curtains in his room, and he inquired about it to the master of the house.

"You will not find curtains in any honest house in this city," the latter replied.

"Is it a tradition or some vow like with the gondoliers in Venice?"

"Not at all. We simply have nothing to hide. We have no need to conceal ourselves. But if you wish, I can have curtains installed in your room. Where you're from, in that nest of fornication Versailles, it's all too understandable that people should want to hide themselves from the eyes of their fellows. The shady machinations of the papists all but demand it."

Van Boon, his noble, aquiline face dominated by a sort of beak formed by his hooked nose and jutting chin, spoke in a tone quite appropriate to the surroundings. The large liberality and freedom of Amsterdam was unimaginable in Paris. Uncensored religious pamphlets circulated; the monarchs were publicly rebuked; there was nothing one was forbidden to think about, speak about, and find fault with.

On one of the first days, the state councilor accompanied Theodor on a stroll across the Flower Market to the Dam. The great man walked past aldermen, beggars sitting in the dust of the streets, wasting away from their festering wounds, as well as legless fiddlers on little wheeled carts, and he doffed his hat to them all in friendly equability.

Theodor, who always suffered a bad conscience at the sight of misery, tossed them a coin. The wealthy van Boon didn't give them a farthing.

"It's not pleasing to God to be so miserable," he explained.

"Why aren't they cleared from the streets, then?" Theodor asked.

"Oh, we're more tolerant here than the French," the merchant opined. "They've got a right to live, too."

While Theodor passed his days in upstanding, solid Amsterdam, carrying out negotiations on Görtz's behalf, his inner ferment grew more and more intense to make his story public, disclose his game, in order to snatch from the admiration reflected in the eyes of his listeners some reward for the fact that he had not become a little lieutenant in the French army.

His two trunks full of stylish clothing and *accessoires* stood constantly open and he spent whole afternoons choosing what to wear in order to find a packaging for his self-esteem that was both elegant and ostentatious. In his opulent get-up, a sensuous display of carded wool and damask, silk, cambric, Brussels lace, and finest leather, worthy of a concubine, he would go out into the streets, and he grew bitter at the Dutch phlegma toward everything and everybody, and especially toward him. He couldn't blabber out the well-founded reason for his get-up without endangering his mission. The longer he had to keep his mouth shut, the more he was provoked by the Calvinistic black-and-white and wished to see just once that even these people could let themselves go.

Truth to tell, by "these people" he actually had in mind primarily his hostess, Mijfrouw Els van Boon, the cool and much younger second wife of the once-widowed state councilor. Her generous proportions somewhat resembled those of la Valentini, but her face was more coarsely modeled, more with charcoal pencil than red chalk, so to speak.

He was almost certain that Els—who was always dressed in black and withdrew yawning into a corner, prayer book in hand, whenever he was chatting—he was almost certain that she, to express it in the words of a Versailles courtier and Jesuit, had "showed him the instruments."

Without going further into whether it was really so or Theodor only imagined it, nevertheless he could have sworn that two or three times in his presence, the lady of the house had let hidden regions of her skin show, which hardly admitted of any other interpretation than as clear invitations to his pluck: a few seconds of bare ankle shimmering between the hem of her skirt and her shoe, the edge of her areola, dark as a birthmark, in a lightning-quick slip of her décolleté. And once, in his presence, her long fingers insistently kneaded the knob of her chair arm . . .

In the colloquies he conducted with Russian councilmen in a cabinet in van Boon's house, his thoughts strayed again and again to the question of what relief there might be for his distress. By now, he had a clear understanding of the political situation: the real reason for Görtz's presence in Holland was to negotiate with the Russian czar, currently sojourning in Amsterdam, about the conditions of a possible peace treaty. The Swedish minister, still comfortably stranded in the Hague, had prepared a written message for the czar which Theodor was supposed to hand over to him in person, but first he had to breach the ranks of Russian officials on the strength of his charm and of genever.

When he finally stood before the future emperor, a small man dressed in black—shorter than Els Boon, it crossed his mind—with long, thin hair, a drooping mustache, and a white center part in which lay flakes of dandruff, the imposing figure of the Swedish minister shrank to midget size in comparison with the aura of this man.

Pyotr Alexeyevich stood in a shaft of sunlight falling aslant through the window and clouded with dust, his hands clasped behind him, rocking on the balls of his feet in intense concentration, flanked by two scribes or secretaries holding before their chests wooden boards on which paper was stretched.

He listened to the words Theodor spoke while the young man vainly attempted to penetrate the taut, protective carapace of this man and create a common basis for conversation. Once Theodor accidentally touched on something that interested the czar, and it was as if a light was ignited in his eyes. He began to speak and briefly sounded Theodor out, but after a few minutes, he let the subject drop—in disappointment, as it appeared.

He had wanted to talk about facts, and Theodor only for the sake of talking, and that wasn't enough.

The conversation with the great man was too concrete to be pursued in his *à-peu-près* style. One needed to possess expert knowledge in order to communicate with him. Insulted, Theodor said to himself that the czar would rather have talked to Sternhart than to him, even if the result would have been stubbornly stolid professional jargon—deadly boring for any outside observer—about ship-building and construction engineering.

"My time is short," said the Russian, "I thank you for your remarks," and extended his hand, in which Theodor laid Görtz's sealed letter. Then he was dismissed.

Even before he had recovered from his annoyance at himself and the brusque man so far superior to him (at least there had been no witnesses!), it dawned on him what to do. He would arrange a celebration. In van Boon's house. A fest in honor of his host. A gigantic feast. An orgy among the Calvinists.

What an idea! What had motivated it? Was it that Theodor, humiliated by his meeting with the czar, wanted to celebrate in hedonistic excess the pointlessness of his own existence? Did he need a large scope in order to seduce Els van Boon undisturbed, in the eye of the storm? Did he believe he could only demonstrate his advancement and good fortune in this way, or on the contrary, was he driven by a secret anarchic desire to smash what he had achieved, pulverize five years of a lieutenant's salary with one blow and stand there with empty hands, if only to be able to grasp what he had possessed in the realization that he had it no more? Was it the fear of having already reached his goal and the belief that only hope drives life forward, but when results and conclusions are reached, hope can no longer flourish? Or was it perhaps a somewhat infantile protest against the appalling Calvinist philosophy that success was pleasing to God? For as Mortagne was fond of saying, success was cause for shame.

The celebration took place on three floors of van Boon's patrician house, at the end of the eighth week of Theodor's stay in Amsterdam, and included over two hundred guests.

Theodor had engaged an orchestra and an entire theater troupe from Paris to perform a pastoral play and ballet. He had ordered barrels of red wine from Burgundy and a thousand bottles of champagne. Two entire oxen would be roasted in the huge fireplace on the ground floor. An entire fluttering, screeching wagonful of chickens and pigeons arrived in the Herengracht.

Larbi had been criss-crossing the city for days, delivering invitations, and with the additional assignment of finding fifteen of the most beautiful prostitutes, decking them out like royalty, pledging them to initial good behavior, and mixing them in with the guests. Yards and yards of cloth panels and drapes were sewn to hang on walls and windows and produce atmosphere. Hundreds of candles were dipped to create the impression of drifting through a sea of molten gold.

The optic nerves of the guests were strained to the point of hysteria by bustling stewards, tumescent flower arrangements, the orchestra's billowing wigs, scything bows, and walnut-hued violins, by swelling draperies, glowing damask, and shimmering platters laden with crispy, yellow-brown poultry. Their nasal mucosa were excited by a mixture of smells: roasting and baking, punch and liqueur, perfume and flowers and candle wax and crowded, perspiring humanity. As the evening progressed, the worlds of sound that were clearly distinguishable from each other became compacted into the kind of hum an apoplectic hears in his head.

A few guests escaped before it was too late and regained their senses in the sobering night air of Amsterdam. The rest, however, ate and talked and the longer the evening lasted, the more powerfully they fell under the spell of this Catholic, sensuous *Walpurgisnacht* over which Theodor presided, clad in black and white, a sacral-sober Mephistopheles with gleaming eyes who caused dish after dish to be brought out and commanded that even more of the unusually heavy wine be poured down the throats of the patricians.

The pastoral play with its sultry ballet interludes infected the audience; hands and mouths became independent of their owners; the music turned shrill and then ingratiating and then shrieking again. The dignity of the guests disintegrated into lascivious, drunken sensuality, tipped over into hysterics that gradually subsided in alcoholic coma. People in dishabille had fallen asleep beside and atop each other, their makeup streaked, their white shirtfronts stained red with wine. They lay on the field of battle amid amputated roast chickens and legs of mutton gnawed down to the bone. Digestion and sleep descended upon the dying night through which a dockside whore toddled back to work, carrying a year's earnings and roughly dragging the velvet train of her moss-green dress behind her like a puppy tugging at his leash. Mijnheer van Boon was sitting at the table of honor which he had not left the entire evening. He had fallen asleep hours ago, his head lying on the oak tabletop and watched over by empty dark-green bottles, his arms wrapped around two snoring ladies. Stewards were emptying the leftover food into potato sacks. A violinist and a spinet player were still playing, their eyes closed, mechanical as a music box. The thin sound echoed spectrally through the house.

This was Theodor's hour. The gray gleam of the dawning day shone through the rippling lengths of tulle.

He had danced much and talked much, not with Els van Boon, but where she could see him doing it. Several times, their clothes had touched each other in passing, and he could feel in his fingertips that she was waiting for him. Now he approached her and she stared at him with reddened eyes, between drunkenness and dream, at once slack and sensuous. He closed his eyes. The path to the end point of indiscretion, the final frontier of strangeness, had to be crossed without his volition. He felt he was being sucked toward it, opened his eyes, and the patrician's wife had laid sleep-heavy arms around him. She sat up on the edge of a table, opened her legs, pulled up her dress with both hands, and clamped it between her teeth. Her naked thighs smacked against a tabletop wet with spilled wine. Her arms lay on his shoulders like lead weights. Her legs closed around his back. She pulled him to her, opened her mouth, and her dress fell over the moment of their union.

As they wordlessly disengaged from each other and put their clothes back in order, Theodor read in the eyes of Els van Boon, to his greatest satisfaction, a sort of astonished horror in whose center the tiny pupils signaled exhausted, feline gratification.

Here at least, Theodor told himself, he wouldn't be so quickly forgotten.

In the early morning, he accompanied the merchant Jacob Cats, whom he had commissioned to procure the supplies for the party, on his way home. Cats was all keyed up. His calculating soul kept getting into conflict with a lust for life which had been freed from its Calvinist chains and couldn't stop talking in an excited babble about the memorable night.

Theodor moodily drew the balance: Amsterdam was an excellent location for money and business. And with a little encouragement, for pleasure as well. His five annual salaries were now in the pocket of the man walking beside him, a man who would never forget him. He himself was impoverished, weightless, full of expectancy. That same day, Baron Görtz was released from detention, traveled to Amsterdam, and offered Theodor the post of private secretary. The young man, feeling he ought to take leave of Amsterdam for the present, agreed.

Görtz informed him they were headed for Mecklenburg. Theodor asked what his salary would be. The large, bearded man told him. It was what a lieutenant in the Régiment d'Alsace earned.

Chapter VII

THEODOR WAS RIDING NORTH across endless plains at the side of Baron von Görtz. A blanket of dove-gray clouds stretched from horizon to horizon. To the east it bulged dark and heavy and hung low over the black fields. It was raining over there. It was an icy rain, and the wind blowing across the flat landscape ruffled the gray-green grass like an animal's fur.

The rain fell sometimes in heavy drops which crashed against one's forehead like hailstones, sometimes in a finely sifted mist which penetrated one's clothing and textured the horizontality of the natural world with silvery, diagonal hatching. They rode past black fields of burned stubble. A buzzard rose from a hedgerow, heavy wings flapping wetly. Irrigation canals slanted toward the road and disappeared again in the mist on either side. From time to time, a tall, gray silhouette would emerge from the damp air, becoming blacker as it approached, a medieval knight armed for combat that revealed itself to be a windmill with a wood-shingled cap glistening with moisture.

Theodor wiped the wet from his face and mentioned Cervantes and Don Quixote. "What sort of nonsense is that?" said Görtz brusquely. He was in a hurry. His king had arrived in Stralsund and that's where they were headed. After months of inactivity in Amsterdam, he was back in his element: politics and war, war and politics. Theodor felt lonely.

Private secretary of the Swedish plenipotentiary sounded more splendid—much more splendid—than it was, and that was in any event some consolation to Theodor on this uncomfortable and martially frugal journey, when he was assailed by doubts if it had been especially smart to exchange the career he had just begun as a secret agent for the prestigious but miserably remunerated position at the side of a prominent politician.

Görtz declared that the plan was either to isolate and conquer Peter or to make common cause with him, and he went on to expound that diplomacy consisted precisely in simultaneously pursuing one strategy and its opposite until imponderable contingencies forced one to leap onto one or the other of the two saddled steeds. Theodor recalled the Russian courier who to his very great surprise had paid him a visit a day before his departure from Amsterdam and handed him a plump purse as a reward for his role as intermediary. Theodor had consulted Cats about the best use of the money and decided to have him invest it in Law's newly founded *Compagnie d'Occident*.

At the border of the Duchy of Mecklenburg-Schwerin they encountered a troupe of Swedish cavalry who informed Görtz of an impending battle. As darkness fell, they reached the place where the two armies were encamped in anticipation of combat. When someone handed Theodor a telescope and he scanned the bonfires blazing in the enemy camp, his stomach contracted in fear.

Larbi whispered to him in French, "*Maître, on ne peut pas se tirer d'ici?*"

Görtz, who was standing nearby, replied without looking around, his eyes staring straight ahead into the wet darkness in which watery flames were flickering, "*Non, mon petit. Vous allez vous couvrir de gloire ou mourir.*"

The minister seemed to find pleasure in crawling into his bivouac still clad in his wet, stiff, outfit of stinking leather. Bearded men in uniform brought him a bottle of rum. "Wake me two and a half hours before sunrise," he commanded.

Theodor was led to the officers' tent and assigned a cot among drunken, snoring, whispering lieutenants.

"*Mon pauvre Larbi,*" he said hoarsely, "*on est faits comme des rats.*"

The camp bed was narrow and hard as a coffin. Bathed in sweat and sleepless, Theodor listened to the rain drumming on the tent roof and was certain he was spending the last night of his life. He stank. He longed for a bath and fresh clothes. He was freezing. It's quite possible I'll catch incurable rheumatism here he thought, appalled, until he remembered that he was to die a bloody death on the morrow. It was an infuriating thought. Half asleep, Larbi mumbled smothered reproaches.

Theodor listened to the rain and attempted to take stock. In view of what he had achieved and experienced up to now, was his demise acceptable, or would he make himself ridiculous if he died now? How good that he had never forged any long-term plans that would now be left behind as half-finished ruins.

Someone shook him by the shoulder and he cried out. It was five o'clock. The tent was full of hectic activity: curses, coughs, the clatter of weapons. It was still dark but torchlight played across the canvas. Commands were shouted. He must have slept more than four hours. He tried to slip into his boots without success; they were stiff from dampness. Larbi had to help him, and once he was standing in them, his legs threatened to buckle beneath him. He tensed all his muscles and stepped out of the tent. Go to your death with dignity, he told himself. Don't show you're afraid. Go to your death with a smile on your face.

"Well, Baron," Görtz said, "where would you like to witness the spectacle? By my side, or among the lieutenants in the cavalry?"

"Whichever you prefer," said Theodor with a charming smile, took a deep breath of moist, frosty night air and exhaled it, trembling slightly.

"Better stay with me. I still need you," joked the Holsteiner.

Theodor bowed, walked stiff-legged to his horse and mounted. They rode at a walk to a rise with an abandoned windmill from which they could survey the battlefield once dawn had broken.

The gloomy, rainy day of death began with the enervating sound of dry drum rolls and regimental flags snapping in the wind. Theodor had a sour taste in his mouth and his stomach ached. He hadn't been able to get anything down; the thought of dying on a full stomach was nauseating.

The plain between the hill on which he stood with Görtz and the two low knolls on which the enemy general staff had taken up their position was a gray-green, blurry sea. To their left, a line of poplars along a stream marked the horizon. A stone's throw down the hill, cannoneers stood at their gun carriages, chatting. Görtz was talking to the commanding general in Swedish. He swept his hand in an arc.

"We're going to have the rising sun in our eyes if it ever breaks through the clouds," said Theodor, attempting to sound professional. He felt helpless and confused. His mind was continually jumping back and forth between the perspective of a painter of battle scenes and that of an infantryman hopelessly wedged in his marching column.

"We have the stronger mounted force," Görtz replied. "They're only Schweriners. They don't have enough money to deploy a cavalry worthy of the name. To tell the truth, the outcome's already decided. While they poach some of our foot soldiers, our cavalry will advance along those poplars, fall upon their flank from behind, and disable their cannon on that hill there to the left. By this afternoon, they'll be running up the white flag, unless there's a genius commanding them and something special occurs to him. You never know, and that's the spice in such an engagement."

All this in a conversational tone, the braiding on his wet tricorn fluttering in the wind. An orderly to his left held the bridle of his horse, another to his right the telescope.

"As soon as they're within range of our cannon, we'll open fire on the column to our right," said the general, who held a smoking pipe in his teeth.

Theodor looked from one to the other and recalled the games of the village boys, when they set fire to anthills and watched the patterns made by the wildly fleeing, half-scorched insects or put barriers in their path. They were cold, indifferent gods, and he sensed he didn't belong with them just as he hadn't belonged back then.

A shot, a tinny fanfare, the abrupt gallop of several messengers down the hill, the incipient, funereal boom boom of the drums, and the army crept forward like a crocodile into the rainwet plain with banners aflutter. The muzzles of the cannon flashed and thunder rolled over the fields.

Theodor stared spellbound at the broad, undulating formation that moved forward, sergeant-majors in the lead, each footfall a fraction of a second behind the dull thud of the drum. The soldiers sank into the wet hayfield. Legs and hearts were now being driven forward by the drumbeat alone. *Boom-boom-brrrt, boom-boom-brrrt.* The enemy fire increased, falling far short of its targets. Fountains of earth spurted up against the silky curtain of rain.

The pincers of the enemy infantry opened. The Swedish soldiers advanced toward them, step by step, without hurrying, *boom-boom-brrrt, boom-boom-brrrt.*

"Fire," coolly commanded the general next to him. The word was repeated three times like an echo, then Theodor's eardrum almost burst. The cannon jumped back like a kicking donkey. He looked back down toward the rainy, gray-green field, where the sudden spout of geysers marked the impacts. An invisible magnet in the middle of the plain was drawing the armies toward itself, and they approached each other in bovine lethargy until they could see, as the saying goes, the whites of each other's eyes.

Theodor is in the midst of them, his muscles and joints frozen in fear. Everything within him screams, Get out of here! Let me out! But there is no freedom, only the fatal march toward each other. Eyes wide open, trapped between his terrified, sweating fellows, on a collision course with death, and conscious of the madness and senselessness of it all. Death that slides cold steel into your belly, your soft insides, and steals your life away in a gush, while to your right and left the grass ripples in the wind and the birds twitter and a stream runs down to its mouth, and you could step out of line and run away and live, but you can't. You can't do it.

Then began the rattle of musket fire. The order of march dissolved; the armies reached each other, intermingled, wedged together. The drums had fallen silent or their sound could no longer be distinguished: a teeming tumult, the burning anthill.

The thunder of the cannon had become a matter of course, and every time Theodor expected the next explosion in the usual rhythm, it didn't come until a moment later, just as his expectant nerves were relaxing again, and he flinched as if in an epileptic seizure and almost fell from his horse.

He saw the lips of those around him moving, but heard nothing except the detonations until directly beneath him, down the slope, the skin of sound tore open: one of the cannoneers had not gotten out of the way of the recoil, lay there with his chest lopsided and collapsed. Blood trickled from his mouth and his screaming soon ceased.

On the horizon, the cavalry now emerged from the shadows of the poplars, fanned out as they moved forward, and panic began to spread among the Schweriners' rearguard.

The wind had clearly shifted. The shouts of those screwing up their courage and the screams of the wounded reached their ears like a chorus of yowling hounds of hell, the shove and countershove of the carnage parodied a contra dance accompanied by the castanets of crackling musket fire. As red as if dipped in blood, the flags flashed and then disappeared again in the surge of bodies.

The pincers of the enemy infantry had bitten off the head of the Swedish army, but now they were being wiped out from the rear. This was the moment for Görtz and with him, Theodor, to ride down and direct the end of the battle from close up. Bloody uniforms, bodies piled grotesquely on top of each other, like lovers murdered in the act. So many staring, white eyes, so much broken off, splintered wood in bellies, thighs, necks. Only occasional musket barks were still to be heard. Powder smoke and rain combined in a thick incense. A mounted messenger right next to Theodor suddenly fell from his horse without a sound. Only when he was lying stretched out on his back could you see the black hole in his smooth forehead, an expression of surprise on his face.

Everywhere around them soldiers were still running, shouting, stabbing. The Schweriners were fighting for their lives, the Swedes, now in the majority, liberated themselves from the grip of mortal fear in hate and bloodlust.

Mounted couriers rode up and spurred away again. Cavalry officers gave their reports. Then someone pointed to the distant hill: they were waving the white flag. It was still raining and hadn't brightened up all day.

Then the plundering of the corpses began. They were rolled over, disarmed, stripped of clothes, tossed onto piles. Their pockets were emptied, and in the evening, as fires blazed and the defeated general had been sitting at the palaver in Görtz's tent for two hours already, the moon appeared from among the clouds and shone dully down on hundreds of naked, pale bodies, lying there contorted, with arms extended stiffly in rigor mortis, as if to implore or praise the nocturnal heavens. Insects took possession of everything soft and swarms of crows flapped and hopped around among the dead. A reminiscence of powder smoke and the sweetish stink of wounds hung in the air.

Theodor found Larbi by the field kitchen and had him bring meat and rum. He was as hungry as a wolf.

In Stralsund, he got a look at the Swedish king, still a young man only ten years older than himself. At his express command, the Swedish army had not been quartered in the city, but was encamped outside the gates in the rain and cold.

The king wanted no comforts; he wanted to be among his men. He smelled of horses and dried sweat. Theodor was reminded of a scene in the palace of Versailles when the future regent, la Palatine's son, was sitting for a portrait on horseback and Theodor had stood among her retinue of passively admiring spectators. Philippe sat on a sawbuck holding the reins like a large, pudgy child on a rocking horse. At the artist's command he had to make giddy-up, bounce up and down, and the hat fell from his head. It was a degrading spectacle. The Swede, restlessly wandering about among the officers of his general staff with two pistols in his belt, was another big child. And he was playing at war. And the bloodier the game, the more men fell over, the louder he laughed and clapped his hands.

Theodor inquired from Görtz how he meant to use him in the future and received the bitter answer that, lacking any particular diplomatic missions, he would probably be ordered into military service for the present.

After a sleepless night, he tried talking to the minister, bargaining with him. Finally he even offered him his shares in Law's company in order to buy his freedom and in the end fell to his knees before his master.

("Larbi," he said in a cold, toneless voice on the road to Glückstadt, where they would set sail a week later, "if you ever utter one word to anyone about that scene, you're a dead man."

Larbi confined himself to an "*Entendu, monsieur.*")

Görtz, half amused and half repelled, finally entrusted him with a mission to Spain, but warned him that he would have to figure out for himself how to get near enough to the prime minister, Abbé Alberoni, to submit His Majesty's proposals to him and make them palatable.

Theodor didn't care that he couldn't speak Spanish, that his cash on hand for such a trip was laughable—indeed, shockingly so—that the voyage was not without danger, the future uncertain. He engaged a cabin on one of the merchantmen of his friend Cats and traveled with Larbi to Bordeaux and from there overland to the Spanish capital.

Having arrived in Madrid, however, Theodor had exhausted his energy, and he holed up in rented rooms with a patio. He knew no one, couldn't speak the language, was like a lost child, and decided to get sick.

If he was suffering from anything, then from a sort of frenetic boredom, which is to say, a combination of various fears which engendered a hopeless lethargy and paralysis. This, in turn, made him more nervous and fidgety with each passing day spent in idleness, such that hardly had he sprung from his bed like a man possessed, with the words, "It's finally time to get something done," before he immediately had to return to bed in order to calm himself down.

Fears, thought Theodor, staring at the whitewashed ceiling which shimmered gray in the half-light, I'm plagued by fears instead of thanking heaven for having delivered me from dying in the thick of battle among those warmongering madmen.

But his joy and relief were already exhausted by the time he got to Bordeaux and felt firm ground beneath his feet again. And then there was the foreign city he didn't know his way around in, the cold walls between which he lost his way, the gauntlet of malicious and threatening looks he ran until he stumbled over his own feet from concentrating so hard on them, the conversations he overheard but didn't understand in bright doorways or through high, open windows; so much that was incomprehensible, that threatened his own being with disintegration; fear of the aggressive, loud, flagellant religiosity that flashed from the deep cisterns of these people's eyes.

He sat up in bed, shaking his head and murmuring half under his breath and with that benevolent forbearance, that admiring and approving curiosity he could always muster for his own person, even when disturbed by the oddest and least exemplary of his qualities: I have a real talent for fear!

On second thought, in his case, that ignoble word designated not cowardice, but rather the highly respectable combination of knowledgeable interest in his own person—which moreover was nothing but an expression of respect for the miracle of his life—and a sober-eyed realization of the dangers that lie in wait for an existence exposed to the public eye, dangers which indeed may even be attracted by such an existence.

But a talent for fear also meant being able to muster enough imagination to identify—and thus already half avert—all threatening eventualities that might be encountered along his path. It meant not placing much trust in the future, his largest creditor. For after all, the future had the freedom to thwart the mission that justified his existence. So his fear was a mark of respect, a tactical kowtow before the autonomy of the future.

By no means, however, did he consider it up to him to justify his existence. Quite the contrary, Theodor held it to be the duty of Fate itself to thank him for his respect by putting a certain amount of mental effort into a benevolent appraisal of his case and placing at his disposal an attractive goal for his life.

Admittedly, he had no idea what sort of goal that might be. It could hardly be his present assignment for Sweden, and it was with a certain contempt that Theodor had Görtz's letter, which in these parts might well not be worth the paper it was written on, simply delivered to the palace by messenger.

No, he didn't know what his mission would be, and when he reflected upon it, he didn't even want to know before it revealed itself. It was enough to know that it would have to be something extraordinary to which his contribution was not to undertake some insulting, banal activity that would divert his expectations and block the great plans that Fate had in store for him.

What he needed was simply time, and his fear was thus in the end a fear of being cheated of time by death.

But even Theodor knew there was no cure for death, and you needed luck if it wasn't to track you down before your time.

The Madrid doctor he consulted was groping in the dark, trying to discover what was wrong with him, and decided to bleed him.

He said the fluids that were poisoning his blood needed to be flushed out, took out his lancet, and placed his cupping glasses on the table.

Even two weeks later, Theodor—in the meantime aboard a Dutch merchantman on its way to Genoa through the glittering Mediterranean—was still pondering his relationship to fortune. For just as the doctor was getting ready to go into action, he was interrupted by a reprieve in the form of an unexpected leather purse containing two hundred pistoles.

Larbi held the bag of gold coins in his hands in disbelief and approached his master who was delirious with fever. The latter cracked open his eyes and had Larbi read him the letter, personally signed by Cardinal—so he had become a cardinal in the meantime!—Alberoni and inviting the Swedish envoy to a conversation in the *Descalzas Reales*. Theodor bid Larbi hand him the money, took a quick look into the purse, placed it nonchalantly into the drawer of his night table, and sat up in bed.

"My constitution has always had its resources," he explained to the nonplussed physician. "I have no more need of your services."

The next day he sought out a tailor and had a new wardrobe prepared for himself at the cardinal's expense. In the evening, he dined with Larbi in a bodega. Two days later, his clothes were ready and he paid his respects to the prime minister, who immediately and without further ado drew him into a political discussion in which Alberoni explained his strategy and its various contingencies to Theodor with the help of several maps and charts unrolled on an ebony table.

On paper, everything looked doable. Big changes were in the offing, and it wasn't just he who said so: la Farnese said so too. Her astrologer had done the calculations, and the neurasthenic king had at least nodded assent. Then the cardinal's ring-bedecked finger dropped onto a single point on the map. Here, exactly at this point, he needed a base on the mainland of Italy. If he was to remain open to an alliance with a Sweden which was, after all, on the downslide from the height of its former glory, then this was the price: at the least a promise that the Republic of Venice would remain neutral, or even better, would provide support for the Spanish expeditionary fleet.

Theodor didn't need any persuading, the less so, since Alberoni was a more generous employer than Görtz. And Theodor spoke Italian, too! So off to Venice!

He was obviously someone who considered having good luck as an essential part of his being and his fate and allotted it the place others reserved for personal merit. How much more exciting it was to be able to say, I was just lucky, than to have to clench one's jaw and say, I gave it my all.

But whoever considers good luck a character trait, whoever snuggles trustingly into Fortuna's lap and acts like her pampered darling, if his luck should ever fail, then he will have to see himself as accursed, the scum of the earth, or as someone the gods are punishing for being what he is.

In the future, Theodor would have every opportunity to experience in the flesh the vicissitudes of fortune like a series of cold and warm showers. He would have long, idle hours in which to imagine what would have happened if he had made a different decision when the opportunity arose—except, did it ever really arise?

He had not yet reached Venice when he got wind of a naval battle between the Spanish and the English at the southernmost tip of Sicily. A few days later, this rumor acquired solidity in the news of the defeat at Cape Passaro. He found himself in the midst of the Venetian carnival when he learned that the Swedish king had fallen in the battle and the man who was still his master, although Theodor had already half forgotten him, Count Görtz, had been taken prisoner and shortly thereafter beheaded. No sooner was he back in Madrid in the summer when Alberoni, under pressure from the ubiquitous English, was forced to sign a declaration of abdication. In the meantime, Theodor had learned that Cats's investments in the stock of Law's company had made him a rich man. But when he returned to Paris to withdraw his capital, he got caught up in the bankruptcy troubles of the central bank and discovered a few days later that he was again as poor as he had been in his youth.

So then what was his reason for entrusting himself, for better or for worse, to luck—which is as much as to say, to chance?

Only luck burst the fetters of causality. Only with the help of luck could hurdles be leaped over, limits exceeded, and goals achieved that no effort, no disciplined work would ever accomplish before one was old and dead.

Besides, the person who masters life by planning and preparation finds himself forced into a single track. If he comes through, then he's only achieved what he'd always planned to achieve. Theodor had no interest in a fulfillment that followed so narrow a path, and as a last resort, he arrived on his own at the insight that what a man is and does as the sole architect of his own fortune doesn't amount to very much, and that to make something beautiful of your life, it takes more than your own efforts, namely, the influence of higher powers.

Seen in the right light, the *a priori* invocation of or reckoning with Fate's indispensable help for everything one did was an attitude of humility, and it pleased Theodor to think of himself as a deeply humble person, the brother of hermits and saints, so to speak.

And it was this quest for a happy frame for his life, for a beautiful image to present to the eyes of the watching gods, that led him—once he had learned that they were to reach Venice by the overland route and thus in some sense from the back, through the swamps—to persuade his fellow passengers by means of a generous bribe to have their route changed, so that, having poled down the Brenta, they finally arrived at Chioggia, where Theodor engaged a boat in order to reach the long dreamed-of city in the only appropriate way: by water, across the lagoon.

As he sat at the bow on a shiny black wooden chair, listening to the gurgle and slap of the six oar blades dipping into the water with almost perfect precision and driving the boat forward in gentle surges, as he looked in turn at the cloudless sky and its rippled reflections in the brown-green-golden water of the lagoon, took in the pilings and stilted huts of the scallop fishermen as a dark, vertical grain in the otherwise purely horizontal structure of the scene, as he glided through swarms of tiny gnats which one puff of wind would swirl off into oblivion, as he squinted his eyes to search the horizon where sky and lagoon merged in pastel streaks of color and haze so he could be the first to spot the silhouette of the city, the scene before his eyes was suddenly torn apart by a simultaneously stabbing and gnawing pain in one of his left lower molars.

Tears sprang to Theodor's eyes. He pressed his lower jaw with both hands and turned to Larbi squatting behind him on the luggage.

His servant carried with him a sort of portable apothecary from which he handed his master two dried cloves, instructing him to place them on the rotten tooth and bite down.

For several minutes, the color drained out of the sky and the water turned black. Every time the boat rocked his skull threatened to split open and Theodor had the feeling he was being poled across the Lethe.

In an acute concentration of all his senses, sharpened and honed by the pain, with a mixture of disappointment at his spoiled pleasure and simultaneous heightened awareness and receptiveness, he now watched the campaniles of San Giorgio Maggiore and San Marco rise out of the haze, at first like columns of smoke ablaze with sky-blue and turquoise, then slowly acquiring sharper contours.

The impression of a city melted by the sun and then slowly regaining form as it cooled, the increasing number of ships which, the closer they approached, soon became a forest of long oars and tall masts, and the racking pain in his tooth all augmented and intensified each other and took such deep root in his consciousness that holding his cheek, he whispered tonelessly, "I'm twenty-four. I'm arriving in Venice. If the pain doesn't stop, I'll have to get this tooth pulled. I know I'll never forget this moment."

"You see, Baron," said Respighi three months later as the two men sat in a gondola being punted down the Canale Grande, past the Ca'd'Oro and the Pescheria to the Palazzo

Vendramin, "Venice has fulfilled its function as an asset in the world's balance sheet and has survived. Now its only function is to put itself on display."

Theodor let his hand glide through the slate-gray water and waited for the moments when the amber radiance of the sun broke through the clouds. He looked attentively at the merchant and friend of Jacob Cats, hoping he would continue to talk.

From the very first day, with a painful jaw and a sensibility as exposed as his odontic nerve, he had adopted the city as his own, and what Respighi told him about it consoled him for his present condition.

His travel budget had been seriously depleted by receptions and clothes, balls and operas and daily life. With Görtz and the King of Sweden dead, and Alberoni, because of his military defeat, unable to take action or pay him, he had no one worthy of the name of employer anymore, and no more diplomatic mission in Venice.

"So what is the home of San Marco good for anymore?" Respighi asked and immediately provided the answer to his companion's receptive eyes. "In order to demonstrate the beauty and endurance and dubious nature of human existence. It's an old city, after all," he added, with the same relish as if he had said, "She's a young woman, after all."

"And age," he continued, "is a strange thing. Intelligent people always claim that the course of one's life leads toward reduction and clarity, but isn't it really exactly the opposite?"

He looked at Theodor with raised eyebrows and then continued in an authoritative voice, "Here in Venice it *is* the opposite." And after a pause, "Isn't it true that in reality, the older one gets—the older the human race gets—the less clarity there is and the more *ambiguité*, the more—how shall I put it?—*chiar-oscuro* . . . ?"

Theodor looked at the dark figures standing still or scur-rying along beneath the arcades on the banks of the canal and Respighi's words rustled as quietly as the water gurgling at each stroke of the gondolier: "certainties . . . differences . . . between water and light . . . truth or dream . . . clear identities . . . appa-ritions . . . The symbol, that is, the mask, first covers the face and finally replaces it . . ."

Masks—the party, one of the many festivities, music waft-ing from each of the high-ceilinged rooms, billowing curtains, twilight, the unreality of the surging crowds dressed in the most expensive brocade that only to a ruthlessly clear eye revealed all its darned holes and mildew spots—a theater wardrobe awak-ened to nocturnal life. Theodor's costume with its ruffles and jabots in the latest Parisian fashion was too explicit, not ironic enough, in the midst of this splendiferously shabby round dance of masks. Everything was blurred. The depth of field shifted as in a dream, as if one were dancing in place and the room drew closer and then pulled away again.

He was excited by the anonymity, the impression of blind-ness or blurred vision in the presence of all these masks and missing faces. For Theodor, the proximity of uncertainty, of the unknown, was erotic. The mummery helped him not get dis-tracted by whatever personal traits might be concealed beneath it, nor by the yearning in his lips and fingertips, a yearning to touch rather than to comprehend, a yearning that wouldn't be satisfied with insight and understanding but rather wanted to be both fulfilled and assuaged and yet continue to yearn.

The mask who had chosen him for a dancing partner was a tall woman with shimmering silver fish scales worked into her bog-green dress. When she invited him to leave the ballroom with her, he remarked her deep, almost masculine voice. He offered her his arm and she placed her hand upon it, a long, small-boned hand in a glove of open-work lace. He saw its white skin and blue network of veins as if beneath a wafer-thin layer of ice. It glimmered like the nacreous interior of an oyster shell. They reached an empty room whose two round-arched windows stood open. The smell of the icy, nocturnal water rose to their nostrils. It made Theodor half crazy not to be able to kiss her, like finding the very first door of a whole suite of rooms locked. His hands slid over her costume in barely restrained desire. Through rustling twists of silk, with a noise like rain or the wind in the poplars, for the twinkling of an eye, he caught sight of pale skin beneath the green material. As his fingers flexed or stretched, groped or plucked in their search, quite abruptly a fissure opened between the moire fault lines. Shoving aside, pulling apart the heavy, crackling material, a slit was revealed, a hem his fingers could shinny their way up, until the touch of startlingly warm skin made his fingertips start back in surprise. All this was happening while they circled and snaked around each other, two spirals threading together, and Theodor, whose searching gaze was not met by another pair of eyes but rather refracted by the black holes of the mask, watched with half-closed lids the hand clad in the open-work glove and its fingers which operated with the speed and confidence of a spider. Then he leaned back powerlessly against the mask's bent arm, noticing even in his clouded consciousness that in this position, the two of them resembled a sort of pietà. His head hanging down over her soft upper arm was gently lowered to the ground, the mask separated itself from him, stood up, went to the window, peeled the glove from her right hand, held it between thumb and forefinger, and let it drop into the canal. He watched her, and as she sat down again, she said in her beautiful, somewhat hoarse alto, "I have more gloves where that one came from . . ."

Later she asked him, "It's carnival; why aren't you wearing a mask?"

His lips brushed her pinna, and he whispered as he had before, "My little horse." It was the tender childhood nickname their mother had given his sister Amélie, and in the embrace of this invisible woman Theodor had been existing simultaneously in a different time and place, had been here and there, now and back then at the same time, and every one of his words reverberated through a sort of echo chamber which conquered time and distance. And so he multiplied and enriched his own happiness in a recession of mirrors created by words, without his nocturnal companion having thereby lost anything of herself.

"But I *am* wearing a mask!," he finally replied.

On his way home at the crack of dawn, in a square with buildings on three sides and two steps leading down to a narrow, brackish canal on the fourth, two men in masks suddenly appeared before him, pulled daggers from under their capes, and demanded his money.

In Paris, Theodor would have raised his hands and thrown the men his purse, but here in the twilight dawn of Venice, between night and day, masque and reality, theater and street, in a dreamy mood after love with the unknown woman, and tortured by his toothache, still wandering in the mist between times and worlds, he drew his sword without a word, sprang into a lunge, stretching forward as he had been taught, and his blade entered the body of the nearest robber.

The sword slid and slid through the flesh without meeting any resistance, as if Theodor's arm were being pulled, so perfectly and effortlessly that he experienced a satisfaction that must have resembled that of his old friend Sternhart when one of his equations came out even. But that was probably an inappropriate simile, for when his forward motion came to rest with the hilt against the man's breast so that Theodor's face almost touched his mask, the robber was dead.

Bright blood trickled out from under the mask and onto the black cape. He must have pierced the lung. The blood smelled sweetish, like horseflesh, and the smell mingled with the morning odor of excrement from the canal. The other robber fled in terror.

Theodor pulled his sword out of the corpse, which had sunk to its knees. With his foot, he pushed the body into the water and watched it sink. A more atmospheric stage than Venice on which to run a man through was hard to imagine, he mused, only half awake.

By the next intersection he had almost forgotten the incident so that he stopped and asked himself if he were perhaps dreaming. This was the first man he had killed and it called to mind his rotten tooth. The first sign of physical degeneration and the first man dead by his hand: like a cold wind a feeling of passing time and approaching age swept over him.

Back in his room in the Palazzo Respighi, he stroked his host's yellow cat, which had taken up residence in his room for the duration of his stay. It was sitting on the windowsill and following the pigeons flying by with what seemed to Theodor longing eyes. The rising sun suffused the gray, pock-marked facade of the palazzo on the opposite shore with hammered silver and bathed it in blinding light. He scratched the small, ever so fragile skull of the well-fed, purring beast. It felt like a fur-covered walnut and tenderly, he called her "*Poverina. Poverina.*"

"Yes, it's a city of masquerades," Respighi repeated. "First the mask covers the face, then it replaces it."

Theodor nodded, lost in thought, his hand in the water.

The gondola docked at the landing by the Palazzo Vendramin. For financial reasons, the family had put their collection of paintings up for sale and Respighi was interested. "A painting, my dear Baron, is an excellent investment quite apart from its aesthetic value," he declared and rubbed his hands together. Pressing a clove between his teeth and with his gaze sharpened by pain, Theodor returned again and again to a medium-sized painting hanging in a wide corridor between two doors framed by long velvet curtains.

"That's a Giorgione," said Respighi as he passed. "*La famiglia del pintore.*" He gestured toward the painting, "*Quest' uomo è il pastore dell'essere . . .*"

Theodor nodded absentmindedly.

Nonsense, he thought, made cross and aggressively sensitive toward everything and everybody, including himself, by the toothache that had suddenly begun to rack him again. And in inexplicable envy, he thought, That's not a family at all, and if it is, then not the painter's.

He stood before the painting like a captain on the swaying bridge of a ship in distress and held onto the picture with his eyes for dear life.

The landscape was bathed in the turquoise light of a stormy sky. In the background, a town was ranged along the right bank of a river traversed by a wooden bridge. In the left foreground stood a young man in holiday dress. He was just departing the town through a grove, past an ancient ruin. To the right sat a young woman in a meadow, a thin white cloth draped over her shoulders, and nursed the child she held in her arms. The young man was looking over at the woman, who for her part gazed absentmindedly out at the observer.

Through the towering green storm clouds fell the first lightning bolt of the impending storm. The row of houses along the riverbank still lay in sunlight and was reflected in the water on this side of the bridge.

The gaze of the observer, falling indecisively into the picture's empty center, wanted to pull the couple toward each other, let them come together. But in this moment before the storm broke, when everything trembled, quivered, stood still, neither of the figures made the slightest move to take two or three steps and overcome their unbearable separation. Instead, the young woman seemed not to notice the handsome young man at all, and he seemed to find satisfaction in looking at her pleasurably, but without thereby forgetting his journey, wherever it might lead, or even wanting to interrupt it for a time.

The young woman was beautiful. Her rosy skin had a velvety sheen and was shadowed in the wedge of her groin. She held her child with that off-handed, protective serenity that makes young mothers into such strange, admirably strong, and self-sufficient beings—into a unified image that the young man, too, didn't want to disturb. At the far end of the town stood a severely simple church with a dome.

Theodor was captivated by the expression of heartfelt love on the face of the mother. Furious with the pain of his toothache, he cried, Why don't you go over to her? What are you waiting for? Never again will happiness be so close, within reach!

He held his throbbing cheek. Respighi was standing behind him again. "Would you like to buy it? It's more than two hundred years old."

"No, no," said Theodor almost in annoyance, "What made you call him *pastore dell'essere*?"

"He's obviously a shepherd," said Respighi with a shrug, pointing to the young man's staff. "You can still see baggy white shirts and embroidered knee-britches like that at country fetes."

"A strange picture," said Theodor with his painful mouth. He fished for his little pillbox with the cloves.

"Yes, it's been puzzled over a lot, instead of people just enjoying it. It's expensive, by the way. I just heard someone say that the young man is Hermes, god of shepherds, and the girl is Io or maybe even Isis. In any event, the myth is painted in the al fresco colors of modernity, and our questions remain unanswered. Look at the ancient ruins there, Baron, that our Hermes has just passed—destroyed beyond recall. Perhaps by the storm that's just about to break."

Theodor smiled, which the painful half of his face turned into a mere lop-sided grimace. The thought that here in Venice it was not crazy to regard the past as imminent, not yet happened, pleased him. And the thought that he found a painting more important to his life than anything else he had seen and experienced in the past twenty years enchanted him. He thought of his mother: never confuse reality with truth.

"What are your plans now, Baron?" asked Respighi on their way home.

"I must have this tooth pulled and then return to Spain," answered Theodor.

"Come visit us again," said the merchant.

Chapter VIII

$\mathscr{I}$T HAD BEEN MORE than five years since Theodor had seen his sister, who in the meantime had become the Countess of Trévoux. It seemed to him they had both still been children, and now Amélie was rocking her two-year-old son and he himself had traveled so much and served so many masters that he hardly knew any longer where he was coming from and where he was going to.

Joyous anticipation of their reunion and a vague sense of fear hurried and retarded his journey up the valley of the Rhône. He reproached himself that this visit, so important to him, was only coming to pass because it lay on the route of an assignment about which he had of course said nothing in his letter to Amélie. Baron Ripperda, a Dutch soldier of fortune who as Alberoni's successor enjoyed the favor of the quick-tempered Farnese, was Theodor's new limited partner in Madrid and had dispatched him to Paris with messages whose content Ripperda had not revealed to him. It was the first time since his debut in the service of the regent that he didn't know what was in the sealed letters he was carrying. He didn't really care a fig, incidentally, but it wounded his pride. Paris—another reunion in the offing!

In Lyon he would buy gifts, gifts for his sister, for her husband (whom he wanted to know nothing about), and above all, gifts for his nephew: a little uniform complete with fringed tricorn, a sword, little top boots, and a lace jabot that would certainly look most charming on the manikin whom he involuntarily imagined looking like himself as a boy. Most charming: a phrase he would never have hit upon under normal circumstances and which now popped into his head in anticipation of the reunion. That's my state of mind, he thought with a shake of the head: sentimental in word, thought, and feeling.

He would give him lead soldiers, a whole regiment of them, a drum, and a rocking horse—no, he'd already sent him a rocking horse—so a puppet theater like the one he'd seen in Venice, with all the stock characters, and the music box with arcadian scenes and a flute-playing shepherdess rotating slowly on its little domed lid, which he'd already purchased in Madrid.

If only everything would turn out just as he had rehearsed it countless times in his mind. If only everything would turn out as it had always been, and there would be no estrangement between them, and her husband had not changed her and would remain as invisible as possible. The nearer he came to his goal, the more tense he became, until he was even plagued by olfactory hallucinations: the smells of their childhood garden, the scent of the rollicking, sweaty Amélie among the roses and the mignonettes, under the honeysuckle hedge in the damp shadow of the wall.

Will she recognize me, he wondered, with my jaw grown narrower from the loss of four molars? A shiver ran over his skin, but he had forgotten the pain. What did appear before his inner eye every time he recalled the toothache and the bloody extractions was the painting with the scene of the impending thunderstorm. Then he had to recall his mother and was a bit dismayed to discover that at some moments he got confused about who it was he was returning to.

From the very first moment, everything was exactly as he had wished it to be. He was already pleased at the sight of the chateau, situated on a rise beyond a grove of oaks. Actually, it was not a chateau but a little castle from the times when it had still been necessary to be able to take refuge and defend oneself in one's house.

The way led quite steeply uphill, through the tall oaks, turned toward the right at the crest, and beyond a tall wrought iron gate became an avenue of plane trees leading directly to a compact courtyard. Tubs of flowers hung in the former embrasures of the gatehouse, and this was so clearly Amélie's doing that Theodor's heart rose.

To the left and right of the avenue lay walled orchards and vegetable gardens. A boy with a basket stood on a ladder picking cherries. A woman knelt on the ground pulling weeds.

As he dismounted and walked through the archway followed by Larbi leading the horses, the house door opened on the other side of the smoothly raked inner courtyard adorned with little boxwood parterres, and Amélie emerged, followed by a nurse carrying the boy.

Theodor took his sister in his arms, closed his eyes, and inhaled the old familiar smell at the nape of her neck. He felt it necessary to ask her forgiveness as he had asked forgiveness of his mother, whose demanding love one was never worthy of, no matter what one did.

But then he stepped back from the embrace and knelt down to the boy who was now standing on his own two feet, gripping the cotton skirt of the nursemaid with one chubby little hand. Knitting his finely drawn brows and puffing out his cheeks, the child examined the face of the strange man.

"*Allez, dis ce que je t'ai appris,*" said Amélie.

"*Bonjour, Monsieur mon Oncle,*" lisped the lad, and Theodor sat down on the ground in front of him, gallantly removed his hat, and returned the greeting. Then he stretched out his hands, and as his nephew hesitantly took them in his, Theodor began to sing, to the astonishment of the others.

In a soft but full and, as usual, a bit nasal baritone he sang an Italian song and swung the child's hands back and forth to the rhythm. Frédéric's features relaxed, then he shrieked with delight. Out of the corner of his eye—not because he wasn't concentrating completely on his nephew, but because he had a need to simultaneously take in everything that was happening—Theodor saw the look with which his sister was inspecting him and read in it a kind of astonished and approving attention, to which his thoughts responded, Yes, we've both come quite a ways.

At the same time he resolved to prove himself worthy of this look of approval during his stay here and to extend the mixture of warmth and freedom that had come to him quite naturally in these first moments into a leitmotif for his behavior.

He was still sitting on the ground when, after a polite interval of respect for the siblings' reunion, the count himself appeared in the arched doorway of the right-hand wing and approached him with outstretched arms. A very slim, small, gray-haired man, no taller than Amélie, with a noble, gray Caesarian head and flattened nose. His light tread betrayed a horseman who indulged in the hunt. Theodor sprang up, picked up Friedrich in one arm, brushed off his trousers, and submitted to his brother-in-law's somewhat stiff embrace.

"My dear Baron, it's a joy and an honor to make your acquaintance," said Trévoux. "I've been waiting a long time for this moment when the family is finally all together."

Theodor bowed and returned the compliment.

"By the way," continued the count, "you are missed at court as well, where many ask after you."

Theodor pricked up his ears. Hardly credible, but very flattering if without his knowledge he really had gained something like reputation and renown during his absence.

In view of the respectful courtesy of his brother-in-law, Theodor abandoned his reservations and considered what he could do in his turn to please his host. Most immediately and most honestly, he expressed his admiration of little Frédéric who was just inspecting the presents his uncle had brought him.

But while he complimented the father on his son, it seemed to Theodor that he was congratulating the count for something that he had actually accomplished himself, just as in the exuberance of victory, a satisfied general whose plans have all worked perfectly might congratulate a little lieutenant in the hussars as if it were he who had won the battle all by himself.

He felt the need to make everyone a little happier with a friendly word. He was even cordial to the servant girl who had been assigned to him on the two floors of the former tower where he and Larbi were housed, and after she had arranged his luggage, turned down the beds, and lit the fire, he slipped her a coin out of all proportion to his present means.

In the evening, guests had been invited in his honor, some local gentry, provincials whose talk and ideas were as narrow-minded and obtuse as their clothes—Parisian fashions of five years ago—were risible and inappropriate. Theodor, who still had had no leisure to devote himself to his sister and his nephew, had to control himself and keep his impatience in check in order not to run the company off. At least he could recount secret missions, larded with fantastical exaggerations and battles reeking of blood—he had almost decided the engagement off Cape Passaro in his favor when a fleet of Turkish galleys full of cannibals attacked . . . —and answered the guests' commentaries and questions with a gentle smile: Is it true people up there in the north wash themselves in cold water? They must be a rare breed, if their skin can stand that. Are they very hairy? Or: I've heard your real Venetian is coarse and libertine, is that your experience? Does Venice belong to France, or who's actually the king there?

But if Theodor inferred the intellectual level of his host from that of his neighbors, he was mistaken. Once everyone had left, the evening continued in Trévoux's library, filled almost exclusively with works on theology and the philosophy of religion, where the count drew Theodor into a discussion of those same topics to which he dedicated all his leisure hours.

It turned out that Trévoux had an insatiable need to talk about these subjects, and before long he launched into a sonorous lecture that completely exhausted Theodor's already weakened powers of concentration. In his time-tested strategy, he contented himself with stoking the fire of conversation from time to time by tossing into the flames the log of a name or an opinion he had picked up somewhere or other.

All evening long, Amélie displayed the same even-tempered, self-contained friendliness toward her husband as well as toward Theodor and the guests.

Trévoux was just speaking of Bernard de Clairvaux, the crusades, and the architecture of the Cistercians when Theodor discovered that his sister, a piece of needlework on her knees and sitting still and smooth in the candlelight like a Vermeer painting, was soundlessly moving her lips, and a short time later, he was almost sure she was reciting the count's speech by heart.

But he didn't want to trust his initial shock too much—was his sister's marriage such a hell of boredom? His observation didn't necessarily have great significance, and after all, it was an advantage to have a husband familiar with religious matters—all the more so, since Amélie had always been pious, although more in deed than in bluster.

Moreover, he knew that she knew he was watching her, so he turned his head ostentatiously back toward Trévoux and out of the corner of his eye caught her in a quick, surreptitious yawn. He was dog-tired himself. But the count uncorked yet another bottle and raised his glass to his brother-in-law. Only now did the thought occur to Theodor that here in the provinces, Trévoux probably hadn't many people of education and urbanity to talk to and was perhaps somewhat neglectful of courtesy from an excess of gratitude.

Amélie said good-night and the gentlemen rose, but then Trévoux sank back into his chair with such a sigh of contentment that Theodor didn't dare to withdraw as well.

On the following morning, however, he feigned a slight case of traveler's nerves to escape the hunt the count had invited him on. Amélie had been astonished the previous evening, for she remembered from Mortagne's time how much Theodor abominated hunting. Now she understood immediately the cause of his illness. Hardly was the hunting party out of sight when Theodor sprang from his bed, declared he already felt much improved, and ordered a generous breakfast, which he ate in his tower room in the company of his sister and little Friedrich or Frédéric.

And so there arose tableaus of harmonious family life, worthy of being captured by a society portraitist, although Theodor had no need of one, for he was already living through this day as if he were gazing at a picture from the distant past or future: the young man, the young woman, between them the lad, ambling hand in hand through the avenue of plane trees past the sunny orchard wall, strolling on the gently undulating meadows from linden to chestnut tree, feeding the tame does in the deer park.

The same three on a white blanket, waited on by Larbi serving roast chicken, wine, and bread from wicker baskets, and the boy playing dreamily in the tall grass, an explorer in a tropical jungle.

In strongly contrasting light and shadow inside the house: the young man at the spinet, the young woman playing the viola, eyes closed, mouth puckered in concentration, brief glances of musical communication from one to the other, in the doorway the nursemaid in a light blue dress and white apron and cap, listening raptly with the child on her arm. His sleeping head rests on her shoulder, one little arm hangs down.

What no painter can capture, but only memory, producing itself from moment to moment: grease dripping from the chicken legs and the intense smell of freshly baked bread, then the shadows of clouds sailing across the sky and the sough of the wind in the tall grass, undulating like an ocean swell and melancholy because it reminded one of autumn, or his sister's eyes swinging quickly back and forth between him and Friedrich.

He felt compelled to ask the question that had been burning like a canker on his tongue since the previous evening. He had already formulated it dozens of times in his mind so when he finally said it, it would sound unambiguous but also as casual as possible.

After the music, a little out of breath, their skin flushed, and dissipating their concentration in hearty laughter, his moment had arrived: "Are you happy, Amélie?" Not even with the intonation of a question, but as though he were stating the obvious.

She turned a serious face toward him. "Yes," she said in surprise. (A warm swell of relief.) "Yes" (and turned around to look for her son, as if Theodor had asked where he was instead of about her happiness). "Yes, I don't look back. I live forward."

Theodor shook his head, annoyed at this addendum.

"But forward, up ahead, there's nothing there. Your memories have to make you happy. They are all we have."

Amélie looked at him as if she knew exactly what he was talking about, better than he himself knew at this moment. His gaze fell onto the white cradle with finely turned spindles in which the boy lay sleeping, a white cap covering his reddish-brown pixie's hair and his enviably smooth brow.

"Memories are chimeras," said Amélie.

"Not at all!" her brother vehemently contradicted her. "They are images and feelings and sounds and blissful states . . . All that's missing is the philosopher's stone that would make them tangible, the way I can touch you now."

"Do you think a lot about time passing?"

I think about nothing else, Theodor almost said, but that would have been too easy an answer. The passing of time was one of the subjects he was unable to comprehend, that slipped through or unraveled the net cast out by his intellect. Instead he said, "When old men die, an enormous treasure is lost. With children, it's not so terrible . . ."

"And Friedrich, whom you claim to have fallen in love with?" Amélie hissed at him. "Wouldn't you sacrifice your own life if he were in danger?"

Involuntarily, Theodor looked at the carefree brow of the little child and asked himself whether in a crisis the love he felt for Friedrich would be deeper than his instinct for self-preservation. Give up my painted images for blank canvases? he thought, recalling the mysterious Giorgione.

"For whom else would I do so if not for him or for you?" he answered after a while, and they began to talk of other things.

He told her about Venice and the parties and the fashions, the opera, the dances, about things he thought would interest a woman more than politics and wars, and observed—at first with surprise but then with growing admiration—his sister's imperturbable, alert, not easily impressible interest. To inflame her, to bring her to the point of agreeing without further ado to give up her opinions and convictions in favor of others, to make her feel that everything was more beautiful or more important elsewhere, and that one ought to go there on the spot—all that was impossible.

Even as a child she had possessed a certain indolence, a calm forbearance. And if he were a seagull gliding above the oncoming, protean, chameleon breakers of life, borne up and ruffled by the wind, from time to time diving into the waves like an arrow, only to beat his wings up again, with or without a catch, then she was—an unchivalrous metaphor he didn't utter aloud—a seawall. The surf broke against her. She faced equally the fury and the seduction of the elements, unperturbed, and behind her there was calm and protection. To live in the lee of Amélie like little Friedrich, that was the very definition of peace and happiness.

Nevertheless, when his footlockers were opened and Amélie took out the dress of Venetian satin, interwoven with threads of gold and silver and embroidered in a rhomboid pattern iridescent as the eyes on a peacock's tail and held it up with outstretched arms, her gaze wandering from bottom to top as she raised her chin, a change came over her, a rejuvenation. The soft fog was dispersed from her eyebrows, sunbeams were reflected in her irises, the tip of her tongue clucked pinkly in the corner of her mouth, her fingers—accustomed to wielding embroidery frame and prayer book, plucked and fluttered, played with the air like blackbird tails, girlish jerks and twitches loosened up the rigid trapezoid of neck and shoulders, her thin shoulders rose and fell, and beneath the skin in the shadowy depression directly above her left collarbone, an artery was beating.

Amélie drew the prize to her breast with both hands and twirled once around her own axis, oblivious, infatuated, and elated by the feel of the silky soft material on her skin, and the dress swung around her like a dancing partner.

Theodor watched in satisfaction. More than hearing that she was happy, he needed visual confirmation that she really was still able to be happy.

As they walked hand in hand through the park, they were again playing prince and princess (but only he knew it, or was their inner affinity so great that she too was silently playing along, reduplicating her childhood self?), and he reined in his desire to exchange the same words and caresses with her as before. Trévoux was only a pale trompe-l'oeil figure on the threshold between being and appearance, his monologues on faith and God resounding through porous time like distant church bells.

Little Friedrich fit quite naturally into Theodor's production, for he lived completely and intensely in a world of play whose reality had an infinite number of angles of incidence and reflection. He evinced the droll, almost religious seriousness of well-brought-up children, forcefully weaned from their mothers, in whom the etiquette of politeness they have learned by watching their elders ennobles their native play instinct with a certain grave concentration. Even while they sneaked around tree trunks together or crept through the tall grass, a fine membrane of touching formality remained between them, for even with his face hot with excitement, red cheeks, and tousled pixie hair, the little fellow always called Theodor *"Monsieur mon Oncle"* and Theodor used the formal *vous* for him as well and addressed him with *"Mon petit bonhomme."*

Theodor sat on the ground and pretended to be the harbor of Rhodes. His spread legs were the jetties, his upright torso the colossus, and the grass waving in the wind smoothed itself into the ocean through which ploughed Friedrich, both galley and Captain Demetrius in a single person, and made his triumphal entry into the harbor. On all fours, Theodor became a horse—no, he corrected, he was Chiron, a centaur. *"Qu'est-ce que c'est, Monsieur mon Oncle?"* asked little Friedrich suspiciously, and then rode on him, led him, and when he began to wrestle with him, Theodor sensed without any words needing to be said that he had surreptitiously undergone a further metamorphosis into a bear, a mountain, a fortress.

Amélie, who watched them indulgently from the blanket as if she were looking after two children instead of one, and Larbi, the flute-playing Pan, who hopped in a circle from one foot to the other, became giants, trees, rocks, mountain ranges, sleeping lions, sphinxes, and pyramids, or simply became invisible. Proportions were also in constant flux, and if one minute they were poor human creatures lost in the immensity of nature, the next they were titanic gods, gigantic eyes looking down from the sky, looming over a continent no bigger than Theodor's hand, a tiny scrap of sandy earth with a few blades of grass, a world before the birth of Man, and terrifying monsters—ants, beetles, and snails—traversed the sunless steppe shadowed by Theodor's forearm, in search of feeding grounds.

When darkness fell, they set up the Venetian puppet theater and Amélie and Theodor's servant played music while

Theodor himself put on a show for the huge, dark, shining eyes of his nephew whose father sat quietly by the fire, a Bible in his hand, and gazed over toward them.

On the following evening, Amélie showed her new dress off at a soiree in Lyon, and during their return home that night, when Theodor learned from his host that the latter had to leave for Paris and the court the next day, Theodor declared on the spot that he would accompany him.

She could at least have said something! She would only have had to ask him or reproach him. Instead, this morose silence, this expression of wordless disappointment eating into her features like acid. It laid a pall over the happiness of the final evening, even if it seemed dissipated in the morning, so that their farewell took place in obvious love and tenderness. Ought he to have uttered a redemptive word of explanation? But it was too complicated to try to explain his decision to leave. Like all his decisions, it had been uttered before he had consciously made it, as if he hadn't the least notion of it until he heard himself saying it. In the coach, sitting across from the count who was reading, Theodor shook his head and thought, I never have reasons for doing anything, only after-the-fact justifications.

For one thing, he needed to finally get to Paris and carry out Ripperda's instructions. For another, through Trévoux he had a good opportunity to get back into the court's good graces, which he had presumably squandered by his breach of faith in working first for the Swedes, then for the Spanish. But the main reason was different: the hours and days with his sister and his nephew, even with the count himself, had passed so harmoniously that any extension of his stay could only mean an inevitable decline. A slackening in the tension of happiness which Theodor (so it seemed to him now in retrospect) had kept perfectly level and tight, like a taut rope, for all those present. Now his arm was getting tired, and he had to put an end to it.

Just as you put an end to everything and transform it into a memory, before you really learn something about people and things and how they change, he thought as they reached Paris. It was strange and sad the way people remained episodes in his life and disappeared before they could become reality. It's painful to think, he thought with a vague smile, that it probably functions the same way in reverse. But if he was honest with himself, it seemed more important to him to leave an indelible mark in the memory of others than himself to participate too intensively and in too much detail in their lives. So that in addition to being surprised he had felt a strange sort of joy at the sight of Amélie's sulking.

But who was she and what did she think when she wasn't thinking of him? Amélie's lips on that evening before retiring to bed, compressed as if tied with a string. Amélie's bright eyes catching the sunlight, her hands clasped behind her back, as she tried to spy a lark against the blue-black sky. The tilt of her head when she looked down at Friedrich playing with his governess. Her bolt upright posture when she was getting into the carriage and stretching her right hand out and a little upward, bent at the wrist, to take Trévoux's, who was helping her in. Her eyes calmly surveying him. Her infrequent, bubbling laughter. What did she expect from life? In contrast to him, Theodor, she had never been sick. He had never seen her lying sick, doing nothing, dreaming.

Trévoux reintroduced him at court, where everything had changed since it had moved back to Paris. On one occasion, Theodor drove out to Versailles. None of the fountains was functioning any longer. A leaden stillness lay upon the park, in which the buzz of mosquitoes was so loud it hurt his ears.

Discreet and reliable as always, Theodor accomplished Ripperda's mission, drew up a report encrypted according to the system of Vigenère, sent the key word to Madrid by separate courier, noted down his observations about French politics, was praised by the regent for the success of his first trip (the fact that Görtz had thereafter been executed could hardly be blamed on him), and received new, smaller assignments: sounding out a foreign diplomat here, a confidential message to be delivered in the empire there. He was approached with the request to conduct inquiries about Spanish plans the next time he returned to Spain, and so little by little, a new and very practical rhythm entered the shadowy work that was to carry him back and forth across the continent during the following years. There was little that was earthshaking about it, although one often couldn't tell that right away. Apparently banal things often proved in retrospect to be the core of something important. But in general, it was less about war and peace than about the everyday trade in diplomatic secrets and intrigues, where what was important was to speak well without saying too much, engender trust, practice discretion, or broadcast selected indiscretions. As Theodor once jokingly told an Englishman in confidence, this trade was gradually giving him the physiognomy of a greyhound: a streamlined head to let him slip between all obstacles, and slightly rounded shoulders—a little hunchback—for he was always forced to keep his head down, either so as not to call attention to himself by his alert gaze, or not to lose a trail he was following, or because he was constantly, a priori, bowing and scraping: to his masters and his enemies, to his employers and those he was employed to sound out, to sovereigns and villains.

Theodor's sojourn in Paris coincided with the scandal of the collapse of Law's bank, and when he tried to exchange his shares for cash in the rue Auincampoix in order to purchase a house in

St. Mandé, he couldn't get through the screaming, gesticulating crowd. Even though Ripperda was his master for the time being, he didn't trust that indelicate soldier of fortune further than he could see him. He boasted of his affair with the queen when everyone knew that la Farnese was not in the least choosy about the origins of her lover-advisers—first the shopkeeping boor from Italy whom she had elevated to cardinal and now this pipe-puffing faun in wooden shoes. Theodor wasn't about to pin all his future hopes on Madrid.

He hadn't even moved into his house when his shares lost their entire value, and he plunged into a whirlwind of speculating, borrowing on credit right and left with mostly fictitious collateral in order either to multiply his current losses by ten or transform them into a hundredfold profit.

Cats, his Dutch friend and business partner, had in the meantime opened a branch office in Paris as well as a bank for credit and exchange and provided him with good advice, but quickly lost his overview of Theodor's frenetic transactions, which seemed to owe less to a legitimate desire to enrich himself than to a boyish desire to be the wildest of the wild in a mock tussle.

With a combination of willful fury and the most naive carelessness, Theodor borrowed money, ran up fantastic debts, won ten thousand livres in one night and lost them again the next day. In the spring of 1721, as a result of these wild ups and downs, he was finally forced to leave Paris in the dead of night so as not to be dragged before a judge by a horde of creditors and thrown in the Bastille.

The question is—and his behavior allows of either conclusion—whether he didn't understand the laws of finance, or whether he didn't want to understand them and whenever it suited him, ignored them as contemptuously as an aristocratic estate owner ignores the grumblings of peasants crushed by the burden of his taxes.

The money he needed for a lifestyle appropriate to his person had to be there. He neither wanted to hear nor have to think about whether or not it was covered, whether or not it belonged to him.

And sometimes it happened that as he emerged, dressed like a dandy, from the opera or the *Comédie italienne*, he would be forced to deal with people, to talk and argue and even be abused by them in an insane surge of screaming buyers and sellers. He held a handkerchief to his nose, his hat fell from his head, he was jostled and shoved, and later he would throw himself onto his bed, sobbing from humiliation, and be sick for three days while his creditors scratched at his door. Larbi would have to serve him lime blossom tea, an abbé was called, and Theodor would make a tearful confession.

Instinctively, his servant understood that connections existed between the idyllic sojourn on Trévoux's estate, Theodor's precipitous purchase of a house, and the insane speculations that were undermining his reputation, and that this self-laceration would only come to an end when they had once again set off on a journey or were forced to flee. And this time it would be a flight from several quite different furies.

At the calm bottom of his soul, Theodor, buried in his pillows and disgusted with himself, knew quite well what was bothering him, but without being able or wanting to do anything about it: he was waging a kind of war with himself, wanting to forcefully graft Amélie's more settled existence onto his life of traveling and at the same time taking pains to nip in the bud any possible success for such an endeavor. But it was a sore point and he didn't want to think about it too carefully and possibly understand the motivation for his actions.

Beyond these self-imposed limits to his thinking, it was the actual limitations of his analytical faculties that made him furious. He didn't understand what was happening. He didn't understand how it was possible for tangible assets to be destroyed overnight, poor people to become rich, debts to be canceled or balloon immeasurably.

Cats explained to him that what was happening in an anarchic way in Paris had long since taken place smoothly in Amsterdam and London. But if Theodor was taking it so much to heart (something that otherwise hardly ever happened) that he didn't understand things—Law's bankruptcy, the role of paper money, and the development of modern trade—things that were taking place before his very eyes and that were part of today, the times, part of life, then it was also because in this Parisian autumn and winter his entire conception of himself and the world was being shaken up from an entirely different direction and to such a degree that he felt like an outcast from his own time, and that went against his dignity.

It had all started with an anonymous manuscript circulating in the Parisian cafés and clubs that autumn before being printed, which Theodor read all atremble in his bedroom in St. Mandé, his eyes wide and cheeks puffed out in astonishment. Moreover, as he laid each sheet aside, it was picked up and studied by Larbi (who already knew how to read and write when he first arrived in France from North Africa) as well, and not to the benefit of the moderation appropriate to his rank. From time to time, Theodor heard him through the closed doors, snorting with laughter and slapping his thighs.

A copy of this manuscript had been handed to Theodor in one of the cafés or clubs where he spent his free time between financial escapades and political and social contacts. The men enthusiastically discussing the work belonged to his generation, he thought in dismay, and yet were a completely different sort than the gallant, blasé, sharp-tongued, pleasure-loving fellows he had known in Versailles, who loved only themselves and the monarch who was at first aging, then ancient. Theodor had quite automatically thought of them as the very embodiment of youth.

How acutely he now realized that he would have had to stay in one place, this place here, and himself cultivate the impulses of the age in order to understand and appreciate their first fruits! There was a tone prevalent among the young, there were words being spoken of such impertinence, such caustic criticism, that not only had he never heard the like of it, but would never have thought it possible.

In a certain sense, the men he met were Sternhart's relatives. They explained the world and the circumstances of life in a frighteningly materialistic spirit, and as if berserk, they tore apart the cobwebs covering the mysteries that were so precious to Theodor. For no one, they said, should have to look through a veil to see what was directly behind it.

A bit reserved as he was toward people who so clearly constituted a group, an *équipe*, people who have learned things together and send up sprouts from the strong roots of their knowledge like trees in the spring, he listened to how their words complemented each other and again was reminded of Sternhart, the *studiosus* from years gone by with his ears glowing red with the thirst for knowledge. What had become of him?

He recalled how Sternhart had first approached him, at a salon, with his large eyes and the quantum of charm he was capable of, mistaking Theodor for a young nobleman and patron of the arts and sciences, a dolt with money from whose pocket he could coax a monthly stipend for the price of a few crumbs of intellect. Such was the beginning of their friendship, and it had ended with a confidential investigation initiated by the *Académie des Sciences* apropos Sternhart's application for membership. On this occasion he, Theodor, whom his friend had named as a character reference, in the midst of eulogies for Sternhart's capabilities, quite casually let drop his heterodoxy (Sternhart was a Protestant, after all), and thus robbed him of any chance whatsoever of becoming a member of the society. If it had in fact been Theodor's intent back then to keep his friend down, it had essentially been unsuccessful, for almost at the same time came the resounding call from the Prussian Academy.

Yes, Theodor was astonished, impressed, and put off by these relatives of Sternhart. What was the reason these men talked as they did and seemed to have lost all respect and any sense of fear?

Was it the court's return to Paris, the liberal regime of the regent, the lifting of the sarcophagus lid from bodies and minds following the death of the Sun King, or was it simply the times? While Theodor trembled at his creditor's threats to have him thrown into the Bastille as if they were threatening him with capital punishment—my God, anything but the hell of the Bastille!—he observed how these young men, a motley mixture of nobility and Third Estate, without powdered wigs and in cheap, monotone clothing, cracked jokes whenever one of their own got picked up by a patrol and once again placed under arrest.

Arouet, the former notary's clerk, who under his *nom de plume* had scored a theatrical triumph two years ago with an "Oedipus," a little man, ugly, with a long hooked nose that swallowed up the rest of his face, brown, deep-set, sparkling eyes, and a lock of black hair that kept falling across his forehead, sat there with his white shirt open at the neck when the uniformed officers came to pick him up yet again, and raised his arms in greeting.

"Ah, *messieurs*, I've been expecting you!" Short and skinny as he was, he sprang to his feet, and his friends lined up in a guard of honor and applauded him. Two weeks later, they again formed an applauding cordon as the sinewy man with the head of a sparrow hawk was released at the gate of the prison with a shove that made him stumble. He exaggerated the stumble for comic effect, but the push really had made him lose his balance. Theodor was watching and saw only the two deep lines running from his enormous nose down to the mouth with its bad teeth, which then broke into a grin.

The fellow's gritting his teeth, thought Theodor in the midst of the cheering onlookers, and he has teeth to grit. He had something of a tightrope-walker, the way he moved. Into the Bastille, out of the Bastille. Exiled to Sully-sur-Loire, and then back in Paris. And they laughed about it.

The manuscript, the story of the two Persians, Usbek and Rika, with a brazen portrait of Louis as the "Great Magician," was purportedly the work of a nobleman from the provinces, a certain Baron de Secondat from Bordeaux. And it was not just the critical barbs of this work which shocked Theodor, its critique of the monarch, the prevailing conditions, and the Academy, or its ridicule of religion, but above all its treatment of love and the role of women—both in the manuscript as well as in these gentlemen's lives, as he understood.

For Theodor had his eye on a blond young woman from Arouet's clique and had decided to make a conquest of her. He took her to the theater, dined with her, they regarded each other across the table in silent erotic challenge, and when Theodor brought her back to her house, he was looking forward to a few weeks of tingling excitement full of yearning, dreams, and conversational beating around the bush. She said, "Come on inside. I want some too."

"You want some . . . ?" he began tentatively.

"Yes," answered the blonde with a smile. "I want you to do it to me now."

Theodor swallowed hard and replied, "Your words certainly have the charm of the unambiguous, I must say."

While she unbuttoned his pants, groped around in there and then pulled her hand back out, said, "Well, well!" in a mischievous (and not, as Theodor had feared, a sarcastic) tone, grasped his hand and pulled it under her dress, as if to prove to him that she had already covered quite a bit of ground and he mustn't dawdle but should put on some speed himself, Theodor was thinking of intoxicating and being intoxicated, of how a gaze of bashful dreaminess smoothes out, beautifies, and elevates reality, of closed-eyed yearnings, religious epiphanies, the fulfillment of waiting and trembling, the mixture of uncertainty and sensuality that was the religion of seduction—in a word, of his own philosophy of love which was here and now being pursued ad absurdum.

He was seized by the alarming suspicion that Sternhart had been right back then and even young women were after nothing but being rhythmically impaled. With provocatively ironic curiosity they waited to see whether the dog that knew how to sit up was also capable of taking care of this little piece of business and then, when it was all over, could have a hearty, unblushing laugh about what had occurred.

"Why do you want to be mine?" Theodor asked. "Explain it to me. Put your desire into words that will make it comprehensible and transmit it to me."

"You're Baron Neuhoff, aren't you?"

"Indeed I am."

"I've heard so much about you. The crazy baron, they call you."

"You've heard talk about me?"

"Yes, in all the cafés."

"That's a different story, then," said Theodor, "and I won't keep your curiosity on tenterhooks any longer."

They don't take the Bastille seriously, nor the king, nor tradition, thought Theodor afterward, and they think just as little of the mystery that billows around and between all living beings, protecting their innermost identity from questions, even and especially from their own questions.

One's own questions! In the conversations he had in the *Club de l'Entresol*, he came to realize that he had actually hardly ever asked questions, at least none of higher importance.

The single, decisive question it had never occurred to him to ask, the question that was now permeating and corroding everything, ravaging all certainties like dry rot in the walls, consisted of a single, simple word: Why?

It was true, he took things for immutable fact, God's work, whether true or false, pleasant or unpleasant. That's just the way it was, and instead of scrutinizing the facts to test their solidity, he tried to tack his way between them. Never in his life would it have occurred to him to analyze or criticize the facts, to call them into question, ask after their origin, their justification, their reality, and possibly to change them. It's true, he admitted to himself, if everyone were the same as me, we'd all still be sitting in caves and howling at the moon—although it would be a highly melodious howl.

One time during those days, a captious objection occurred to him, and he asked, "If one casts doubt on the perfection of the world, that is, if one calls God's creation into question, isn't it actually in order to distract attention from the chasm that separates us from our own personal perfection?"

All around him there were smiles—wordless, but still perceptible for Theodor, and so humiliating that he decided to avoid these people. It was the smile of people strengthened by their shared past, and one of them asked him what they should think of a personal perfection that an imperfect world and society prevented nine tenths of humanity from attaining: *vide* the burden of taxation on the Third Estate, the misery of the rural population, *vide* the moral corruption of those whose profession it is to mediate between God and us.

Theodor was happy that new assignments and the pressure of his creditors were finally driving him from Paris. And yet he didn't forget this experience, tried to defend himself against it and to maintain his meandering path. How is it, he wondered, that I who have seen more of the world than all of them put together let myself be intimidated by their theorems? Nevertheless, he resolved in the two years of travel, secret missions, and espionage that followed to take to heart the seriousness of the underminers and their culture of penetrating questioning.

What can one say? He envied them. He envied them the way he had envied Mortagne, Sternhart, or Görtz. He also forced himself to read, to read a lot, but then his great resolutions flagged again and he contented himself with his memories, images, and anecdotes, for in the year 1724, he fell in love and got married in Madrid, all within the briefest time, and whatever he had heard in the cafés of Paris vanished as if he had finally triumphed over it.

Chapter IX

$\mathcal{T}$HEODOR BEGAN HIS *COUR* of Jane Ormond, an Irish lady-in-waiting to the Spanish queen, conscientiously and without passion.

He felt like an official transferred to the provinces and provided with a house he neither chose for himself nor had built, and for whose attractions (although such houses seldom have any) he is blind. It's too big and too little at the same time, crowded with someone else's furniture, and the view has a stale look because too many eyes have seen it already.

And yet you couldn't say Jane Ormond was ugly. Her small, heart-shaped face would surely have deserved to be called attractive. It was just that the sun never seemed to fall upon it, especially not the sun of an amorous gaze from her suitor. And then, she was no girl anymore. She was in fact—and this was a considerable shock to Theodor—a year older than he.

As he strolled with her through the parks of Madrid, making desultory conversation, she looked at him out of eyes that were admittedly large and sea-green. Their purity, however, was marred by a few tiny, burst capillaries, just as the skin of her face and neck did not look as marble-smooth as one would have wished. Together with a faint whiff of alcohol on her breath when he happened to get closer to her from time to time, the sight of the bloodshot whites of her eyes, her not entirely pure, thickly powdered skin, and a sprinkling of raised pores like the skin of a plucked chicken on her otherwise elegantly formed and graceful neck added up to an impression of—Theodor had trouble forcing himself to think the word—of dissipation, although you had to wonder where the excesses that would have left such traces could have taken place at this dreary court.

To be sure, they discovered a common interest in music and belles lettres, but their conversations about them petered out in quotations.

"Why are you so sullen?" Theodor burst out in annoyance one day during a walk.

"It's a sullen life," replied Jane laconically.

But it was not primarily life nor the Irish countess herself who was lackluster and morose, but above all the mood of her suitor. For however proud he was of having made a rational decision in a man-to-man conversation with Ripperda, he now felt unwilling and unable to put it into action.

Involuntarily, he equated rational motives with a lack of imagination, and therefore—bearing in mind the old banker's wisdom *On ne prête qu'aux riches*—he confined his exertions to flexing his financial muscle by inviting Jane Ormond on carriage rides (for which she had showed an interest—passion would be too strong a word for it) and to the theater.

As yet not a word about marriage had been uttered, and if he had hoped that the lady-in-waiting would provide him an occasion for a proposal or possibly even bring up the topic herself which, even if unexpressed, was quite obviously the only reason for them to continue boring each other, he was sadly mistaken. Lady Ormond sat through their shared afternoons as if through a bad opera, and it was not clear whether it was only politeness toward her host which kept her from leaving the performance early or because she was hoping for a scintillating finale after all.

It was the diplomatic successes of the Dutch prime minister with his shock of white-blond hair that had given Theodor the idea of lending his life gravity and stature by getting married.

What Alberoni had failed to accomplish with military force (although admittedly, it was a difficult feat to interpret the passionate outbursts of the Farnese *in politicis*, channel them into strategies, and finally "sell" her the results in a way that led her to approve of them), Ripperda seemed to achieve with discreet negotiations in which Theodor in turn played an important part.

Meanwhile, the boat in which they all sat, the Kingdom of Spain, was rocking alarmingly, not so much in political storms as because of the depressive king who was boring holes through the planking from within.

Just when Ripperda was in Vienna, beginning to woo and intrigue for future Bourbon hegemony over Parma and Piacenza, Philippe declared his intention to lay down the burden of sovereignty in favor of his minor son and devote his life to penance and meditation.

"What do you think of that, my dear Neuhoff?" asked Ripperda one morning, emerging directly from the Farnese's cabinet. The stubble on his cheeks looked like a fine layer of mold on pork that has stood out too long. "Is he serious this time? Is he really going to quit? Who does he think he is, Charles the Fifth? If Elizabeth is to be believed, he hasn't had any willpower for years. Or is he more clever than we think, laying down the crown here so that he can all the more easily have it put back on again beyond the Pyrenees?"

"Did you intercept Daubenton's letter?" asked the baron.

"Didn't intercept it, but I read it. That damned Jesuit! Writes to Orléans every single word his penitent said to him in confession, hoping that the uncle will make his nephew see reason and the father confessor can hold on to his power."

"All the better," said Theodor, "because the former won't do it and that will trip up the latter. Two birds with one stone . . ."

In the event, the problem solved itself within the year through the death of the infante, but the entire situation—the rickety ruling house and the dangerous game of diplomatic provocations on the one hand (in those years, Theodor shuttled back and forth a dozen times between Madrid, Vienna, and Parma) and the example of his master on the other, who only a few years ago had been an anonymous soldier with blood on his big, bony hands and in the meantime had risen from baron to duke and grandee of the empire and, what's more, become a multimillionaire in the process—led Theodor to the decision to plant a few stakes of prosperity and security in the ground for himself.

If Ripperda's policy succeeded, Theodor's future in Spain was ensured in any case, and who knew, perhaps he could even follow in his shoes some day. And if the Dutchman failed and everything collapsed, it was better to be a general in the army and a landowner than a creature or marionette of an ostracized politician.

The Dutchman granted him his first request, the rank of colonel, after a five-minute conversation, but Theodor needed, in his own words, "an even broader chest," and if he didn't want to have to wait, it could only (and with the least trouble) be acquired through an advantageous marriage.

"Would you know anyone who might be a candidate?" he inquired of the prime minister.

The Dutchman sucked on his pipe. "Hmm, in addition to money, she needs to have a certain name, of course, and would have to be available. That essentially boils it down to one of Elizabeth's unmarried maids-of-honor."

"That gaggle of geese in half mourning?" said Theodor with little enthusiasm.

"I wouldn't recommend the Spanish women either," Ripperda declared. "You wouldn't have much cause to laugh, although the one thing has nothing to do with the other. . . . What are your desiderata?"

Theodor raised his hands in a fatalistic gesture. "Someone who doesn't stand on ceremony. After all, the whole thing shouldn't turn out to be a lot of work."

"Well, there's this Englishwoman, or more precisely Irishwoman . . . Lady Ormond. No longer young, exactly. Yes, I'd try her."

"The daughter of the Stuart loyalist?"

"Precisely. They had to emigrate back then, but who doesn't in this life, from time to time? Her father died a few years ago. She's got a first-class name."

"Could Your Grace order a discreet investigation of her financial circumstances? I want to be sure it makes sense before I commit myself excessively."

"I'll see to it if you promise to throw a big wedding celebration so we'll finally have something to make us laugh again. I get ulcers from being entertained by Catholic chorales and the howling of that castrato Farinelli who brings tears to Philippe's eyes."

Ripperda's taste in music was not exactly exquisite.

To shake off his morose mood after a few weeks of half-hearted courtship, Theodor decided on short notice to attend a reception at the English embassy, one of the few places in Madrid where one was certain to have a good time.

He arrived late and squeezed his way between groups of standing, drinking, and chatting guests in search of a familiar face. Suddenly he heard laughter from an adjoining room whose door stood ajar—a wave of sonorous, hoarse, snorting, knee-slapping, braying, spluttering male laughter, while above it like a crown of foam danced the bright giggle of a woman before breaking off in a fit of coughing. As Theodor stuck his head through the door, he could hardly believe his eyes.

Closely surrounded by six men, Jane Ormond sat perched on a table, her back hunched and her legs spread beneath her dress like a man ready to scratch himself. In one hand she held a glass of sherry and with the back of the other, wiped tears of laughter from her eyes. Beside her stood the half-empty bottle.

"Let's have another one!" someone cried. "Yes, another one, please!" agreed the others, and pushed in closer.

"All right, gentlemen, one more, but then that's enough for today."

Lady Ormond drained her glass, set it resolutely down on the table, and began:

> *"There is a young wrestler in Greece*
> *From whom every foreigner flees.*
> *He's awfully unkind,*
> *Gets on top from behind,*
> *That's why he fights covered in grease."*

And she accompanied this recitation with descriptive gestures and at the last line, even jerked erect as if she had sat down on a pincushion. Jane herself joined in the new eruption of laughter, and although Theodor was standing too far away, he felt as if he were looking directly into the rosy depths of her open mouth, all the way back to its leaping uvula.

Then she slid from the table and plunged in the throng of men crowded so close around her that there was a considerable amount of shoulder and upper-body contact. A wreath of laugh lines encircled her green eyes. She caught sight of him, surveyed him with a somewhat tipsy look, and cried, "Ah, monsieur le Baron, now you've caught me red-handed!" But Theodor was too absorbed by the glances of the chattering men to react. He saw their eyes, their gestures, and their postures, and it was not hard to read them.

One would have to call it a cuckoo's love, Theodor later confessed to himself. A love, in other words, that couldn't lay its egg until a nest had been prepared for it somewhere, even if the nest hadn't necessarily been meant just for it. His feelings arose from his perception and appropriation of the feelings of others, and only the eyes of those men upon Jane enabled him to appreciate her himself.

That is, he honored feeling wherever he encountered it, but not necessarily those who felt it. Toward them, in a case like this, Theodor's ruthlessness could assume enormous proportions.

He fell into one of those trances familiar to him from earlier years, becoming temporarily blind and deaf and able to overcome distance without noticing it. He forced his way in among the male bodies into the center of the laughter, grasped Lady Ormond by the arm as the cries of protest from the others simply bounced off him, pulled her out of the room and into a corridor, and proposed to her.

She regarded him for a while, then cleared her throat and accepted.

After this scene, they couldn't very well part and agree to meet on a later date. And while Theodor was still standing there in disbelief, recapitulating in his mind what had just happened, Jane said with her Anglo-Saxon knack for the practical and self-evident, "Let's go to my place, Baron."

She lived in the palace, for she needed to be at the beck and call of her mistress, just as he once had as the page of la Palatine. First she introduced him to her three cats. "This is Harriet" (an aristocratic chartreux who inspected and apparently approved of him). "This is Gordon" (a big tiger street cat with a kink at the end of his tail where it had gotten caught in a door). Gordon jumped right up on Theodor's lap and started to purr. "And this is Friday" (a young black and white cat; Jane had of course read Defoe). Then she turned around and introduced him to the beasts, "And this is Big Cat."

She was the first person since his mother to give him a nickname. But not just him: the cats to whom he had been so formally presented all had nicknames as well. Harriet was only called Harriet when she was being fed or when she was sharpening her claws in the soft wood of the cherry secretary. Otherwise she was called Titi. In everyday parlance, Gordon's name had been shortened to its initial, Gee, which in the light of his purring sensuality always sounded like an avowal of rapture. Jane usually called Friday Fry; the black-and-white was so skittish he would pop up and then disappear again before one had time to get out both syllables of his name.

But they weren't here, thought Theodor somewhat dispiritedly, to talk about cats. Although they had to talk about something so as not to talk about the matter at hand.

Up to now, Theodor's erotic encounters had never been with women whom he had had previous social interaction with, chatting about this and that. And like an actor suddenly struck rigidly dumb in the center of the stage by an insurmountable lapse of memory, he saw himself incapable of coming up with any decent transition from their conversation about music, books, and cats to the few, crude words with which people announce the imminent beginning of sexual relations.

For a while, Jane Ormond watched as Theodor squirmed, then she hitched closer to him, narrowed her eyes, and declared that another limerick had occurred to her. Would he like to hear it?

Nonplussed, but relieved that she, too, obviously shrank from an embarrassing shift in tone and preferred a friendly chat, he nodded.

"Madrid's big fat cat had a pole," Jane began, drawing even closer.

> *"Madrid's big fat cat had a pole*
> *For which he'd not yet found a role.*
> *When into her house*
> *He followed a mouse*
> *Who said, might it not fit this hole?"*

While she spoke, she was gathering up her *modeste*, the uppermost of her three skirts, a long, rustling work of art made of velvet and satin and embroidered with silk, which caressed the palms that touched it. Gathered up on the left side, it revealed the two skirts beneath it, each tighter-fitting than the last: the *friponne* and the *secrète*, knit from *tabis*, a light and airy moire which her hands now pulled up higher and higher, until it covered her head, so that at the last syllable of the limerick word and image, signifier and signified coalesced in such a suggestive way that the answer to the question could no longer be in doubt and any splitting of hairs was superfluous.

The wedding took place on the eighth of June, 1724, and cost Theodor the better part of the money with which he had intended to outfit a regiment. Even Ripperda's report a few days after their first night together could no longer prevent the union: "The common wisdom is that these Scots are just miserly and hide their money, but there really isn't much there. Paltry, very paltry, my dear Neuhoff."

"I thought she was Irish, not Scotch," Theodor replied.

"Irish or Scotch, she won't make you a rich man in either case."

At once defiant and relieved, the Baron declared, "You'll never know it from the celebration, Your Grace."

A few weeks after the wedding, Theodor's cuckoo infatuation acquired a foundation of real feeling. He was about to take Jane to Mass on a Sunday morning when she said, "Go without me. I don't feel like it." She seemed very small and lost on her big chaise longue.

"Why not?" asked Theodor in astonishment.

"That damned Catholicism robbed me of everything, Big Cat: my country, my money, and my father, who never felt at home here. Catholicism took everything away so it could have all the room for itself. Must I thank it for the favor every day as well?"

At this moment, with an animal's fine sensorium for moments of unusual emotion, Gordon appeared, jumped onto her lap, circled himself into place with great circumstance, and began to purr. Jane stroked his head with a vacant stare.

A wave of pity for the exiled and impoverished woman washed over Theodor, pity and indignation at the injustice of fate. He swore himself an oath that he would do everything in his power to make her happy.

One needs to have concrete feelings for another, and then you can call it love, for the word *love* is just a collective term for a combination of more precise sensations, chief among them in this case a sympathetic pity for a plucky creature battered by misfortune.

Moreover, he was by no means alarmed by the fact that for the first time in his life, the happiness of another human being was dearer to his heart than his own. On the contrary, he experienced this unexpected enlargement and expansion of his heart as a moment of happiness, one of those experiences that enrich one's life and come close to an epiphany, imparted only to those who do not seek them out.

From now on, however, he no longer carried out his assignments with the same peace of mind as before, for traveling is more onerous when you are constantly haunted by the image of another person. More precisely, it was the image of Jane surrounded by the laughing men with glowing eyes which haunted him when he was away from Madrid for weeks at a time, and he wondered what would have happened that evening if he hadn't proposed to her.

When Ripperda sent him to London for secret negotiations whose goal was to get England to assume sponsorship for the planned transfer of the Duchy of Parma and Piacenza into Spanish hands, Theodor conceived a plan to desert and shared it with his wife who, just as he had hoped and expected, was delighted to put Spain behind her.

Suddenly, he had lost faith in the future of Ripperda's policies, on whose success, after all, he hung like a marionette from the fingers of a puppeteer, nor did he believe that England would come around, a doubt which Jane seconded.

His intention was to sell all the information he possessed about Spanish policy and begin a new existence with a new employer—to be employed at last by the government whose diplomacy, guided by reason, he had respected for years.

But that longed-for Mecca turned out to be the scene of a considerable defeat. As usual with Theodor, he let the decision itself take the place of meticulous preparation, and so when he divulged his great secrets in London, they were met with a shrug of the shoulders. He came to the unwilling realization that in these parts, there was no call for the sort of secret diplomacy he had first observed in Versailles and since then perfected. In England's highly organized network of foreign-policy informants, full of well-paid and thus hardly bribable agents with clearly designated tasks, there was no place for flamboyant masquerades and intrigues. Jane consoled her husband with the observation that her countrymen were "terribly down-to-earth." They already knew everything that Theodor was able to report about Ripperda's cabals, and what they didn't know didn't interest them. He had to concede to himself that he didn't possess what was expected of a secret agent in the country with the most modern diplomacy in Europe: the painstaking ability to work with statistical information.

That is, perhaps he had to concede it to himself, but he never would have admitted it.

They had spent barely a month in the English capital when Theodor declared to his wife that he had had enough of the occupation he had pursued the last few years. He was heartily sick of it and wanted to lead a completely different sort of life, one in which he would no longer have to demean himself with clandestine, thankless work for the greater glory of someone else. Jane had no objections, even though she had just pawned her family jewels in order to procure the rent money for a small apartment they were inhabiting in a dubious section of London.

Fortunately for both of them, Theodor had the gift of perceiving the last escape route of a cornered rat as a royal highway of free choice. And now, face to face with the void and having to earn a living without possessing either a job or a skill, he mustered ten times more imagination and activity than he would probably have needed to continue his previous occupation here in England with satisfactory results.

Whenever the charming, witty pair received an invitation to one of the London salons, which happened more often than it was possible for them to accept, for they often lacked the funds for the appropriate clothes (high society by no means cut Theodor, but it clearly knew all too well how to distinguish between the baron's entertainment value and his practical usefulness)—whenever the two were invited, therefore, Theodor, supported by Jane, made use of the opportunity to uncover sources of income.

He worked the parquet of the town houses as a sort of traveling salesman for himself. It wasn't easy to combine the uninterested—if not indifferent—cynicism, the urbane ennui, and the nonchalant wit expected of guests like him with the hungry and watchful eyes of a footsore predator in search of vulnerable prey.

The pressure such evenings imposed upon them, of which no one else was (nor cared to be) aware found an outlet in the overheated eroticism of all lonely couples living in the romantically shabby rented rooms of a semi-legal present and an uncertain future.

On one occasion, Theodor was telling stories about the young Handel and his organ and harpsichord duels with Scarlatti in Venice. A flaxen-haired nobleman, barely into his majority and made bold by too much medeira, thereupon challenged Theodor to a contest of their own. A clavier was brought in and Theodor, deploying eyebrows, shoulders, flaming eyes, and gaping mouth as theatrically as his hands themselves, gained a unanimous decision over an opponent admittedly unequal to the task. His family thereupon invited Theodor to spend the summer weeks on their country estate near Reading.

Before he accepted, however, he made sure that all members of the family were equally unmusical. Then, for afternoon musicales and evening harpsichord recitals, Jane made him up with dramatic eye shadow, and gesticulating wildly, he ornamented the simplest pieces with trills and arabesques, and repeating daily his entire repertoire in constantly changing modulations, was able to maintain the illusion for three weeks that he was a second Handel.

Once back in London, they worked off their tension (would he make a mistake, would they discover that he was playing them the same compositions every evening?) and their relief (alone in their room they threw the gold coins into the air and then crawled around under the bed, giggling, to retrieve them) in jolly evenings spent in cheap dance halls near the docks where there was no risk of encountering one of their potential patrons.

Once the income from such employment had been expended on rent, clothes, and carriages, they stood in the drizzle outside the opera and the concert halls, listening to the distant, muffled music in silent embrace, and later returned home convinced that no opera heard from a box had ever moved them so much as those scraps of music interrupted by the patter of rain and the clatter of hooves.

Another lucrative employment Theodor chanced upon in the same way was as an art connoisseur and buyer of paintings in the service of an immensely wealthy lord who had a love of art like others of his kind had a weak chest.

The work was as well paid as it was relaxing. For the lord, though perhaps not very bright, advocated division of labor and had a pronounced sense of realism. He turned each of his enterprises over to proven experts whose judgment he trusted implicitly, and gave Theodor complete freedom within the scope of his assignment to acquire pictures that were "beautiful" and whose value would increase with time.

The latter traveled around, purchased hunting scenes for the trophy room, still lifes for the dining room, two gigantic mythological works from Rubens's atelier for the grand hall, and commissioned a Venetian sojourning in London to paint a portrait gallery of his patron's ancestors in mythological dress and undress. Then, however, he violated the unwritten contract of bad taste and presented his master with a Watteau that neither he nor Jane could resist.

"Sir!" cried the lord.

"Sir?" answered Theodor with the lifted eyebrows of a continental suckled at the breast of Art.

The painting finally landed in the boudoir of the lord's mistress in Kensington and, with the purchase of this first genuine masterpiece, Theodor's employment came to an end.

Without a doubt, his strangest assignment of this time came from the parliamentarian Redgrave, who belonged to one of the new Masonic lodges.

Theodor had listened with interest as the politician discussed the *Ancient Charges* of the Reverend James Anderson and the useful connections to be made in the London Grand Lodge, and the baron had picked up a few phrases that struck him as strangely familiar and which he could improvise upon.

When he thereupon held a short discourse on alchemy, larded with terms like *conjunctio*, *maza*, *nigredo*, and *citrinitas*, Redgrave immediately pricked up his ears and approached him, making a curious sign which Theodor didn't respond to.

"I see that you are not yet a member of the Lodge, but yet without question, you're an initiate, Sir. Would you not care to join our brotherhood?"

It soon transpired that Redgrave was willing to sponsor him, but had an agenda of his own, namely to find out if the baron's knowledge of alchemy was extensive enough to initiate Redgrave into the art and possibly perform a transmutation of the lower order, that is, of a remunerative sort.

An alarmed Theodor, who from his time with Vanzetti could recall just enough about alchemy to use it in conversation, as he just had, still had enough presence of mind to counter with the enormous investment and considerable expenses involved, but Redgrave waved such objections aside: "That will not be a problem."

And so the baron found himself, together with his wife and a few dim recollections of the hours spent in the witch's kitchen of the marchese, housed for an indeterminate time in an empty castle in Gloucestershire. He leafed through books to plug up the holes in his knowledge for the time being, wrote shopping lists, surrounded by twenty discreet domestics whose only job during the week was to see to the well-being of the two guests (Larbi had been loaned out, so to speak, since the beginning of the London adventure; Theodor had sent him off to hire himself out somewhere or other, until better times returned), and then wondered what progress or results he should present when the master of the house arrived for the weekend.

At first, an explanatory inspection of flasks and receptacles, neatly arranged stones and metals sufficed. Tables with zodiac signs and their associated chemical reactions were elucidated, or rather, transmuted by incense and mysterious-sounding words into important steps along the path to the final work. Mondays, once the satisfied sponsor had departed, they fell into fits of nervous laughter.

"In my mind's eye," Theodor gasped for breath, "I can see the last day of our stay here. We'll place a red velvet cushion at the end of the last glass tube, the last copper pipe, and lay a few of Redgrave's own gold coins on it. And then, when he picks them up, we'll say, 'Sir, creating gold from English limestone isn't the only thing we know how to do. No, our skill also makes it appear with the portrait of His Majesty George I. already stamped upon it . . .'"

At some point, however, Theodor's own interest became ignited. His intensive study of the ancient texts had convinced him that there could possibly be more to the thing after all. For his own better understanding, he drew an *arbor philosophica* and began such incautious experiments with sulfuric acid that his hands got burned.

But what interested him was not the extraction of grains of gold from Redgrave's bars and their transplantation into base metal or stone, but rather, in fact, the *magisterium*, his own transmutation, the process of purification, the attainment of perfection, the thought of being able to give birth to God within oneself. Suddenly, everything seemed to hang together logically—the elements, astrology, mysticism—so that Theodor thought he could already discern the shape of the mystery like the outlines of a monument before its unveiling, and had only to pull off the final veil separating him from understanding.

The practical consequence of all this was that he neglected to continue throwing up clouds of dust to fool his paymaster and actually spent the money—and then diverted some money of his own as well—in the service of the work, so that Jane's only recourse to salvage at least some of their funds was to purchase a coach-and-four.

In exchange, during Redgrave's weekend visits, Theodor was now able to keep him so spellbound with inspired disquisitions on Hermes and Osiris that the politician forgot all about increasing his wealth by alchemistic means at the prospect of sanctifying his soul.

Despite, or perhaps exactly because of their fear, constant uncertainty, and shared solitude, this long London summer became—without their realizing it and as expressed in a song popular at the time which they had often danced to in the dives of Whitechapel—"perhaps their love's most beautiful time."

As if Theodor guessed something of the sort, after a year in England he seized upon the first opportunity that presented itself to begin a really new life, and left Redgrave to seek perfection by himself.

An envoy from the Elector of Saxony had spoken to him with misty eyes of the Pietist movement. He told him about Francke in Halle, with whom the man had studied, and about his friend the law counselor Count Zinzendorf, who had founded an ecumenical community on his estate at Berthelsdorf. The envoy urged Theodor to join the circles of supporters and friends of Herrnhut that were springing up everywhere, for at the moment, the baron once again had the look of someone with the necessary means at his disposal. The former alchemist replied—and he knew how to make a persuasive impression, especially on a Saxon protestant—that it would both advertise the cause more broadly and attract more adherents if a man like himself, with all his fame and contacts, would settle there as a practical demonstration, so to speak, and function as an example and model.

The Saxon, quite smitten by the idea, arranged a correspondence between Theodor and Zinzendorf. Thanks to the count's enthusiastic yet at the same time urbane and well-educated personality, their letters soon took on a friendly tone and culminated in Zinzendorf's offer to sell Theodor and his family an estate that was part of his own property, and to welcome him to a life of sympathetic confraternity as brother among brothers.

In letters and conversations, Theodor promoted Zinzendorf's community and in return received a generous sum from the count which enabled him to pay off his London debts, bring Larbi home again, and move to Berthelsdorf, with cats, in a manner befitting his station.

Their journey to the Electorate of Saxony took place in the spring of 1726.

Chapter X

At first, only the harsh call could be heard. It came from nowhere, as if the air had set itself into agitated oscillations. The peasants looked up from their plows. The cats fled into the house, their bodies pressed to the ground. The dog barked. Jane ran out onto the terrace, and Theodor laid aside his book and stepped to the dormer window of the library to see what was happening.

High, high up in the sky a wave was passing, as if drawn in the blue with a fine nib and tapering to a point. It moved forward, spread out, drew together again, and trembled in the light. The cries sounded so near, they hardly seemed to have anything to do with the vague sight of them. Then the flickering wave crystallized into a wedge of perhaps forty cranes coming from the north and heading south, flying past far, far above their heads.

Already they had passed the watching humans, disappearing beyond the roof of the house, flying over the next hill on whose summit stood Zinzendorf's house surrounded by elms and lindens, and dissolving into the dusty light.

The first formation was barely out of sight when the bright cry arose again, and Theodor, who had come downstairs and was now standing next to Jane on the terrace, extended his telescope and looked north. The next flock fluttered in the wind like a forked banner: the lovely bodies, long necks extended, the majestic tranquillity of their rhythmically flapping wings. The point of the wedge held its confident course southward in utter calm and blind obedience to instinct.

In all, four flocks migrated past that day. One wedge deformed into a spiral: the lead birds fell out of line and all the others followed them into the spin like an airy train. The flock waited for stragglers, flew a few loops high above the two or three estates on the flanks of the hills, the little hamlet and its church in the swale, then the lead bird climbed steeply into the sky and crying excitedly, the other cranes fell back into formation, each staggered slightly behind its predecessor, and resumed their route.

They flew quickly. From the moment one could make them out in the north until they faded into the washed-out blue at the southern horizon, barely two minutes passed.

Jane watched them go and said, "Travelers above the wind . . ."

That was in October of their first year in Berthelsdorf. In late February of the following year, they heard and saw the cranes on their return flight north, and Theodor felt like a father welcoming his children back home from a great journey.

In the following years, of course, the joyful shock was less. The music of the cranes had been an epiphany only that first time. But the crying and the banner fluttering by above their heads in the cold wind of late October always seemed like the handwriting on the wall that winter was on its way. And the first flock flying below the deep blanket of February clouds brought the hope of renewed life. And Theodor always recalled what his wife had said: travelers above the wind.

The day of their arrival in Berthelsdorf had itself been memorable. Once their coachman had finally found the right road after repeated inquiries, and Theodor and Jane climbed down at last—dusty, sweaty, and bruised from the jostling— they were received at the door of their future home by Zinzendorf and his wife, who stood waiting hand in hand under the portico. They came up to the coach and welcomed the strangers with a fraternal kiss; it was disconcerting, although it did break the ice. But then they went on to embrace the dumbfounded Larbi and called him Brother, so that later that evening Theodor whispered to him, "Don't get any foolish ideas. You are my servant and you'll stay my servant." And the Kabyle servant, whom years of intimacy had made cheeky and articulate, bowed and replied, "For a trifling increase in my emoluments I am willing to forgo the status of child of God conferred upon me by strangers ignorant of the realities."

That first day, taken up with an inspection of the house and farmyard and a ride through the adjoining meadows and woodlands, came to a close a mile away at the Count's home, where the newcomers were introduced to the members of the circle that had formed around Zinzendorf.

Their friendship with the founder of the community and his wife Erdmuthe Dorothea developed quickly and naturally. According to her usual habit of bestowing first a nickname and then a shortened version of it, Jane was soon calling the Countess Zinzendorf Dorothy—"I can't pronounce Erdmuthe," she apologized—and then Dolly, and the name stuck to its bearer, so that even her husband the Count used it, at least among intimate friends.

During the first year of their life in Berthelsdorf, Theodor regularly carried out his initial assignment to attract benefactors, friends, adepts, and patrons to Zinzendorf's project of a community living together in shared belief. Theodor traveled to Hamburg, Dresden, and Vienna, corresponded with Swabian Pietists, Parisian Jansenists, merchants, noblemen, the Patriotic Society in Hamburg, and university professors, and did what he was best at: using his charm to interest people in something that under normal circumstances would not have interested them in the slightest—to get them to look favorably on something their natural inclination would have turned a cold shoulder to. But the more Theodor himself became integrated into Zinzendorf's singular little world of fraternal kisses, Bible readings, public declarations of repentance, ecstasies of God's children that sometimes tottered on the edge of prurience, and precise, Protestant bookkeeping of the lower realms of life, the more he and Jane became components of this home sweet home and international enclave, the more his public relations function and diplomatic role slowed to a standstill. The work he had performed as unofficial foreign minister of the community became increasingly superfluous as the machinery set in motion by the founder and über-father began to run with a well-oiled purr.

After only a short time, Zinzendorf himself stopped asking Theodor about his undertakings. He and Jane simply belonged, like the handful of other noble families who had settled around the little hybrid parish of Herrnhut, all brothers in Christ's spirit: Lutherans, Pietists, liberal or disaffected Catholics like him and Jane, if somewhat more privileged Brothers than the bulk of Moravian settlers and tenant farmers who constituted the village proper.

The great and unspoken accomplishment of Theodor's years in Berthelsdorf was the metamorphosis of time.

Whether one regarded time as a mill wheel through which the seasons ran, grinding their days to fine meal, or as a spiral slowly threading itself higher and higher toward hypothetical consummation and certain death, or as a parabolic arrow arching directly toward the Sacred Heart, as Zinzendorf insisted, or as a straight line, a sort of ant trail one crawled along blindly, jammed in among the others, farther and farther away from one's origins, toward some inevitable demise along the roadside —whichever belief, whichever point of view might be the right one, Theodor was trying to suggest something else to himself and those around him.

He had long been familiar with the phenomenon that all eyes will follow the glance of an individual who is staring fixedly at some invisible point, so that everyone adds his own light to the beam of this first stare and sees the same images that the hypnotic gaze has etched in nothingness. Sometimes it seemed to him that with nothing but the muscles of his eyes, he ought to be able to bring the wheel, the spiral, or the flying arrow to a stop and force it into the motion he wished: the motion of a pendulum, to make time into a gentle, symmetrical swing across a purely imaginary, perpendicular axis that was its static heart and home.

Unlike his father and mother, he had escaped death, had not caught it in the chest by living in cold military forts. No cholera had dried out and rotted him, no plague spots had grown on him, and he had evaded cannonballs, bayonet thrusts, gangrene, and the bone saw of the regimental medic. The keen scimitars of thieves and murderers in nocturnal cities had perforated others;

the rats in the Bastille had not gotten him to gnaw on; it was not his blood and sweat that saturated the racks of the Inquisition. He had survived the past and here in Berthelsdorf, he had also deprived the future of its dangers by castrating the wild beast of his eternal hopes and taming it into an unchanging present.

Now time swung peacefully back and forth, its amplitude clear, and in its quiet center stood Theodor Neuhoff pursuing the contemplative life.

It was an existence that reminded him of certain performances staged in the park of Versailles in his youth, the tableaus vivants in which, to the astonishment and aesthetic delight of the onlookers, the bodies of the performers who had been strolling or dancing around suddenly coalesced, as if magnetically drawn to one another, into a mythological group familiar from a painting or sculpture.

Such a tableau would remain for several moments in utter, motionless silence. At most, one saw a chest quietly rising and falling. After a few seconds, a face frozen in the grimace of a smile or shriek lost its grotesque appearance when, as inevitably occurred, you forgot your connection to the person—perhaps an acquaintance—in favor of the allegorical representation. And the illusion, magnified by the barely perceptible trembling of the living bodies, became an epiphany burned onto your retina which you carried away with you even after the spell was broken.

Theodor was developing into a collector of the tableaus vivants of his own life.

One of them was of course the "travelers above the wind," the first sight of the cranes in combination with the smell of paper in his study as he heard Jane's call, her eyes squinting into the bright sky with crow's feet in their corners, the cat scurrying away in panic, his telescope's smell of metal and lubricant, the grayish brown, turned-up October earth, the peasants in their wooden shoes and brown jerkins peering upward, their horny hands on their hips, the indifferent ox in his yoke, the sight of the birds flying by above Zinzendorf's estate.

Another of these living tableaus was an opera performance in Dresden they had gone to see by themselves (Zinzendorf was no fancier of Italian opera), which Hasse himself had directed while his wife Faustina Bordoni—whom Theodor greeted warmly after the performance, having met her years ago in Respighi's house—sang the lead to great acclaim. The king was not in attendance, and in the hall, lit by hundreds of candles, there were wild goings-on. Ladies on sofas were carried into the hall by their lackeys; gentlemen had card tables set up in the back of the auditorium; pipes of tobacco and drinks were being handed around. In the loge next to theirs, there was a rustling of clothes behind the closed curtains, and the moaning only died down when la Bordoni sang a da capo aria: the curtains parted as in a marionette theater, two flushed faces appeared, and the hands that went with them were clapping wildly. The stage set was splendid beyond compare. As if the end of the world were near, sun and moon raced across the sky, Pallas Athena floated through the air in her coach pulled by owls, Jupiter and Apollo were enthroned in the clouds, and ghosts and monsters spewed forth from the mouth of the underworld. When one of the curtains caught fire during the second act, panic ensued, but several plucky fellows pulled down the cloth, stamped out the fire, and the performance could continue.

Theodor and Jane held each other by the hand the whole time, frozen in noble senectitude by their aesthetic concentration, while those around them just wanted to enjoy themselves. The couple watched the swaying musicians, the play of light on their wigs and the necks of their fiddles, and listened spellbound to the voice of la Bordoni, following every one of her coloraturas just as closely as her husband, who conducted the performance with gloved gestures from the harpsichord.

Mostly, however, there were calmer images—bucolic, pastoral moments of peace, prisms of happiness: Jane in the great kitchen, wearing a dove-blue house dress, with the light falling through the window panes turning the limestone walls saffron yellow. Baskets in graduated tones from ash gray through chestnut brown to the color of ripe wheat hung from the ceiling and looked altogether like a bellying fish net. On the shelves were rows of stoneware vases and cheese strainers. Beside the fireplace hung redly shimmering copper *braseros*, and Jane was pouring milk into a mug from a grayish blue jug that matched her dress. A few drops that had splashed out gleamed like pearls on the scoured tabletop. Jane held her head at a slight tilt, parallel to the angle of the jug. Her hair fell to the right and left past her ear that reminded him of a cameo.

Or one of their quiet evenings by the fire when the hour of bats had just passed and outside there could perhaps still be heard, according to the season, a last cricket's chirp or the trills of a nightingale. Jane sat there with her embroidery frame in her lap, and the profile of her back rising to her shoulders, her neck, and the back of her head formed a fine line, as if drawn with charcoal pencil, and Theodor's hand traced it dreamily in the air. A stack of periodicals lay next to him and he read to her from them, from the *Hamburger Relations-Courir*, for instance, and she raised her eyes from her work and looked attentively at him, with slightly raised eyebrows and parted lips.

At such moments he was reminded of her loud laughter in the midst of the tight circle of men in Madrid. Now that laugh had given way to a gentle, understanding smile. Was she happy too? She often said, "But we're not going to stay here in this hole forever." And yet it was she who taught in the Herrnhut school, visited the orphanage twice a week, looked after the trellised roses that would outlive them all, and unlike him knew by name and could tell apart all the peasants, domestics, Herrnhut settlers and their families and all the preachers, while he undertook less and less and, in cozy happiness, watched her in the lovely, meticulous execution of her daily rounds.

When he looked at Jane, his gaze sank into the depths of time, and with a slight start as in a dream, he saw her in a black dress, her hair knotted at the nape of the neck, emerging from the Herrnhut orphanage as she did every week, a look of relaxed composure on her face and with two empty baskets in her hands. He almost ran to her as he had back then, long, long ago, clasping her legs in his arms and burying his face in her rustling skirts. He could almost feel her cool hand on his hair, her admonition to control himself.

"What are you thinking about?" asked Jane when his empty stare had lasted too long.

"That I've always loved you," he answered.

"That's nice. And what else?"

"I'm thinking about Nikolaus," said Theodor. "He works so hard at being good that he must get calluses on his soul the way people who ride too much get them on their backsides."

He often compared Zinzendorf's religiosity to that of his brother-in-law Trévoux, involuntarily contrasting them to himself as older, more serious men. But then with a little shock he had to remind himself that Nikolaus was six years younger than he. Wherever he went, he was so used to being the youngest or at least younger—still but a boy, turning cartwheels past the adults and forcing them to stop their work—that, having always lived in the expectation that the future would cast his destiny into a form suitable to him, it seemed alarming and hardly believable that younger men than he had already built and accomplished things that were visible, functioning, well-planned, while he was still playing the country gentleman for his divine audience, costumed in the wool and tweed, felt hats and corduroy breeches he had seen in England and imported to Saxony, and wondering whether they would congratulate him yet once again for his good fortune in life.

Trévoux read St. Augustine and then went hunting or banqueting. He loved to encounter great ideas as others love meeting great men, as if after their embrace a dusting of sublime glitter remained on his shoulders. He took delight in the language of the theological poets and was inordinately fond of quoting them—and that was enough for him, whereas Zinzendorf considered reading as a summons to action and change. Theodor's friend Nikolaus had read the Bible and this encounter demanded—to use his favorite expression—a reaction, and a reaction that transcended one's private life. No, not just a reaction, a revolution, something that would change the world and society for the better. And the astonishing thing in this regard was that it was taken for granted that Zinzendorf's own life of fulfillment was the model for everyone else.

At their joint meals, that made it a little difficult for Theodor to maintain the style of conversation he preferred: a voluble parlando between bites and swallows in which one showed oneself to be informed by bringing up current events, while immediately relativizing their importance with a bon mot. One chatted about books, but the books themselves were less important than one's witty description of them. One made good-natured, sharp-tongued fun of absent acquaintances, honored the meal one had just enjoyed with carefully chosen words of praise, and for the rest didn't dwell pedantically on a topic or an opinion, especially not one's own.

To be sure, Nikolaus and Dolly lacked neither education, nor wit, nor cordiality—on the contrary, there was perhaps even too much of the latter. The count's friendliness was excessive, ubiquitous, enthusiastically monopolizing, and quite often found expression in tears, which Theodor found particularly repugnant at table. And yet those tears were only the overflow of a soul filled with God, but that was precisely the problem for Baron von Neuhoff: as long as God filled this soul, there was no room for anything else in its body either, and while Zinzendorf started off on impromptu praise of the Lord, the potatoes got cold and the perch turned mushy.

"You're too critical," said Jane. "He's just aflame with enthusiasm for God. They all are. It has the freshness and ardor of all new beginnings. The drive toward a breakthrough to even greater purity. Remember that his fellow believers are still being persecuted all around us. Recall the dungeon that is Catholic Spain. And don't you agree there's something enviable about throwing yourself entirely into a youthful love of God?"

"Of course, of course," said Theodor. "And I esteem him as well, but it's still a fact that it requires living your life with utter self-confidence, standing by your convictions—in the end inhabiting your body like an old suit of armor—to speak and act with so little self-irony! You know, there are fraternal kisses that maintain the hierarchy more strictly than a caning."

"You're too fastidious, Big Cat."

"Could be, but he who never doubts himself knows nothing about the nuances of the human heart."

"And anyway, why shouldn't he inhabit his own body with utter self-confidence?" asked Jane. "His body is not ugly . . ."

Theodor's smile was more like a grimace.

If only she wouldn't talk about bodies! As with Orpheus and Eurydice, everything depended on not looking back. Just as in the old days his mother had hoped to banish hunger by not mentioning it, it now seemed to Theodor that the price of their happiness was to avoid any mention of the erotic, unless of course Zinzendorf mentioned the topic in one of his sermons. Then it was so absurd that you could laugh about it.

And yet he loved and respected Jane's body more and more with each passing year, enjoyed the sight of its slim flexibility, delighted in the tilt of her head, the way she held her arms, was touched to see with what equanimity her skin bore the slow work of time, and the deeper his knowledge of this form and covering—its smell, its little afflictions, its sensitivities—the greater grew his tenderness and esteem and the more his desire ebbed away.

This troubled him as little as a boatman who finally reaches calmer water yearns for the rapids just passed.

For it was a strange thing he often pondered: that with love, one's bashfulness toward the other grows greater rather than less.

Jane's loud, vulgar laugh while she sat on that table was only a distant echo in the fog of the past, as was the abandon of their first days together, their chiliastic casting aside of all inhibitions as if there were no such thing as the future.

When he recalled certain things they had still done with each other in London, he blushed as if he had stumbled upon a pair of strangers, and he told himself that he was no longer capable of such things today. How could people who trusted each other commit such indiscretions with their own and with the other body and still look each other in the eye with love and respect their whole life long? For it was Theodor's strangely melancholy realization that self-respect and lust, constancy and lust, love and lust do not go together in the final, deepest analysis.

Jane looked at his smiling mouth expectantly. He pursed his lips and said, "I fear that that body is already spoken for . . ."

"What? . . . But of course! For heaven's sake! I didn't mean that . . ."

"You mistake me. I'm not talking about Dolly. I mean, it's dedicated to our Lord Jesus Christ."

Jane laughed and shook her head, "You'll always be a jester, Big Cat."

This was the kind of laugh he could join in.

And by the way, speaking of bodies, one had to admit that Theodor had somewhat neglected his own during their years in Berthelsdorf. First, he had fallen out of the habit of wearing his cumbersome corset. Too lethargic to bother getting shaved every day by Larbi, who imperceptibly was becoming more and more Jane's servant—who just gave him more things to do— Theodor allowed his beard to grow, a beard that was not necessarily combed nor kept clean of bits of food at all times, day or night. Meanwhile, on some days his habit of dressing like the English gentry deteriorated into something looking more like a peasant, both in terms of the clothes themselves and their cleanliness.

Once he had completed his not especially time-consuming daily duties as estate owner and member of the community— visiting the peasants at shearing time, marking trees to be felled, a ride to the sawmill, communal Bible study and penitential rounds—Theodor liked to sit in his library, at an open window when the weather allowed, and devote himself to reading and writing letters. Through his initial diplomatic activities, his correspondence had grown enormously and by this time had become a substitute for Theodor's journeys back and forth across Europe. In a single year at Berthelsdorf, he wrote more than in his entire previous life, and awaited the arrival of letters, books, and journals like someone dying of thirst.

He had subscribed to the *Spectator* and the *Patriot*, he read pamphlets sent to him from Paris, ordered Pope's *Essay on Man*, studied the annually appearing installments of Brockes' *Irdisches Vergnügen in Gott*, read with fascination Reimarus' *Triebe der Tiere*, and possessed a beautifully bound copy of Mattheson's novel *Des Ritter Ramsay Reisender Cyrus*, personally inscribed by the author himself.

It was impossible to talk to Zinzendorf about what he had gleaned from his reading, for while the Count had literary ambitions of his own and filed away at the texts of lyrical prayers and chorales which he then rapturously recited at table, the amateur author would tolerate no competition from others. So the only thing left was dialogue with the writers themselves, at least with those who were still alive and willing to correspond with him, and with Jane, of course, who was also the only person with whom he could make fun of them. What a pleasure it was from time to time to let slip the tight Herrnhut leash of spiritual purity and Christian morality and diction and indulge in sarcasm, cheek, unfairness, ridicule, and exaggerated mimicry, to have a hearty, liberating laugh and clap the dust of humorless good behavior from one's clothes.

For the length of one evening, in Hamburg, Theodor found the man with whom precisely this was possible, as it had earlier been possible every day under other, more easygoing skies.

If Theodor and Jane undertook journeys during these years, then it was primarily for the sake of music. As they had heard Bordoni sing in the Dresden Opera and listened to

Handel's newest works—*Radamisto, Ottone,* or *Alessandro*—in the Royal Academy of Music in London whenever they had enough money, they also traveled to Hamburg and there encountered at a performance of *Pimpinone* (a creamy wedding cake of an opera buffa, covered with frosting and topped with meringue) the *Meister* himself, who was not only music director of the opera but also of the five main churches, cantor at the Johanneum, and who knows what else.

At supper afterward, Telemann joked about it himself. "I have three hats at home: a choirmaster's cap, a court composer's cap and bells, and as director of the opera, a gigantic woolen cap I carry around the theater after performances, collecting alms so that the rotting gridiron backstage doesn't fall on our skulls. The Hamburgers are clever folk. They've said to themselves that a man can only expect one salary, even if he's got five jobs. But then they mustn't complain when my organ concertos sound like *Tafelmusik* and my *Tafelmusik* like Neapolitan opera . . . But that's the wonderful thing about our mathematical cabalism: nobody dares to interfere in what we do because nobody understands the language of music, at least nobody who pays people like me. I can't tell you how glad I am not to be a poet. Anyone who's memorized the alphabet feels called upon to let you know you can't write your own language. . . . I certainly hope the story didn't offend you as a married couple, but I assure you, fat old Pimpinone represents Hamburg and the innocent Vespetta is me, of course. . . . By the way, did you see how the Hamburgers amuse themselves in my operas? They play cards!"

"Not all of them," Theodor replied. "Three of the gentlemen at that card table were staring in such fascination at the stage that the fourth was able to pull his trumps out of his sleeve with no trouble."

"How were you able to see that?" Telemann asked, feigning a pout. "I thought that you at least were a real music lover."

"To my misfortune, that's exactly what I am. I was one of the three!"

The musician laughed. "Unfortunately, I don't get a cut of the winnings."

"It's very civilized here compared to Venice," said Theodor. "There, they take care of other sorts of business during the performance."

"Oh well, in my operas they eat, and by the time digestion sets in, I've already run out of notes."

"Perhaps they misunderstand Telemann's reputation as a composer of divine movements."

Their host smiled and bowed. His paternally benevolent way of regarding the piece of meat on his fork made the others hungry too. He liked to dine with a handful of guests of his own choosing, not too many, so he could keep track of them all and talk to each one. He was one of those people—and this immediately won Theodor over—whose modesty increases with success.

"Of course," he declared, "otherwise people would hate me, and rightfully so. To be lucky and in addition need to always be right—it's more than a good Christian can bear . . ."

As they were saying their farewells, Telemann said, "And by no means pass up any opportunity you have to hear Cantor Bach in Leipzig. I think the world of him and did my part in getting the town to honor him with the post they had actually intended to offer to me. But how much more can I undertake? And besides, he can do it better than I. But don't forget! He really has no peer as an organ virtuoso!"

It was an evening in February 1732, the beginning of their sixth year in Lusatia. That morning, the resounding, metallic cry had been in the air and they'd come out of the house to watch the returning flights of pilgrims.

It had rained in the night, and the air was filled with the intense odor of humus and fermentation. The coffin lid of the earth's crust was becoming porous and the first green was breaking through. The Zinzendorfs had been there for high tea and despite Nikolaus's troubles with the government, their conversation had been lively and cheerful. Now their guests had left and the hour of bats already passed. A fire burned on the hearth. The large salon, painted in pale blue and warm yellow tones, lay in the flickering twilight of the dancing flames. The dog was half asleep, drying off in front of the fire, muzzle and body flat on the ground and curled up as if to wrap himself as tightly as possible around his own center. Now and then, at a soft snap or crackle from the fireplace, he opened one eye. The servants had withdrawn.

Jane was sitting on the chaise longue in a black dress and humming a melody. She wore her hair in a bun, pulled back tight and slightly graying at the temples. Overwhelmed by tenderness, Theodor gazed at the silver threads interwoven in the warm chestnut tones. On one temple, a bluish vein meandered beneath the transparent skin. His black Madonna. He stood up again with a sigh and went outside.

The starry sky exerted a pull on him, like looking over the edge of a deep well. At the bottom of the balustrade sat Fry, graceful and upright as a heraldic beast, staring fixedly into the darkness. Without asking permission, Theodor put his hand under his belly and carried the struggling, scratching tomcat back into the house, closed the door with his shoulder, shot the bolt with his elbow, and put Fry down. The cat hissed in annoyance, but then scuttled ahead of Theodor with his tail raised and thrashing, sprang onto an armchair in the salon, cleaned himself, circled twice, rolled up, and settled down to sleep.

Standing in the door for the space of a moment before sitting down again next to his wife, Theodor took in the peaceful scene that presented itself to him.

Happiness is a perfection of images that resonate together in harmony for the space of a moment. A painful flash of "Now" and simultaneously, the wish for stasis and in the flame of plenitude the blue core of sadness at the evanescence of the moment. The future is the enemy of the moment of happiness, although it's also its creator.

On the other hand, if one feels unhappy, thought Theodor, one's perspective contracts down to Now. You roll yourself up against time like a hedgehog defending itself, to offer less surface area for an attack, and you battle your way forward. One's most powerful, vital impulses come from unhappiness.

"Do you know what I'm thinking about?" asked Jane. "The music of Cantor Bach. You recall the cantata *Vergnügte Ruh, beliebte Seelenlust*? Sometimes I tell myself that's what Zinzendorf is always seeking and never finding. He never can find it . . ."

"What, 'blithe peace?'"

"No, I mean what that music does to you that no words, however good, can ever achieve."

Theodor remembered the impression the notes of the Leipzig composer had made on him, and when he tried to express it in words, he suddenly was reminded of his distant first days in Madrid, lying in bed with a high fever. Larbi perched on a chair next to him and killed time with a puzzle. You had to turn and tilt the top surface of a wooden box to coax jade marbles into the right holes, and Theodor remembered how in his fever he had heard the endless clicking and clacking of the marbles rolling across the wood and Larbi's breathing and had thought he would die if his servant didn't finally succeed and leave him in peace and quiet.

And he had left the church of St. Thomas just as if his brain and his soul were this board full of rolling marbles which the music had directed into their appointed places in peaceful, limpid movements.

"Let's go to bed," he said to his wife.

PART TWO

La speranza è quella sola che consola
ogni meschino già vicino a disperar.

Hope is the only consolation
for any wretch on the brink of despair.

Casti, *Il Re Teodoro in Venezia*

Chapter XI

THE IMPERIAL AMBASSADOR CROSSED the Ponte
Vecchio and strolled toward the Signoria. The little clouds high
up in the blue sky were like cockle boats and gondolas on the
surface of a clear sea, seen from below.

The sunny facades glowed a dull ivory, the light glittered
on the piazzas as if on desert sand, and they reflected back the
blinding brightness, so that when your eyes peered into arcades
and entrance gates, you were blinded and saw nothing but grainy,
blue-tinged specks of anthracite, and the whole city seemed a
bizarre chessboard of quadrants of light and black holes.

Theodor's gaze, made hungry by his empty stomach,
snatched at the people along his path: the water carriers, fruit
sellers, messengers, tradesmen, strolling ladies and gentlemen,
and the artisans in the dark caves of their open workshops. It
smelled of coffee and urine. From under the arches of the arcades gray tongues of water licked out onto the street, and you
could hear the whisk of brooms. The splash of emptied pails
mingled with the soft murmur of the fountains.

The shadow of the Campanile fell across the Signoria like an outstretched index finger pointing at Theodor. He traversed it and stood in the sun again, breathing a sigh of relief. He felt as though he were floating above the vast square and if necessary, could leap over the heads of the passersby with a single bound. Just a moment ago he would have been capable of crossing the mud-yellow Arno, withdrawn into its deepest, slime-green furrows, in one jump. He felt as light and free as if his heart and soul had been surgically removed.

Only once or twice a day—on one of these sunny Italian days with the prospect of tea and irony in the English trade mission, a supper replete with frivolous chatter, nocturnal mysteries of groping lust, and the flight from postcoital melancholy into the dawning day; on Florentine days such as these with a bit of paperwork and official conversation in a box at the opera, or whenever he indulged in a Mass and the whole licentiousness of the Catholic soul, giving a conspiratorial wink to whatever pale sanctity was left amidst all the gold and incense—once a day it was certain to happen that he would suddenly be catapulted from the aquamarine South into the pitiless penury of a February morning in Saxony and the voice of the Lord, weary and disgusted, would speak to him: What hast thou done? And once again, Larbi would be staring at him like an innocent man condemned to death. How old he suddenly looked, gray-haired and stooped. And then he began to weep—that had been the most unsettling thing. Larbi had been his servant for fifteen years and Theodor had never particularly given a thought to his emotional life, and now—the shadow of his master—he was doing precisely what Theodor was incapable of: he was crying. Larbi stared at him, they were standing outside by the stables, intense smells were steaming from the warm stalls, horse hooves pawed the hard earth, a swallow in monk's habit zigzagged low over the ground, raindrops drummed on the shingles, water gurgled in the rain barrel, and Larbi stared at him, tears filling his eyes. He couldn't understand why his master was absconding.

Theodor had had to turn away, and he realized that he couldn't take the servant along with him, the servant whose presence would remind him for the rest of his life of what he had done. Above all, Larbi's tears had robbed him of any courage for explanations, which in any case didn't exist. Perhaps he was simply fleeing the perfection of images.

Theodor had not gone back upstairs to Jane again. He hadn't spoken to her again. He had simply mounted his horse and ridden south.

Now, if while strolling or taking a ride he happened to see an ox in the yoke being whipped until its nostrils bled or observe a donkey having its forelegs broken, then he felt Larbi's tears as though the pain were his own and saw Jane's gray skin and infinitely weary eyes against the white sheets after she had survived yet another exhausting miscarriage, while on the other side of the hill that accursed Erdmuthe was bearing her Zinzendorf his eighth or ninth heaven-sent brat.

If a peach tree stood along the road, heavy with fruit and stretching its branches toward him almost like the arms of naive country lads who give away for free the luscious fruits of their labor, distributing them right and left to any passing stranger, out of sheer gratitude for having received so much from God, then he lowered his eyes in shame and gave his horse the spur so that the white dust of the road obscured his backward glance.

Such things happened once or twice and day, and he got used to them, just as in his youth he had gotten used to his plump hips, inadequate powers of logical comprehension, and later to his rotting teeth and graying temples. One gets used to all one's defects. You have to live with yourself your whole life long, after all. You can't just leave your skin, flesh, and bones standing in your boots somewhere and inhabit the first likely body you happen upon, like an incubus. The less so, since there was a risk one would end up in the body of a decent, deadly boring fellow whose path through life led toward no destiny.

And so Theodor accepted it when he saw a woman in a window stroking a yellow tabby lying on the sill, or a fat nurse-maid waddling along the lane with four children, or caught sight of the back of a woman kneeling in church with a long, slim neck and her hair in a knot, or when the wife of an English whole-saler poured tea and began to chat in her mother tongue, or when in a concert, amid all the distracted and uninterested chat-terers, he suddenly discovered a young couple clinging to each other, then he accepted being seized and shaken as if by an at-tack of malaria. Such spells passed quickly, the sun warmed him anew, and he was soon back in the midst of life.

And in this life, he once again had the exciting feeling of being the intersection and node of the streams of information and news that circulated through a metropolis. Granted, Flo-rence had outlived its era of greatness and as a marketplace for political commodities now lay on the European periphery. Nevertheless, he saw himself as a sort of weir, able to control and regulate the direction and volume of the information flow-ing across his desk.

The list of his appointments for today was long. The conversa-tions would extend into the evening. The Viennese legation was the unofficial central control station of the city and grand duchy, for the grand duke himself—referred to by everyone, in eloquent disrespect, as Gian-Gastone—was a catastrophe.

Theodor had a weakness for this fat, pathetic, and effeminate weakling. One never knew whether what ran from his eyes and was dabbed away by a graceful youth wielding a lace handkerchief were tears of emotion unleashed by an opera or an ephebe, or merely white wine.

On the occasion of taking up his office, Theodor had indulged in a half-serious joke and given the grand duke a little gold jar with a tiny beak in which tears could be caught and collected, and on later visits, observed with an emotion bordering on a fit of laughter that the jar stood next to the soft, upholstered couch from which the grand duke arose less and less frequently.

With a pathos by turns comic and serious, Gian-Gastone celebrated the decadence of being the last of his line, the consummation, whose death would bring to an end the dynasty, its sovereignty, history, the whole world, and Theodor admired it as a theatrical performance by a natural-born actor. Behind everything other people found revolting—his conscious lack of restraint, his wallowing in filth, sin, sodomy, and the songs of castrati, the lascivious spiritual and physical putrefaction of his still-living body—Theodor believed he could discern a variety of honesty, a protest against the human condition requiring the sort of courage you only discover once you've overcome all concerns about *qu'en dira-t-on*, once you've laid aside the shield and armor necessary for life among men.

Ecce homo, thought Theodor, every time he took his leave, somewhere between a shudder of disgust and an expression of respect, but of course it was exhausting all the same to spend an hour with the grand duke, and Theodor didn't very often allow himself to be led into temptation.

After all those years of penurious, sober, Protestant communication, all those encounters with people who always said only what they meant and—oh *sancta simplicitas* and holy bore-dom!—always meant what they said, it was an entirely welcome change of the intellectual bill-of-fare to eavesdrop on half-truths and rumor, gossip and slander, furtive character assassi-nations and calculated indiscretions, and depending on his mood and whim and how useful they were for the interests of the empire, he reported on them *in extenso* or in bits and pieces, with bias or word for word, or kept them in reserve as political letters of credit and speculated on a bull market.

Theodor was astonished himself to discover how many professions he still had at his command. Like an actor who has retired from the stage and years later makes a comeback, smells the glue of the sets and the mothballs in the costumes, sees through the ridiculous vanities of the young lovers and knows in advance how it will turn out in the end, who can't suppress a certain fear that perhaps he won't be able to remember his lines anymore or that his jaws and joints have gotten rusty, and then realizes, as soon as the curtain rises, that he still knows his role by heart, that the words pearl from his mouth like clear water from a spring, that his frugal, symbolically deprecatory gestures are much more powerfully expressive, more deeply penetrating than all his youthful exuberance of years gone by, who senses that where love, faith, and enthusiasm have withered, experi-ence has sprouted and grown into mastery. This was exactly how he felt and what he experienced since that February morn-ing when he turned his back on Berthelsdorf.

Not only had he lost none of his ability to enter a room and calculate immediately and precisely the hierarchies of those present, to say the right things to the right people and win their trust. Much more important was the fact that he himself had not been forgotten. People remembered him, and thanks to the language of secret signs he had picked up from Redgrave—to which several people reacted even though Theodor, lacking a second sponsor, had never been officially admitted into the London Grand Lodge—after less than a month in Vienna he had received an invitation to the Hofburg, where he was offered the post of ambassador to represent the interests of the House of Habsburg and the empire in the Grand Duchy of Tuscany.

He thought of himself with a certain romanticism as one of those men who has been tempered by the fire of life's suffering: men of action, unsentimental, free of passion, like the ones he had often encountered in the past and found to be inaccessible. Men who have sacrificed their idealism on the altar of youth. Men who have been deceived by friends or lovers and have pledged never to trust anyone again, are friendly but closed-mouthed, who give orders rather than make requests. Men whom life has embittered, but only at their core, which has become hard and unyielding. The need to survive, however, keeps their exterior flexible as a willow wand, and their behavior is guided by only one thing: facts, not feelings.

And indeed, he was such a man, even if he had to admit to himself that it was by no means life's disappointments that had steeled and isolated him. Actually, life had always treated him well and handled him gently, had given him a soft bed to lie on so that he had never been forced to practice asceticism or exercise discipline. So if he had become an embittered man, knowing and single-minded, then it could only be on account of his own faithlessness. Unlike the others, he had not walled up his heart, but rather pawned it at life's gaming table to see how it would be to live without it. And it proved to be decidedly easier.

If the eye apprehends the world in three dimensions, the heart adds to everything a fourth. If you look at a tree, you don't just perceive it as an object in sharp focus against its background. At the same time you recall it in the spring when it was a perfumed butterfly cloud of white-pink blossoms delicate as a baby's breath. You see it in the winter, bare and dead with wet black branches, or after a lightning strike. You remember kisses in its shade and you feel it growing as you grew yourself beneath the transitory and revolving skies of fear and hope. Now, everything he looked at was flatter. Sometimes he had the impression that the whole world was as flat as the horizon of a stage set. The one dimension in which joy reigned—but also fear—had become invisible. Which didn't mean he wasn't enjoying these days.

Whenever he gave a party or a dinner, all of Florence thronged to the door of his palazzo: the old patricians, the English wholesalers, the Jesuit latifundium-owners, the purple and violet crowd of princes of the church, the noblemen who possessed vineyards in the surrounding hills, ship owners from Leghorn, diplomats from Savoy, Sardinia, Genoa, France, and Naples.

Parties and suppers, picnics, pleasure cruises, and receptions at the embassy were amusing and diverting as long as they lasted, but afterward, Theodor always lay awake with the feeling, like a stale taste in his mouth, that he was performing lovely jumps over hurdles that were too low, which looks even more grotesque than tripping over ones that are too high.

It was like at the gambling tables. On cautious days, one doesn't wager much and doesn't win big. But how paltry the satisfaction at a moderate win compared to the expectation when you make a large bet, bet it all, bet more than you have, with every nerve fiber aquiver, face flushed and brain tempered to clairvoyance—and then lose it all!

For Theodor had begun to gamble again in Florence, was getting into debt and like a proud, unrepentant sinner recalled his days in Paris when he had acted the same way, knowing full well he would have to leave the city sometime or other, once he had reached the end of his tether with all his creditors.

He was well on his way to falling back into a comfortable jog trot, if one can call it a jog trot when you goad life like a chained-up watch dog until it tears itself free and you have to flee head over heels. For only extraordinary behavior could justify the betrayal he had committed. After all, if he had sacrificed love, then it had to be in order to free his arms to embrace something great and exceptional.

But what must I do to hear you say that all the pain was worthwhile in the end? he would ask himself while fleeing into the arms of some woman or other whose limbs, words, or gestures he had fallen in love with while carefully avoiding any look at her as a whole human being. Once the local fire of his lust had been extinguished, his love was also reduced to nothing but a little pile of ashes which scattered in all directions as soon as morning came and he opened the door to leave.

Later, he would be incapable of saying exactly when it was that time began to accelerate and individual events to gather like thunderclouds. Nor could he say whether or to what extent he himself had contributed to these climatic changes and, awakening from his lethargy, had given history a nudge, so to speak, by adding his own speed to that of time. That is, he wasn't sure whether without him, without his at first completely involuntary, inconspicuous, and trivial assistance things would have taken the same course.

One thing at least was clear: contrary to all the subsequent legends and commentaries that came to his attention, in this summer of 1732, when Theodor was dispatched to Genoa during and immediately after the Congress of Corti, he had no plan, no opinion, no intentions, and at that time as good as no knowledge of the problems the Genovese Republic was having in occupying its possession, the Island of Corsica.

With mixed feelings, he was only capable of remarking that the free time in which he could dream, in which he encountered beautiful and terrifying images around every corner in the labyrinth of memory and envisioned new futures for himself—that these moments were becoming less frequent. Some days he took pride in that fact. He would soon be forty years old. It was time he undertook a patronizing excursion into the kind of existence under which most people suffer, that is, already by the age of fifteen, twenty, they are consumed by their work, which deprives them of any leisure to digress from or annotate their own lives.

In Leghorn, Theodor met General Wachtendonk, a military man through and through, so that to make conversation possible, the ambassador immediately transformed himself into a veteran and, with some exaggeration, reported on his father's campaigns in Worms, Speyer, and Heidelberg and narrated how, arm in arm with Mazeppa and under the command of the glorious Soldier-King Charles of Sweden, he himself had fought at Mohilew and Poltava.

As Theodor correctly guessed, there was no one the general mistrusted more than salon politicians. But now Theodor's tales—credible and gripping not least because while in the midst of inventing them, he would have sworn on a Bible that he was retrieving them from his own memory—loosened the general's tongue, and he launched into cumbersome explanations the way a heavy hay wagon starts to roll when pulled by just one ox.

"You see, Baron, in the final analysis this Corsica is a simple problem. The topography of the island—just mountains and gorges and forest and *macchia*—makes it utterly impossible to conquer it completely and clean it out once and for all. I've got four thousand men stationed over there, powerful Hessians not afraid of anything, but even with forty thousand I'd never clear the island of all its insurgents and bandits. That's in the first place. In the second, there's nothing there. No money, of course, but no agriculture either, no mining, no trade—nothing. In the interior, the populace survives on chestnuts. That means that Corsica needs its ports as lifelines. Now, Genoa fortified those harbors, and wherever the rebels occupied them, we reconquered them. That's all quite straightforward. We have the ports, and the insurgents go into the mountains where we can't get at them. If we leave the ports, the Corsicans come back down from the mountains and try to recapture them. If we come back, the Corsicans go back up into . . ."

"I think I understand," said Theodor.

"All right, but there's something else. When I say 'the Corsicans,' who am I referring to, anyway?"

"This riddle would give pause even to men more educated than I, General, but I assume you mean the Corsicans."

"Wrong, Baron, completely wrong! I mean *certain* Corsicans, but not always even the *same* Corsicans."

"I'm afraid I don't completely follow you."

"What I mean to say is, if Genoa has repeatedly been able to put down various rumblings and rebellions for the past hundred years, the reason is that if there's one thing the Corsicans hate more than the republic, it's the thought that other Corsicans might possibly achieve more power and more wealth than they themselves. Genoa's greatest allies are the clan feuds, the never-ending power struggles among patrician families and between *pieves*, as the towns are called. Whenever some patriarch or other sounds the trumpet for a war of liberation, you can be sure that the *capo* of some other family will inform the authorities about it, and for a healthy remuneration and the promise that the land of the man he has betrayed will be turned over to him, he'll enter into an alliance against his own compatriots—for a limited period, of course."

"But then everything's in order, isn't it?" Theodor asked.

"Not completely," replied the general and wiped his mouth with a coarse gesture. "Who's going to pay for it? Neither the state nor the banks can afford to maintain an army such as mine. Is Vienna going to take over the costs? Not on your life! The empire is arming against Fleury!"

"If I've been correctly informed," Theodor continued, "the Corsicans are also refusing to pay taxes, so that Genoa lacks the wood, so to speak, from which to cut the clubs to punish the Corsicans."

"So to speak," replied the general. "Most of the ones who have money are sitting on the mainland anyway and hire themselves out. Some of them, by the way, to the republic, which they then oppose as soon as they get back home to their island . . . To pacify the place once and for all, you'd need to distribute a standing army of twenty thousand men among the port towns and garrison them there until Judgment Day. But there's neither the funds to do that nor, in all honesty, the will."

"And if I may ask, what's your personal impression of this quarrel, General?"

"Personal impression? I'm a soldier!" blustered Wachtendonk. "I fight for whoever commissions me. Today I'm fighting the insurgents, but if Vienna sends me against Genoa tomorrow, then I'll fire grape shot against the republic. But since you're asking, Herr Baron, I'd rather make war against Genoa. They're rational people. With them, you know what to expect. They're human beings like us!"

Thus informed, Theodor set off on his journey—first to Genoa, then to Leghorn, where the representatives of the insurgents were located—in order to be able to report his impressions and suggestions to the imperial delegation at the Congress of Corti, the princes of Württemberg and Kulmbach.

For the first time in his life, he was fulfilling an official and public function and did not have to travel and work incognito, but instead could present his credentials everywhere under his own name as the representative of the House of Habsburg. It was his intention to practice modern diplomacy as he had watched the English do, greatly admiring their clear-headedness and unambiguous interests. The only difficulty was finding out what policy line his own side was actually pursuing. And Theodor was only too aware that he could easily be disappointed in his search for that line.

Vienna had responded to Genoa's call for help and was now playing the referee in Corti in order to calm the storms whose seeds it had sown itself. But it was managing everything in a hectic way, with "Yes, yes," and "All right, all right," as if it wanted to cast off this burden again as quickly as possible. It was impossible to discern the slightest strategic intention behind its support—for instance, to grasp the tiller in Genoa with its own hand or to acquire Corsica for the empire and build up the island as a strategic base in the Mediterranean, which at any rate would have made some logical sense if another war with France was imminent.

How could you serve a master who didn't know what he wanted (quite apart from the fact that it would never have occurred to Theodor to actually think of himself as a public servant who owed his employer loyalty come what may). But the fact that so many powers were preoccupied with this island without being able to formulate exactly why was food for thought.

Especially after his conversations with Signor Galeazzi Maria, it seemed to Theodor that there was something dogmatic about Genoa's police actions; they were like a burdensome obligation that had to be discharged in order to obey the letter of the law and satisfy Genoa's honor and traditions. Genoa had boxed itself into a corner, but it's a well-known fact that that's the hardest place to get out of.

Even before his conversations with Maria and the Corsicans, Theodor had wondered (quite at odds with his ambition to pursue Anglo-Saxon diplomacy) whom he would find more congenial. The idea of acting impartially, listening to opposing points of view like some marble Justicia, and then dispatching to Vienna some lame suggestion for a compromise solution bored him to death.

His intervention had to have some effect, after all. It insulted his pride to be nothing but a stone in the stream, washed over by the current. If a Theodor von Neuhoff was going to get mixed up in these troublesome quarrels, then only if he could be a witness to their resolution, one way or the other.

Secretly he already suspected that he would tend to favor whichever party proved most thankful for his presence and friendly to his person. A piece of advice here, a piece of advice there, and whoever ignored it would have squandered his goodwill. He had no real opinion about the Corsican problem, and, as usual, based everything on his emotional impressions instead. Theoretical rights and demands, articles and laws were one thing, but it was pleasant or unpleasant people who put flesh on those bones and gave them a face, and that was all Theodor was interested in.

What displeased him about Galeazzi Maria, who received him like a lord and immediately started speaking French and English, was that the fellow presented him a reflection, a distorted and shopworn grimace, that he naturally sensed was a lampoon of himself. For the Genovese official made use of the same intuitive tactics as his interlocutor, sought to achieve a congruence of tone, word, and gesture on the basis of which it would be all the easier to achieve mutual agreement. Theodor shuddered at the thought that his whole life long, he himself could have been so transparent and appeared so unctuous.

There was not the slightest objection to be made, however, to the assertions of the tall, sleek, patrician Maria. Backed up by titles of legal ownership, his arguments were irrefutable. Theodor's inner self had always been at too much of a boil to make him favor anything but the strictest conservatism and loyalty to traditional, immutable circumstances in the outside world, and so in principle completely agreed with the view that the never-ending uprisings of the Corsicans were constitutionally unacceptable, politically intolerable, and needed to be crushed once and for all.

And then too, Theodor was won over by Maria's brazenly cynical comments about the feuding and the inconsistency with which the Corsicans were forever bashing each other over the head (Maria, incidentally, had never set foot on the rebellious island). He found the ability to joke and laugh about a problem much more congenial than the dry insistence upon one's viewpoint, whatever it might be.

Theodor's meeting with the Corsican negotiators could not have been more different. Ceccaldi and Raffalli received him in their offices on the Leghorn waterfront, technically an illegal location where they sold products from the island smuggled past the Genovese authorities under the benevolently closed eyes of both the grand duke Gian-Gastone and the eternally Janus-headed Habsburgs.

In the cool, vaulted storerooms where one groped around blindly at first after the bright sunlight of the harbor, there was the sour, vinegary smell of fermented wine. Dark, dried splotches disfigured the flagstone floor in front of the barrels, as if a massacre had taken place here and the evidence had been only superficially wiped away. On wooden shelves were stored hundreds of cheeses in various stages of ripeness and over-ripeness and from the back rooms, the goatlike stink of stretched hides penetrated the air.

So this is what Corsica smells like, thought Theodor, holding a handkerchief over his nose until he had gotten used to the effluvium.

Ceccaldi and Raffalli were no born tradesmen. They greeted him with wary courtesy, as if in a mechanical ballet, and maintained a kind of aura, a cultic space, by taking a step backward every time he took one forward.

One of them was a lawyer, the other originally an estate owner who had, however, already served in several armies, including that of Genoa. It was hard to say in what spirit they maintained this quasi-legal Corsican export firm that was at the same time a sort of unofficial embassy for the separatists, a conspiratorial location, and not least of all a symbol. In any case, Theodor had been informed that the business was not especially prosperous, since it seemed to offend the pride of the merchants to advertise their wares or display them attractively, as if that would be tantamount to humiliation and a debasement of their intrinsic dignity. On the other hand, if you showed no interest in their products, you also insulted their quirky sense of honor, for to talk only about the vexatious topic of politics without first admiring the fruits of the Corsican soil made the managers of the place press their lips together, as if they were receiving a beating without protesting.

Their cold civility was extremely formal. They stood there looking like old women at a window, grasping the shutters with both hands and ready to slam them shut at any moment if the stranger's look should become too inquisitive. They gave the impression that candidness and cordiality were the last possessions they had been able to rescue from the Genovese, and they had walled them up so as not to be robbed of them as well.

Each nod, each gesture, each word—and there were precious few of them—was agreed upon through clandestine glances out of the corners of their eyes and celebrated in a deadly serious parody of cultic dignity that seemed more theatrical with every passing minute in this stinking cellar full of wine casks.

Involuntarily, Theodor entered into this strange game, becoming more and more serious and stiff, yet had to fight down an inner desire to either burst out laughing or break off in annoyance.

The marionette-like Corsicans had in fact been steering the ceremony toward an unexpected climax. For at a certain moment in their sluggish conversation, by secret arrangement, both of them strutted to a double door, posted themselves on either side so that it looked a bit uncanny to Theodor, threw open the wings, and as soon as a small, rotund man rolled in, they said in unison and as if heralding the arrival of a saint, "Don Luigi Giafferi!"

The man, who had a full beard streaked with gray and short, curly hair, moved straight toward Theodor like a tiny bull toward a torero, stuck out his hand without a twitch of his full-lipped mouth, bushy eyebrows, or sly, black, button eyes, and said in a tone one couldn't quite decide whether to call unctuous or sarcastic, "Don Teodoro! Welcome!"

Theodor grasped the hand and the other then laid his left hand on top of the two hands clasping each other, waited with furrowed brow until the imperial ambassador understood that he should do the same, and then they stood there like two men

fettered together on the marketplace of a foreign city and regarded each other, at a loss for what to do next.

Sarcasm, compassion, curiosity—Theodor couldn't decide
which contradictory feelings this production evoked in him, and
more than ever he felt he was in a play—half audience, half
actor. The way the two fake merchants had built up the sus-
pense. The way the important man suddenly appeared like a
mounted courier. The way the hieratic solemnity of the extras
had both prepared the way for Giafferi's entrance and at the
same time misled Theodor, in view of the little man who reminded him of a bull calf and now stood before him in a frock
coat, knee britches, and white stockings, with buckled shoes on
his surprisingly small, feminine feet. His hands, too, were small
as a child's. And then the solemn greeting with their interleaved
hands, and the way he looked: like a somewhat down-and-out
gentleman.

It took a while for Theodor to realize that the Corsican
was no longer even thinking of calling upon him as an impar-
tial referee. The little man was courting him! Without beating
around the bush, Giafferi treated him as if he were an independent traveler, an adventurer who had placed himself at the service of the Corsicans. Incidentally, the little man displayed no
sign of surprise nor did he resort to cringing gratitude. On
the contrary, he treated his own fiction with offhanded self-
assurance, as if it were a matter of course that anyone who in
misty bygone times would have set off in search of the Holy
Grail or joined the ranks of the Crusaders in the conquest of
Jerusalem would nowadays unquestionably devote himself to
the liberation of Corsica.

At first glance, Don Luigi seemed more open and obliging than his two comrades-in-arms. Yet his brow, too, was
creased with furrows that expressed worry and obstinate

strength of will; he too was deadly serious. If his eyes twinkled ironically at all, then only to give a modest glimpse of the discrepancy between the sacred earnestness of their cause and the helpless inadequacy of his own person. Nevertheless, Theodor didn't find the conversation with him tedious. Sometimes he even had the impression the Corsican was speaking in blank verse.

To be sure, there was too much spoken dialogue à la Molière and too much pantomime in the commedia dell'arte style for it to be a Shakespearean history play. But don't underestimate this little man, thought Theodor. He has become a well-to-do lawyer on the mainland. He has fought, fired weapons, murdered, been incarcerated several times, and they'll have to kill him to get rid of him. And just as one finds a character in a play sympathetic and decides to trust him, just as a card player bets on a middling hand just because two red queens are smiling at him and he places himself in their protection, so Theodor decided at some point in the course of the conversation to trust Giafferi.

In retrospect, he had to shake his head and admit to himself that the rotund, woolly headed man had ensnared him with his ostentatious openness and his way of acting as if he were laying the fate of the nation into Theodor's trusted hands. But when the Congress of Corti ended in compromises that were either bad or only sounded good on paper—the recognition of Genovese sovereignty on the one hand and a general amnesty, a promise of equal economic rights for the Corsicans and the establishment of a Corsican court of justice in Bastia on the other—and not three months later Giafferi, Ceccaldi, and Raffalli, having all returned home, were arrested and chained to the walls of a dungeon, Theodor abandoned his role of mediator and rushed to their aid.

Why in heaven's name am I taking sides? he asked Jane in his mind, Jane, whose sober, deliberative point of view he missed. And which side would you advise me to join? Even if I'm combating the injustice being done to them, the Corsicans are just too foreign and irritating for me.

He recalled his boyhood games, how he would kneel in the grass and, filling their firmament like a god, watch ants attacking a bee heavy with pollen. By no means did he rescue the bee: in his childish cruelty he was much too eager to watch the spectacle. But the bee had his sympathy, so he put obstacles in the ants' way and—judge and executioner in one person, like every god—killed some of the incorrigible insects and then, once they had completed their murderous work at last, he left the scene in disgust and strange sadness, crestfallen and guilty, and made large detours for days to come to avoid returning to it.

Generously interpreted, everything he did continued to be within the scope of his assignment. When Vienna, on the basis of his report, forced the republic to release the three freedom fighters, it was still a neutral act to pick them up from the Savona Fortress and accompany them back to Leghorn, even if Galeazzi Maria's cordiality had turned to ice.

Only Giafferi himself and his companions had a different reaction. "Don Teodoro, we place ourselves under your protection," said the rotund little steer, as he emerged squinting into the sunlight. Everyone could hear him say it, and then he stood on tiptoe and gave Theodor a resounding, fraternal kiss on each cheek, and after him the stiff, formal Ceccaldi and Raffalli, who had apparently been given nothing to eat in prison but garlic.

Without Theodor being able to do anything about it, their return journey turned into a triumphal parade joined by more and more Corsican exiles whose hands Giafferi shook through the windows of their coach and who withdrew their hats and made deep, comical, but deadly serious bows before Theodor.

The almost daily visits of Giafferi and his men in the ambassador's residence got on Theodor's nerves and at the same time flattered his vanity. They asked his advice, wanted his opinion, profited from his wealth of experience. Much too delighted to turn them away despite a pretense of resistance, Theodor discovered with not inconsiderable pride how many sensible things he had to say, but was simultaneously plagued by misgivings that he might be squandering his wisdom on the undeserving.

Would it not have been more advisable and fitting to support the Genovese? But neither Maria nor Doria, neither Venerose nor Gripello nor Rivarola, had ever asked for his support. What sort of image was he projecting as an adviser to Corsican rebels whom everyone considered more troublesome and laughable than as a threat to be taken seriously?

Sweating and tossing restlessly in his bed, he thought: If only I had a real opinion or conviction about the whole thing! The attempt to fathom his own depths yielded only a frightening abyss, and since his plumb line found no solid ground during those oppressive nights and he refused to take refuge in illness this time around, he sprang out of bed and fled to a secret house in Florence.

There he hid himself from the torture of being forced to make a decision, hid under the cover of the sweetish, humid-smelling twilight, the heavy, dark velvet curtains and soft ottomans, where the only sound was the gurgling of the water pipe he was sucking on.

"You need money more than anything else," he had lectured Giafferi. "You must export the fruits of your island. You must buy arms, ammunition, uniforms, supplies. You must organize, man, or you'll never get beyond trifling skirmishes. You've got to make a serious impression, and not just on the republic. And stop ogling at Madrid or Vienna. You'll get no help from them. The powerful only support undertakings that can get established without their help, and only when fate has already decided in their favor."

"What we need first of all, Don Teodoro," was the answer, "is someone to unify us. A leader, an experienced man we can all trust because he's not involved in our feuds and of whom no one believes he wants to enrich himself at the expense of one of the families. That's the kind of person we need."

Silence. They looked at each other. Theodor was the first to speak. "Where do you intend to find such a person?" Giafferi turned away. "I don't know . . ."

Hadn't he already made quite enough decisions in his life? He was reminded of a story Larbi had told him on their flight from Stralsund. The grand vizier comes running to the caliph in panicked distraction and begs leave to go to Basra. In the marketplace he has encountered Death, who looked at him threateningly, intending surely to take him away. Now he wants to run for his life. His request is granted. Shortly thereafter the caliph himself meets up with Death and asks him about the incident. Nothing was further from his mind, Death replies, than to frighten the vizier. He was only surprised to see his servant here in Baghdad today when he had an appointment with him tomorrow in Basra.

Theodor pulled on the opium pipe as if a single puff could extinguish all images from his memory.

He lay on the ottoman, too weak to clench his hand into a fist. Slim, childlike figures approached, helped him remove his clothes, wrapped him in a silk gown. Short, plump children's fingers stroked the back of his neck, his back, his throat, his arms and palms.

It was not like having a woman caress you; the fingers explored his body like animals. Like worms on a cadaver, he thought. You'd have to not want to be a man anymore to seek your pleasure here.

Where's my daring, thought Theodor and felt his muscles tense defensively, where's my curiosity, love of life, my youth? Have I really become such a eunuch, a lethargic jellyfish, an anemic old man finished with life?

He jumped up—the figures retreated into the shadows—put on his clothes, paid, shook the opium fumes from his head, left the house, breathed in the mild night air in deep draughts, and ordered the coachman to drive to the palazzo of the widow of the banker Malerba. It was two a.m.? So what. His need to prove he was a man would brook no delay.

Chapter XII

$\mathscr{A}$T SOME POINT IN the course of numerous council meetings (which is what one was gradually forced to call the gatherings at Theodor's residence of the Corsican freedom fighters seeking his help) the word *independence* had been uttered. In fact, it turned out that the partisans had already progressed as far as the outlines of a constitution, drawn up by Dr. Costa.

It was one of those words whose reverberant, richly allusive resonance was an inspiration to Theodor, and without listening to the rest of the discussion, he began to spin around it a dense cocoon of his own thoughts. An independent Corsica, free by self-determination.

The associations kept flashing before his eyes like a meteor shower on a moonless August night: the critical conversations of the salon *philosphes*, their ludicrous efforts to obtain employment and earn their bread from those they despised, the great traditions of the Lodge, theory and practice, Montesquieu, Jacob Cats, the general political atmosphere,

Genoa, Spain, Savoy, Vienna. Not to mention the English. And Fleury's interests. We need someone to unite us.

"What are you thinking about, Don Teodoro?"

"About the right of a people to self-determination. A great and noble idea . . ."

Giafferi gazed at him as if anticipating a word of redemption.

But Theodor was lost in thought again. It was a chess game. Sixty-four squares, thirty-two pieces, and mathematical, logical planning. A clear view of both flanks and insight into the center of the battlefield. His concentration flagged and he had to admit himself incapable of it. Things only stayed in focus where his gaze was directed and his imagination ignited. At the edges, all was blurred and dark.

It was a chess game, but he was a card player. His common sense, which, lacking an overview, was nothing but fear and hesitation, told him to fold. His temperament told him to bluff, but how could you bluff in chess?

On the other hand, there were those words: *independence*, *freedom*. A great idea. A grand challenge in which he would grow and which matched his family motto: *Ubi libertas, ibi patria*. Or was his ambition simply seizing the first opportunity that presented itself and building it up into something worthwhile?

Wachtendonk and his troops had left Corsica. Another rebellion was raging on the island, and vast stretches of the inhospitable mountains were in the hands of the insurgents.

"This draft constitution—it's full of great and beautiful words," Theodor said, "but they're only on paper and in theory until someone translates them into deeds. Do you realize at all what kind of strategic importance Corsica could have in the Mediterranean? For example, don't you think that Elizabeth

Farnese would pay her weight in gold if you offered to let Spain use Bastia as a naval base?"

"Don Teodoro," protested Giafferi, "we're like functional limbs without a head to decide when the hand should grasp a pen to write down great words and when it should clench into a fist. You must help us and advise us with your knowledge and experience; you must act as our head."

"You don't need a helper and adviser whom you will pay heed to as long as he tells you what you want to hear, but run away from when he makes demands on you. And you need more than a minister of trade or a mercenary commander. What you need is a leader, a man in a position to get you the support you need from abroad to free yourselves from the Genovese, and someone you yourselves can look up to."

"The question is," Paoli interjected, "what can we offer such a man, assuming he exists."

"The crown," Theodor answered airily. "Corsica needs a king."

"And do you think, Don Teodoro," Giafferi asked just as casually, "that such a man, assuming he exists, would be satisfied with nothing less than the royal title?"

"I think that a man in possession of the capabilities to make the Corsicans respect him and the connections they are in need of—that such a man would also know he could only convert his talents into action if he had the title and the authority of a monarch."

"Does this man exist, Don Teodoro?" Giafferi asked beseechingly.

"If he exists, he won't come begging to you. You'll have to ask him."

Theodor had now ventured dangerously far out on a limb. Just a little further, he knew, and the roles would be reversed.

For heaven's sake, remember that they want something from you, not the other way around! But it was almost too much to bear, his head was so abuzz with the sound of the word *king*.

At their next meeting, Theodor was still able to control himself, even when Giafferi himself asked, "Don Teodoro, couldn't you be the man to unite and help us to free ourselves from the usurpers?" He literally had to put his hand over his mouth so as not to start blabbering and promising things that would later make him a laughingstock for the whole world.

But he owed them an answer, so he gave them an impromptu lecture on how they could break Genoa's economic stranglehold. For the next meeting, he had prepared a detailed plan, but didn't notice the embarrassed look on their faces. When the sherry was brought in and Theodor paused in his exposition, they had something to confess. Without their knowledge, without the knowledge of the "Noble Twelve"— or at least half of them—Canon Orticoni (the same Orticoni who had prepared for Theodor a memorandum on the history and circumstances of the country), was en route to Spain as the official emissary of a faction of patricians to offer the island to the Bourbons if they would free it from Genovese dominion.

Giafferi and his fellows sat there like naughty schoolboys, dishonored, mortified, duped, circumvented by their own compatriot and forced to admit what a sorry state Corsican unity was actually in.

Theodor looked at them with a mixture of contempt and sympathy, but his thoughts were headed in a completely different direction from what his self-appointed wards assumed. Inwardly, he was in ferment.

By no means did he take this unexpected news as a salutary warning to keep out of the Corsicans' disputes. All he could see was Orticoni at the bow of his ship, on his way to Spain with a letter of recommendation from Alberoni that would open the right doors for him and with Theodor's visionary strategic plan in his pocket, and he calculated the canon's chances and decided they were quite good. What could he do about it? Keep calm, but that was more than he could manage.

They were staring at him, so Theodor gave them a reassuring smile and said, "If the canon succeeds, then all your problems are solved. If his mission is a failure, then I shall liberate you from the dominion of the republic and by force of arms gain independence and happiness for your island as your king, the King of Corsica."

So there it was. And Theodor, who as usual had been the first to utter the words that filled his mouth and only began to plant them in the humus of thought once their reverberations had started to die away, winced briefly to himself but continued to speak with no noticeable pause to cover up the fact that it had been he who had offered himself after all, instead of waiting for an official and possibly even written repetition of Giafferi's request.

But wasn't this word the logical consequence of all their discussions during the past year? In its spell, Theodor went back over everything he had always told them, but this time the fog had lifted from the apex of the logical pyramid and like a cross on a mountaintop stood the shining word, giving wings to his rhetoric, wings with which he swept Giafferi, Paoli, and the others along with him.

At the same time, Theodor was appalled by his own pretensions, or rather by having revealed his secret and now being dependent on their answer, and deprecated his offer in every other sentence, promoting the accursed Orticoni and his mission to Spain and wishing it every success, but in such a snidely patronizing tone of voice, that his auditors, for whom in any case the canon's bold move was a dagger to the heart, saw themselves compelled to become more and more emphatic in support of a potential King Theodor, despite his torrent of words against his own claims.

"But no, Don Teodoro! Success for Orticoni is not at all what we prefer. Please believe what we say!"

"I know of no one more worthy than our benefactor and protector, Don Teodoro, to be our king as well," cried Giafferi. Emphatic words indeed, but more of a challenge, a question, than a conclusive declaration. And whoever knew the Corsicans knew that, in any case, they didn't see a question as a proposition to be discussed, but either as something to be silently endorsed or as in and of itself an insult to their honor, in which case they went home without a word, there to ponder in the bosom of their clan how to wash away the affront.

So Theodor was aware that the lack of objection to Giafferi's statement did not automatically signify a stamp of approval. Instead, he found himself for better or worse chained to Giafferi and Paoli. Whether he wanted to or not, he had to trust them and count on them. Conversely, it was a bit of a relief to realize that they were running just as much of a risk as he.

Above all, he would be forced into negotiations unless the Spanish crown, that is, the Farnese woman and her new adviser Patino (although the policies of his old friend Ripperda had met with success, the latter had not: he'd been deposed and had disappeared somewhere in Africa), took pity on the Corsicans. Once again, without it being his fully conscious intention, he had made a momentous decision.

The first thing he did was to overstep his authority and send a letter to Cardinal Alberoni in Rome, signed with the seal of the imperial legation, in which he wove into a bouquet of compliments the warning that Vienna regarded the journey and efforts of Canon Orticoni with the greatest displeasure.

Less than three months later, the news of the emissary's failure flew ahead of his ship as it approached Corsica with drooping sails. Before Orticoni reached his native waters, Theodor was already in Leghorn harbor, embarking with official authorization to procure the means for a successful revolt of the people of Corsica.

"When I return, you will name me king and I shall free you from Genovese dominion," he said in farewell, summarizing their agreement in one sentence.

"Yes, Don Teodoro," answered Giafferi, beaming. "You will free us from the republic and we shall make you the King of Corsica."

His eyes were already too focused on a vague and distant greatness, he was already in too much of a rush to sail off in pursuit of his visions and plans, to react to the tiny, subtle difference in the sequence and priority of these words of farewell. Picturing to himself the faces of his future interlocutors when he introduced himself as the representative of the Corsican freedom fighters, he recalled a story the Count de Mortagne had told him in his boyhood: on a rainy day, in the company of beautiful ladies and sharp-tongued gentlemen, a nobleman clad all in silk and velvet and lace cuffs slips and falls in the mud. In the most remarkable example of presence of mind one can imagine, he forestalls any ridicule of his clumsiness or jeers at his besmeared and stinking exterior by pretending to have a seizure. He tries to sit up, falls back into the muck, writhes around in it face down, gurgles and rolls his eyes up into his head, so that without daring to laugh at the dripping bundle of filth, everyone is obliged to plunge into the mire themselves to save the possessed fellow. As soon as his friends are just as muddy as he and thus all embarrassment removed, he quickly regains consciousness.

There is an enchantment in departure that expands and then suddenly contracts the solar plexus in rhythmic spasms of fear and desire. It's there in the gentle rocking of the ship still moored in the harbor, the smell of seaweed from the jetty, the deafening screeches of gulls flying white zigzags among the yards like a mobile set free against the porcelain blue Mediterranean sky. And then putting out to sea, leaving behind the anchorage and the tiny humans on the other ships, when the waves, edged with the finest Brussels lace, gleam green and opalescent where they face the sun. The more pleasant the life one leaves behind, the more precipitous one's departure, and the more uncertain the future—the deeper and more frightening and joyful the enchantment.

Theodor's mission would occupy him for almost a year. He sailed up to Holland, sojourned in Den Haag and Amsterdam, traveled overland to Hannover and Hamburg, and from there to London and Liverpool, came through Amsterdam again on his way back, and returned to the Mediterranean via Lisbon.

At every stage of his journey, in anecdotes and adumbrations, he related what he was about to do and become. These outbursts of vanity, kept in check by self-deprecation, this delight in gossip that clammed up in embarrassment halfway through its story, were too delicious to resist. And after all, none of his indiscretions was committed just for its own sake: his assignment required him to attract people's interest and woo them to the cause. The realities of Corsica and the savings entrusted to him by the Corsicans were in and of themselves not enough to induce anyone in Europe to risk an investment. And so Theodor could hardly proceed with modesty and restraint.

His intention was not to soften hearts, but to tickle business instincts and awaken appetite for future profit.

There was neither time nor opportunity to let things develop in such a way that accomplished facts came first, along with them guarantees, followed by investments, in their train results, and, thanks to the results, the settling of debts. Instead, he had to sketch castles in the air, beginning with the staterooms, and make them livable without anyone noticing that the foundations were missing and couldn't be laid until the rent payments started coming in.

To attack the problem of Corsica, he reduced it to two facets. There were at most one hundred fifty thousand Corsicans, and a ruler would need perhaps two-thirds of them on his side. Thanks to Giafferi, Paoli, and the others, half that number were already loyal to him. But he had rejected out of hand the idea of convincing the remaining fifty thousand to support his plans, thus first uniting the Corsicans behind himself and then together gaining independence by military and economic means. No, he first had to go it alone, provide the means the future state would need, and only then weed out the remaining skeptics. Begin by establishing facts (which incidentally would make the Corsicans more dependent on him than they were at present), and then resolve the question of trust and unity.

Despite Orticoni's memorandum, Theodor knew little enough about the island and, for the present, had no desire to know more. Corsica was a blank canvas that would be filled in according to his dreams and conceptions. It would be quite out of place to concern himself too deeply with the mentality of the population. Knowing too much means understanding too much, and at some point only exceptions to the a priori rules are left over.

Theodor had copies made of the bonds entrusted to him by the Corsican freedom fighters, signed them with the names of various Italian bankers, and invested them with northern European banks and securities traders, thus multiplying them by a factor of ten. He multiplied by twenty the actual export goods of Corsica and sold English and Dutch trading firms exclusive rights to them for cash in advance. He put his signature on more patents for branch offices than there were ports in Corsica. He had concessions for the mining of silver drawn up and entered names of towns on them without even knowing whether they lay in the mountains or on the coast. Giafferi had told him that somewhere on the island there was a mine being worked by Corsicans employed by the Genovese, but with no appreciable output. He simply multiplied it, extrapolated it statistically, so to speak.

And yet what he was doing was not a lie and a swindle, at least not in a higher sense. Everything he sold and promised could within a few years in fact be amortized and become reality, if only he was able to play for time and create the necessary financial and military conditions.

He knew very well that banks and creditors treated no one with such kid gloves as they did their largest debtor who, if he drowned, would pull them down with him to their own ruin, and Theodor signed with his own name and without the slightest hesitation—except with his friend Cats, whom he asked for advice, but not for money. For the rest, he already meant Corsica when he said "I" and vice versa.

Which may also be the reason he had not the slightest hesitation, either, to appropriate the entire cash savings of his wards and future subjects for his own use. For one thing, he calculated that no one would trust a supplicant unless he acted more lordly than his financiers; for another, Theodor felt it had been too long since he had lived in a manner appropriate to his position.

While en route, he quartered in stately townhouses; engaged flocks of local domestics and secretaries; gave receptions and banquets; hired the Hamburg Opera for a private performance; tipped coachmen, confectioners, and chorus girls; canceled business appointments to take a look at six matched grays for an equipage (if he liked them, he would give them to his sister or his wife)—in short, within seven months he spent down to the last penny the money accumulated in fifty years of saving by thirty Corsican patricians. At the end of this time, however, he had a million *louis d'or* at his disposal, enough to supply Corsica with food, weapons, and ammunition for a year and throw the Genovese off the island.

Later Theodor would often muse that he had never lived so regally, had never made so kingly an impression as during those months when his vision was still undisfigured by compromise and unsullied by reality. It was the euphoria of anticipation, the euphoria at the sight of the longed-for coastline shrouded in mist.

He sensed that the time had come for him to reap the fruits of his entire life. Yes, he said to himself, this is the golden opportunity that makes a man great. To be sure, one needs the aptitude to stumble upon it at the right moment. And so the meanders of his life suddenly proved to be the only path that could have brought him to this appointment with destiny, neither too early nor to late. All the heterogeneous subjects and skills he had partially grasped, casually learned, or impudently aped suddenly constituted precisely the store of knowledge about the world and its inhabitants on which he would have to draw as the ruler of an endangered little kingdom in the Mediterranean.

Half materialist philosopher, half oriental storyteller, he detailed his visions and plans for an ideal future Corsican state to the growing host of professional listeners and hangers-on who flocked around him and reported on the course of his odyssey toward power for readers of the weekly and monthly periodicals.

In particular, there were two English travel diarists or journalists who—from August 1735 on, when he had purchased unusual quantities of muskets and cannon in London—never left his side. Later, they were joined by a German poet, if only intermittently, for he was a real scaredy-cat and shied away from waterfront taverns and nighttime alleys as well as long ocean voyages. He was a private tutor who had set off on a grand tour but run out of steam in Geneva where, bedazzled by Theodor's grand scheme and the crumbs he garnered from his table, began composing odes and poems to him. He disdained the two Englishmen and their factual prose as inferior competitors for his place in the sun of the object of his admiration. He never openly rebelled against them, however, but only made snide remarks and wrote carping verses, in all seriousness considering himself to be Theodor's privileged confidant and, as his countryman, dearer to his heart than the cynical Anglo-Saxons.

This Ludwig Overbeck shrank from joining the return voyage to Corsica in November. They passed the Straits of Gibraltar and four days later were captured by corsairs who escorted Theodor's ship, cruising fully laden under the Dutch flag, into the harbor of Tunis.

Meanwhile, a letter from Giafferi had informed the future monarch that Corsica had declared its independence and, as a free state, placed itself under the protection of the Blessed Virgin. The insurrection was fully underway, the Corsican Council had been notified of Theodor's imminent arrival with aid and was prepared to declare him King. To substantiate their earnest intentions, the General Assembly's first order of business had been to condemn thirteen traitors and have them impaled. Giafferi waxed lyrical in closing: the stakes were lined up along the anchorage as a guard of honor, awaiting the arrival of the King of Corsica.

In the narrow harbor of the corsairs, the high-decked Dutch ship was enthroned among all the feluccas with their faded red sails and the leafless forest of banked galley oars. Its bridge towered over the white walls, roofs, and awnings of the waterfront, so that the sandy-golden palace of the bey, shining in the sun, looked back at it across the maze of alleys like another, proud commando bridge.

Here Theodor's traveling companions, the correspondents of the *Gentleman's Magazine*, Mr. Charles Sweeney and Mr. Jeremiah Upworth, proved their true worth. For of course, they were already familiar with Tunis, just as they had already been at the Vierwaldstätter Lake, in the Meran Valley, or Heidelberg, Istanbul, and St. Petersburg.

"By the way, Sir, Tunis here is a wonderful place for your holidays."

"Holidays? What do you mean?"

"Well, for instance, when you get tired of work and need to recuperate, but your own garden bores you, then you can travel somewhere nice and rent yourself a house for the summer," Sweeney explained.

"If you go in the winter, I recommend the French Riviera," Upworth added.

"I think it makes more sense to work in the winter and travel in the summer. Weggis is my favorite," said Sweeney. "Do you know Weggis, Herr Baron?"

"No more than I do Tunis," Theodor said, looking toward the soldiers standing along the wall of the embankment.

Sweeney gave a sympathetic nod. "And what now, Sir?" he said, as he always did when a decision was imminent.

"Yes," Upworth added, "our readers are wondering what the baron will do now." And the two pulled out their pencils like two tiny daggers.

"It seems to me I've already given you enough material to fill up a whole book about me, gentlemen."

"The only question is, Sir," said Upworth and pointed to the armed guards, "will it appear posthumously or will something occur to you to save our lives, our freedom, and our cargo?"

"While you think it over, Sir," Sweeney suggested, "we shall look for a pub here on the waterfront and then pay a visit to the English consul."

Whenever it seemed necessary to them and with their English sangfroid, the two journalists switched from Theodor's side to neutral terrain and back again, like disembodied beings who float from army to army over a battlefield and then up into heaven to report to the gods.

Turning to wave back at Theodor, they disembarked down the gangplank and with the words, "We are subjects of His Majesty George II, King of England," walked past the bey's guards. Upworth called back, "See you this afternoon."

"Hopefully!" Sweeney added, and the two of them disappeared into the crush of the harbor bazaar.

Theodor watched them vanish. He liked to use the two as sparring partners in the gradual fabrication and testing of his thoughts in the act of speaking, and in the present situation as well, their mention of the English consul had indicated the possibility of turning the capture and confiscation of their ship into a satisfactory business for all concerned.

When a troop of janissaries arrived at midday to escort him to the palace of Bey Husain Ibn-Ali, Theodor was wearing a tight-fitting, uniform-like navy blue tunic, partly in honor of his abductor and partly from his love of show. It was decorated with the Swedish and Spanish medals he had been awarded in days gone by as well as with English ones he had had made up in London for good Corsican gold.

The insignia of the London Grand Lodge, which he as good as belonged to, hung discreetly round his neck, and from the mighty hold of the merchantman he had the crew fetch up a crate with forty brand-new muskets, shiny with oil, which he intended as a gift for the bey.

In the flicker of light and shadow beneath awnings fluttering in the wind, the smell of salt and seaweed gave way to the odors of mint, coriander, and saffron. Everywhere, traders had shaken little gleaming piles of spices out onto the ground, with a little silver measuring scoop stuck in each one. From an unseen minaret intoned the guttural call of the muezzin, audible far and wide, a noise that startled at first, then unsettled, until it finally sounded like the call of a giant fairy-tale bird. Thinking of the church bells of home, he grasped that for the first time in his life, he had stepped outside the Christian world.

As Theodor, followed by his secretaries and servants hauling the crate and surrounded by the escort of janissaries, entered the lofty hall with its mosaic tiles, the bey surveyed him with wakeful-weary ruler's eyes, his blue-lipped mouth encircled by a black beard that tapered to a point beneath his chin. Through the delicately filigreed windows the sunlight fell upon the floor in golden drops. Outside on a patio, a fountain burbled.

Although the bey's head and torso remained motionless and only his eyes moved, going back and forth between two rear-view mirrors mounted on a framework fitted over his shoulders so that he could see in every direction at once in order to be ready for any assassination attempts, the impression he made upon Theodor was not of ponderousness. The lifelong use of his eye muscles had hollowed him out as surely as heavy physical work would have, but it also kept him taut and limber.

Husain Ibn-Ali bowed slightly without lowering his eyes. Theodor bowed more deeply and betrayed not the slightest surprise (and was in fact not particularly surprised) at seeing Mr. Sweeney and Mr. Upworth, seated behind the bey on thick carpets and ottomans, in the company of a third man who could only be the English consul.

Later, in the bathhouse, it turned out that Mr. Upworth smelled of beer. So there really was an English pub in Tunis, called "The Arms of Monastir." A brief sign from Mr. Hamilton, the consul, assured Theodor of Masonic support against the moor.

After that, everything was a matter of Byzantine expressions of courtesy and rounds of negotiation, pursued with relish in the cool shade of the patio, later in the steamy hammam, later still over a series of tagines served in rust-red clay pots shaped like tops, interrupted by peppermint sorbets to make space in their stomachs for more courses to follow.

Husain's overture was as follows: "You are in a hurry, Baron? You sailed across our seas in a hurry, alarming us and making us fear that war was being waged against us, and now you're in a hurry to continue on your way? Allah created the world slowly, Baron. It's still in the process of coming into being. What is time? What is a year in the history of our world? What is the life of a man? A grain of sand in the desert. What is your Corsica with its worries? Nothing but a blink of the eternal eye . . ."

The bey went on like that for half a day with no intention of getting down to the real questions: whether he was asking for punitive damages or customs duty, whether he would commandeer the cargo of Theodor's ship or buy it, whether he would prefer to sell them something or perhaps intended to hold the baron himself hostage and extort ransom for him.

But this kind of conversation immediately won Theodor over to the careworn, haggard, nervous man. In any case, he was in no hurry for his present, comfortable life, blessed by the expectation of a great future, to come to an end too soon. He, too, could trace ellipses around the entire word, and so he began from the opposite end: "Honored Sir, our God made the world in six days and gave himself no rest. Our English friends here have a saying, 'Time is money.' Every single day in far-away London, half the city—as big as your entire realm—gets torn down and built up again. And for what? For nothing. Just to keep in motion. We Europeans have a faster heartbeat. We don't live as long. Something we sowed the day before yesterday has to ripen today. You, wise Bey, and we children of unrest —we are so far removed from each other that I must plead for the help of your patient God so that hurry and leisure can coexist for the common good, just as the dignified sun stands still and shines upon the hectic earth which circles it."

"I know very well what the sun does for the earth, but how is it the other way round? Does the latter have anything useful for the former?" asked the bey in a lordly tone of voice.

"Well, who would ever know about the sun and its blessings if there were no earth to do homage to it? It is the hasty, spinning world that lends leisure (which a more ignorant man might call indolence) its dignity."

"Woe to it, however, if it gets too close and burns up!"

"It's all a matter of the correct distance, Highness, just as in business. If the seller stands too close to the buyer, he casts a shadow on his own wares. If the buyer stands too far away, he can't see them well enough and some other less finicky customer snaps them up from under his nose. But if the seller keeps his distance so as not to annoy the buyer, then they can't do any business."

Husain Ibn-Ali licked his bluish lips and took Theodor along falconing so they could continue their negotiations.

"And what now, Sir?" asked Mr. Sweeney.

"Yes, the Corsicans are waiting," added Mr. Upworth.

"First off, gentlemen, I shall arrange a place to live, and you would be well advised to invite me to the Arms of Monastir tonight so that I can tell you about my adventures in the great war between the king of Sweden and my old friend the czar."

Theodor stayed two months in Tunis, during which he presented the Dutch ship (without its cargo) to the bey, who in turn, by previous arrangement, sold it to the English consul, who outfitted it with an English flag and put it and an English crew at the disposal of his fellow Mason for the journey to Corsica, without the arms and ammunition ever having left the hold.

"Feel free to use it for the return trip as well, by the way, should your expectations be disappointed," he said.

Still largely in ignorance of Corsican topography and the island's network of roads, Theodor purchased a white mare from Ibn-Ali's stud with the last money he had and, having noticed a decrease in his visual acuity, ordered a pair of reading glasses ground by the bey's optician, for which his host gave him a silver case.

"I can think of no greater gift for a friend who must negotiate with the infidels than to enable him to read the fine print,"

Husain declared with a prophetic smirk while Theodor was being fitted with the spectacles.

And lastly, in the conviction that such things would certainly never occur to the Corsicans, he ordered from a tailor a coronation uniform, cut to his own design. He personally chose its material and color and supervised the application of passementerie, to the approval of both the bey and the Englishmen.

In the first days of March of the year 1736, the Dutch merchantman, rechristened *Sea Rover*, put to sea and on March fifteenth, after an uneventful voyage, reached Aleria, a village (as the disappointed Theodor ascertained through his telescope) no bigger than the port of Leghorn. Nothing but a church tower rose above the low housetops and on the outskirts the ruins of a Roman settlement emerged from the grass like the bleached bones of some prehistoric animal.

Once in sight of the harbor, Theodor had the blue and white striped pennant run up, the agreed-upon signal, and while he stood in the bow of the first longboat and was rowed ashore, the whole town assembled. Giafferi stood on a barrel, waving both arms above his head in greeting.

Theodor had spared no expense for this first, psychologically important entrance. He wore a costume made in Tunis along with the royal uniform: a long caftan of scarlet silk with Moorish pantaloons and yellow slippers. A Spanish hat with a feather covered his head, and his brown hair, without a wig, fell to his shoulders. He had had it curled on the *Sea Rover*. A pair of richly inlaid pistols were stuck in his sash of yellow silk, a long sword hung at his side, and in his right hand he held a scepter.

As a narrow path opened for him amid ah's and ooh's and hurrah's, Theodor distributed to the right and left coins, dates, and, first and foremost, guns. Immediately, the entire port crackled with musket fire and bluish powder smoke hung above the crowd like incense. Theodor recalled reports of how the savages in America also started firing into the air as soon as they were given muskets.

His first performance had gone off befittingly. Theodor withdrew to a house that had been prepared for him. But he would begin to be annoyed the very next day—namely, when Giafferi informed him that a *consulta* was being held in the episcopal palace of Cervioni (from which De Mari had fled) to work out the details of the constitution under which the free Corsicans would choose him as their king—and the vexations would continue to mount with each passing day.

Theodor was taken aback. There had been no talk up to now of the constitution circumscribing his rights. He sensed obstacles being put in his way. And as usual, he perceived them as being directed against his person, his very being. They were so abhorrent to him that he would have liked to flee to some place of complete freedom.

But that was impossible now, unless he wanted to make a fool of himself in front of the whole world, represented by Upworth and Sweeney as well as a correspondent of the *Journal des Scavants* newly arrived via Leghorn, all of whom kept tabs on and reported every move he made.

Ceccaldi, Gaffori, Paoli, Aitelli, Luca Ornano, and Dr. Costa joined them in Aleria, the canon Orticoni, Casacolli, Raffalli, Fabiani, Arrighi, and others traveled directly to Cervioni. Ludwig Overbeck, the poet, had also greeted him at the dock, pushing his way forward to recite a poem in his honor:

> *True majesty is never achieved by luck. Instead,*
> *This Golden Fleece our own endeavor must for us gain.*
> *Are we then elevated when we the crown obtain?*
> *It's we exalt the crown that weighs upon our head.*

There were eleven more strophes which he declaimed as they proceeded. The poem lasted all the way into the entrance hall of the palazzo and no one understood it, since of course it was in German. Sweeney and Upworth made onomatopoetic fun of the court poet's verbal music, a whole barnyard of gurgles and gobbles that forced Overbeck to bellow louder and louder and stick out his chest while he walked along, resulting in a sort of lopsided hop.

Since they weren't going to Cervioni by sea and the road was in the hands of the *mécontents*—as the French journalist dismissively called the freedom fighters—the poet joined them on the journey.

In obstinate silence, Theodor rode along the coast on his white Arabian mare. From time to time, Giafferi caught up with him and after a few words about the landscape or the journey, fell back again.

By the time Theodor had regained his inner tranquillity, they were on the winding mule track of the Castagniccia, which traversed dense stands of chestnut trees as it spiraled round the mountain. The landscape thrust itself into his sight, forcing his vision out of the vagueness and blindness of thought into the concrete and immediate.

Bluish mist hung over the northern end of the valleys, lending a shimmer of turquoise and violet to the succulent spring ferns. When the sun emerged, the dew drops on their leaves glittered like glass rosary beads. Blackthorn, hawthorn, and holly bordered the path. The chestnuts had prickly leaves, sharp as lancets, and Dr. Costa rode up next to him to say that when dried, they were the ideal remedy for a cough.

The leaves of the olive groves fluttering in the wind made the cultivated valleys gleam with silver. Women in black bowed deeply to the slowly passing cavalcade with its pennants, banners, clattering sabers, and loaded donkeys trundling along in the rear.

Theodor halted on a rise and gazed off across the forested slopes and the green hills cascading down to a narrow band of ink-blue ocean deep in the distance. This is my country, he told himself. He had to smile. He couldn't believe it himself.

Upworth and Sweeney walked beside him, leading their mounts.

"Beautiful landscape, isn't it?" said the smaller of the two, the corpulent Upworth, breathing heavily.

Cervioni lay in a narrow valley. The yellow, densely jumbled houses hugged the flanks of the mountains. Swaths of fog hung above the town like a raised canopy of silk and began to sparkle and glitter as soon as the sun rose above the ridge. Then, as the mist dispersed and light flooded the valley, there was an explosion of color in the dew-soaked olive trees, chestnuts, and hollies and on the facades of the buildings.

The Corsican nobility had been arriving for two days already, and the inhabitants crowded onto the small square on which stood the cathedral of San Erasmo, closely surrounded by houses, and the episcopal palace attached to it. They shouted and shot off their weapons—even from the windows there was shooting—just like in the harbor of Aleria.

One after the other, the men crossed themselves before entering the church. Theodor, surrounded by his guard, was still standing there waving to the crowd. The acrid smell of powder slowly dissipated, the rhythmic cheers echoed in his ears, and somewhere a pig was squealing. Charles Sweeney held the door for him and said ironically, "The conclave is beginning."

Overbeck, who as a Protestant would not set foot in this papist temple, remained outside and attempted by gesture and word to make known that he was the hungry court poet of His Majesty, in need of a free meal in a tavern.

Theodor hesitated a moment in the gloomy porch beneath the rood screen, dipped his hand into the stoup, and thought of his sister to whom he had written for the first time in years from Aleria, informing her of his advancement.

But you really couldn't call it advancement during the following two weeks that the "conclave," as Sweeney had called it, lasted.

Each day—and the Corsican patricians were late sleepers —began with a Mass. Then they moved on from incense to kitchen smells and tobacco fumes. It was rare that they all sat down together around the refectory table. Individuals jumped up excitedly, conferred in adjoining rooms, withdrew with their families behind closed doors, returned, waved sheets of paper in the air, read out resolutions and ripped them up again in fury. Whole casks of sour Corsican red wine were emptied. The windows were thrown open to dry eyes streaming with tears from the smoke and excitement. Delegations of the populace of Cervioni knocked on the door with petitions. The roast pork was ready and got passed around, then cheese, then coffee, then herbal schnapps, and finally they withdrew for a siesta or discussions in small groups. At five, the gentlemen began to trickle back in. The priest and the mayor complained about the throng of ladies of easy virtue attracted by the council. An official text condemning their presence was drawn up and a building requisitioned to house them. It did a brisk business. Toward evening, the cigar and pipe smoke thickened. They couldn't seem to wrap things up. They fidgeted on their chairs, whined, haggled, grumbled, rubbed their hands together, wrung them, kneaded them, folded them, raised them in the air, traced orbits and curves with them. Men stood up and declaimed passionate appeals to

their fellows, sat down again and looked around in embarrassment. Circles and coteries and coalitions came together and
swayed a while on the rope bridge of a common strategy, until
the rotten ropes gave way.

Theodor, who had expected homage and thanks, was
assailed with demands, confronted with questions, buried in
petitions. They gazed at him beseechingly, mistrustfully, in-
credulously, fiercely, arrogantly. He put on his Tunisian reading spectacles to skim the documents they handed him and tried
to calm the cacophonous chorus of patricians drunk with their
prospects and demands.

"Don Teodoro, you guaranteed . . . Don Teodoro, you
promised . . . Don Teodoro, we assumed . . . Don Teodoro, my
family and I absolutely cannot accept . . . Don Teodoro, you've
made a start, but . . ."

Or demanding and threatening: "Where are the mercenaries, Don Teodoro? . . . Over my dead body! . . . Never, Don
Teodoro . . . What do you want from us? . . ."

Or, as soon as he had spoken: "You can't expect that from
us, Don Teodoro . . . I have a family, Don Teodoro . . . I'm only
a simple farmer, Don Teodoro . . . You've got to understand,
Don Teodoro . . . Put yourself in our shoes, Don Teodoro . . ."

And when there was a difference of opinion, it always came
down to the same old song: "Don Teodoro, you don't really know
Corsica very well yet: our homeland, our traditions, our state of
mind. Therefore, allow me to point out to you . . . Don Teodoro,
you're not a Corsican. You can't grasp, comprehend, feel that . . .
Don Teodoro, your experience on the continent doesn't apply
to Corsica . . . Don Teodoro, you've got the wrong idea . . ."

"Now you can imagine, Sir," said Upworth one evening
with a smirk, "what your cousin George has to put up with in
Parliament every single day."

Theodor lost control and snarled at the journalist, "Devil take you, Jeremiah, why don't you go look for a pub somewhere?"

Often, the Corsicans forgot about Theodor and the constitution altogether and raised their voices to each other: "I refuse to talk with traitors . . . Whose family was it who collaborated with the occupiers? . . . You can't reach any agreement with Corsicans from the other side of the mountains, from the south, from the north, from the Balagna . . . You're just afraid of losing the privileges the Genovese granted you . . . A Corsican who lives too long on the mainland is not a real Corsican anymore . . ."

In the evening, Theodor locked himself in the prior's cell, gazed through the open, barred window at the narrow strip of sky between the mountains, listened to the foliage dripping with fog, and thought, I have to get out of here. I don't want to do this anymore. Why did I ever get involved in this madness? But as soon as morning came and the noise of the street began, he had to start bargaining and negotiating again if anything was to remain of his kingdom.

He succeeded in getting them to agree to install him, and any subsequent descendants residing in the country, on the throne. Over the Corsicans' objections, especially toward Greeks, he held fast to his plan to expand the population through immigration from abroad, but had to concede that no foreigner would ever be allowed to hold any office or government position.

The Corsicans demanded a diet of twenty-four patricians without whose assent the king could make no decisions about taxes or wars. If Theodor succeeded in obtaining a palace guard of his own choosing and permission to engage foreign troops and militias, he was granted this prerogative on condition that every foreign soldier must leave the country after the victory over the republic. He also had to promise to expel all the Genovese and grant economic privileges and tax breaks to the native propertied classes, who were childishly absolute in their demands.

As if Theodor were a tradesman with whom one could haggle over the price of merchandise one didn't necessarily have to have—haggle beyond any bounds of decency—some of the council members escalated their requests to an absurd, shameless, even fantastic degree.

"The king may not impose taxes on transportation! The poll tax may not exceed three—no, two livres per family! The annuity for widows and orphans must be abolished! The salt the king provides for the people must not cost more than two *seini* per bushel! The king has the duty to see to it that the Corsican university enjoys the same privileges as all other European universities and has a reputation equal to theirs! But no foreigner will be permitted to give instruction here in our country and then draw a state pension!"

They began to get involved in things of which they had no understanding: military strategy, import and export, monetary policy, morality, and agrarian reform: "Never will I permit a single square foot of the ground that has belonged to my family for twenty generations to be ceded or sold to a foreigner who will defile our sacred Corsican earth . . ."

It was the tenth of April. Theodor rose from his seat with the words, "Gentlemen, I believe I have made a mistake. I wanted to help Corsica gain its freedom. I promised to export your products and bring you arms and ammunition. I have kept my promise. But it's not my impression that you intend to keep yours. You know the motto of the Neuhoffs: *Ubi libertas, ibi patria*. If I'm to be Prometheus bound, then this is not the place for me." Thus he spoke, and left the chamber.

No one moved, but Theodor paused a moment on the stairs and could already hear the storm breaking out. He was very calm, as serene as he had ever been since setting foot on this island, for he realized that inwardly, he was finished with the idea of wanting to be the king of these people. In two days, he could be on a ship to Leghorn or Lisbon, Marseilles or Tunis. He was free.

Two hours later, there was a knock on his door. It was Giafferi and Paoli who had fallen between all stools during the *consulta*, torn back and forth between dual loyalties: their friendship with Theodor and the patriotism that forced them to extort humiliating concessions from their sovereign. But now the shocked delegates, suddenly awakened as if from a drunken dream into a hungover morning, had come to their senses and in contrition, had sent them on ahead. As Theodor reentered the chamber, they kissed his hand but avoided his gaze.

It's like spending a night of love with a stranger, he thought, when you make the mistake of staying until morning. Without shame, you've exposed yourself in an erotic frenzy you now want to forget, but the expression on the face of your partner keeps reminding you of it. You can't help feeling awkward and hostile toward someone who has looked into the maelstrom of your soul.

The coronation took place on April fifteenth in the monastery of Alisgiani.

At moments during the Mass, the deep stillness of the forest with its basso continuo of crickets and arpeggios of songbirds was encapsulated in the rhythmic cheering of thousands like air bubbles in a glass sphere. The cheers, Orticoni's psalmodizing recitatives, the encomia of the Corsican male choruses who stood before him in broad ranks as if they had it in for him, their throaty polyphony that reminded Theodor of the call of the muezzin in Tunis—all this put him into a kind of trance in which he experienced the ceremony as if he were under water, where only wavering images and distorted sounds reached him.

The procession of the Twenty-Four who knelt before him and kissed his ring, the feel of the laurel wreath (like a crown of thorns? like a bird's nest?) that Giafferi and Paoli pressed onto his hair amid the swelling jubilation. "Long live the King of Corsica!" Stand up now. Wave. Smile. The grandeur of being elevated. He had to force himself not to play it, but to feel it. Or was feeling always a conscious effort of the will? The greatest moment of his life. If only one could take it seriously! I wish they were all here and could see me: Jane, Amélie, Mortagne, la Palatine, Görtz, Sternhart, the Swedish Charles, the czar, my lovers . . . But how serious was it to be the king of Corsica? Could the king of this island of brigands be compared to the king of France, for instance? Giafferi's voice from the previous day: "Don Teodoro, I'm on my knees to apologize, but you have to understand them. They are men who have had their honor stolen from them. For generations they've been humiliated, fobbed off, swindled, patronized, kept in ignorance. Their whole life consists of compromises and self-delusion. Nothing hollows a man out like contributing to the loss of his own dignity. A man can call you a swine and it doesn't matter, but if he forces you to call yourself a swine, then something breaks inside of you. Don Teodoro, Your Majesty, please understand. They're your children now, your people."

He heard the choruses: Theodor, Baron Neuhoff, unanimously proclaimed King of Corsica. A wave was carrying him higher and higher, toward the sun, then he was plunging down into the shadow of the trough. This risible rock in the Mediterranean, still ruled by Genoa, and he himself: an exotic bird, an adventurer, a laughing stock for the educated readers of the *Gentleman's Magazine*, and he was ashamed of this farce here, half peasant wedding, half Handel opera. Now the scepter, then the charter. Where should he sign? My glasses, please.

I have completely forgotten about love, haven't thought of it for months. Is that a sign of maturity and dignity? Or of age and decay? His palms felt the warmth of smooth skin, glided over the soft, gently pulsating, slightly moist inside of an elbow. His index finger stroked the delicate down on an arm far, far away from all this.

Chapter XIII

$\mathscr{I}$T WASN'T THEODOR'S PERSONAL lust gushing out while his curious gaze wandered over the flushed face lying beneath him, framed by a crown of black hair. His eyes slid over to the barred window and took in the threadbare, faded Persian rug here in the bishop's roomy bedroom cell. No, it was the seed of the king which was at this very moment bringing to a climax and culmination a kind of official sexual act, the hot sealing wax of *Theodorus Rex* in the loins of this unknown girl.

She had not budged from Cervioni since the coronation. She stood in every crowd, witnessed every audience, was leaning against the nearest wall whenever Theodor stepped into the street—indeed, she was so intent upon lying with the king that Theodor felt much too flattered to turn her down, despite Paoli's frown and Giafferi's most humble reservations ("Please, Don Teodoro. We have no idea who the woman is. It's possible she's a whore from Bastia. In any case, she's not from here"), despite Orticoni's compressed lips. Theodor felt certain the canon was crossing himself behind his back.

But if he couldn't travel to Florence to talk about the fact that he was king, if it was utterly unthinkable to invest the event with reality by his presence in the capitals of Europe, then he did not intend to forgo at least having his elevation notarized by the intimacy of eyes rolling up in ecstasy.

For little Angelina, perspiring with excitement as the door of the bedroom closed behind them, was the only person (besides a black-clad, hollow-eyed old woman who had fallen to her knees before him after the coronation, kissed his dusty boots, and croaked that she had lost her two sons in the war of independence and now the Blessed Virgin had sent him, the king, the savior of the country—an embarrassing scene, he later thought) who saw him and the king so much as one and the same being, that Theodor, shaking his head in astonishment, laughter, and triumph, could say to himself, Yes, I am. I guess I must be.

This head-shaking triumph, this astonished laughter at the palimpsest of royalty upon his skin wrought a basic transformation in Theodor's lovemaking. Where had the moment of delirium gone, the weakness in his limbs, the dimming of his sight? Whither had fled his delight in detours and tangents, the ellipses and orbits of eroticism? What had become of his preference for mule tracks traipsing off into the underbrush rather than the royal highways and official pilgrimage routes which always led in a straight line directly to the grottoes, cathedrals, and temples where one was expected to deposit one's mite in the offertory box?

It was broad daylight. The double subservience of adoring eyes and loins greedy for a trophy provoked his desire to treat the girl, so enamored of his majesty, as his subject. By making the girl happy with his love, Theodor was also honoring her with his scepter, or he was making her happy by honoring her. And in a mood far removed from delirium and blindness, Theodor observed how Angelina weighed the imperial orbs in her hands like an experienced merchant.

It was the sort of masculine lust he had observed years ago in Jakob Sternhart and shaken his head at its strangeness, an eroticism that utterly lacked self-irony and had its source in religious amazement, in intimate, apprehensive awe before the mystery that one had to approach as the captain of a small vessel approaches an oncoming storm: entrusting one's soul to God and relying a bit, but not too much, on being a good swimmer.

Less like a king and more like a sorcerer's apprentice wielding his master's wand for the first time, he had decreed, "I do not wish you to wear clothes in this room," and ever since, Angelina got undressed without a word as soon as she stepped over the threshold, fled in feigned terror of him behind the bed, clung breathlessly to one of the four turned bedposts, stared at his naked body, and squealed, "You satyr!"

Of course, she wasn't usually so familiar with him, but he didn't quibble at such moments, calling to mind instead antique frescos and vase paintings showing nymphs being pursued. The thought of being a part of this tradition of virile vitality was just as satisfying as the act itself.

With an acquiescence only a ruler can grant without losing the feeling of being his own master, he made a live sacrifice to the blind, eternally hungry god several times each day, a sacrifice that was accepted, ingested, and then in the end peevishly spit out again.

His love for the small, sturdy girl, the sight of her broad pelvis, which reminded him of a Roman arched bridge, her thick black hair, and the darkly shimmering down on her upper lip and back, where the two white full moons of her buttocks rose—all that failed to tire or bore him even after several weeks, perhaps because he desired to know nothing about Angelina the person, who for her part neither importuned him with questions nor told him her life story nor made any attempts at conversation.

He sat on the bishop's bed in the palace, requisitioned from Monsignor De Maris and converted into his residence, and let his eyes wander over the landscape of Angelina's naked body. And with the leisure of a flaneur traversing a pleasant, familiar quarter of the city, he concentrated on something else, namely, the ideal form for his existence.

Theodor could not deny that Angelina's loins were the starting point of his deliberations. Of course, the Corsican girl was no substitute for Jane. But now that his elevation to king had at least justified, if not obliterated, his guilt, what if he were to appeal to the intelligence and magnanimity of his wife and ask her to come to Corsica and live with him as his queen? Naturally, he would respect her privacy and she would live beside him like a royal sister, so to speak. Surely he could arrange to assuage his baser instincts with Angelina in appropriate discretion, and at the same time have the queen of his spirit by his side for conversation and thought, official acts and occasions, concerts and travel. And in addition a son, even if this third member of his ideal family would not come to him in the classic way, but rather from very sad circumstances which Theodor strictly forbid himself to think about.

He had received a letter, a document composed with a quill pen in elegant handwriting, which addressed him trebly as Esteemed Sir, Your Majesty, and Dear Uncle and Father, in which the Vicomte de Trévoux, his nephew Friedrich, informed Theodor of the death of his mother Amélie and expressed the wish to be allowed to spend his future life at his uncle's side.

If Theodor had had a single calm moment in which to open himself up to this news, he would have broken down and turned melancholic or gone crazy. The only thing he took cognizance of was the announcement of Friedrich's imminent arrival. How old was the boy, anyway? Sixteen, seventeen, eighteen? As old as he himself had been when he'd given up a secure, boring future as a lieutenant in the Régiment d'Alsace.

Theodor imagined to himself Jane, Angelina, and Friedrich —first wife, second wife, and son—drawn from various eras of his life and happily ruling their land.

Such were the images in his head while his lips ferreted out sweet dried figs and Turkish delights from where Angelina had hidden them in apposite locations on her body, and sucked them into his mouth against a slight muscular resistance. "How do they taste, Your Majesty?" asked the girl eagerly, and Theodor answered, "Like prunes wrapped in bacon, my child."

Yes, wanting and needing these hygienically royal orgasms was an impoverishment of the imagination and a dumbing-down, but at the same time a sign that Theodor's elevation and exaltation had changed him.

And not just his erotic technique, which had become hasty, virile, and single-minded; the king within him—or rather, en-closing him—of whom Angelina's fascinated devotion had made him aware, was also taking possession of the remaining prov-inces of his soul.

Theodor was astonished to discover that, while his talents may have made it possible for him to attain the title of king, it was even more the title itself which enabled him to think and act like a king. He had first to become King of Corsica, to be-lieve that he was king, in order to feel the royal power and zest for action growing within him.

There was an urgent knock at the door and Theodor re-called that it was the morning of April twenty-seventh and the officer of his guards was calling him to an execution he himself had ordered.

He was just having himself dressed when Giafferi and Orticoni sent in word of their presence in the antechamber, which meant that Angelina had to be removed, for she was a thorn in the side of the two Corsican patricians. The execution made them uncomfortable too. All his advisers had either lapsed into embarrassed silence or hemmed and hawed, but no one had raised an objection to it.

The charge against the condemned men was nothing more than a family vendetta of the kind that was a daily occurrence on both sides of the mountains. With malicious pleasure, Theodor could read in the eyes of his councilors the conflict between his lofty arguments (the blood feuds which were de-populating the countryside were the basic cause of Corsican disunity) and their uncanny sense that given the right circum-stances, this could have befallen any of them.

Theodor couldn't resist conducting this first real official act as a direct strike at the wasp's nest of their conflicts and bad consciences. It was also a kind of revenge for the way they had treated their king during the *consulta*.

"The villages of the condemned will naturally make com-mon cause with the Genovese, Don Teodoro," Paoli cautioned.

"So what if they do?" answered Theodor. It could hardly make a difference from which side of the conflict the inhabit-ants of tumble-down goat sheds in the mountains demanded tribute before showing the troops the best path through the Macchia.

The law that Theodor had issued specifying capital pun-ishment for clan murders, about to be applied here for the first time, showed them he was serious. And this morning, his path through the cordon of curious onlookers, growing more and more quiet the closer he came to the gallows—whose cross-beam seemed to bump against the low-hanging clouds—made Theodor aware of his power and the concrete consequences of his thoughts.

He watched as the two unshaven men, their white shirts dirty and torn, their hands bound behind their backs, their feet chained close together, were pushed toward the gallows and stumbled forward unwillingly. He could smell that one of them, who sank to his knees in front of the platform, had lost control of himself; at the same time, he inhaled the fresh aroma of damp forest. He could hear the sentence being read, heard the drum roll, saw the whites of eyes turned furtively toward him, heard a woman's mournful wail.

The drumming echoed through the stillness that followed. The second man was stoically calm. Both were led onto the platform, and the nooses placed round their necks. The legs of the man who had lost his nerve were trembling so hard that his pants shook. Then the hangman pulled the lever and the trap-door swung open with a bang. The shout from the crowd failed to drown out the sharp snap, like a rotten branch, with which the neck of the fearful man broke. His eyes rolled up into his head. He was out of his misery in a second. The other one wriggled and croaked and turned on his own axis and fought against death. His face turned red, his neck muscles swelled, his eyes bugged from their sockets, his bound legs thrashed in the air, seeking a footing. Theodor watched and waited for the man to die. The patricians behind him looked at the ground. The soldiers in front of him prodded the muttering crowd from the prisoners' village with the butts of their lances. Theodor tried to keep his mind on the straight line leading from his thoughts about how to prevent the self-mutilation of the Corsican people, to his law, to this man here, valiantly dying.

It was one thing to kill a man in fury or the heat of passion, as he had done years ago on a dreamy night in Venice. It was quite another to stand at the head of a chain of command at whose other end a man was being executed. Not that he had any regrets at all.

Now the hanging man was getting weaker, opening his mouth like a baby bird waiting in its nest to be fed. Theodor caught himself awaiting some unforeseen interruption of the performance, but then the man appeared to be choking up something large and black, and Theodor narrowed his eyes to see more clearly. It was his tongue, which death was sticking out at all of them in an obscene grimace. Then his torso twitched and his limbs hung limp and swaying.

The corpses were cut down, thrown onto a cart, and turned over to their relatives to transport back home. The royal delegation returned to the episcopal palace.

It was just as hard for Theodor to concentrate on the execution and experience its full reality as it had been earlier with the plans for his family. If the demands of the day jostled aside thoughts of the latter, the memory of lovemaking with Angelina and behind that of Jakob Sternhart constantly interfered with the execution. And the sword-swallowing act Theodor had been performing with the Corsican girl reminded him of his old friend because he had recently heard from Sternhart again after twenty years.

On the very top of the pile of petitions that arrived every day he had discovered a letter from the erstwhile Prussian professor, whose ornate handwriting and equally eccentric salutation, which seemed to creep along on its belly and yet bow at the same time, were the floodgates that let in a tide of self-pity and undeserved bad luck.

Theodor read with knitted brow and twitching lips how thanks to the intrigues of colleagues, Sternhart had first lost his professorship, then thanks to the intrigues of his wife's family his house, and in the end his health as well. Which was probably, thought Theodor—completing the lamento that was silent on this last point—thanks to the intrigues of *filles de joie* and flagellate organisms.

For the sake of old times, the unhappy man was asking for a bit of financial aid, a letter of recommendation to one of the imperial principalities, or perhaps even a position on the Mediterranean island, about whose heroic struggle for independence one could now read and hear about everywhere.

Theodor had paper and pen brought and wrote a personal reply, standing at his high desk: the memory of their cordial friendship, unchanged since youth, was preserved in his heart. The honored Herr Professor had by no means been forgotten and should feel free to make as much capital out of his, the king's, name as he did out of his own. Theodor's name should prove not unfamiliar to most of the relevant establishments.

While the pounce dried the ink, Theodor reread his letter. His lips were drawn into a thin smile and the laugh wrinkles formed coronas at the corners of his eyes.

But reading and answering letters was not all there was to it. During the first weeks of his incumbency, Theodor issued a general amnesty from which only treason to the Corsican cause and vendetta murders were excluded. From the Twenty-Four of his diet he put together a government. He ordered the appointment of judges and attorneys, took the first steps toward establishing a department of revenue and finance, and decreed the conscription of a regular Corsican militia which he would lead in liberating the harbors and fortresses still in the hands of the Genovese.

But it was still not enough, not enough by far. For already some Corsican patricians were beginning to demand new deliveries of arms and ammunition, seeds and farm implements. What in heaven's name had become of the first delivery in these few weeks? Shrugging of shoulders, lamentations, attempts at explanation that trailed off into ellipses. Theodor suspected they were hoarding things in order to resell them, perhaps even to the badly equipped and perennially hungry Genovese troops in the forts, which consisted partly of Corsican volunteers, but assuredly also in order to lay in massive supplies for their clan warfare.

The king had to correspond with business partners whose continued support was contingent on the expulsion of the current occupiers, and that would only be possible via additional weapons and ammunition if the wastage were to continue at the same rate as it had begun. Nor had Theodor yet abandoned the idea of the patronage of a powerful state, although support from Spain would infuriate the empire, and help or opposition from France depended on the fate of Genovese diplomacy, so that Theodor preferred to pin his hopes on England, since he didn't want to run the risk of making a pact with the Sublime Porte. It was completely impossible, however, to accomplish anything in London without putting in a personal appearance, but leaving his island citadel was out of the question at the moment.

The other thing he had need of was expert assistance, for he had no great confidence in the abilities of his Corsican councilors, a fact he could hardly reveal to those tetchy men whom he had to employ in subsidiary theaters of engagement to give them the feeling that their king depended on them.

In search of advice, he composed letters to Baron de Secondat in Bordeaux (Montesquieu had already shown interest in Costa's draft constitution) to learn from him how best to effectuate the separation of powers and the rule of law. Above all, he devised a bold plan to win over the erstwhile genius of the rue Quincampoix himself, the Scotsman Mr. Law, to be the kingdom's minister of finance. But all his letters to Law were returned to Corsica marked "addressee unknown" or "no longer residing at this address" and after months of postal odyssey, Theodor learned from his old friend Respighi in Venice that the long-forgotten financial wizard had died seven years ago in the city of lagoons, miserable and penniless.

When this news reached him in Sartè at the beginning of September, it was another one of those moments Theodor loved so much. This time it was a letter, but it could have been the perfume of a flower, the ringing of a church bell, or some melody that suspended a tightrope over the abyss of time: Law dead in Venice! That stretched all the way from memories of his youth in Paris to his own dream-like days in Venice, from whose background emerged in sharp illumination the painting that had been so inscrutable to his yearning spirit. Theodor could see it clearly in his mind's eye: the girl nursing the child, the hesitating shepherd or wanderer, the approaching thunderstorm . . . Yes, it could have been a moment to muse on time and life's strange pathways, but there was no time for that. For in the midst of the traumatic campaign against Bastia, Theodor had convened the diet in Sartè in order to found the Order of the Redemption, and he had as little leisure for memories and dreams as he did now, in the final days of April in Cervioni.

The paradox he was experiencing was that his overfilled days were producing not life, but emptiness. In Berthelsdorf, to take a counterexample, he had lived. He had not the slightest difficulty in conjuring up the vivid colors, sounds, and smells of long evenings spent in contemplation of the constellations, of conversations, hours of idleness, and their infrequent excursions. By contrast, he could not remember one single day since he arrived on Corsica and would not have been able to say what had actually been stolen from him in those lost hours. Even later, when he thought back on these months, many blank spots remained. He could only say for certain was that he had been king, but he had to make up almost all the other details.

Bivouacked near Isula Rossa in June, Theodor awoke one morning before dawn, shivering and with aching bones, and exclaimed, "What a struggle!"

Before he even had time to think about the day to come, he was brought up short by his own words. It was true, he was struggling since becoming king. He had to struggle every day.

As banal as it sounded, this realization was a true revelation. When in his life had he ever had to struggle? I can do it! he said in astonishment and looked around to see if there were anyone else in the tent he could tell his discovery to who would congratulate and admire him for it.

Like the shadow of a cloud, the suspicion crossed his mind that his current condition was perhaps not in harmony with his true nature. For what was struggle except a willful and impatient violation of the boundary between one's own sphere and the realm of the gods? One kept moving ahead, but not too far, and trusted that they would meet one halfway in return. To cover the entire distance alone, with eyes wide open and not leaving anything to chance, was for someone like him, possibly, criminal hubris.

Theodor stepped from his tent. Two soldiers were squatting before it, on guard. Sharp gusts of wind blew in his face. The ridgeline of the hills to the east looked like black lace against the rosy dawn. It would be a long time before the sun would rise over the mountains, in whose shadows lay the slopes of garigue, sparsely covered with rosemary and gorse. Waves crashed against the rocks and the wind smelled of salt.

Two campfires still glowed weakly. The warm aroma of animals wafted over from the horses and oxen. Awakening soldiers cleared their throats, others tossed fitfully in the final moments of sleep. The battle flag with its moor's head snapped in the gusts. Far to the south lay Algajola. Theodor's gaze took in the encampment, the sea, the hills, the dusty road, and the harbor in the distance, and he could not help but think that the whole of this present moment was actually already past.

He recalled his nephew's letter. Its news of Amélie's death really should have brought his own life to a halt as well, but instead, he went to bed with his mistress and then on to this campaign.

Involuntarily, he thought of the man who had impressed him more than anyone else he had ever met and for whom he had proved so inadequate: the Russian czar whom he had encountered face-to-face many long years ago in Amsterdam.

Now he understood that it was impossible to both make decisions and have feelings. Feelings needed the air of time and contemplation. Today he, Theodor, was not yet finished being astonished at the wonder of his own birth and existence, would have preferred to brood on the curious paths of his childhood and youth. Men like the czar, and to a lesser extent his current self, simply had too much to do to also be able to feel anything. Before the feeling associated with an act could really come into its own, there was a new decision demanding to be made. If you were a doer, you couldn't be a liver, Theodor thought. Not in my understanding of life, anyway. That's the tragic truth.

No one admired him except Angelina. But how was he expected to go on without being admired? Why should you bother to reconstitute yourself every morning if no one's there to say: How beautiful! The Corsicans all just wanted something from him and doubted he was capable of getting it for them. Maybe Angelina wasn't much, but she looked up to him because he was the king, and he needed this wide-eyed admiration from the girl when she woke up in the morning, and her fingers, moist with excitement, had only to touch him to awaken to life the monarch within him.

Beyond all his dreams and ruminations, he knew that he must rid the island of its occupiers by autumn, before the Genovese appeals for renewed help from abroad could yield results. Once they were gone from Corsica, no one in the world would help them win it back.

Now the two cannon were brought into position and began firing. Clouds of smoke and the biting smell of powder and hot grease befouled the clear morning air. Theodor, in a flowing Berber costume, mounted his horse and simultaneously the steps of the Paris Opera, accompanied, as now along this strip of coast, by English journalists, a German court poet, and an Italian history painter whose specialty was battles. A cousin of His Most Christian Majesty, offhandedly regaling the listening court ladies with his triumphs. He reined in his white, whom the noise was making skittish, and also had to curb his own high-flying imagination. If he weren't victorious here, if he couldn't liberate Corsica, he would never again be able to show his face anywhere and would end up a defeated, contemptible beggar, at whom every stinking burgher would feel free to hurl the slanders Genoa had been circulating for quite some time: Neuhoff the swindler, the bogus nobleman, the king of gambling debts, the fortune hunter, Neuhoff the thief, Neuhoff the sodomist,

Neuhoff the syphilitic. Rhythmic choruses of contemptuous scorn, cascades of derision broke over him, echoed in his ears, and he writhed and squirmed in the dust of the street like a worm. A man who had cheated, wagered too much, and lost his nerve had been brought low by the Furies, one whom Fortune had lured onto the highest peak and then stripped naked and exposed to ridicule.

He gave his horse the spurs, drew his saber, and the be-fuddled Corsican cavalry followed him into the even more be-wildered Genovese troops who, accustomed as they were to being ambushed, had been expecting an exchange of cannon and musket fire—as English gentlemen exchange their calling cards—but not that on this island (where they did business today, got spat at tomorrow, and were embraced day after to-morrow) they would simply be mowed down.

The battle was not what Theodor saw with his inner eye: no magnificent clash of two massed armies, no attacking forest of lances or cannonades that went on for minutes on end and tore gaping wounds in the trembling earth. The Genovese avant-garde cowered behind the cadavers of two dead horses, fishermen's huts were burning, the white-eyed Corsican line shouted as it stormed forward, there were muzzle flashes and the rattle of musket fire sounded like fireworks. All the same, horses reared and sabers flashed in the first rays of the morn-ing sun rising over the mountain ridge.

The mournful mooing of oxen in the long interval between two cannonades and then a venomous slaughter with knives and pikes and the panicked rout of the Genovese into the gorse-covered hills, where they tore their clothes and got cut down from behind. Some even fled into the sea where they came to a stop, hip-deep in water, paddled with their arms, and were sit-ting ducks for the Corsican sharpshooters. Wisps of fog from all the expended powder and the usual sight of solitary shoes and abandoned caps on the battlefield, the bellowing of dying animals, soldiers kneeling and slitting the throats of the dying enemy and plundering their bodies, a blazing morning sun climbing higher and higher, so that by midday, everything was already reeking sweetly of decomposing humans and animals. The liberated fishermen stood before their smoldering huts, smiling sourly, and waved a tentative hurrah to the royal army that was moving on toward Algajola.

On this and the following days, Genoa would have more than five hundred dead and wounded to mourn. Theodor himself was no longer present at the ensuing engagements and skirmishes, but already on his way to Ornetu to establish the new mint, with the Englishmen and the poet in tow, although Filippini, the history painter, complained that everything had gone too fast for him and was left behind to make more sketches on location.

In thought Theodor was still sitting in bed with Angelina, before the Balagna campaign had begun, and was telling his cow-eyed listener of his plans and visions for the island.

Despite being himself the descendant of one of the most ancient noble families in the Mark, he told her, it had taken him a long time to finally hit on the cure for all the clan feuds, vendettas, struggles for power, and cockfights of his subjects: he would found an order of knights! An ideal that would be more binding than all the bonds of blood. Of course, the example of the Masonic lodges had played a part in his idea. What did she think of it? But she thought nothing, said not a word, perhaps didn't understand all he'd said, neither his witty Italian nor his complicated vocabulary.

"A knightly order, appealing to the highest human virtues, tailor-made for the exclusive Corsican nobility, an honor and at the same time an obligation, an attempt to refine all their baser instincts into a higher aspiration. Of course, I'm not so naive as to think that the whole thing won't need to be modernized a bit," he quickly added, "and if its purpose is also to put the patricians under personal obligation to me, then there's got to be something in it for them, too. That's how well I've come to know them by now. But that's an expense that can be recouped by also inducting foreign monarchs and dignitaries into the order (the former for free, the latter in exchange for an appropriate fee), which would in any case contribute to its reputation. What do you think, Jane? Does it make sense and will it succeed, or is it absurd?"

He was already well into the next sentence before he realized that he had called Angelina Jane. Of course, he'd been speaking to his wife from the first, through the membrane of time and space, and was just using his Corsican mistress as a resonator, but saying Jane's name out loud interrupted his train of thought. However, Angelina had obviously not heard the English name in Theodor's flood of words.

It got more difficult to maintain the fiction when Angelina, after a brief moment of thought, actually began to express her opinion of an order of knights. He wouldn't hear a word of it, gently put his hand over her mouth, and began once again to detail his plans to her—the other one.

Why did he bother, anyway, to have pillow talk with one woman who was absent and another who was unqualified about things that would surely meet with much more interest and understanding from his confidants and ministers: Paoli, Costa, or Giafferi?

He got an indirect answer to this question on the thirtieth of June in the monastery of Favagna, where the first casket filled to the brim with shiny new silver thalers was hauled in

front of his travel throne, a folding chair of mahogany with lions' heads at the end of the arm rests.

Theodor plunged both hands into the coins, pulled one of
them out, and peered at it as though it were a mirror, which in
some sense in was. One whole morning long, while signing edicts
and laws in the episcopal palace of Cervioni, he had sat for the
sculptor of the half-length portrait. Below the royal profile on
the smaller denominations stood the words *T. Rex Corsicae* and
on the obverse, the image of the Virgin with the motto *Monstra
te esse matrem*. The larger coins—for want of gold, they were not
yet golden—bore beneath Theodor's likeness the line *Theodorus
D.G. unanimi consensu electus Rex et Princeps regni Corsici*. When
one turned it over, there was a crown borne up by three palms
and the words *Prudentia et industria vincitur tyrannis*. And finally,
the smaller copper coins had to make do with a *T. Rex* on the front
side and the promise *Pro bono publico Corso* on the back.

Mr. Sweeney, reacting with more spirit than the Corsican
ministers, who were obviously incapable of getting enthusiastic about anything at all, congratulated Theodor and his advisers on what they had achieved so far with the words, "Very nice
piece of teamwork, Sir!"

But to tell the truth, that was precisely what it was not,
mused the king. He had thought everything out all by himself,
jealously kept it secret, talked over his plans and reflections with
his wife through Angelina, listened for her answer across the
boundaries of space, time, and logic, and then presented his
completed plans to the cabinet, hoping for enthusiasm but expecting fault-finding and opposition.

On the one hand, he felt it his duty to give birth by himself to ideas for saving the country. Indeed, he thought that in
a certain sense, he owed it to those who had chosen him to justify his elevation to the throne in this way and to make a gift of

his findings (if not fetch them like a dog) to the surprised patricians. And in return, it was no more than fair to expect thanks and praise. But it wasn't just that.

His secrecy was of course also an attempt to outfox those who had forced him to accept the constitution by presenting them with finished conceptions which they would have to give their blessing to, whether they wanted to or not, because they lacked any realistic alternatives. Theodor had not the slightest interest in concerted cooperation or division of labor in a spirit of mutual trust—of teamwork, as Sweeney called it.

It's mine, he thought, and I want the whole world to find out just who is turning this country (which he still had not taken the trouble really to study) into an exemplary modern state, an experiment all of Europe is watching with baited breath.

He washed his hands in the casket of money and then held one of the coins out to Sweeney and Upworth like a consecrated Host. "This is what you must report, gentlemen! Corsica has its own currency."

"What's it worth in relation to the pound?" asked the smaller of the two journalists.

"I'm aiming for parity," Theodor replied loftily.

At least the small, rotund Giafferi and the others looked moved.

"For this historic occasion I have written an opera," announced the Venetian librettist who had turned to account Theodor's yearning for some music other than "polyphonic braying," as he called it, and obtained a commission at court. Grumbling, the German poet turned his back. "*Il re di Corsica.* All that's missing is the congenial composer Your Majesty has promised me. Would Your Majesty care to read the transfiguration scene? The chariot of the Sun King, drawn by Pegasus, rises into the air, the four elements join in the chorus . . ."

"Yes, yes, of course, another time perhaps," the king cut him off. He also had to keep his court poet at a distance, for the latter felt obliged to justify his gargantuan meals with effusions, hymns of praise which grew daily more hypertrophic and inflationary. Besides, he had just been sent a book about himself recently published in Frankfurt am Main, a biography written by a person he had never heard of. Absurd as it must necessarily be, Theodor nevertheless regretted having no time to read it. A distant cousin whom he had also never in his life set eyes upon and who claimed to be related to him through Count Drost—someone else he didn't know, although he knew his name (they must have been distantly related through his grandmother)—was publishing letters by Theodor in German gazettes, letters he couldn't for the life of him recall having written. Ah well, he thought, grasping in his closed fist his dreams concretized in bite-tested silver, my name's on everyone's lips at any rate.

He had just laid his hand on Angelina's lips to keep her from interrupting the dialogue between him and his wife with her own views. Now she bit him gently in the heel of his hand, usually a pleasurable pain which excited Theodor. This time, nothing of the sort. He had to think aloud and needed the sight, but only the sight, of the girl in order to do it.

"You see, ideas and thoughts and grand theoretical constructs—moral precepts as well—have always bored me when they come from books whose authors (take it from me) are usually their own worst possible advocates and warrantors. However, these thoughts obviously possess a life of their own, quite independent of their originators, otherwise how would I have suddenly been able to recall them in my deliberations about how to help this beautiful island become more lively, enthusiastic, productive, and rich?"

"Why do you want to change Corsica, Your Majesty?" asked Angelina querulously. "It's the most beautiful country in the whole world."

"Yes, yes, my child. It is indeed a very beautiful country. It just needs a bit more activity. By the way, are you familiar with any other country?"

"Of course not," cried the girl proudly, and Theodor patted her cheek, completely satisfied with the logic of her answer.

"For example, Corsica has harbors, mineral resources, the fruits of its soil, and an ideal strategic position in the Mediterranean. But sitting on all that are unfortunately only your compatriots who don't know how to exploit it. Now if one were to allow foreigners to settle here in large numbers, build new towns, establish industries and trade, one could pay for all that in the beginning with the confiscated Genovese assets that are already covering our court expenses, and then the land could flourish within a very short time. Two problems: What bait would there be to lure them here except, as you said, the beauty of the country? There would have to be absolute and enforceable freedom to practice their religion and its observances. There isn't a Jew or Huguenot I know who wouldn't be interested . . ."

"What? You want to let Jews, heretics, and Saracens into the country?" cried Angelina, falling into the familiar form of address in her indignation. "When Genoa has already sent over its convicts and killers, to say nothing of the damn Greeks!"

Theodor smiled. "I can already see what's in store for me, but I was talking about the real problems, and this is the second one: How can I arrange matches between the land's new citizens and its old ones? If the immigrants, like the Greeks who are already here, start paying taxes to us instead of to the Genovese, the Corsicans will be quick to see their advantage.

These people will bring skills, money, bread, and foreign exchange to the natives, and once they start working together, then one can have confidence in the effect of time, which ultimately intermingles everyone who lives close enough together. The political rights of these newcomers are of course another matter; they must be as narrowly circumscribed as their religious rights are broad. But what Jew lusts for a government position as long as he can transact business and observe the Sabbath? The administration can perfectly well be left to the Corsicans. They won't knock themselves out . . . On the other hand, Locke mentions the problem presented by atheists, who can't be put under oath and do not recognize the authority of the supreme court. Do you know what Secondat wrote to me on this subject?"

Angelina, bored by Theodor's monologue, pouted and rolled over onto her stomach, showing him the undulating view from the rear, but he was oblivious. His gaze glided vaguely over her skin and off onto the white wall.

"People like the Herrnhuter would come here, too. In Saxony they were always living with one foot in prison. Protestant textile factories and weaving mills, Huguenot furniture makers, Greek oil and wine merchants, Jewish mine owners and bankers—all would become Corsicans in the course of three or four generations and help dilute the hot blood of the original inhabitants."

Kings, as one had known them up to now, he thought, would be incapable of such visions. But he, Theodor Neuhoff, *Rex Corsicae*, was no keeper of the flame of constraining traditions. Even if he did honor the values of class and religion and had a nostalgic and affectionate respect for genealogy, he was no longer able to believe in them seriously. While reserving his right to have principles, eccentricities, and topics he refused to think about, no royal blood grown sluggish over the course of generations condemned him to an etiquette of paralysis. Only a revolutionary king like him, only a stranger to the land, only someone living at the turning-point of two epochs, was able to look backward and forward with the same unprejudiced eye.

Using all the best the Occident had to offer, no matter which age it came from, he would turn this island into the treasure chest of Europe as soon as it was liberated. Perhaps he was indeed destined to become one of the great men of the century.

His gaze snapped back into focus and fell directly onto Angelina's black fleece. She stood before him, reached down into the thickly curling hair with three fingers of each hand, and pulled it open like the women in the port of Tunis drew aside the strings of beads hanging at the entrances to their dens of pleasure to lure strangers in.

"No, no. Not now," Theodor said gruffly. To his own surprise, he felt not the slightest desire. "Go away, Angelina. Some other time. I have to work."

It was the first time in her presence that he hadn't sooner or later succumbed to the temptation to horizontality, and as he set off on the campaign through the Nebbiu, he worried about how that was possible and whether he was no longer kingly and disciplined enough to assign love its place in his daily schedule just as he did the other obligations he had to fulfill.

Only when he finally interrupted this restless, nomadic existence between campaigns and short-term residences in the provinces and returned to Corti for the trial of Casacolli, while the army of Colonel Fabiani moved into position for the siege of Bastia, did his imagination again separate Angelina's body far enough from Jane's mind to renew his desire for it.

But after they had made love, she began to weep uncontrollably, so that Theodor began to doubt the quality of his caresses and became as sober as if the girl's tears were a splash of cold water on his forehead and neck. He was about to send her away in annoyance, when she threw herself onto the floor in a gesture that was too theatrical to be completely impulsive and began to tear her hair.

Theodor, ever scrupulous in matters of thespian skill, said impatiently, "What's wrong, child? Don't torture me, just get to the point. I don't have much time this morning."

"Your Majesty, Don Teodoro, my beloved, please don't beat me, even though I deserve it. I'm a spy, a miserable spy. Genoa pays me. Punish me, kill me—quickly and with your own hand, but don't have me tortured, I beg you. I'm so afraid of pain. Yes, an officer of the town commandant approached me in the port of Bastia, where I was working. I was supposed to get near you and then tell them everything you do and think. I'm so ashamed, holy Mother of God, take pity on me, now and in the hour of our death. It was so much money and I have nothing and a child to feed. It's staying with a wet nurse and can't yet . . . But I've fallen in love with you, Majesty, my beloved, liberator of my country. I did on the very first day and my soul has died a thousand deaths every time I reported something. It wasn't much, nothing important, but of course, I deserve to die anyway. But I loved you immediately, Majesty, hopelessly, just like a girl from the docks would love a king, and you raised me up and showed me respect and wrapped me in your kindness, Don Teodoro, beloved, and how did I thank you? For thirty pieces of silver I sold you. But now, when you were gone all these weeks, I couldn't stand it anymore. I wanted to die. I had to confess to you, even if it means my death. I only ask for one thing, Majesty, don't let them torture and burn me. I'm so afraid of pain, except the little pains you inflict, beloved. They are sweeter than honey and I long for them and for your eyes and your hands and . . ."

"You're a spy the Genovese sent into my house?" Theodor interrupted her in astonishment and deep delight.

More sobbing, more batting her eyes red with weeping below her disheveled black hair. "Oh mercy, Your Majesty! Don't burn me! Don't have my eyes poked out!"

"Please stop talking about such horrible things!" Theodor commanded and gave a tipsy laugh. "So Genoa actually set a spy on me?! Are you telling me the truth? Aren't you just showing off? Now, I want you to tell me all about it. Here's my handkerchief. Blow your nose and calm down. I can't understand a word you're saying!"

Angelina told it all again, with less hemming and hawing this time, and in between sentences looked at Theodor with growing incomprehension, rolling her eyes in dismay at his insatiable desire for details. Again and again, he made her repeat the exact orders the Genovese had given her, describe the tone in which they had talked about him, and what she had reported to them, and his mood grew better by the minute.

"Really? Seriously? So they damn well do have some respect for me and everything I'm doing here! What an accolade! And so you regularly tell your contact everything you observe here, and then he takes off, does he? Or haven't I got it right? Have you written reports yourself?" But no, she couldn't read or write. She had to deliver everything orally. "Yes," said Theodor, "the Genovese knew that I was a man with a weakness for beautiful women, my little sweetheart. I can just imagine them sitting there: We can't get at him by military means or with money, but maybe a young girl . . . My compliments, gentlemen! This is just wonderful, completely delicious. Now tell me once more how it was. They talked about me with respect, did they? I'm giving them a lot of headaches . . ."

Angelina, still not quite sure what was happening, found Theodor's exuberance infectious. Already half convinced that her imminent death was no longer a certainty, still dizzy from the completely unexpected change in her situation, now cried out a bit more brashly, "Oh, and I told them what a great lover you are, Majesty. I told them how strong and insatiable you are and how sometimes you take me like a wild animal in heat and impale me and lift me right off the ground just with the strength and power of your manhood and then flood me like the Nile floods its delta until I think there must be a spring bubbling within me, a warm mineral spring like in the mountains back home, and I shouted in their faces what a man our king is, how tirelessly he flings me into the seventh heaven of pleasure four, five, eight, twelve times in succession . . ." (now she's exaggerating, and quite a bit, thought Theodor with a certain disapproval, for the fantastic superlatives at the end of the sentence threatened to rob the beginning of its credibility) ". . . and that any opposition or resistance to such a man was pointless, and he was a great sovereign . . . but wait, aren't you going to kill me, have me tortured my lord, my master, Your Majesty, haven't I forfeited my life?"

Theodor did not answer. Before his mind's eye was the portrait she had painted of him—her short little fingers aflutter, obviously excited by her own exaggerations—the portrait of him as a wild bull. To her bafflement, he called her Europa and snorting, invited her to mount him.

Gradually, however, memorable moments were accumulating into a more and more stable royal consciousness: the sight of his likeness on freshly minted silver coins; the long, pleasurable minutes spent having his hair washed and his scalp massaged by an African slave girl; getting his face rubbed with aromatic essences and oils; having the barber shave him in clean strokes of the razor and then color, curl, and twirl his mustaches; the daily horoscope, determined by the conjunction of planets and constellations shining down upon him and drawn up by the royal astrologer; and now the revelation that Genoa was spying on him.

A few days later, his compassion touched by Angelina's confession that she didn't know how to read and write, and still in a high-spirited but also, as it would turn out, naive mood, he suggested to his mistress that they compose and write her next report together.

"To the Doge and Senate of Genoa, my greetings!" Theodor just shoveled irony and sarcasm into the document. Angelina stood behind him, leaning over his shoulder. Her warm breasts rested against the back of his neck and her tongue flicked playfully in his ear. She had him read her what he was putting down on paper, and giggled. "In the name of God, please be so good as to tell me how you have earned the title of a monarch and prince, since heretofore your republic was nothing but a bunch of mercenary pirates."

"And now listen to this, at the end: 'I must ask one more favor of you, namely, to see to it that in any future engagements between my troops and yours one of your countrymen be present to command them. I fear that your officers are so busy being extortionists that they have little time left to be courageous.'"

And so on and so forth, with Theodor and Angelina having all sorts of fun, until the letter was finally sealed and ready for the double agent to hand over to her contact.

It was to be foreseen that the recipient would find this document less than amusing, just as it ought to have been clear that if one could not lay hands on its author, one was all the more certain to take revenge on the conveyor of this piece of impudence.

In mid-September, Theodor received news that Angelina had been found in an alley in Sartè with her throat slit. He paid for a proper Catholic funeral from his private purse, a funeral he did not, however, attend. The doctor who had declared her dead confided to him that the murder victim had been pregnant. With some certainty, Theodor could assume that he had been the father of the unborn child. The death of the unfortunate girl was all the more curious since the very next day, Theodor's nephew Frédéric de Trévoux arrived on the island.

I've had everything, the king thought sadly, but never all at the same time, like other, happier men.

One might have thought it was Theodor's self-satisfied, tipsy mood on the morning of Angelina's confession that made him so soft and conciliatory that he asked the diet to pardon Casacolli. But instead, it was his expansive mood that enabled him to assess and describe the situation clairvoyantly. At the most, this mood kept him from speaking as sharply, threateningly, and intimidatingly as necessary to get the assembled patricians to submit to his arguments, and unfortunately they had jurisdiction as long as the court Theodor had instituted had yet to meet.

Casacolli came from a noble family from Furiani and had been one of the Twenty-Four until the recent discovery of secret correspondence between him and the Genovese commissioner in Bastia. Now he was accused of high treason.

Theodor had spoken once or twice with this proud and intelligent man whose personal fate didn't interest him in the least. But he knew only too well that the Casacolli clan would make trouble if their chief were found guilty, whether he really was or not, trouble Theodor definitely did not need in his precarious project to liberate and unite the island, already dependent on enough imponderables. Especially not now, when they were moving against Bastia.

But in a diet that was agitated, angry, and not entirely disinterested in its judgments, it quickly proved illusory to argue strategically and for the higher good of liberating Corsica and against the lesser evil of some letters which, in the end, had not harmed anyone.

"But the traitor undermines your royal authority, Don Teodoro!" was only the most innocuous of the objections he had to listen to. The canon Orticoni took the floor and as always when that enterprising man puffed himself up, Theodor pictured La Fontaine's Master Raven cawing on his branch.

"Your Majesty, Don Teodoro," began the clergyman, laying a perfidious pause between the two titles as if he had weighed the first in his mouth, tasted it, found it inapplicable or unappetizing, spit it out, and settled on the less deferential one as more appropriate. "Don Teodoro, this sentence of death is a question of honor, the honor of the monarchy that reflects upon us, its guarantors and keepers. Perhaps you are a bit confused by such questions of Corsican honor since you consort with a woman well known to the entire city as a prostitute . . ."

The others murmured in embarrassment.

"Is it at least your intention to wash away the shame this creature inflicts on your majesty by legitimizing your relationship with her and putting an end to the tittle-tattle?"

Theodor gave a thin smile. "But my dear Abbé," he said, investing this word with all the contempt of a man who had seen priests on the job in every second room in the regent's palace, standing at a canopy bed with legs spread wide and cassock hitched up, practicing their psalms to the accompaniment of a nun or a baker's daughter playing on their block flute, "my dear

Abbé, in this I but follow the good example of the Catholic clergy. For the rest, I'm already married, or is it your intention to awaken my appetite for polygamy with the richness of your own experience?"

Orticoni flinched as if Theodor had slapped him in the face. But such skirmishes—which the king waged in the spirit of his rhetorical apprenticeship in Versailles, where the goal was to get off a telling retort with lightning speed and have the laughter on your side, not to convince an assemblage of twenty self-righteous patricians of the advantages of rational thought— such skirmishes didn't get him anywhere.

Arrayed against him were those gentlemen who, as neighbors of the Casacolli, foresaw benefit to themselves from the elimination of the clan leader and the confiscation of his property. Others were keen to set an example, from who knows what peculiar psychological motives. Perhaps, Theodor thought in resignation, simply from blood lust and prurience. In the end, even Giafferi and Paoli, the most level-headed and insightful of his ministers, spoke against a pardon.

"It's a matter of principle, Don Teodoro, just like the capital punishment you declared for revenge killings. We can't break the laws we have consecrated ourselves simply for tactical reasons if we are to remain credible as men of honor."

Theodor did not prevail. Had he done everything he could? Did he perhaps forgo some ultimate means of persuading them just to let the inevitable take place, so they would discover and have to acknowledge that he had been right all along? They took a vote, and only the loyal Giafferi and Sebastiano Costa voted with the king.

The condemned man was given the opportunity to say his last words, but Theodor didn't wait around to hear them, just as he didn't show up for the execution, which took place the following morning. Casacolli was to be drawn and quartered.

But it was a small town and one couldn't help but listen. Through closed shutters and open windows, the king heard the iron cuffs snap shut and the shouted "Geeho!" to the horses. He heard the curious popping sound of the bones pulling out of their sockets and then the scream of pain from the dying man, who had remained stoically silent up to then. He heard the tearing of muscles and tendons and the gurgles of horror from the crowd. He heard the clatter of hooves from the four straining horses.

In less than twenty-four hours, a blood-stained scrap of clothing was delivered to the royal residence and five days later, while Theodor tarried in Sulenzara where a Dutch ship with a cargo of arms and ammunition lay at anchor, he received the news that Colonel Fabiani, who was supposed to storm Bastia, had been murdered and instead of besieging the city, his leaderless troops were bogged down in exchanges of sniper fire with the Casacolli clan, who were thus playing into the hands of the besieged Genovese, waiting to be relieved by mercenaries from Grisons.

Theodor ordered a troop assembled as quickly as possible to come to the aid of Fabiani's men and capture Bastia while the means to do so were still available. He himself left Corti with five hundred men, another two thousand soldiers under Gaffori's command were supposed to march up the east coast from Aleria, and a message was sent to the part of the army in the Balagna to join the other units at the foot of the Tegime Pass.

The difficulties began on the second day, but on the first, Theodor had the opportunity to experience anew what a welcome simplification of the world life in the field represented: the society of other men with its comradely handclasps, its simple pleasures of sharing a canteen, wiping the sweat from one's brow, and good-natured, hearty laughter in the face of death.

For the first time, Theodor had the leisure to really appreciate the Corsican landscape, which he had to traverse by foot in the narrow valleys. With all its dramatic contrasts between jagged precipitousness and moss-covered hilltops resembling sleeping elephants, between raging torrents and the lunar stillness of sky-blue mountain lakes, between the delicate tracery of orchid blossoms hidden among ferns and the harsh thorniness of the gorse, it seemed as if an angry god had grabbed a lovely continent in his hand and crumpled it into a jagged little island whose crinkles still groaned with their former greatness.

On this first day, Theodor still laughed a lot with his soldiers, who joked respectfully with their king. On the second day, however, their march was halted by meter-deep snow which made the high valley impassable. "Where did this accursed snow come from? It's the middle of summer!" cried Theodor as they showed him on the map an alternate route which would cost them an additional half day.

In the evening of the second day, they discovered that half the donkeys loaded with ammunition and boxes of powder had disappeared, along with their drovers. Supposedly, they had not been paid.

On the third day, the troops were stopped once again, this time by an exchange of fire with a barricaded mountain village whose inhabitants, as it turned out, had a blood feud to settle with one of the soldiers. It was the same soldier who had suggested the alternate route. The only way forward was through crossfire from two houses. There was no way to get through, and only when Theodor had the soldier shot in the middle of the road could his army proceed without further losses. Meanwhile, several riflemen who came from this area and refused to do any harm to the village had run off.

Theodor's shrunken contingent arrived two days late at the foot of the Tegime Pass, but was still the first one there. Gaffori, who showed up the following morning, had similar things to report. The army that finally stood before the battlements of the citadel of Bastia was no longer an army.

Less than two thirds of Theodor's cohort had made it through and Gaffori's troop consisted for the most part of sons of Bastia (which obviously no one had noticed before) who refused to fire upon their own houses and families. The War of Corsican Liberation was like an hourglass whose contents, no matter how often they were turned over, kept trickling away and mounding up on the bottom as a sediment of stubborn inability to learn from past mistakes.

With the perhaps two thousand men who were left, but without adequate ammunition, nothing could be accomplished except a bit of symbolic bombardment of the citadel, which in the meantime had been reinforced by the mercenaries from Grisons, and Theodor had to be grateful that the Genovese didn't attempt a sally, which would certainly have annihilated his threadbare army.

Embittered, the king lay down in his tent on his camp bed and surrendered to fever and apathy. Self-pity was followed by chills and toothache.

I want to be in a civilized country, he thought, in a great, bright city, in a comfortable bed. Gloomily he listened to the rain falling on the canvas, and later on the roof of the palanquin in which he was transported back. The red velvet curtains remained closed. One hand toyed with an open casket of silver coins stamped with his likeness.

In September, he was in Sartè. The generals had requested Theodor to choose a permanent royal residence and leave the campaigns to them. Theodor was happy to have escaped the episcopal palace in Cervioni, which was even smaller than his apartments in Florence. He wanted to be surrounded by a bit of luxury and pomp after the frugal and uncomfortable wandering life of the last few weeks and months. He needed more room for the library he had assembled, for the servants who looked after his bodily well-being. He felt weak and run-down, still dirty even after a bath, and his mouth, from which two more teeth had had to be pulled after the catastrophic campaign against Bastia, had a hollow, bitter taste.

In small things and in large, there are certitudes that exist in latency for a while, without metamorphosing into realities, and the passage of time must, so to speak, catch up with them.

As Theodor lay on his camp bed before the citadel of Bastia and the toothache began, it was a small thing to know that another hour of torture at the tooth extractor's would be inevitable, but he forgot this fact so completely in the following weeks that the pain also disappeared, and so when the day of the operation arrived, it was like a bolt from the blue and plunged him into panic.

As his shrunken army fired helpless cannonballs at the citadel, it was a large thing to be aware that sometime or other, he would have to interrupt his reign, his project, without having secured either one, in order to return to the continent and dig up additional weapons and credits. That was what awaited him, but Theodor had not the slightest intention of seizing the initiative himself, whether in a spirit of reconciliation or resignation, and taking steps to confront what was hostile and inevitable. As long as the moment had not yet arrived, it didn't exist and would never exist.

Thus from September on, Theodor knew that he must leave Corsica, where everything was still just getting started, and yet in a sense that was difficult to grasp, he simultaneously knew nothing of the sort, so that he was able to continue to rule with confidence, blind to the future.

In Portivechju, he personally welcomed the first Huguenots and Spanish Jews and presented them their citizenship papers. Forgotten for the moment were the heated discussions with the patricians. The new settlers luckily had no idea what objections had been raised. For the length of one day, the island showed itself from its most lovely side, eliciting exclamations of wonder from the newly arrived immigrants, and the images from Theodor's dreams of kingship and those now before his eyes were harmoniously superimposed beneath a gentle late summer sun.

In the next *consulta* in Sartè the situation of the kingdom—still not liberated from Genoa, still not universally recognized—was discussed, and Theodor frankly but with justifiable optimism brought forward all the statistics. The towns they had taken, the standing army, the mint and the incipient flow of money and exchange, the reopened mines, new manufactories, the first successes in export, the court that had now been established, and the laying of the cornerstone for the university represented a positive balance they could be proud of, despite all their setbacks and failures.

Nevertheless, there were questions about the king's unnecessarily luxurious personal budget, especially from those who had diverted Theodor's deliveries for their own use. In answer,

Don Luigi Giafferi and Ghjacintu Paoli each laid two sacks of gold onto the table, their personal fortunes, and donated them with simple words to the king and the homeland as a sign of their absolute belief in the victory of their common cause. This rotund little man, thought Theodor with emotion recalling the stinking office in Leghorn, he's spiny and tough as a Corsican chestnut, but from our first encounter he's never deserted me.

Theodor regarded the silence that followed this gesture as one of the high points of his reign, as was the solemn founding of the "Order of Knights of the Redemption" on the following day, the sixteenth of September.

Everything was a bit bigger, cleaner, and more magnificent than the hastily improvised coronation in Alisgiani, and the surroundings a more appropriate place than the humble episcopal palace of Cervioni to present himself, a gilded laurel wreath on his head and clad in a floor-length azure cape, as the grand master and to appoint the prime minister Giafferi and the commanding general knights of the order, while a further fifty worthy Corsicans—some present and some not—and foreigners (for a fee) were named satraps.

The medal that symbolized membership in the Order of the Redemption was the work of the same artist who had designed Theodor's coins. The king wore one on a ribbon six inches wide, the knights and satraps on progressively narrower cordons. It consisted of a green enamel medallion bordered by two stars, one superimposed on the other. The larger seven-pointed star was in gold and the smaller in sable. The medallion showed the nude figure of Justitia, her pudenda hidden by a belt with an oak leaf. In her right hand, she held a sword, in her left, the scales. She stood with her right leg bent, its foot resting on a mountain on a highly stylized map of Corsica. Beneath the sword floated the *globus cruciger*, beneath the scales a Masonic triangle enclosing the letter T. Each ray of the black star contained Theodor's family crest: a bird in flight and the letters U.L.I.P.

When Theodor announced that the Duke of Saxony-Weimar, Count Drost, the Count of Nassau-Weilburg, the Vicomte de Trévoux, as well as the Earls of Montague and Hamilton had also asked to be accepted into the fraternity, the Corsicans were proud and elated in a way possible only when one is celebrating oneself.

Either shortly before this day or shortly thereafter Theodor learned from Giafferi that Orticoni had assembled a third party, with himself as its leader, and intended to get rid of both the Genovese and the king. Money was becoming scarce. Autumn was coming. The times had caught up with time.

Theodor chose to ignore them. Sartè was a good place to live and rule from, and now he had his nephew Friedrich with him too, a dashing French soldier with fifty mercenaries from the Palatinate in his entourage, seeking to join the king's guard and be paid for it.

Friedrich was a strange young man: gallant, educated, more serious than Theodor at his age, his unfinished features ennobled by mourning for his mother. Theodor embraced him like a son and had him relate in detail Amélie's last years, which Theodor had not witnessed. Meanwhile, October passed.

On the first of November, Giafferi informed him that Orticoni had forged a plot to murder him. A hired assassin had been intercepted in Theodor's antechamber and had confessed under torture. Only now did it occur to the king that Angelina had quite possibly been a victim of the scheming cleric rather than the vengeful republic. Giafferi thought the moment ripe for the inevitable trip to the continent, so that they could mop up Orticoni and his machinations upon his return.

The king agreed without quite being willing to accept what it meant. Nor did he realize it yet on November fourth, during the journey from Sartè to Sulenzara, nor on the sixth in the little port town itself. He was looking forward to the continent, looking forward to narrating the last few months to listening audiences in richly elaborated tales, but simply could not get it into his head that this also meant leaving his kingdom. Not even when the little *tartane* set sail on November tenth and drew away from the quay. Not until it was no longer possible to leap back onto land, when even swimming back through the restless water was inconceivable, did the scales fall from Theodor's eyes.

He stood at the stern and to postpone even longer the realization of what had become obvious, he pulled from his pocket the poem of farewell that Overbeck, who was remaining on the island, had handed him on the quay with much bowing and scraping.

He thought nothing more of it than as something to distract his eyes. For a change, the poem had no title, no rhymes, no line breaks. Amazing! Perhaps the poet had finally realized he had no talent for any of that. Theodor read: *"My eyes have often followed the flight of birds above my head. I sensed that I too am but a traveler above the wind. A voice from heaven seemed to be telling me: Man, it is not yet time for you to leave. Wait until the wind of death is rising. Only then will you spread your wings and fly to those unknown regions your heart yearns for."*

Theodor looked up from the page in dismay and made an involuntary gesture as if to really fly back to the island rising round and dark from the morning mist. Standing next to him, Costa started and looked inquiringly at the king. Sweeney, leaning on the rail, had just lit his pipe and its smoke was pulled apart by the wind like a small personal parody of the haze shrouding the coastline of Corsica, above which floated the silhouette of the mountains like a castle in the clouds. A servant approached the king and offered him and the others tea. Upworth sighed luxuriously and asked for milk.

Theodor could not tear his eyes from the island. How unbelievably, overwhelmingly beautiful it was! It was slowly, majestically floating away, and he realized that his feelings had only just arrived on it.

Ubi libertas, ibi patria! This had been his homeland, the homeland of a homeless man, the place he had chosen and created for himself. This is my country, thought Theodor, appalled. He was compelled to think of his mother and his sister, both of whom had died without him, and his wife, whom he had left without a word. The regrets of a lifetime, never again to be made good.

But could he have done anything differently, so as not to be standing on this ship now, sailing east? Nothing occurred to him. He had never had a choice and had made all his decisions with the best of intentions. He had to remind himself that it was not good-bye forever, after all. It was a necessary and long-planned journey and in a few months he would return.

His gaze fell on the two journalists from the *Gentleman's Magazine*. They were standing next to each other at the bow rail and looking in the direction of the mainland.

"Isn't it a pleasant thought that after all these months, we're sailing toward home again!" said Mr. Upworth.

"I must agree with you there, Jeremiah," said Mr. Sweeney. "It's been a long time. I can hardly believe it, but I'm even looking forward to London fog and rain."

"Now, now. Let's not exaggerate," answered Mr. Upworth.

Chapter XIV

*I*N ORDER TO ESCAPE the Genovese bloodhounds and the bounty hunters hired by the republic, Theodor was forced to dodge from one secure enclave to the next, constantly seeking the protection of neutral or sympathetic courts and embassies. At the same time, he had to mollify his biggest creditors as quickly as possible (his personal creditors and those of the wobbly Kingdom of Corsica often being one and the same) by asking them for further advances and credits, juggling what little collateral he had to offer. As a figure notorious in all the banking houses of the continent, however, he was in a more favorable bargaining position than before. The only secure and trustworthy negotiating partner is a creditor to whom one is already so deeply in debt that one's own fall will pull him down too. Theodor thought he could neglect the others for the time being.

With a feeling of relief he couldn't quite put his finger on—was it because he had cast off the burden of day-to-day responsibility or because he looked forward to the chance to

improve upon his first, perforce dilettantish attempt to rule?—
he journeyed to Rome, inducted Cardinal Alberoni into the
fraternity of the Order of the Redemption, and in return received a letter of introduction to the king of Savoy.

The latter, while not in principle precluding support for
the struggle for independence, nevertheless revealed that he had
learned from Campredon and Amelot that Fleury was inclined
to respond to the republic's call for help. Having accomplished
little or nothing, but at least with the hope that Savoy was a
potential, if not particularly weighty ally, and above all reassured by the ceremonious way he had been received, Theodor
and his little entourage of twelve continued on toward Paris.

After a quarter of an hour spent at his sister's grave, at a
loss and not feeling much of anything, he reached the French
capital in the last week of January, settled into his quarters, and
sent a letter to Fleury in Versailles, requesting an audience.

There he met with a disappointment all the more sobering because his expectations, already raised by his visit to Turin,
had been more than exceeded during his first days in Paris.
Visiting cards fluttered into his apartments one after the other.
Journalists, sensation seekers, and high-class courtesans followed on one another's heels. Bankers and merchants fought
to have him at their table for supper. He spent his evenings in
the opera or the Théatre Français and his nights in the cafés,
surrounded by a clutch of chattering, drunken wits, supposedly
the most brilliant in Paris.

If he had been in a position to analyze coolly which circles
found him so attractive, he would have noticed it was above all
youthful philosophers, pamphleteers, young authors—in short,
the critical, intellectual elite—for whom he represented a hero
of freedom whose constitutional monarchy they celebrated as
revolutionary for its right of self-determination and rhetoric of

equality. Theodor, for whose taste there had been altogether too much constitution on Corsica, could only give a sour smile in response. The higher nobility and the courtiers, however, hung back noticeably, and no invitation was forthcoming from the palace.

But he didn't think about it, for he was spending his time with the young Diderot, got introduced to Marivaux after a premier in the "Français," and went out drinking with Prévost d'Exiles, the author of the story about the Chevalier des Grieux and Manon Lescaut, which Theodor had read on the sly in Berthelsdorf in times gone by. The writer, dressed like an abbé in a long black gown and clerical bands, was also the translator of Richardson's *Pamela* and appeared in public with his Dutch mistress Lenki Eckard, who struck Theodor as a more cosmopolitan version of Angelina, a young woman with flaxen hair and large incisors who when she bowed revealed a décolleté whose lace trim encircled her nipples like petals around a pistil.

He spent most of his time, however, surrounded by ten or fifteen intently listening men and a few young women, debating the theory and practice of government with Montesquieu—that is, from time to time he would intersperse quotes from Locke and anecdotes from Corsica into the flow of Secondat's words.

But his sojourn in Paris reached its apogee on January twenty-ninth when two pistol shots were fired at his carriage on its way to the opera. Or rather, the evening would finally reach its high point once he had overcome his shock—the balls pierced the wooden paneling and buried themselves in the blue upholstery of the seat opposite Theodor—for his two Corsican bodyguards on the coach box fired back wildly into the darkness, the horses shied, panic broke out on the street, and the news that there had been an attempt on the life of the King of

Corsica ran like wildfire ahead of Theodor in the direction of the opera. There, the beginning of the performance was delayed on his account, the crowd on the steps opened a cordon before his slightly trembling steps, and as he entered his box, the hall rose with ooh's and ah's and applause before the orchestra finally began the overture.

All this was poor preparation for the next day, when he drove out to Versailles under the protection of his bodyguards with muskets at the ready and pressed his visiting card into the hand of a bored secretary.

In the course of the following hours, he traveled a *via crucis* through three antechambers and was repeatedly asked to identify himself. King? Of Corsica? But that island was a possession of the republic of Genoa, not a monarchy . . . So he was the Baron . . . eh . . . the Freiherr Neuhoff. From where? Westphalia? He waited, growing more nervous by the minute. He peered around, blushing, to see if anyone was making fun of him, stared down into the inner courtyard, and watched the shadows lengthen on its buildings angled this way and that, its arcades, staircases, and shortcuts, where thousands of courtiers lived out their pent-up lives. It was like in his boyhood, when the duchess had ordered him to stand all day at just such a window, watching the movements of certain persons, and noting down whom they met and at what time. His first assignment as a spy.

Fleury did not receive him. Amelot was supposedly not in. His note was returned.

He remained not one more day in Paris.

But the humiliation in Versailles was nothing compared to what awaited him in Amsterdam. To be sure, he became careless in the city of his patrons and financiers. He somewhat lost sight of his mission, or if not his mission, then the speed with which he ought to be carrying it out if he were to return to his island and establish facts on the ground before France had a chance to intervene. In the prosaic light of Amsterdam, in the cool wind off the canals, it was simply impossible to imagine such romantic dangers as a pistol shot at a velvet-lined coach on its way to the opera. Theodor stayed in a house on the Prinsengracht and recovered from the disdain of the French politicians by telling elaborate stories about Corsica. He yielded a bit too much to the almost irresistible urge to reap the rewards for all his trouble from the admiring eyes of his listeners and from the town gossip they brought with them.

In the night from April sixteenth to the seventeenth, he played cards and then walked home through the moist morning air, somewhat poorer than he had been at the beginning of the evening. At the door of his lodgings, he was arrested by four men in uniform while his bodyguards looked on helplessly. That is, if Theodor had guessed or been able to believe that he was actually being arrested, he probably wouldn't have gone along so peacefully. He only realized his situation when they wouldn't answer any of his questions, there was no official to explain things to him, and they shoved him into a filthy cell with a barred window, where he stumbled and fell to the floor. When he got to his feet, there was a big, wet, smelly stain on his cloak.

Two hours later, in an office on the second floor of the same building, he learned what he was being accused of. A former creditor, utterly forgotten in the meantime, had gotten wind of his presence in Amsterdam (which was not at all difficult to do), produced a ten-year-old promissory note that had never been paid off, and demanded that it be enforced and Theodor put into coercive detention. It was a matter of a few thousand gulden.

Theodor reacted with biting condescension and all the corrosive sarcasm a king imprisoned on account of five thousand gulden is capable of. With a careless wave of his hand, he named a banker who would cash the letter of credit he drew from his pocket. The official was impressed by his behavior, but only until a messenger returned late in the afternoon with the news that the banker had declared bankruptcy and was not in the position to make any payments whatsoever.

A judge with a face as yellow as a quince, an ill-fitting full-bottomed wig with gray, wiry hair sticking out from under it, and brownish, equine teeth, declared succinctly that if he could not pay off his debt, monsieur the king would remain under arrest until his case could be heard. Theodor was given two rooms, a bedroom and a living room cum study, and was permitted to have a valet and his secretary with him, but the door remained locked.

He only became aware of the full extent of his situation the following morning when the newspapers were brought in, at first only the *Gazette of Amsterdam* and the *Utrecht Gazette*. At least the headline in the former was "King of Corsica in Amsterdam Debtor's Prison," but the latter called him "the German adventurer Baron Neuhoff" who "attracted so much notice last year when he had himself crowned king by Corsican rebels."

The journalists who had accompanied him over the course of the previous years as devoted Eumenides were transformed into Erinyes whose torches and serpents were rhetoric and malice. Every blow of their whip drove him to madness. He fled through both locked rooms, knocking over the table and sending papers sailing to the ground and the inkpot to shatter on the floorboards. He threw himself against the heavy oak door, broke the stained glass window, and cut his wrists. "No, no," he stammered, "don't let this happen on account of five thousand gulden!" With every blow of their whip, lurid, indelible images of an abyss of ridicule exploded before his eyes. Much more than the cell, he wanted to escape the narrow chamber of time, the mousetrap in which he was caught.

The reverberations of his imprisonment were commensurate with the interest his projects had aroused in media and society throughout Europe. Like an addict, Theodor devoured every line of it. He held the newspapers with trembling hands, his wrists wrapped in thick bandages. He got drunk on gin. He vomited. His stomach was as tense as a vibrating cello string. His toothaches started up again. He fell into bed with a fever. He sweated and suffered. Don't perish like this, he thought. If I've got to die, then by my own hand. The most humiliating thing was the healthy appetite that returned as soon as his fever let up.

Meanwhile, his debts had quintupled, for the Genovese consul was combing the city, looking for old creditors who could be mobilized, and every day Theodor passed under arrest produced a new one to add his name to the list of those who had lost faith in him and now wanted to see him bleed.

Theodor had already secured the noose (a sturdy silk cord used to tie back the canopy of his bed during the day) to the ceiling of his study. His lunch had been delivered, so that no further disturbance was to be expected before tea time. He had dismissed his colleagues. To get a sense of the gruesome death he was about to die, he fingered his neck, and the tender warmth and gentle pulse of life beneath his skin were so overwhelming that he broke into tears of sympathy for this poor, lovely body, his only protection and hiding place. And was it now his intention to mistreat it, cause it pain, extinguish himself and abandon his own skin, condemning it to black, shriveled, stinking putrefaction? No, he couldn't do that to his body. He shook his head while the tips of his fingers still gingerly stroked the large-pored skin below the edge of his beard.

In his mind's eye, he saw the larger-than-life carnival figures in Venice, with small men—and sometimes women—on
stilts concealed beneath their robes. In the same way, he retreated behind his skin, which suddenly seemed much too large
for him, and through its eye holes he cast furtive glances onto
the outside world.

But you can get used to anything, even to newspaper articles, and after three weeks in prison, his interest in reading
waning with each passing day, Theodor had to admit that his
ability to think and plan was returning. Some encouraging written testimonials—a letter from Costa as well as several articles
in a respectful tone that counterbalanced the initial malice—
did their part, as did the return of Jacob Cats from England,
who promised to put up bail.

On the seventh of May, the King of Corsica left his cell in
the Stadhuis, pushing his way through a crowd of people. Cats
threw a party in his honor, at which, among all the beautiful
young women, Theodor's eye fell on a matron with a puffy face
disfigured by brownish spots who seemed to be examining him
with narrowed eyes almost hidden behind rolls of fat. He felt
her gaze following him and took refuge behind his host. Did
he really not remember her, Cats asked with a thin smile. It was
the widowed Mijfrouw Els van Boon.

Back in his rooms, his face aflame, Theodor ran to the
large mirror above the mantelpiece, candle in hand, to reassure
himself that the years had not deformed him as well.

Further letters from Corsica informed the king that Genoa's
attempts to use his imprisonment as propaganda by broadcast-
ing it from the battlements of the citadel in Bastia had not only
failed, but had caused his subjects to bombard the city around
the fort into rubble. With a smug smile, Theodor exploited the

dialectics of publicity which had gained the king, imprisoned for debt but released in the end, a whole new cohort of financiers attracted to his oft-repeated name. He outfitted a ship with arms and ammunition and set sail on the thirtieth of June. At the beginning of August, a half-day's sail beyond the Straits of Gibraltar, he was captured by Spaniards who escorted him to Oran and confiscated his cargo. On the nineteenth he was freed by an edict of the Spanish crown and allowed to continue to Sardinia, from where he returned to Holland without having accomplished a thing.

In February of the following year, French troops under the command of the Marquis de Boissieux landed on Corsica. According to all reports reaching Theodor's ears, they wreaked more havoc than the Genovese ever had. There were rumors of massacres and pillaging and somewhere on the island there was still Friedrich, his nephew and son.

Then in October, after a sojourn in Florence, Theodor was on his island again for the length of a day. Giafferi and Paoli had been forced into exile and reported that the Corsican people still stood behind him, but for the moment, it was illusory to expect to reestablish the monarchy. For Theodor, in any event, saving his Frédéric was much more urgent. But the young man had disappeared into the Macchia with a few partisans and was inflicting many casualties in skirmishes with de Boissieux's soldiers. Theodor had in his possession a letter from General Wachtendonk, commander of the Habsburg garrison in Tuscany, to the French high command, demanding safe conduct for the young Trévoux.

De Boissieux died in February '39 and was replaced by the Marquis de Maillebois, a much more judicious man, who succeeded in pacifying the Corsicans with diplomacy and courtesy, whereas his predecessor had failed with murder and terror, although he had kept them in check. In Florence, Theodor was finally able to wrap his nephew in an embrace and arrange a commission for him as a colonel in Wachtendonk's regiment. From there, then from Venice, and again from Amsterdam, he followed Maillebois's policies with increasing panic. Every guarantee that the Marquis granted, every concession he promised to make tamed the battle-weary Corsicans a bit more and won more of them over to the idea of French sovereignty, especially since the Genovese had no more say in the matter and the islanders derived no small pleasure from maligning and intriguing against their old masters with their new ones.

As he had five years earlier, Theodor organized the rebels' illegal trade from Venice and Florence, corresponded with them, gave advice and encouragement, so as not to lose the legitimacy he still enjoyed among the people, the only thing left from all his efforts. It was the only way he could continue to speak to banks, trading houses, and hesitant governments in the name of the Corsicans, touring Europe in the role of their king.

He had sunk from laurel-crowned monarch to Amsterdam convict, and had escaped the purgatory of humiliation like a phoenix minus only a few feathers. He had become less thin-skinned vis-à-vis his personal dignity and majesty. In his letters and personal appearances he had hit upon a tone that combined supplication and demand, and joined the spirit of sovereignty to the spirit of barter.

The recovery of his throne became an idée fixe and although Theodor did not have a good feeling about it, he sensed that it was nevertheless too late to let it drop. Never before did I bet everything on one card, he thought, for I knew that this is exactly what would happen. Every day that goes by is a lost day for any other activity or alternative course of action, one more day of disappointed hopes in the only thing that matters, where success becomes more and more necessary the longer it's postponed.

He had given up the idea of ever liberating Corsica from within by himself, at the head of his people. Monitoring the diplomatic situation in Europe and sounding out diplomats, devouring newspapers, pursuing political astrology and geometry, and reading tea leaves, he was looking for a chance to gain the help of a great power in consolidating his pretensions to the throne. The island itself was reduced to a pawn in his calculations.

The vanes of the propaganda windmill he was forced to operate turned and turned without rest, while he himself sat in their middle like the pivot bearing. He just had to wait. Meanwhile, as he told himself repeatedly, he was getting older and older.

In December 1740, the Prussians invaded Silesia. At the same time, England was engaged in a half-hearted naval campaign against Spain because an English captain had gotten his ear cut off, and for the first time in fifteen years, the seat of the prime minister was starting to totter seriously. The following spring, Maillebois was recalled to France because Fleury had formed an alliance with the Prussians (after their victory at Mollwitz) and the Spanish for the purpose of hemming in the Habsburgs, and that took precedence over his support for Genoa. Around the middle of the year, the French troops left Corsica and with their departure, the republic reasserted its former unjust sovereignty. In January, the English king dismissed his prime minister Walpole, who had little taste for war, and the "Patriotic Whigs" came to power and formed

an alliance with Vienna. This was the constellation that
Theodor had to exploit.

He composed a twenty-page memorandum, part strategic white
paper, part offer of an alliance, part letter of extortion, and journeyed to Vienna, arriving early in May. What he had to offer
was a liberated Corsica, under his rule, as a naval base in the
Mediterranean to patrol the shipping lanes and keep Tuscany
and Sardinia from falling into Spanish hands, and if worse came
to worst, as a strategic staging area for conflicts with France or
the Turks. He went so far as to suggest that if he were to die
without male heirs, Corsica would devolve upon the empire
(which didn't exactly correspond to either the letter or the spirit
of the general capitulation he had signed with the Corsicans in
days gone by). Nor did he mince words when asked what the
consequences would be if the empire refused his terms, and thus
ensured his own downfall: with grim certainty, the island would
fall into the hands of the Bourbons, the Habsburgs would
sooner or later lose their Italian possessions, and trade in the
Mediterranean would be dependent on the whims of Madrid.

Theodor stood at the map table, pointing, explaining, elu-
cidating with cold but charmingly packaged logic and listened
to himself as if listening to a complete stranger. The room
slowly filled with ministers and generals, the air grew heavy with
the smells of wig powder, pipe smoke, and horse manure. There
was an atmosphere of lethargic panic, with much nodding,
murmuring, and clearing of throats.

In what seemed but a heartbeat, a blink of the eye later,
Theodor found himself sitting beside John Carteret in an official box adorned with golden plasterwork, looking up and to the
left where King George II had just been brought to his feet by
the fanfares of the Hallelujah Chorus, followed a split second

later by his foreign minister (whose raised eyebrows signaled Theodor to do the same) and the entire audience of Covent Garden.

So much was coming together at this culminating moment in Theodor's life. The tropical storm of the present was crashing against the jetty wall of his memories, the receding waves meeting the oncoming ones in a thunderous burst and instantaneously rearing up together and clambering over each other, crowned with foam and explosions of spray. Theodor stood listening to the jubilant chorus and tears began running down his cheeks, registered approvingly by those around him as a tribute to the music of his German countryman.

He recalled how he had stood outside Covent Garden almost twenty years ago, leaning against the wall and listening to the echoes of Handel's Italian operas with Jane. And now, not three weeks ago, the empire in the person of the Archduke of Lorraine had become his ally—not in writing, to be sure, for "we can't risk doing *that*, my dear Baron!" An enormous sum of money, however, had been allocated by Vienna to outfit an English naval fleet so that the King of Corsica could reconquer his land. Accompanying the money was a message in secret code (Theodor smiled nostalgically at the sight of de Vigenère's cryptographic tables) to the English government. And so Theodor had come to London to spend his ample resources and with the power of two European courts behind him, to take at last what was rightfully his.

In a willful attempt to sound out just how much the gods were prepared to spoil him, he had diverted his route toward the English capital so as to pass through the Electorate of Saxony. He had intended finally to fetch his wife back and enthrone her at his side as the Queen of Corsica. You see, he was going to say to her, it was worth disappearing in the dead of night. And then, frozen in disbelief, he had stood at her grave in the little Herrnhut cemetery. The slanting rays of the spring sun fell on the light-colored stone. Engraved on it in four lines of gold letters were all her names and titles. No trace of his name. Here lay a Lady Jane Ormond, not a Baroness Neuhoff.

Oh thou of little faith, he had murmured, shaking his head. What are ten years? You should have known I would come back. You should have trusted me, but instead, you just went and died.

Outside the cemetery wall, on unconsecrated ground, there was a single grave. Here lay Larbi, passed away a month after Jane. Having served his mistress to the end, the servant had done honor to his master to the end.

And today, his master was listening to Handel's oratorio in the box of the English foreign minister after having dined with the English king, who was delighted to be able to speak German and complained about having to conduct business with his ministers in a kind of bastardized Latin. In the afternoon, the young Horace Walpole, son of the previous prime minister and for years a avowed partisan of Theodor's, had taken him to the newly opened swimming baths.

"Isn't it magnificent, Your Majesty?" he had said, "It's the first one of its kind in the world, as revolutionary in its way as your Corsican constitution."

Theodor's admiration cooled considerably when he learned that the large pool was by no means meant only for private use, but rather there were as many people floundering through its water every day as there were goldfish in the pond of Fontainebleau. "So they swim back and forth, do they?" he said. "Well, there must be something symbolic about it for most of them."

All well and good, including that he would now become King of Corsica in a different way than he had the first time—

not by bargaining and brawling, without humiliation, intrigue, or rancor, and also without having to take the sensitivities of the natives into account. His former idealism had given way to a conception that seemed more like a cross between Maillebois's style of rule and that of the Genovese high commissioner. And as the oratorio came to an end, Theodor concluded with a certain bitterness that there was a huge difference between expectation and gratification.

I'm turning forty-eight this year. I'm an old man, no Alexander. I get what I want, but I get it late. Only a young man can find true happiness, one who has never been thrown off course by defeat. Later in life, it's as if the pile of gold were only concealing a cesspool. It shines and shimmers, but the stink still comes through.

The image of a golden cesspool was apt, but although he may have thought it up in a moment free of illusions, still it wasn't the sort of insight the helped one continue to live one's life. The fact is, that a few months later, standing on the bridge of the *Revenger* next to Captain George Barclay and inhaling the spicy air deep into his lungs, not the slightest smell of excrement reached his nose. And even though he was forty-eight years old, what he felt there on board his Majesty's ship of the line, in sight of the Corsican coast shimmering in the haze, was expectation and not gratification. Afterward he would often tell himself that in that instant, at the moment when what he yearned for was near enough to touch and he felt in complete control of the situation, God ought to have held his breath, so that the moment could have become an eternity.

From June to October, he had planned the reconquest of Corsica, financed by Austria and executed by England. Several ships carrying everything needed by the rebellion, led by the *Revenger* and the *Salisbury* under Captain Peter Osborn, had sailed into the Mediterranean via Lisbon, chock-full of English soldiers and under his own command. Whatever was happening on the continent had only been of peripheral interest to Theodor during that summer and fall.

In the waters off the Corsican coast, they had sunk the Spanish warship *San Isidoro* with a hundred and twenty cannon, captured a dozen smaller Genovese vessels, and welcomed the repatriated Corsican leaders Giafferi and Luca Ornano on board off Isula Rossa, given them instructions, and landed weapons, ammunition, and uniforms.

Theodor had ordered that Bastia was to be attacked and taken on the eighth of March, unless the new Genovese high commissioner raised the white flag.

On the evening of March fifth, a *tartane* sailing under the British flag made fast alongside the *Revenger* and the English ambassador to Florence, Mr. Horace Mann, boarded up a rope ladder.

"I assume you would like to be present as we begin to reconquer the island tomorrow?" said Theodor.

The ambassador fixed his eyes on a striking clock on the wall and shook his head. "I'm afraid not, Sir," he answered.

Theodor, sitting so that he could look through the tall cabin window at the coast, calmly asked what the other meant by his answer.

He had been delegated by his government, Mann explained, to express to the baron their regret that on the highest authority, no British ship was to attack sovereign Genovese territory.

"And whence this change of heart?" asked Theodor, still calm, his gaze still resting on the coast, which was so close he thought he could count the leaves on the trees.

He was not able to tell him for certain. A change of priorities, Sir. A direct affront to Spain was no longer considered opportune. Mr. Mann's voice trembled a little. "No longer opportune?" Theodor repeated with an ironic undertone.

Quite right, Sir, so he had been told.

"Whom do I have to thank for this? Carteret?"

He only knew this much, that neither Carteret nor his front man Compton were having an easy time of it at present. Public opinion . . . Mister Walpole . . . Obviously, someone had convinced the king that a land war against France was the most the Exchequer could be expected to support . . . The eventuality of naval warfare against Spain and perhaps France as well . . . His Majesty must surely understand that. Perhaps next year, he had been told. After all, they continued to have interests in common with—

"*Perhaps next year?*" Theodor interrupted him, drawing out each syllable. Hastily, the ambassador continued: it went without saying that compensation, an indemnity, had been reserved for His Highness. He had been instructed to issue him this letter of credit. Moreover, there was no question but that they would pay the cost of an appropriate domicile . . .

Theodor asked the ambassador to step outside with him, onto the narrow catwalk outside the captain's cabin. "Can you smell the air?" he asked. "There's an offshore breeze: thyme, mint . . ."

The ambassador nodded. They were silent a while. Then Mr. Mann started speaking again. Lord Carteret had also asked His Majesty to think over another suggestion. He had much experience in—eh—secret diplomacy . . . And the foreign minister wondered whether perhaps, since the Corsican matter was not going anywhere for the moment, he might feel inclined to be of service to the English crown and—how should he put it?—take a look around in Savoy, Naples, Florence?

"Why not," said Theodor. "We could certainly talk about it. Might I ask you a favor in return?"

The ambassador bowed.

"I would not want my people's last sight of me to give them the impression that I was shamelessly leaving them in the lurch. Is it within your power, before we depart for Leghorn or wherever it may be, to allow us to circumnavigate the island so that my subjects might derive courage and reassurance from the sight of me on this ship and continue their just and holy struggle for freedom?"

And so it was to be. In several harbors, the flags of the royalists fluttered. Cannonades were shot off in tribute, and Theodor stood on the bridge and waved.

As the *Revenger* and the *Salisbury* then fell off before the wind, set a southward course, and widened the gap between themselves and the rugged coastline, Theodor leaned on the rail. He had already taken a step toward the cabin door, but could not or would not yet tear himself from the sight of the island. His left hand rested on his hip. The contours of Corsica dissolved in the evening mist. He squared his shoulders, completed the step he had adumbrated and initiated hours ago, released the coast from his gaze, and stepped inside.

In the spring of 1744, Theodor was living in Siena. He called himself Baron von Bergheim and employed ten men as valets, secretaries, and stewards. He maintained a large establishment and paid in English pounds.

In the fall of 1745, he appeared at the Savoyard court in Turin with a white paper on the liberation of Corsica. He wore a collarless violet dress coat, its lapels and pockets trimmed with brocade. On his breast was the medal of the Grand Master of the Order of the Redemption and around his waist a green-gold satin sash. His suggestions were rejected.

In July 1746, back from a journey to Vienna where he had hoped to find renewed support for his pretensions to the throne, he sublet lodgings from a furniture maker in the suburb of Volterra.

In February 1747, he traveled again to Vienna with the same object, disguised as a priest, and was given a bed and handouts by various lodge brothers, but was not received at court.

In August 1747, a detachment of soldiers sought him out in the cheap boarding house in Florence where he occupied a room and presented him with an expulsion order.

Toward the end of the year, he was in Cologne, staying with his distant relative, Baron Drost. From there, he shuttled back and forth between Amsterdam and Hamburg, both avoiding and seeking his creditors, since they were his only source of money. He called himself Baron von Stein, Sir John Palmer, Abbate Lacenere. He gambled, sold off his Corsican medals and coins, and performed various services.

In January 1749, he arrived in London with a letter of recommendation from the Dutch minister Hop which gained him access to high society and diplomatic circles. He called himself Baron von Stein, but made sure everyone knew who he really was. The Republic of Genoa was still demanding his extradition, but Thomas Pelham refused to carry it out.

The now gaunt, gray-haired man who had been king for the space of one summer became the attraction of the London salons for the space of one summer. The Swiss ambassador Schaub paid Theodor a princely sum to lend brilliance to his receptions. In his presence, the young Horace Walpole presented his collection of *Neuhoffiana*, as he called them, which turned Theodor into an historical curiosity, a man who only had his past to look forward to.

They called him "Your Majesty" again. They talked of the extravagance of his attire, the dignity of his public appearances. He was already beginning to think he was a made man again, when at one of Schaub's receptions on the evening of December twenty-first, he was arrested for having run up several million pounds of debt.

The leader of the uniformed officers, a youngster who was looking around uncertainly, asked him, "Sir, are you Baron Neuhoff, the King of Corsica?"

Theodor, much too aware of the New Testament connotations of the scene to be able to resist a bon mot, stretched out his hands, lowered his head, and answered, "Thou sayest it."

The onlookers laughed and continued to applaud until he had been escorted from the room.

Chapter XV

THE KING SURVEYED THE set: plank-bed, nightstand and oil lamp, the latrine in the corner. In the middle of the room, the desk with a pile of half-finished letters and the stack of white paper on which he actually had intended to write his memoirs. Up to now, not a single word of them had flowed from his pen. Something within him refused to discuss his own person in the past tense. Beyond the desk, the rough-hewn board, bowed beneath its load of books. New works of belles lettres he hadn't read yet, historical treatises, periodicals. In the second cell, into which a little daylight fell through a light well, the heavy, tasteless piece of furniture which was to a real throne as an unconsecrated wafer is to the body of Christ. Next to it, a place for his visitor to sit. The psyche. The musicians sat against the wall with the barred window, waiting for their signal.

"Where are the mandolin players for the Vivaldi?" asked the king severely.

Two men rose from the shadow of the vault, still gnawing on chicken bones. Theodor nodded. "Did you get enough to eat and drink?"

"Certainly, Sir! Thank you, Your Majesty. It was enough for yesterday and the day before. For today's hunger we'll eat next week!"

"William," the king asked, "what can we offer our guest as an aperitif?"

"Only the sherry Mr. Walpole left here last time, Sir."

"Notify him to send some wine and cognac," said the king.

He took his place on the throne. He only knew the famous tragedian from seeing him on stage. Who would he appear as today? The light-footed Harlequin or the lame Richard? No, there's only one king here. *Ha? am I king? 'Tis so.* A line that stays with you. *O bitter consequence.* And yet he had lived worse in recent years than he was living now. The dialectics of freedom. Fate had seen to it that he was able to live as he had always dreamed of living: ruminating undisturbed upon himself, without being distracted by the demands of the day. He had to confess to a certain inconsistency in not being satisfied but wanting to escape this confinement. But no matter where he had spent time in his life, he had only been able to stand it because he could leave any time he wanted. And yet, once the arc of a journey had reached its longed-for goal, you always found yourself in the same old place: surrounded by four walls that differed from the present ones only in their details. Ah, the world of details!

The idea for this meeting was a product of Horace Walpole's fertile brain. He was doing everything imaginable, everything in his power to get Theodor out of prison. Since it was illusory to think Theodor would ever repay his debts, only a pardon could help. And Walpole thought a pardon would be more likely if London society and the court were applauding David

Garrick in a tragedy that the actor would write and perform: the Tragedy of the Glory and Misery of the King of Corsica. The cathartic tears of an entire city might float Theodor back out to freedom. That was the plan, and now it was up to Theodor to win the actor and playwright over to it, that is, win him over to himself, ignite his inspiration and give it a leg up.

Garrick was announced, Theodor gave the musicians a sign, the mandolin concerto began, and he watched as the man, his face hidden in the shadow of his hat, came through the door and involuntarily matched the rhythm of his steps to the music. Before Theodor's throne, he doffed his hat and bowed so deeply that its feather brushed the floor. Then he lifted his face into the light.

"Your Majesty," he said in a loud, clear voice, and the king admired how the words hovered between affirmation and question, how the first, third, and fourth syllables emerged quickly and naturally while the second was retarded by a slight suspension, as if the speaker were listening for an instant to the echo of the first. Theodor heard how palatal it sounded, as if it had already been thoroughly masticated and its taste and appropriateness tested for this situation. On stage, thought Theodor, this is how one addresses a king whose fate has already been decided. Not cynically, not even ironically, but stretching the ominous word out enough to keep all options open.

While the theater owner's hat and coat were taken and a chair offered to him, Theodor studied his face from up close for the first time, without having his features distorted by thick makeup.

It was a doughy face, not in the least gaunt (which would have limited its range of expression) nor chubby either, but literally doughy: moldable. That raised the question of how Theodor should behave and present himself. If he were sitting across from a man made of granite, then it would be easy to wrap himself around the other's personality and respond to it in the same tone and mood, making communication possible. But what do you do when your interlocutor is himself a master of kneadability?

"Mister Garrick, it is an honor and a pleasure for me in receive you here in my throne room. May I offer you a glass of sherry? The circumstances preclude my bar being better stocked."

"I was longing for a sherry in any case. May I offer you a Havana in return, Sire? The house rules do allow you to smoke, don't they?"

"They only forbid me fetching some for myself. There are advantages to possessing an empire."

"Unfortunately, it's not my personal possession. My own realm is restricted to the Drury Lane Theatre."

"Whose fame is hardly less than that of the other."

Garrick gave a slight bow. For a moment, both were occupied with sniffing, cutting, and lighting their cigars. The actor rose to give the king a light. The smoke was drawn toward the candle flame and gathered above the table in a violet cloud. Transparent veils billowed toward the musicians.

"Dear Drury Lane Theatre," resumed Theodor. "How does it look? Is success still its constant companion? What are you putting on this season? I'm completely out of touch. Nothing is more detrimental to one's social life than a spell in prison."

"Oh, success, success," croaked Garrick in a choked voice and grabbed his throat. "Pardon me, Your Majesty, but I have a touch of pharyngitis from constantly bellowing into cold, damp halls. Yes, success. It's a tricky business . . ."

"You astonish me, Garrick. I've never been in your theater when there wasn't a full house."

"But once you subtract the free tickets for friends, critics, schnorrers, freeloaders, and aristocrats, Sir—and don't forget that Shakespeare's plays are unmanageably long, complex, and require a horde of actors who all need to be fed . . ."

"Which one are you rehearsing for the upcoming season?"

"*King Lear*," said Garrick, looking straight into the king's eyes. "Surely you know it . . ."

Theodor shook his head, "No, I've never read it. What's it about?"

Garrick stood up as if it were impossible for him to think sitting down. "It's the story of a king who . . ."

Theodor leaned forward, "Is it similar to the play you're planning to write about me?"

"Not exactly. The king goes mad, and so do I, for the fact is, Lear won't fill my cashbox."

He stood leaning forward, resting his arms on the back of his chair, and looked toward the musicians as if seeking their help before lifting his glass to his lips.

"May I be permitted to recite to you, Sire, what I have written as a prologue for the upcoming season? I would be pleased to have your opinion of it."

"By all means," Theodor urged.

"Sacred to Shakespeare was this spot design'd
To pierce the heart, and humanize the mind.
But if an empty House, the Actor's curse,
Shews us our Lears and Hamlets lose their force;
Unwilling we must change the nobler scene,
And in our turn present you Harlequin.
Quit Poets and set Carpenters to work,
Shew gaudy scenes, or mount the vaulting Turk.

"And then my conclusion:

> *Sublimity's soon forgotten. 'Tis no puzzle,*
> *That what we really long for is to guzzle.*"

"Hmm," answered Theodor, "*guzzle* isn't very pretty. How about,

> *With stomachs grumbling, actors drop their rhyme,*
> *But given three square meals, they are sublime.*"

It took the astonished Garrick a moment for his features to catch up with his astonishment.

"But you're a poet!" he cried at last. Theodor waved his hand in deprecation. He was displeased when anyone expressed surprise at his talents.

"As far as eating is concerned, you'll be well compensated this evening. There's to be mince pie, Yorkshire pudding, a rack of lamb, a Moorish sorbet, and finally a crème caramel flambée and Stilton. But to return to our subject, tell me how you rehearse a role like King Lear. After all, you're not someone who portrays the common human passions with symbolic means, like the actors I've seen in France, but rather with concrete affect. In England I believe it was Mr. Betterton, was it not, who emphasized beautiful linguistic cadences, undergirded by correspondingly static gestures."

"Yes, that old mummy!" cried the thespian, his face getting red and splotchy. "Where do the passions begin, after all? Where do they appear? In the body! What's your reaction to fear, fright, or surprise? Cold sweat. And arrogant dummies like him want to present hot passion with Olympian calm! A mime may sweat, or a stagehand, but such a thing is beneath the dignity of an actor!

They make their mouths as round as if they were kneeling before their friend and pleasuring him. And their vacant, bovine eyes! They stand there as if they had no knee joints and their arms were brass pendulums. Their necks are so stiff they can't move their heads. And then those dull, dry, dreary voices, that in the end put the audience to sleep more effectively than a dose of opium. No, it's work to be on stage, Sire, physical work, you see. To play Lear, for example, or the play about you . . . but we really do have to talk about that. What should I know, what do I need to discover? A certain something, a gesture, a certain way of lifting and turning your head, a heaviness, or perhaps a lightness of movement which I must absorb until I've mastered it, something characteristic of a sovereign alone, the core from which everything else develops organically. Why do you think I'm so often sick, Your Majesty? Because I place inhuman demands on my body. Would you like to hear all the things I suffer from? Bilious colic, gout, jaundice, flatulence, black tongue. Can you imagine, Sire, what it means to be flatulent on stage?"

Garrick's remarks were getting a bit too physical and personal for Theodor, so he raised his eyebrows and said, "Giving the body free reign upon the stage must needs be part of the new epoch that esteems freedom, in and of itself, more highly than public decency. It seems to me only natural that an age that raises the banner of man's right to be however he wants, also releases the body from the control of the intellect, most especially on stage, where the public, for its instruction and delectation, gets to see for the first time what will soon be happening in the streets."

"But freedom, Sire," interjected a deflated Garrick, "isn't that the star that shone above your kingdom of Corsica? The preamble to your constitution was published in gazettes all over Europe . . ."

Theodor felt he needed to put a stop to the actor's liberal flatulence, and said, "In my opinion, freedom belongs to the realm of the spirit, not the body. It belongs to the soul, not the state. As idea, it has a good chance of being able to retain its irony. As deed, it quickly slides into anarchy and barbarity."

"But your preamble, your Corsica," cried the actor indignantly.

"A playbook, and you of all people should know that everything depends on interpretation, on tone. Although I will concede that you're more likely to get the tone right if the script is good. We should all get a chance to live out Shakespeare's texts, instead of just having to toss each thought into the foggy sea of words like a fishing line and hope we'll catch something."

"I confess that I never feel more confident than when I'm on stage, speaking my lines."

"Yes," Theodor answered, "that's because these stage words are the most profound thing you have the privilege to express."

"Indeed. Sometimes when I remove my makeup after the performance, I fear I shall wipe away the face beneath it as well."

"That wouldn't be so tragic. One of the greatest insights of my life has been that makeup is the most important thing."

"And who are you, Your Majesty, without makeup?"

"That is a secret. And I have much too much respect for secrets to wish to reveal them. Especially those I keep from myself."

"But Sire," continued Garrick, leaning forward with his tongue between his lips and obviously thinking he was on the brink of grasping that certain something he so badly needed to put him on the right thespian track, "when you're all by yourself, sitting here all alone in silence, what do you do then? What do you think about?"

"Then I wallow in what I call time-sickness."

"Nostalgia for past greatness," said Garrick solemnly.

"Perhaps, but nostalgia is only the melancholy side of yearning. If you want to call it nostalgia, however, it's of a slightly different kind than my young friend Walpole has."

It was high time to bring the conversation back to the play via this detour, if Garrick was not to fritter away the entire evening with his chatter.

"He's making half of London rebellious, Your Majesty. He puts papers, coins, and all sorts of other things from Corsica on exhibit. Wherever he goes, he asserts that England and his father left you in the lurch and he's trying to bring the wheel of world history to a halt . . ."

"Quite a successful attempt," said Theodor.

"He organizes donations and benefit performances. Between you and me, he's a whirling dervish of activity who suffers from not having a passion of his own, something that affects him directly."

"Don't think any less of such a person," Theodor countered. "Our age suffers from a surfeit of passion. I find a fleet-footed spirit, with more curiosity than passion, very congenial. You musn't always try to penetrate to the crux of all existence, especially when you can't be sure what awaits you there. An amateur, a dilettant can achieve wonderful results in the course of his life. To quote yourself, my dear Garrick, one doesn't necessarily need to feel the cold sweat of an epiphany on one's brow to grasp that one is alive. A man like young Walpole is attracted by anything that turns up, and occasionally, when he leans over the edge of a deep well, he falls right in. The important thing is that he find his way back out again."

"I'm the same way," put in Garrick, who felt this witty encomium of Walpole to be a distraction from talk about himself.

"I'm as at home in St. James as I am in St. Giles, and I observe people wherever I go. It's the goal and purpose of my life: to slip, body and soul, into ever-changing figures and costumes, to be a different person over and over again."

"You see Garrick, in my case it's exactly the opposite. Me—an army of strangers who usurp the body and destiny of Theodor Neuhoff in order to plumb the depths of possibility in both."

"Shall I play Walpole for you?"

Theodor smiled and raised his hands. "Whenever I'm in his presence, I already feel like one of the Gothic cathedrals he so admires: a large, dilapidated ruin of a building from a purer age. He scratches away my moss and makes me look even more foreign."

Garrick laughed. "I'm certain, Sire, if you'll forgive me, he would also like to have you miniaturized and carry you around with him like the model of his house, or pull you out of a cabinet like one of his majolicas and hand you around the table while he provided learned commentary."

"Let's get to our play, Garrick," said Theodor.

"Exactly, the play," replied the thespian, and under the compulsion of an inner turbulence, he jumped up from his chair in order to walk off the thoughts that were weighing upon him. He halted before the psyche with an inquisitive look. At first he saw nothing in it at all, for his senses were disconcerted by the music and Theodor's slightly nasal baritone. The candles cast restless, flickering light onto the silvery surface, in whose depths he finally descried the king's face with the two deep-black cisterns of his eyes, as if it were floating on the surface of a lake. Garrick placed himself so that his own face covered the king's. The full moon is rising, he thought bitterly, an empty disk marked by the flat craters of smallpox scars. His eyes were more like muddy puddles. He grimaced, producing the expression a critic of the *World* called his "sardonic smile."

"I must confess, Sire, that what makes me anxious about the scheme is the fact that the hero of my play is sitting in person right here before me. I feel as though I were commiting treason or burglary."

"Think nothing of it. I myself regard my life as a fiction, to such a degree that anyone else's interpretation of it gives me new, unexpected insights. And besides, it's not the first time that I've been written about. At least this time I'm being asked for my own personal opinion, since here and there I might be able to contribute an occasional marginal note. Have you found a title for the tragedy? You must always begin with a title."

"So Your Majesty would not be angry if I allowed myself a certain amount of poetic license?"

"Will you acknowledge the dignity and grandeur of my aspirations, Garrick?"

"But of course . . ."

"Then in all else, you are free to do as you please. The one thing I can't stand is not to be taken seriously."

Garrick stared at the man with thinning hair, enthroned on his chair in a faded velvet jacket.

"Yes, dignity and freedom," he said tentatively, "I know what you mean. For it's a strange thing, our dignity. Gentlemen of high estate admire our freedom and our art and send flowers and sweetmeats to our dressing rooms, but on the street they won't even shake our hands. God knows I've mucked out my theater and enforced rules and tried my whole life to gain dignity and respectability for the stage. I can assure you that my private life is above suspicion and reproach. The times are long gone when they used to call us scoundrels and catamites and footpads and prostitutes. And yet, and yet, our profession still doesn't stand in good repute, as if the freedom we claim for ourselves were incompatible with dignity."

"Whoever fears the freedom of others (and his own freedom most of all)," Theodor replied, "must of course deny freedom its dignity and permit it only under the strictest social conventions. But the freest man I've ever known—so far removed from healthy conventionality that they would have been quite justified in beheading him for his excesses if he hadn't been a prince—was also one of the most dignified. To be sure, the dignity of Gian-Gastone de Medici was only to be found beneath a swamp of self-abasement and self-destruction. He exposed the piteousness of the human condition with his own body, and that possessed dignity, if not in the bourgeois or Christian sense of the word."

"He must not have believed in God," said Garrick.

"Likely not. He once told me, 'Neuhoff, my confessor really believes there is no God. Me, I don't even believe that.' But that would be a role for you!"

"A skeptic, a modern man. A tragedy can't do justice to someone like that."

"No, Gian-Gastone, God rest his soul, would have wanted to be the hero of a comic opera. But let's not get ahead of ourselves. First, the play about me."

"Very interesting, what you just said, Sir, for as far as tragedy is concerned . . ."

"Oh, you mean because I'm not dead?" Theodor interrupted. "Let me reassure you on that score. You need not hesitate to have me die. With any luck, I'll be able to hear my own *consolatio* from my loge. And as for the rest, make way for Melpomene!"

"Of course, Sir," Garrick squirmed, "but it's less Melpomene I'm worried about than Fate. We need a hit, if only in the interest of the benefit performances. A tragedy after the manner of Shakespeare ... with five acts ... the dignity and grandeur of your aspirations, to be sure, but do you know what people catcall from the audience at the most heart-rending moments of *Hamlet*? 'Get it over with and bump him off, you bore!' That's what they say ... And you, Your Majesty, a modern man ..."

Theodor watched Garrick's face crumble with shame and antipathy at having to say out loud what he would rather have had his interlocutor guess. He observed how skillfully—right down to the cold sweat!—the tableau of inner struggle was represented. And suddenly, he understood and cried out instantaneously, "You want to write 'Harlequin in Corsica'!"

"*King* Harlequin," whispered Garrick tonelessly, and then a little louder, like a bright tongue of flame suddenly shooting up from embers dying on the hearth, "the role of a lifetime."

For the space of a moment, Garrick disappeared, the musicians disappeared, the dungeon disappeared, and Theodor felt, like a phantom pain, the same pull toward an abyss of ridicule he had felt thirteen years ago in Amsterdam. But this time, it was only a memory, and he suppressed the response that had been on the tip of his tongue. It was up to Garrick, not him, to speak and get himself out of this corner.

"I can see from Your Majesty's face that you don't think much of my harlequinade. And why should you? You, a man of education and experience, must think it a sign of contempt or possibly even derision to turn a drama inspired by your life, your star, into an apotheosis of Harlequin. But just between the two of us, Harlequin is my alter ego, my favorite child, my twin brother, and whatever the critics may say, my only figure that really breaks new ground theatrically. I implore you, Sir, let me try to explain. Hear me out and then you be the judge."

"But why so much tremolo, my dear Garrick? You don't think I consider myself one of Shakespeare's tragic heroes, do you? Do you really imagine I am oblivious to the irony of the surroundings in which we meet? Life is a longing for clarity and purity, around which irony always buzzes like an annoying fly around a light. And God is a playwright whose works (with their obscenities and inept longueurs) would never stand a chance on the French stage. The only truth is the simultaneity of tragedy and comedy, and any attempt to divide this unappetizing, living mishmash into good and evil, light and dark, serious and comic, is a lie, a pretense that life is only the one thing or the other. And it's the same in the theater. I want tears in my eyes, but some of them must be tears of laughter. Your play should have irony *and* pity."

There now, thought Theodor, whatever he serves up, I'll be able to say with a good conscience that I was his inspiration and set him on the right path. And he'll have to admit it, too.

"Thus I may be allowed to hope for your understanding," said Garrick, "for I and my Harlequin seek nothing but to speak the truth in laughter and in tears, such that the subtleties of great dramatic speeches are mitigated and made palatable to human understanding through the exaggeration of gesture. As well-traveled as you are, you must surely be familiar with Monsieur Molière's Scapin?"

Theodor nodded impatiently.

"Well you see, my Harlequin is a very similar sort of figure. He is loved by the public in the cheap seats, for he's one of them and speaks truth to power. But he is also loved by the powerful, for they like hearing the truth as long as it's just on stage, and take pleasure in feeling the cane as long as it leaves no marks on them. Whereas a tragic figure would suffer in noble silence, Harlequin squawks. He shows in pantomime what it's impolite to talk about, but gets beaten for it. And when he gets the chance, he hits back. He is the Holy Martyr of all mistreated bodies, Your Majesty, and the public understands that and loves him for it. That's why they come in droves and pay good money to see him. And now just picture this Harlequin liberating Corsica from the yoke of the republic, right under the noses and without the help of the great powers, who look on opportunistically. Can you imagine all the possibilities for deeper meaning beneath the humor, for bitter truths sweetened by laughter? Harlequin, a better king than all our rulers? But then of course—since you can't make Harlequin into a paradigm for princes—he's got to be thrashed and driven off the stage . . ."

"Yes, yes," Theodor replied with a smile, "but it wasn't exactly a thrashing . . .

"I was standing on the bridge of the *Revenger*, at anchor off Isula Rossa, and I saw the coast where a few years before I had ridden at the head of my soldiers and destroyed a mighty army. Snow lay on the cloud-washed peaks, glittering white. I stretched out my hand and could feel that wild and beautiful island which belonged to me and had become my homeland, the way a peasant digs up a handful of earth and sniffs it to see what kind of year it will be. And I smelled that the year would be good. All my time and effort had finally crystallized, had come to fruition. The silver coins bearing my image would circulate as currency around the world. I stood on the solid oak planks of the English flagship, supported by a world power that followed me in blind obedience. My faithful associates, the indomitable champions of freedom, little Giafferi, wise Costa, gallant Paoli, and my own son Friedrich were also on board, at my side, men of the most varied temperament whom I had gathered into a fist to carry out my will. They had all awaited my return, waited for this moment of apotheosis. And then . . ."

Theodor, who had spoken into empty space as if talking to himself, turned casually toward Garrick, raised his right hand, and made an almost soundless little pop with his index and middle fingers.

His lower arm had moved with lethargic grace—neither slow nor fast—and he had not used his thumb to make a more dynamic snap. One could only call the gesture one of resignation. That is, one could have called it resigned if there hadn't been something so light and playful about it: like brushing away a piece of ash or when an Italian winds up an anecdote with an "*ecco*" as if to say, "And you see, I'm still here to tell the tale." But at the same time, it was like the last sound from a harpsichord, that mischievous "pling!" of release that makes gentle fun of the heavy, final chord. The gesture of flicking a speck of dust from one's fingernail . . .

Garrick was unable to keep his composure. He jumped to his feet. His ears were burning. He spread his arms and took a step toward Theodor as if to grasp him by the shoulders and pull him up.

"That's it!" he cried. "Just so! Could you perhaps repeat . . . But no, of course not. You weren't even aware of it yourself. Thank heavens I didn't miss it. My eyes are sharp and my attention never flags! My God, it always comes down to just such a tiny spark."

"What are you talking about, Garrick?" Theodor asked calmly.

"Your gesture!" the actor said excitedly. "That extraordinary snap of the fingers. That's the sign of the king! That's the action from which everything develops—the character, the man! It's the umbilical chord between your body and mine!"

"What sort of gesture was it, then?" asked Theodor in amused astonishment.

"Just a moment, Your Majesty, and I'll show you!"

And in less than a second, Garrick was transformed into someone else before Theodor's very eyes, namely into him, so that the king was looking at his own reflection. The physical differences between the two men vanished and Theodor watched as Garrick's little pantomime ended in an absolutely exact replica of his finger pop. And he was well able to judge its exactness too, for it had by no means been an unconscious gesture.

Come to think of it, his whole speech had had no other purpose but to lead to precisely this concluding gesture. He would not have been able to say what exactly it was he wanted to express thereby, but that wasn't the important thing. It was much more crucial that this gesture be open to all interpretations.

With the best will in the world, there's really nothing more I can do for him, thought the king.

"The tragedy of a ruler betrayed, an entire people cheated in its hopes for freedom—a snap of the fingers," said Garrick all atremble, having turned back into himself again.

Theodor looked up as if waking from deep dreams. "Most likely I will never have another day like that, don't you agree?"

Garrick regarded him. And if he had still been full of admiration for this man a moment ago, he now saw a broken old fellow for whom he felt pity and a bit of repulsion.

"Perhaps not," he said. "But nevertheless, fate still assigned you a leading role."

"Obviously," answered Theodor in amusement, "but one can never be sure, for our script is part of God's plan for salvation. Only the director gets to see it. The rest of us have to improvise."

Garrick's hands traced a sort of dome in the air and he said, "That's our tragedy. Even after the most beautiful, most moving performance, we eventually have to leave the proscenium

and step back into the awful darkness of the wings, not knowing if it was good. The play goes on. But we don't, Your Majesty. Soon enough, we exit. We are hardly visible in the aeons
upon aeons. We're ants, monads . . . But on the other hand,
there's some comfort in that. The jeers and curses can't follow
us into oblivion. No, there's not much to us!"

He shook his head and repeated, "There's not much to us,
Sire."

"My dear Garrick," said the king, "I'm afraid this most
extraordinarily fruitful conversation must be brought to an end
for today. I'm expecting my confessor, you see. In the early
morning hours, I'm always sentimental and ready for reconciliation, and he exploits that. What can I do?"

When he was alone once again, Garrick's last words echoed soundlessly through the vaulted rooms. *There's not much to
us.* Yes, he had something there. Theodor repeated the sentence
to see if he could warm up to it, the thought of making peace
with himself and the world. "There's not much to me," he said
out loud. What an insight at the end of this evening. Let's just
hope it's not the last and most profound insight I'm granted.

The Penultimate Chapter

*O*N THE SIXTH OF December 1756, almost seven years to the day since his imprisonment, the king mounted the clammy staircase. The gate to the inner courtyard was unbolted and he heard the fine whisper of rain. The man supporting him was not the long-gone William, for the jailers here didn't stay around as long as the prisoners.

For a moment, he hesitated to step out into the rain, as if no longer certain of the effect of the elements on the human body. Perhaps it would dissolve him into his constituent parts.

He shook off the jailer's arm, his knees sagged for a moment, then he regained his balance and took two steps forward onto the cobblestones of the courtyard. He took off his hat and tilted back his head.

The sky has changed, he thought. It was an autumn London sky, leaden gray and smooth as the alchemist's soup he used to stir up, in hopes of straining gold from it.

The guard, whose patience was not unlimited, grasped his arm again and the hand was not unwelcome, for the cold gave him cramps in his limbs and his legs felt like those of a marionette dangling from the fingers of a weary puppetmaster.

He was wearing the same clothes he had on when first imprisoned: the black tricorn, the black *houppelande*, the dark brown suede knee-britches, white silk stockings, buckled shoes, a white shirt and a woolen jerkin. The years of imprisonment had not been kind to his things, although they had stayed drier than he had himself. The greatcoat and jerkin had moth holes through which the rain reached his skin. The silk stockings had become so thin they felt like cobwebs on his calves.

A tall figure was awaiting him in the shadow of the wall, by the porter's lodge. As soon as his eyes had gotten used to the twilight of the gateway, he saw that the fellow was shorter than he was himself, but was wearing a black top hat. He held a book and a pen in his hand.

Doing it all standing up, thought Theodor. Suddenly they can't get it over with fast enough. He had to sign a statement acknowledging that all his personal possessions had been returned to him and promising not to file any future claims for damages. He signed himself "Theodorus Rex" and as the notary opened his bony mouth in protest (he seemed to have no gums at all in his upper jaw, just yellow teeth which tapered up and disappeared into the jawbone), Theodor cut him off with a determined glare.

"You are free, Neuhoff. God be with you."

Theodor smiled ironically. His skin was so stiff with cold that it felt like his facial expression had to break through a layer of clay. The guard who had led him from the cell stepped aside. With great effort, the king stepped forward. All that mattered in life at present was not to trip or stumble before these two men, a prison official and a warder, nor simply sprawl full-length—like falling into water or bed—and go to sleep, which seemed the most natural thing to do in view of the enormous weariness which increased with every breath he took, as if the foggy air were a rag soaked in ether.

Every one of the perhaps ten steps it would take to escape their gaze had to succeed. Step, he told himself, step. Head up. Dignified. Gaze into the distance. Lips together. Clasp hands behind back . . . no, for then you'll fall on your face.

Six steps brought him to the gate. He stopped, slipped his hand casually into the pocket of his jerkin so that if he found nothing there, he could take it out again unnoticed. But his clammy fingers found a coin.

He turned his head toward the man at the oak door that was cut into the larger double doors to let pedestrians through. He felt like he had to operate a series of gears and pulleys to make his head complete the quarter-turn. "Here, for your trouble."

He flipped the coin at him. The dumbfounded warder watched it sail through the air, then his hand snapped shut on it like a frog grabbing a fly. "Thank you, Sir! God bless you!"

Better already, thought Theodor, and walked forward until he heard the prison door slam shut. Then his strength deserted him and he leaned against a wall like a worn-out cart horse. He tried to take slow, deep breaths, but he couldn't get enough air into his lungs. Weariness and weakness seemed to skew the axis of the world.

He tried to concentrate and form clear thoughts, but he couldn't get them beyond an initial gelatinous stage and had the impression that the rain was washing them off him and down into the gutter before he had time to form a shell around them.

Had he nodded off for a moment? The feeling of awaking with a jerk frightened him so much that he was able to stand up straight again, cross the street, and take shelter from the rain beneath an arcade.

From there, he looked back onto the rain-darkened brick of the prison wall. No one had come. *Neuhoff,* the official had called him, disparagingly. Not *Sir,* not *Baron,* not *Your Majesty.* Just *Neuhoff.*

Officials are always a good barometer of our social status. No one had picked him up. How often had he pictured this moment to himself since that first night in his cell: the equipage of his cousin, the King of England, drawn by twelve horses. He could smell the scent of perfume and powder beneath the braid-trimmed tricorn he would have worn, while the cheering folk formed a cordon. Or educated London, under Walpole's leadership, had forced a debate in parliament. Freedom for the King of Corsica! And a delegation of gentlemen crying "Long live the King!" had come to fetch him at the gates of that laughable building that had been unable to confine him. Or Garrick's play had stirred up the people, who chanted his name and rattled the gates until his pardon came, then carried him through the city on their shoulders.

Later, his releases had become quieter, more discreet: a signing of papers, handing over of a visa and letters of credit, a mood of solemn deference or silent courtesy. And as usual, his imagination had gotten ahead of the facts by at least two degrees of the conditional mood. It was true, he had lost touch with international politics, but he would be able to win over some empire or other as a supporter of his cause. He had never felt so much the king, so committed to fulfilling his calling and liberating those awful Corsicans, than since his imprisonment in this country.

Ah well, it hadn't turned out that way. And the Corsicans hadn't sent anyone to meet him either. But then, they'd always been like dogs running after whoever waved the biggest bone at them.

The only friend who occurred to him was Walpole, but obviously no one had informed him of Theodor's release. He could regain his strength in Walpole's house and turn back into a human being again. He seemed to recall where the townhouse was, even if he'd never had to reach it on foot back then.

The first minutes of walking were a completely inward experience. The city simply provided the bars of the playpen toward which the newborn tottered. You are the King of Corsica; you will now walk to that cornice. You are Theodor Neuhoff; you owe it to yourself to cross this intersection and reach that rain-wet brick house.

For one second, the blanket of clouds opened and a flat fan of light fell like a ramp into the chasm of the street. The raindrops glittered like a whirlwind of silver dust, a breath of warmth he perhaps only imagined brushed his cheek. He stopped, but the phenomenon was already past.

He groped his way through the labyrinth of a city that had been a living being during that second of sunlight, but had now become an abstract, three-dimensional projection with cubes, pyramids, truncated cones. Axes tapered off toward vanishing points, vectors darted into his field of vision like comets and veered off in various directions at angles that didn't harmonize with each other. Can you follow me, Baron? asked de Broglie. Ashamed, Theodor shook his perspiring head. *Appliquez-vous, Baron!* I forgot my compasses, whispered the lad and widened his eyes, but the straight lines sagged into curves, rolled themselves up into spirals, bulged out, and collapsed. He remembered that he hadn't closed the door, so the kittens were sure to have run outside. How was he ever to find them now? And if he caught one he'd have to carry it with him while he looked for the others, and it would squirm free and get lost for good. Larbi, I can't solve this equation, he said to his servant, who was wearing a brownish woolen *djellaba* and a black top hat that made him taller than his master. He had grown a little beard that encircled his fleshy lips like a fine poppyseed bagel. *Come here, you merry tipplers,* he cried. *Up, up you young dogs! Come, we'll empty one more glass. Our doom approaches with giant strides, the final cup is near.* Why are you running so fast, Larbi? Your sister is on her deathbed, we've got to get there before she dies! How could he have forgotten that? He'd had his hands so full with the runaway cats that he hadn't remembered the most important thing. But how could Jane be dying if she'd just let out the cats? Then it occurred to him that he wasn't allowed to see her until he'd solved his problem. I'm not waiting for you anymore, called Larbi in an insolent tone he never would have used before Theodor's imprisonment. Beneath Theodor's feet there were no more cobblestones, just mud that sucked at his shoes with each step and made it impossible to lift his legs. The angle of the rain to the wall of huge gray blocks of stone increased more and more, like a scissors opening. The concentric circles of the puddle in which he stood formed a well shaft in whose depths he saw a face looking at him imploringly. He plunged in to rescue it.

Shoving a pushcart in which lay a brass chandelier wrapped in old coats, several locks and keys, some wrought iron fireplace implements, and a set of copper saucepans, Jeremy Larkoszi was on his way home to Soho, where he lived with his mother behind his second-hand shop in the basement of Little Chapel Street No. 5.

He was a small man of delicate build with olive skin, dark eyes, and even darker rings under them. His flattish forehead sloped up to an almost bald crown, cross-hatched with wisps of black hair. He wore a skullcap on the back of his head and when he did sums, he chewed on one or the other of his *peyos*. If you asked after his health, he knit his brows in care and worry and answered, "Quite good, actually. I can't complain. I'm not the man I used to be, of course, but I'm getting on all right."

Now, in view of such cautious assertions, one could have assumed he was a well-to-do man who didn't want to attract the evil eye by sounding too confident. However, that was not the case, yet for exactly that reason, with the example of Job in mind, Jeremy Larkoszi didn't want to start arguing and complaining.

Today he had done excellent business, under the circumstances. He huddled all the deeper into his cloak as he walked along. He would have preferred to disappear into it altogether for fear that someone could read in his face as in a ledger his satisfaction at the profitable transaction. He stared at the mud underfoot and whispered, I'm not here, I don't exist, I've suffered a defeat and I'm slinking home to my mother, God preserve her.

And thus he happened to see the man lying unconscious in the filth of the street.

Why me! was his first thought. Why does it have to be me who happens by when someone's lying there, some poor starving beggar? Why doesn't a rich man come by at such a time, why not some doctor? Maybe he's already dead? Or just drunk?

Jeremy cursed himself for not being able to continue on his way, pass by the collapsed man without looking at him, and get home with his wares safe and sound. He set down his pushcart and bent over the figure whose greatcoat and shoes were soaked and dirty. Passing coaches had spattered the *houppelande* with yellowish mud.

"*Oy veh*, why me?" said Jeremy out loud, rolling the body over. He gazed into the haggard face with wet gray hair plastered to its forehead. The man was breathing. He didn't smell of alcohol.

"We care for sick animals too, don't we?" said Jeremy. "So why not people? What have you got there, hanging around your neck, my friend?"

He looked at the star with fourteen points. There was a medallion in its center showing a nude with sword and scales. He hadn't the foggiest what it meant, but the chain was possibly gold-plated. "Where'd you snitch this from, m'boy? But now it's time to wake up. How's a dwarf like me supposed to get such a hulk as you onto his feet, eh? Come on, wake up."

With his small hand he slapped the unconscious man lightly on his cheeks, left, right, until he opened his eyes.

"Come, my friend. You can't keep lying here," he said to the awakening face that looked vaguely at him.

Slowly the king rose from deep in his dreams back to the surface of consciousness. He tried to remember and get himself oriented.

"Walpole?" he asked.

"Let's stand up then, first," said Jeremy impatiently and took a quick look around. Above all else, he wanted to avoid attracting attention. He was already cursing himself for his good-natured weakness.

"I am the King of Corsica," Theodor managed to say, his eyes still glassy.

"Of course, and I'm King David. And now please stand up and don't make a fuss, and we can ride to my palace."

As he helped the confused man to his feet, he was startled at how light the tall body was and realized that in this weakened condition, he would never make it to Little Chapel Street on his own legs. While he brushed off the king's greatcoat, his thoughts raced ahead and he explained, "My mother will not be pleased when I bring home another mouth to feed. She thinks I should be bringing home a wife who can put things in order. She thinks you find a wife the way you find door locks and used clothes, or if you have to, you can pry one off a facade with a crowbar. Don't pay her any mind. I'll guarantee you a meal and a place to sleep for the night. Haven't had anything to eat in a while, right?"

Theodor, still in a soft and transparent world midway between sleep and full consciousness, replied politely, "It doesn't signify, Sir. It's very kind of you." For the second thing he remembered after Walpole's name was his inner command to display dignity and poise.

Shaking his head and muttering under his breath, Jeremy lifted the chandelier out of his cart and maneuvered the king into it. Then he covered his knees and lap with one of the old overcoats and pressed the six-legged brass spider into his hands.

"Hold onto it tight. Don't drop it, hear? That's my week's wages."

"Certainly, Walpole," said Theodor mechanically. "As soon as we have dined and I've rested a bit, we shall rethink our strategy. Above all, I need arms and ammunition."

"*Oy veh!*" Jeremy groaned, hunched his shoulders so that his head disappeared into his coat collar, and crossed his index and middle finger as a lightning rod to divert the evil eye into the ground. "Arms and ammunition! He's delirious! Let's hope so, anyway!"

And so they reached Soho. Jeremy unlocked the door and raised the hinged shutters. Then he descended the six steps into the basement and called out, "Mama, it's me! I've brought a guest along. Don't worry! Everything's fine!"

"*Now* you come home!" A shrill voice sounded from the darkness of the shop. "Your mother's crying her eyes out. Her son, her only son, is gadding about town all day long, having a good time, forgetting his work, forgetting his mother who could be dying here in the meantime, eaten by rats and worms, helpless, alone, and frantic with worry about him, but . . ."

"But Mama, I've only been gone an hour!"

"And what was that you said?" The voice drew closer, and Jeremy's mother appeared at the bottom of the steps, a powerfully built woman with a red face and unkempt hair. She placed her hands on her well-padded hips and her eyes took in her son arranging his wares and the man sitting in the pushcart holding the chandelier in his lap.

"Jeremy!" she screeched and pronounced the J like the Germans, not the English, as in *Jedermann* or *Januar*. "You've dragged home another of your beggars, and a goy besides! You want we should be ruined?"

"But Mama, the poor man. He'll only just have a crust of bread and a little sleep and then he'll be on his way."

Theodor sat up, carefully laid aside the chandelier, and climbed out of the pushcart. He moved forward, took off his hat and bowed, saying, "Madam, I'm honored. I beg you to forgive any inconvenience."

"Any what? But of course, not at all . . ."

Her eyes flew wildly back and forth between her son and the stranger as if they were acting out a farce she didn't understand. Jeremy tried to placate her by twirling a finger near his temple.

But in the meantime, the king had regained enough consciousness to understand he was not in Walpole's house. He remembered being released and the first few minutes thereafter and concluded that he had fainted from weakness and had obviously been picked up by this little Jewish junk dealer. Now one step at a time, he told himself. Eat and sleep first, everything else can wait. Everything else lay on the far shore of a sea of exhaustion.

"I shall most certainly not incommode you for long, Madam. And you will have no reason to regret it. I am the King of Corsica, and I can assure you . . ."

"Well then, come in," grumbled the old woman and then reverted to her shrill tone, calling, "We'll talk about this later, Jeremy!"

"A *meshuggene*. I had to bring a *meshuggene* home with me," whispered the second-hand dealer.

The basement was a cavelike vault with brick walls and a floor of packed earth that reminded Theodor uncomfortably of his cell. Apparently, he thought, it's difficult for me to leave these subterranean dungeons behind! His gaze wandered about the front room, which was stacked to the ceiling with clothing, hats, pictures, picture frames, plaster figures, lumber from old cupboards, boxes of ironware, oxidized flatware, and rusty sabers, a suit of armor, rugs. In the back room there was a table with four chairs and two alcoves partitioned off with rugs where the beds were probably located.

Jeremy had come down into the room. "You're hungry, aren't you?"

The king turned his head toward him. He wasn't bothered by the little man's familiar tone. He wouldn't reprimand him, but he wouldn't stoop to it himself, either.

"Yes, I had much urgent business to attend to, and I skipped breakfast, if you would be so good as to dish something up . . ."

Mother and son looked at each other. The old woman stood up with a sigh and fetched a loaf of bread from a cupboard as well as a piece of cheese that had seen better days. Jeremy put a jug of wine on the table. Then he cut three slices of bread and divided the cheese into three pieces. His mother shot him a look and he rose and brought back a bowl of pignoli.

"Of course, you're welcome to stay with us longer," said the old woman tentatively, "if you don't have anywhere else to go. It's not expensive here, and you are clearly a man of means . . ."

"*Ma*ma," said Jeremy and put his hand on hers. It was embarrassing, even in front of this burned-out beggar.

"That's a lovely gold chain you have around your neck," the mother continued. "It *is* gold, isn't it? It alone must be worth enough to pay for two or three nights of room and board."

Theodor smiled at her. "Madam, I appreciate your hospitality, but I shall probably not be able to avail myself of it for very long. I have plans and projects that admit of no delay. As for this chain, that's the medallion of the Order of the Redemption hanging from it, of which I am the Grand Master. You will surely understand that it is not for sale. I could perhaps dispose of the chain by itself. I paid six hundred pounds for it several years ago—hand-wrought, eighteen caret gold."

His two hosts exchanged glances. Jeremy twirled a finger near his temple again. He forced himself to laugh. "It's fool's gold, that's what it is. Come, m'friend, stop showing off now and have a bite to eat."

They stared at him. He didn't move a muscle.

"What's the matter? It's all we have. Come on, eat. You're hungry."

Theodor remarked kindly, "Of course. I'm only waiting for the table settings."

"The table settings? . . . You mean, plates and . . ."

"And flatware. Of course, Son, don't be such a dimwit," scolded his mother. "Get the table settings . . . table settings, right?"

"Quite right, Madam."

Then the bread and the cheese lay on a plate, flanked by a knife and fork.

"You've got to bang the cheese on the table to get the maggots out."

Theodor knocked the cheese on the tabletop and Jeremy obligingly squashed the little white worms against the wood. Before lifting the bread to his lips, Theodor began to murmur.

"What's he saying?" hissed the mother.

"I think he's praying," whispered Jeremy.

"Amen," said Theodor more loudly, and added, "That was Latin. I wish you *bon appetit*."

They ate in silence. It required all their concentration to chew the stale bread. Theodor washed it down with wine.

"I thank you for the excellent meal. If you will excuse me now, I believe I shall take a little rest. Madam. If you would be so kind, dear Sir, as to show me my room . . ."

"Of course, Sir," answered Jeremy involuntarily. He rose and accompanied the king to the right-hand alcove, where he usually slept himself. Without being asked, he helped the gaunt stranger out of his clothes and steadied him as he let himself down onto the bed.

"Wait a moment, I'll fetch you a blanket."

"Thank you, my good man. What is your name?"

"Jeremy."

"Jeremy what?"

"Jeremy Larkoszi."

"Jeremy Larkoszi, I shall not forget your kindness. Once I have reestablished my rights, I shall certainly remember you."

"Of course, of course. But now, get some sleep."

"Yes, I shall do that. I am, I must admit, dead tired and a wretched guest. I beg you to ask Madam's forgiveness for my weakness."

Old Mrs. Larkoszi looked over from the table and nodded without a word.

"Good night, Sir," whispered Jeremy and pulled the blanket over the king who was trembling with cold. His gray eyes smiled upon the man, then closed.

Gracious, thought Theodor, I was gracious. But it was a struggle, a very great struggle.

His breath grew calm and he relaxed upon his bed, which seemed to sink like a giant snowflake into the depths of the evening sky.

After he had rested a while, he was wide awake again. The sleep had done him good and he felt strong enough to stand up. He heard the curtains behind him bellying in the breeze coming in at the open window, and he opened his eyes. The air caressing his chest was the same temperature as his skin and the linen sheet covering his body. He stretched, felt the muscles in his thighs, calves, and shoulders, and sprang out of bed.

There it was again, the old urgency to get out into the day and simply exist, go at life with youthful gusto, get a move on, go forward to meet the future. With no planning, preparing, waiting, just trusting in God—and that meant not just self-confidence, but a childlike certainty that the encounter between himself and the world would have a happy outcome.

He wasted no time looking for the right clothing, especially when he didn't know whether he'd be back in half an hour or half a year. He just slipped into the short red and white breeches with the oriental pattern, laced the white linen shirt at the neck, threw on his bright red jacket, grabbed his long staff, and rushed out the door past the bake oven smelling enticingly of fresh bread and down the street whose housefronts shimmered in the ivory and peach tones of the afternoon light.

The gray backs of the cobblestones ran on before him like choppy little waves. He turned off to the right and walked toward the river. People took off their caps and waved. In a garden, fragrant tomatoes reflected the warmth of the sun. A fat yellow cat lounged on a wall whose plaster had fallen off in chunks, revealing the relief map of a strange continent. Pollen danced in the dusty light of entranceways into the dark green of summer gardens. In the shadow of open, semicircular windows, one could almost smell the languid afternoon sleep of young girls like a perfume.

Above the river, the green sky stretched to the horizon. Little gusts of wind were picking up, and the clouds advanced in formation with artillery, supply wagons, catapults, and siege towers. The atmosphere was so storm-charged that if one held up a match, it would bust into flame all by itself. He looked forward to the discharge, the release of the thunder, the splatter of rain, and the steamy warmth that follows, the smells of blossoms, trees, and earth that would rise as if from shattered phials of perfume. The wind rippled the surface of the water, splintering the green reflection of the houses along the river.

Then he was on the path to the grove of acacias and the temple ruins. Even now, a thousand years after it had crumbled, the emptiness between the shattered pillars and the blocks of dusky pink stone with white marble friezes, overgrown with greenery, seemed like the reverse side of the mask of beauty. Swinging his staff in rhythm with his stride, his step was as light as if he had wings on his heels and it seemed that the physical exertion involved was not to lift his feet and set one before the other, but rather to give his body weight enough that it would sink back to earth between each flying step.

Bumblebees heavy with pollen cruised through the acacia grove like gold-laden galleons. He passed the last pillar, which marked the town limits, and paused. An enchanting sight met his eyes, so lovely that the beauty of flowers and architecture paled before it. On a slight rise, not twenty paces away, a young shepherdess sat resting on the grass, nursing her child and completely naked except for a white cloth covering her shoulders and reflecting the green phosphorescence of the stormy sky. She was gazing off into the distance or into herself. All her senses seemed concentrated in the milk ducts, straining toward the sucking mouth of the newborn.

He stood there quite unselfconsciously, watching the seated woman with the same quiet intensity with which she herself concentrated on the pleasant pain of the sucking at her nipple and the warm weight in her arms. But then again, it wasn't quite the same, for in a sort of inner elation, he sensed that while he watched, he was not oblivious to the world around him. The humming of bumblebees and the wind were still there. Out of the corner of his eye he saw the first flicker of lightning far beyond the city and heard the thunder like a distant rockslide in the mountains. He was aware of his own breathing and felt the smooth wood he was grasping, sensed his own living weight leaning at ease on the staff.

Filled with affection and with a desire as light as a dove on his shoulder, he studied the white and rosy complexion of the girl against its green background, the sensuous crease in the skin above her belly which squeezed and elongated her navel, the rhombus of her collarbones and throat (a sight that caused a weakness to creep up the back of his neck and knees), the shadow cast by her left arm, which ran across her belly and into the shadowy delta between her thighs, the two tresses that dangled down on either side of her temples—surely the young mother, when lost in thought, twisted them around her finger and chewed at them.

The thought that fate had already precipitated this encounter with his true love filled him with a joyful gratitude which not even the fact of the child on the shepherdess's arm could diminish. There sat the future he had dreamed of, having lept through the tension of the storm from one temporal dimension into another. He had found his beloved and his son and did not have to seek, conquer, beget them.

He took a step toward the stream that separated them. Then he changed his mind. Just as great as the attraction of this beautiful image was the pull of the journey begun, the road paved with dreams waiting to become, under his footsteps, encounters as beguiling as this one.

The promise of bliss emanating from the shepherdess was tempting, but what she could give him was merely fulfillment. The wanderer, by contrast, traverses the world like a ray of sunlight. His gaze makes everything that has been asleep or nonexistent blossom. It was exciting to encounter wife and child and the promise of eternal delight so soon. But if fate already held such happiness in store for him when he had barely left the town, wasn't there incomparably more promise in not accepting but forgoing it, getting drunk on renunciation, and continuing to wander, seek, bring forth new images?

Renunciation out of abundance, out of the conviction that ever-renewed Hope, not Certainty, was his tutelary goddess and directed his life.

Certain that he would see this beauty only a little longer, he lingered a moment, heaved a breath or a sigh, and then resumed his path without a backward glance.

Behind him, the storm broke out.

He walked on the heights of happiness.